IN THE VALLEY OF THE DEVIL

ALSO AVAILABLE BY HANK EARLY

Heaven's Crooked Finger

IN THE VALLEY OF THE DEVIL

AN EARL MARCUS MYSTERY

Hank Early

NEW YORK

This is a work of fiction. All of the names, characters, organizations, places, and events portrayed in this novel are either products of the author's imagination or are used fictitiously. Any resemblance to real or actual events, locales, or persons, living or dead, is entirely coincidental.

Published in the United States by Crooked Lane Books, an imprint of The Quick Brown Fox & Company LLC.

Crooked Lane Books and its logo are trademarks of The Quick Brown Fox & Company LLC.

Library of Congress Catalog-in-Publication data available upon request.

ISBN (hardcover): 978-1-68331-592-6
ISBN (ePub): 978-1-68331-593-3
ISBN (ePDF): 978-1-68331-594-0

Cover design by Melanie Sun
Book design by Jennifer Canzone

Printed in the United States.

www.crookedlanebooks.com

Crooked Lane Books
34 West 27th St., 10th Floor
New York, NY 10001

First Edition: July 2018

10 9 8 7 6 5 4 3 2 1

This one's for Luke.

1

My mother insisted that when evil left one body, it always jumped into the next. I guessed she based this on scripture—the one about Jesus casting out the demons from a man and into a group of swine. There was a certain amount of logic to this that pleased me when I thought about it, and the older I became, the more I found myself reflecting on the things both my parents had taught me when I was younger. I liked to dissect their platitudes, looking for some pearl of truth, something that might make me feel better about the way in which they had conducted their lives.

It was hard, but sometimes, at least with my mother, I found myself latching onto something that almost made sense.

Like the idea of evil.

If it was a real thing, like so many people believed, why couldn't it go from one person to the next? Why couldn't the evil that had resided in my father—his life was perhaps the best argument for evil I could think of—leap into someone else when he died?

I remember once overhearing Mama and Daddy arguing about some church members, the Edisons. Herbert Edison had died a few days before this argument after a long struggle with cancer, something my father attributed to evil. Cancer, to my father, was always the physical manifestation of evil in the body. When his wife, Catherine, had been caught in Filo Jenkins's barn a week later, with her dress around her head and Filo's face between her legs, Daddy claimed it was the evil in her that had infected Herbert and caused him to die.

This too, was characteristic of my father. If a woman was anywhere near a tragedy or failure of any type, it was her fault.

Mama—though, she'd never say it to Daddy—saw it differently. Herbert—like many of the men who modeled their lives on my father's sermons—saw his wife the way some men see their dogs: subservient companions who should serve their masters. When Catherine had refused to serve, he hit her so hard, she didn't come out of her house for months, and when she finally did, the evidence of her misaligned jaw was still plain enough for anyone to see.

So, for Mama, the evil jumped from Herbert, when he'd died, to Catherine, who'd been dutifully sitting by his bedside.

As a kid, the biases of their viewpoints had been lost on me. As an adult, I saw the bias and found myself sympathizing with Catherine and wondering if perhaps Herbert's evil hadn't jumped instead to their son—one of the cruelest kids I'd ever known. We called him Choirboy because of his vigilant compliance to my father's fundamentalist principals. Later, when he was grown, the nickname became a part of him, something that seemed to shape him somehow, and he became the walking embodiment of everything that was wrong with my father's church.

He was dead now too.

All that evil. Looking for someplace to go.

Why couldn't it just float off, be carried away on some strange breeze? Why did it always have to come back?

Coulee County and these mountains deserved a respite.

But places—much like people—rarely get what they deserve.

* * *

It would have been easy to say that evil came back on the day I waited with three friends in the late September heat for a man named Jeb Walsh—but probably too simplistic.

Because the truth of it was, Jeb wouldn't have ever shown up if the evil hadn't already been here. The more I thought about it, the more I was willing to make the argument Walsh had come here explicitly because of the evil that was waiting for him.

We stood in front of the library steps in downtown Riley, watching as he pulled his white F-150 pickup into the nearest parking space and killed the engine.

The man who stepped out of the truck was nothing like I'd expected. I'd seen the minister and "life coach's" photo on the back cover of the book I'd forced myself to read through clenched teeth, but in person Jeb Walsh seemed younger and more confident than he had in the black and white photo.

He wore pressed tan pants and a light green golf shirt, tucked neatly into his narrow waistband. In Walsh's book, he wrote about working out, cleaning up his diet, and how those changes had saved his life. Nothing wrong with that, except his words were laced with a barely hidden disdain for all who didn't submit to his rigorous ideals of health and what he called "the happy life."

Another man walked a few feet behind Walsh. He was a ragged, unkempt man with thick muttonchops and feathered hair. I assumed he was Walsh's bodyguard. No surprise. Men like Walsh always needed bodyguards. This one looked like a redneck who'd seen too many Scorsese movies. His pants were the bottom half of a crimson track suit, and his faded blue shirt looked like he'd found it in the irregular size section of a soon-to-be-closed Kmart. It was nearly as wide as it was long, swallowing him up and somehow still showing a patch of his hairy belly. I might have dismissed him as a clown if not for his imposing size and the swift, no-nonsense way his eyes glanced furtively here and there, lingering just long enough to let you know he was dangerous.

I stood with my best friend, Rufus Gribble, and one of the library directors, a pretty widow named Susan Monroe, watching the two men make their way down the sidewalk. My girlfriend, Mary Hawkins, was part of our group too, but just moments ago had stepped inside the library to use the restroom.

"They're here," I said to Rufus, who was blind but so capable some people didn't even notice it at first. He stood beside me, nodding slowly, his face pointed toward the two men, his lips snarled in what I knew to be righteous anger.

Rufus had been the one to alert me to Jeb Walsh. He'd also invited nearly thirty people to gather on the library steps to make sure Walsh knew he wasn't welcome, that Coulee County would not tolerate his brand of hatred.

Unfortunately, the opposite appeared to be true. Only four of us had taken it seriously enough to show up. I realized now, we'd all been foolish to expect anything else. It wasn't that there weren't good people here. There were, but so many of them spent all of their time and energy just trying to keep their heads above water, hustling for their next paycheck, their next moment free from the anxieties of this world.

Still, there was a lot for a man like Jeb Walsh to like about this area. Progress and open-mindedness were still regarded with suspicion in Coulee County. The power structure in the county and the city of Riley was pretty much the definition of the "good old boy network," something I had no doubt Walsh relished. Perhaps most importantly, the area was overwhelmingly white and Christian; the only exceptions, a handful of poor African Americans who lived in a narrow valley people called Corn Valley. There was Mary, of course—whose father had been black—but despite our relationship, she'd had sense enough to get the hell out and now lived in Atlanta, where she worked as a homicide detective with the Atlanta PD.

The homogeneity of this area was one of the reasons I'd left nearly thirty-two years ago, and one of the main reasons it had taken me so long to come back. And yet, I'd not only come back, I'd chosen to stay. Chalk that up to the influence of Mary Hawkins and the power of finding a kindred spirit in Rufus.

Walsh was originally from south Georgia and had made a name for himself via some outrageous sermons he'd posted on YouTube several years back. He used the notoriety to get a book deal and wrote two or three screeds in the early two thousands about the dangers of immigration. A couple of cable news interviews later, and the Southern Poverty Law Center had put Walsh on a list with other extremists who preached hate and intolerance. Walsh dropped out of the spotlight a bit and reemerged last year with a new book, directed at kids, called *Live the Happy Life*. While it was, on the surface, a kinder and gentler book compared to his others, some critics had rightly called it out for being even more dangerous because it targeted children, presenting a false correlation between following the moral dictates in the book and being happy.

Then he'd quietly moved to Coulee County, into Sommerville Chase, one of the newest and most exclusive areas in the entire state. In May, the Coulee County school board voted to allow *Live the Happy Life* to be included in the school curriculum. Only a few people noticed. Rufus was one of them. Since that time, he'd been keeping tabs on Walsh. To be fair, though, nearly everyone was keeping tabs on Walsh these days. A few weeks earlier, he'd announced he'd be making a bid for the U.S. House of Representatives in 2018. The damnedest part of it all was that he was already considered to be the favorite would almost definitely emerge the victorious, catapulting him to a position of power that would allow him to hurt more than just Coulee County.

But it was Coulee County that I was worried about now, and like Rufus, I was determined to let Walsh know that life in these mountains wasn't going to be as easy for him as he thought.

As I watched him stroll down the sidewalk, I found his manner to be chilling. There was something off about the man, something that didn't come across on television. But here, in the bright light of unfiltered reality, I saw the stiffening of his jaw, the forced squint of his eyes, and the jerky way in which he moved, nearly robotic, but also somehow simian. Yet, despite it all, he exuded confidence, a man ready for any challenge. In fact, he moved in such a way that seemed to suggest he was quite sure no challenge would be forthcoming at all because who would dare step in his path?

The answer came pretty quickly.

Rufus. Rufus dared step in his path.

I had no doubt that Rufus heard him coming and did it on purpose. Two things happened—neither of which I'd been expecting. First—and almost comically—Walsh collided with Rufus. Rufus braced himself against Walsh and managed to shoulder the bigger man to the ground while keeping his balance. Walsh went down hard.

The second thing was the bodyguard's reaction. He strode swiftly to Rufus, fist raised, but Rufus didn't see him and stood there with the peace and calm that only a blind man could muster.

"He's blind," I said.

The man lowered his hand slightly. People were never sure how much to hold Rufus responsible for when they realized he couldn't see. The bodyguard's eyes narrowed, looking closely at Rufus's face as if trying to prove my statement wrong. He shook his head and stepped back and looked at me. "Maybe you're the one I should punch then?"

I shrugged. "Why do you need to punch anybody? It was an accident, okay?"

Before the bodyguard could reply, Walsh spoke. He was still on the ground but managed to convey a genial sense of control even from there.

"I hope," he said, pulling himself up and dusting off his pants, "you didn't drive too far. I haven't performed a healing in years. God has shifted my focus away from individual healing to healing the ills of society. I'll pray with you, of course."

He glanced around, confused by our silence, and there was a tantalizing flicker in his countenance that seemed to suggest he wasn't sure he'd read the situation correctly.

Then his eyes fell on Susan.

Susan's a good-looking woman. Men notice her. That he noticed her was normal. Most straight men took a second glance, or at least let their gaze linger. Hell, I'm not ashamed to admit, I'd caught myself staring a bit too long once or twice, but what he was doing now was completely different. Over the years I'd had the misfortune of looking into the eyes of some truly depraved men and had found the experience chilling to say the least, but this was something I'd rarely witnessed: this was a predator looking at his next meal. He was violating her, and Susan noticed it immediately; we all noticed it. She stepped away, acting on instinct.

I opened my mouth to say something, to come to her defense, but Walsh caught me off guard by reaching for my hand. "Jeb Walsh," he said, pumping hard.

I pulled my hand away and said the only words I could manage, "We don't want you here."

Walsh's smile grew slowly, the sun taking its time cresting the eastern horizon, until the day seemed filled with it.

"Let me see if I understand. You—you three—came to tell me that? You actually found out when I would be by to meet with the library director about my book signing? I've got to admire that kind of dedication, however misplaced. Truly impressive."

Rufus moved closer now, honing in on Walsh's voice.

"You want to control this guy?" Walsh said, looking at me.

"He's got a mind of his own," I said.

Walsh turned to face Rufus. He opened his mouth to say something, but it was too late.

"You're a pestilence," Rufus said, and the thing about Rufus was that when he said you were a pestilence, you couldn't help but sort of believe him. His voice was a force of nature, the sound of the King James Bible if it could talk. Ancient, stark. Words that dropped on top of you like heavy stones, and that was just his voice. Rufus's appearance could stop traffic. He was a character pulled from a dark tale, gaunt and rawboned, with a mythic quality that he was all too aware of. He favored dark overalls and tattered, loose-fitting sports coats that hung off his stooped frame. His blind eyes somehow seemed alert and distant at once. Combine all that with his uncanny knack of always knowing just where he was in the world, and—most disturbingly—just where *you* were in the world, and it added up to the kind of a man you most *definitely* didn't want calling you a pestilence.

Walsh moved back a step, clearly not interested in getting tangled up with Rufus again, and tried a different approach.

"It appears you folks take some issue with one of my books? Am I correct?"

"I take issue with *all* of your books," Rufus said.

"Well, I have a very simple solution. Don't buy them."

I shook my head. "That's not enough anymore. Now that you've gone after kids, a line has been crossed."

I stepped forward, fists clenched. Was I going to hit him? I didn't know. That had always been both my strength and weakness. Too many times, the deed was done before I had time to think through the consequences. Too many times, I found myself standing over a bleeding man, wondering if I'd acted too fast, if he'd really deserved the pain I'd put on him. And too many times, the reverse: me looking up at a grinning man, hating my foolish instincts and promising to never make that mistake again.

But sooner or later, it always happened, and always without warning.

"Take it easy," Walsh's bodyguard said. His drawl was thick, but not mountain—closer to the Gulf than the Appalachians.

Walsh chuckled again, but I could tell his interaction with Rufus had left him a little shaken, because this time the chuckle seemed forced. "This has really been entertaining, but we do have an appointment. I will pray for all three of you."

"Four," Mary said as she exited the library. I stepped back. Mary always had a calming effect on me. She made me remember what I was fighting for—not just a decent life for me, but for her too. For us.

Jeb took one look at her and nodded. "You're with these people?" What was unstated but implied by his question was his disapproval of whites and blacks being part of the same group.

"I am."

"I suppose you think I'm a racist or something?"

She shrugged. "Well, I did read your book, and honestly, it's pretty much there in black and white."

His bodyguard stepped up and put a hand on Walsh's shoulder, as if to calm him. Walsh glared at Mary. His gaze was different now, but no less disturbing than when he'd looked at Susan. Except now he was the predator looking at prey that would fight back tooth and nail.

"You're all show," he said. "But that's not surprising."

Again, the man seemed to have a gift for innuendo, especially of the racist variety.

My instincts at that point were telling me to step forward and punch him in the face. The problem was the inevitable trouble it would get me in. Not with the law—I could handle that—but with Mary. She'd made it abundantly clear she didn't want me fighting her battles.

So I waited, gritting the hell out of my teeth.

Mary unwrapped a piece of gum and stuck it in her mouth. Her courage had always stunned me; hell, sometimes it shamed me because I knew, deep in my heart, I didn't have half of the intestinal fortitude she did, and this time was no exception.

She smacked the gum for a few seconds and nodded. "It's rare for me to say this, Mr. Walsh, but I read your book, and I can't think of a more pathetic excuse for a man than you. Your words are incapable of hurting me. It would be like getting upset because some kind of wild animal didn't like me." She shook her head, laughing a little. "Actually, I might get upset about that. But not about you."

Walsh laughed, a cruel high sound that seemed almost surreal in the otherwise silent street. "Wild animal? That's rich." His smile vanished. "All God's creatures great and small—I try to remind myself when I see someone I'm tempted to lash out at, God loves them all." He stepped past Mary and started up the steps before stopping and looking back over his shoulder. "But then again, I'm not God, am I? I'm just a poor sinner. Because 'all have sinned and fallen short of the grace of God.' Even little old me, and I'm not going to lie: I love it that God can forgive, brothers and sisters. It means, no matter what I might do, I can stand before the Lord clean and pure as the driven snow. Goodbye. If you'd like those books signed, I'll be here Saturday afternoon. Oh, and after that, we're having a big town square rally in support of traditional values next Thursday. It's already making national news. We're going to have good people from all over the country come in." He looked right at Mary again. "You might not want to come to that one. Some of these boys . . . well, they're angry about what's happening to our country, and I'm afraid they aren't too afraid to point the finger at those who are responsible." He nodded at me. "I'd love to have the rest of you folks join us for that, though."

Then he and his bodyguard were gone, and I reached for Mary's hand. She gripped mine tightly, the only small indication she gave that she was in fact shaken by his words.

2

Late September found north Georgia still hungover from a long, hot summer. The leaves dropped like wild birds, swirling to the soft, still warm ground. The threat of rain was always somewhere, on one distant horizon or the other, and as the calendar slouched toward October, the moon returned, its hooked countenance blooming into the slow sideways smile of a drunk after a long night at the bar.

Despite the run-in with Walsh, Mary and I decided to take advantage of the nice weather and go for a walk, ranging out from my mountain home, exploring the eastern side of Pointer Mountain. It was rare for her to be off on a Monday, so we meant to enjoy the opportunity and spend the day outside. Over the last year, we'd made a pastime out of finding new and hidden caves. They're scattered all over these mountains, and it gave us something to do and something to wonder about. This afternoon, we found two within a half mile of each other. The first was cool and damp and small, a shallow divot in the mountainside. We used it to escape a brief thunderstorm, me holding Mary tight as the thunder shook the mountain. We watched it rain, and I tried to not to think about any of the things that had been bothering me, the thoughts of evil and what Jeb Walsh's presence in these mountains could mean. Unlike so many other times when I tried to focus on the positive, it was so much easier when I was with Mary. Everything seemed a little easier when she was around.

After the storm ended and we stepped out of the cave into the open space of the world, I pointed up the ridge to a large boulder perched precariously on the ledge above a five-hundred-foot drop into pine trees and old logging roads that now lay as dormant and secret as the caves.

"You up for a climb?' I said.

Mary was fifteen years younger than me and in good shape, but sometimes she preferred to walk leisurely while I had a hard time resisting anything that could be explored.

She squeezed my hand. "I think I see another cave up there."

I squinted into the morning sun. There was a dark slash in the rock wall. A cave or maybe just a shadow. "Then we have to go," I said, joking but also serious. If she didn't want to go, I'd come back later with Goose, my Mastiff-Shepherd mix, and explore it on my own. I'd always had a hard time leaving any mystery alone.

She leaned in and kissed my neck. "I'll bet it's private."

I nearly carried her up the hill.

* * *

Once inside, I saw immediately it was a proper cave, not just a little overhang. I pulled out the penlight I kept on my keychain, and flicked it on. The light spread out in front of us, illuminating a stone floor and some mildewed bedding someone had left from a previous amorous encounter. What I didn't see was a back wall.

"This thing is deep."

Mary's hand was resting lightly in mine, and she intensified the pressure just the slightest bit. These were the kinds of things she did that turned me on. Since our relationship had started just over a year ago, she'd taught me to appreciate even the most simple gestures.

I pulled her deeper into the cave. The temperature dropped as we moved, and the darkness seemed to soak into the light that was out in front of us, dimming it and rendering it more ineffectual as we pressed toward the hidden regions of the cave.

When we finally reached the back wall, we touched the cool stone with our hands, mine following hers as she slid it lightly over the dampness. I wondered how deep we were into the mountain now and how many other lovers had stood in this same place, their hands intermingled on the ancient stone. I moved mine over hers, enveloping it, as her body melted against my own.

Sometimes making love with Mary was a kind of sensory overload. Because she lived in Atlanta, our time was tantalizingly brief, mostly comprised of weekends and sometimes not even then if she was busy with a case. I often wished I could remember our lovemaking with more detail when I was alone in the house with Goose, but all that would come to me was an intoxicating swirl of need and more need followed by the sweetest relief, my hands tangled in her short, kinky hair, my mouth pressed so hard against hers, we breathed for each other.

It might have been the same on that morning in the cave, but when our bodies took over, we slammed ourselves into the back wall and something rattled near our heads and then fell, hitting my shoulder.

It landed on the cave floor with a loud thunk.

"What was that?" Mary said.

"I don't care," I said, and pressed her against the cave wall.

* * *

When it was over, Mary found my keys that I'd dropped in the moment of passion and turned on the penlight. She moved it over my face, and I closed my eyes. Somehow the damp stone floor felt comfortable, and sleep was not out of the question.

I was almost there, fading into a blissfulness that my life had too long been without, when Mary gasped. I sat up and found the penlight she'd dropped near my leg. I reached for it, but my hand found something else instead. It was solid and cold and hard. My fingers slipped into a hole, and for a mad second I thought it was a bowling ball, but then Mary picked up the penlight and shone it at what I held.

A skull.

I let go immediately, causing it to roll across the cave with a sickening clatter. When it stopped rolling, Mary knelt, shining the penlight at it for a closer look.

"Is it human?" I said, but I already knew the answer.

"Yeah. And it's been here awhile. She turned it over to examine the other side. "I don't see any signs of trauma."

"Where's the rest of the body?" I said.

"Good question." She stood, shining the light at the back wall again. She moved the light in wide arcs, and that was when we saw the writing: "AOC."

She kept moving the light, and there was another bit below that: "Old Nathaniel."

"Is it blood?" I asked.

She didn't answer.

I touched the letters, sliding my fingers across them. They didn't feel any different than the wall did when we'd touched it earlier, our hands intertwined. The letters didn't feel different, but *I* did. I felt like I'd taken a knife to the gut. All of the wonder and glory from earlier seemed gone now, replaced by a silent despair.

People had made love here, but someone else had used it as a sick kind of temple, a shrine to something dark and unspeakable.

Suddenly, I needed to be free of the cave. I needed to find some light and some air that had been touched by the warmth of the sun.

"You okay?" Mary said.

"Yeah," I said, but I wasn't okay. I was stumbling out of the cave, trying not to think about my father or the cave I'd found him in just over a year ago. The cave where I'd finally confronted him and all the sickness he'd put inside me. The place where I'd sent him to a flaming death.

Once outside, I felt better almost immediately. The sun was shining brightly, and the rain had moved on. I sat down on the ground beside the big rock and wondered exactly what we'd unearthed.

3

Sheriff Doug Patterson was a tall, laconic young man with thick sideburns and an easygoing manner that made me like him right away.

He showed up carrying two water bottles and was accompanied by a deputy who introduced herself in a slow drawl as Lacey Barnes.

"I read about you," Jefferson said. "In the papers."

It was a line I'd heard a lot recently. Ever since the article had come out detailing how Mary and I had taken down my father's church, my fledgling PI business had taken off. Apparently, people around here actually did read the newspapers.

I waited to see where he was going with the newspaper thing, but he only turned toward the cave entrance. "In here?"

"Yeah," Mary said.

Patterson nodded at his deputy, who carried a large Maglite. She flipped it on and started inside the cave. Patterson motioned for Mary to go ahead of him, and I brought up the rear.

Under the glare of the Maglite, the cave looked different. It was smaller somehow. Deputy Barnes waved the light around until it fell on the skull. She held it still as Patterson walked over for a better look. He put his hands on his knees and bent over, studying it.

He grunted and reached for the skull. Once in his hand, he walked to the cave's exit. I followed him out and stood beside him as he turned the skull over in his hands.

"It's fake," he said.

"What?"

He held the skull out. "Look on the very top," he said.

He rotated the skull until I saw a slight crack in the top. "It's a crack," I said.

"Nope, it's a slot." He weighed the skull in his big hand before tossing it out over the ridge. I watched it tumble into the undergrowth below and disappear into the vines.

"Hey, why'd you do that?"

He shrugged. "It's a toy. You take a butter knife and stick it in the slot to pry off the top. Then you put the batteries in. I'll bet the eyes light up or some shit."

"Are you sure?" I said.

"Shit, I showed it to you."

I nodded. Showing it to me might be stretching it a little, but I could definitely see how the crack could have been a slot for batteries. "I'm sorry I wasted your time," I said.

"No worries. It looked real to me too in the cave. You mentioned some writing?"

He followed me back to the cave.

Inside, we found Deputy Barnes and Mary studying the writing.

"It's fake," I said.

"What?" Mary said. "I looked at it myself."

"It was a really good imitation," Patterson said. "Easy mistake to make. Now, what do we have here?"

I looked at the writing again, trying to make sense of it, as Patterson did the same.

"AOC," he said. "Old Nathaniel. Why am I not surprised?"

"What do you mean?" Mary asked.

"They've been showing up everywhere these days. Just last week, I was called out to Corn Valley—you know, the trailer park out there?—to investigate some graffiti someone had sprayed on one of the trailers. One of the kids had recently run off, and the mother thinks the graffiti had something to do with it."

"Run off?" Mary said. "Or was taken?"

Sheriff Patterson shrugged. "Run off. He was eighteen and lived in the armpit of north Georgia. The racists in this county . . . Jesus, if I was a young black man, I'd get the hell out too."

"So what does it mean?" I asked. "Who's Old Nathaniel?"

"Hell, I was hoping you could tell me. I'm a Tennessee boy. According to that news story I read, you were born and raised right here in these mountains. Way I understand it, Old Nathaniel is a local legend. You don't know it?"

"I don't think I do. But then again, I was immune to a lot of the local legends. My father made sure I only got exposed to the ones that took place way over in the Middle East a long time ago."

"I know who he is," Mary said. Her voice sounded abnormally quiet and unsure. I resisted the urge to put my arms around her.

"Granny told me about him when I was a little girl. She said he was supposed to stalk the valley, and he liked to eat little black children."

"Jesus," I said.

"Yeah, it was scary even for me up in the mountains. *Even* when Granny made sure to tell me it was just some made-up thing to scare the kids from coming up and bothering the white folks."

"What about the other thing?" I asked. "AOC?"

"No idea," Mary said.

"Yeah, I'm stumped on that one too," Patterson said.

We were all quiet for a moment. I felt suddenly conscious of the struggles Mary'd had to face that the rest of us hadn't.

"Teenagers," Patterson said at last. "I'll bet that's who we're dealing with."

"Probably so," I said. I looked at Mary. It was hard to read her face in the darkness, but I hoped she agreed. What else could it be?

"Well," Patterson said when we were back outside. "I'm glad I got to meet the famous Earl Marcus, anyway. I'd been meaning to give you a ring."

"Why's that?"

He made a face, stiffening his lip, squinting out across the ridge at a hawk. "I just thought it would be good to meet. You know, in case you needed my help or I ever needed yours."

I let his words sink in. It felt strange to have a positive, mutually respectful relationship with a sheriff. My relationship with the last one had been the complete opposite.

"I'll keep that in mind," I said.

"You do that." He nodded at Mary. "Nice to meet you."

Mary and I stood at the top of the incline and watched as they made their way down the steep slope.

When they were out of earshot, Mary leaned over and kissed my neck. "I'm so glad," she said.

"About what?"

"About the skull being fake."

"Why's that?"

"Well," she said, her voice softening in that special way that made me weak at the knees. "I didn't want to ruin a perfectly good memory with the thought of a human skull."

"Ah, so you enjoyed yourself?"

She didn't answer. She didn't have to. Her lips found mine, and mine found hers, and I knew that it was the only answer I'd ever need in this world.

* * *

That night we saw more storms, and Mary and I stayed up late into the night, sitting on the porch of the house we'd once shared, talking about the future. Goose, the dog whose life I'd saved just a few feet away from where we sat now, lay near our feet, watching Mary closely. He loved her nearly as much as me and reveled in her presence whenever she was around. As usual, it didn't take me long to get around to the thing that stayed on my mind and was frequently on the tip of my tongue.

"You should move back."

She nuzzled my neck, kissing it lightly and murmured, "I work in Atlanta."

"Of course, but you work in Atlanta because the sheriff was a racist here, right? But there's a new sheriff. He's not racist. At least he didn't seem racist."

She nodded. "True. He didn't *seem* racist."

"What's that supposed to mean?"

"It means what it means. You never really know."

"Never?"

I felt her shrug.

"What about me?"

"What about you?"

"Am I racist?"

"Earl Marcus, we're all racist. At least a little bit."

I didn't really like that answer but decided to let it go. Besides, I needed to get back to the real thing I wanted to talk about.

"You could move back in. We could have a life together."

"We already do."

"Yeah, if you count once a week. If that."

"Look," she said, sitting up and facing me. "Let's just let things play out, okay? I'm not the kind of woman to rush into anything. I like what we have here. There's a rhythm to it."

"A rhythm?"

"That's right. And look at you. Just like a man—always trying to rush the rhythm."

"Well, when it feels good . . ."

She shook her head and laughed. "I know. You just can't control yourself."

We barely slept at all that night.

4

I thought I might be in love with Mary Hawkins.

There were a lot of reasons why I shouldn't be, and first among them was that she was fifteen years younger than me. Another was that she lived an hour away in Atlanta and had a busy career of her own. The final reason was that I was not very good at being in love with anyone.

I'd known love once before, as a teenager, but that had been a lifetime ago and had ended badly. Suffice to say, it soured me quite a bit on relationships, and I spent most of my adult life avoiding them in favor of strictly physical encounters, the more frequent and less familiar, the better.

Maybe that's why I was in lying in bed this next morning with Mary, watching her sleep and thinking about how goddamn lucky I was to be with her. And maybe that was why I was so pissed off when I heard the truck approaching.

I lived on top of a mountain, a peaceful kind of place made even more peaceful by the bad roads that connected it to the rest of the world. You needed a sturdy truck with four-wheel drive to get here. What you didn't need was a flashy, jacked-up piece of shit without a muffler.

Rufus said only assholes and kids drove jacked-up monster trucks without mufflers. I tended to agree.

The man approaching now was of the asshole variety, though his emotional IQ was still probably around that of an adolescent.

"What? Mary said, her eyes blinking open. They were the best eyes I'd ever seen, big and brown and luxurious. Looking into them was like slipping into a warm, comfortable bath.

"Just stay in bed," I said. "I'll try to make this quick."

"What's going on?" She reached for my arm and pulled me back into bed. I kissed her but didn't linger. This particular visitor had a way of killing the mood.

"Just stay here," I said. "I promise to make this really quick."

She sat up. "It's Ronnie Thrash, isn't it?"

I nodded.

"Why don't you invite him in? I can make some breakfast."

"Bad idea."

"I think you're too hard on him."

I took a deep breath. Mary didn't really know Ronnie like I did. But it was more than that. The truth was, Ronnie Thrash and I were bound together by a shared secret.

A secret not even Mary knew about.

"Just give me a minute. And don't come out. I don't want you around that asshole."

She shot me a look, and I knew she was disappointed in me. Too bad. I knew Ronnie and she didn't. Sometimes, Mary's ability to see the good in people infuriated me.

I decided to let it go and headed to the front door, where Goose stood, growling at the sound of the truck as it downshifted out in the yard.

"It's just the usual asshole," I said. Goose whined and wagged his tail at my voice. I opened the front door and let him rush out barking. I hoped he might light into Ronnie. I'd been hoping that for some time now, but much to my chagrin, Ronnie seemed to have a way with Goose. Once he killed the monstrous sound from his truck's engine and jumped out of the cab, Goose started wagging his tail. Ronnie knelt and let the big dog lick his face. When he stood up, he was grinning.

There are two things you could count on from Ronnie, come hell or high water: he'd be wearing that shit-eating grin no matter what, and he never came into any interaction without knowing where all the buttons were and just when to push them. He was like a gnat at dusk that won't stop chewing on your skin, or a hangnail you can't ever get rid of because it cut too deep.

He came strutting over like a damned banty rooster, wearing dark blue jeans and some huge, shit-kicking boots. He'd bought himself a new belt buckle too. It was saucer-sized and read "Straight to Hell, Baby." There was something on his face, just above his nose that was new. Some kind of tattoo.

"Like it?" he said, gesturing at the black markings with his thumb. "It's an upside-down cross, on account of this new piece of ass I'm smashing. She's got a fetish for demons and shit." He shrugged. "It ain't real. Just temporary. I figure, why get a real one when me and her will be splits in a week or two anyway?" He patted his shirt pocket and pulled out a nearly empty package of Marlboro Reds. He took the last cigarette out and stuck it in his mouth, then patted his blue jeans. "Shit. Left my lighter at the house. You got a match or something?"

I ignored him. It was my first line of defense against his bullshit. Ignore as long as I could in order to keep the anger at bay. It wouldn't last.

"Well, I guess that's a no."

"Why are you here?"

"Shit, Earl. I'm here because you and me are friends. I don't want to get carried away none, but I'd go as far as to say you're my BFF. Now, it won't hurt me none if you say I'm not your BFF too. Just please tell me it's not that old blind vampire. Now that will hurt."

"We're not friends, and you know that. Please state your business and then get off my property."

"Your property?" He laughed. "Is that what you're calling it now? Jesus, you and the little black deputy about to get hitched? Be careful, Earl, I hear marriage can ruin a good sex life quick."

Second line of defense against his bullshit: get angry.

"I'm going to ask you to get the hell out of here before I call the sheriff."

He looked at Mary's Atlanta PD Blazer parked near his truck. "Looks like the po-po is already here."

"I don't want her anywhere around you."

He nodded. "Cuz I'm vile and reprehensible, right, Earl?"

"You said it."

"Well, that's interesting considering what I helped you do a few months back."

I stepped forward. "You aren't supposed to bring that up."

"Oh, indeed. I'm not supposed to bring that up. Whoops." His smile fell away for just an instant. "You know I've been so good, Earl. Haven't told a soul. I'd hate to let it slip." The smile came back, and I wanted to punch him so much.

Third line: get violent.

Except that wasn't what I wanted, was it? It was true—he had helped me. And since that time, he'd never asked for anything in return.

"I'm calling the sheriff," I said, but my heart wasn't in it.

"That's funny."

"What's funny?"

"You calling the sheriff. You ain't heard, have you?"

"Heard what?"

Ronnie stuck the unlit cigarette back in his mouth. "You sure you wouldn't have a light?"

"Heard what?"

"I'll bet you think the new sheriff is a breath of fucking fresh air compared to the old one, don't you? No ties to your daddy's church, no real ties to these mountains at all. Sounded pretty fucking good to me too. Sad truth is, Earl, he's a real piece of work. Did you know he was busted for misuse of government funds at his old job up in Knoxville? Get this: he used it to buy drugs. Said his wife needed the pot because she had anxiety. They fired his ass, but lo and behold, here he is in Coulee County 'cause any old bastard will do here. Let me ask you something, Earl. What do you think they'd do to a man like me if I was caught buying pot with government funds? I'll tell you what they'd do, my friend. They'd put me under the jail. You know they would."

I just looked at him. I wouldn't give him the satisfaction of telling him he was right, even though I had to agree with his assessment.

"Doesn't matter. He'll still get you off my land."

"Don't it pain you just a little, Earl?"

"Don't what pain me?"

"That the new sheriff ain't no better than the old. That there ain't much satisfaction in putting your faith in anything, is there, Earl? First God lets us down, then our daddies, and now the damned law. I tell you what, there ain't but one man I trust in this great, big, wide world, and that man stands before me right now: the legendary Earl Marcus." He clapped his hands slowly and dramatically and then stopped, seeming to remember the unlit cigarette. "Goddamn, I need a light. Let's go inside. I know you got a match."

"I've met him," I said. "He's a lot better than the last. If he made a mistake, that's too bad, but I won't hold it against him going forward."

Ronnie nodded, still studying the unlit cigarette. "Too bad you don't extend that same charity to everybody, Earl."

I was about to answer, when I heard a voice from behind me.

"Earl?"

Mary stood in the doorway, looking sleepy and beautiful. She wore one of my shirts and nothing else as far as I could tell.

"Hello," Ronnie said. "Ain't you a picture."

"Can we invite you in for some breakfast?" she said.

"No," I said. "We're almost done here."

"I could use some breakfast," Ronnie said.

"Well, I think I could mix up some pancakes . . ." Mary said.

"Hell no," I said, this time like I meant it.

Mary shot me a reproachful look.

"I'm sorry," she said to Ronnie, "for Earl's behavior."

Ronnie nodded. "It's okay. I know he's stressed out by life and whatnot. I don't take it personal."

Mary gave me another look before going back inside the house.

"Be still my heart," Ronnie said. "You are in over your fucking head, ain't you? Beautiful and kind."

"I'm going to ask you nice one more time to state your business," I said. "After that, I ain't calling the law and I ain't talking no more." I squeezed my fists together.

"Sure thing, Earl. It's like this: I need your services."

"My services?"

"Your skills."

"You want to hire me?"

"Well, I was thinking more pro bono myself."

"Pro bono? You can't be serious."

He shrugged and opened up his palms to the deep blue morning sky. "Funds are kind of low right now, Earl. I thought you and me were tight. I thought we were brothers, you know?"

"We're not tight."

He nodded and took the cigarette out of his mouth. He regarded it for a moment before dropping it into the grass. Goose sniffed at it and sneezed.

"That hurts, Earl. Especially because I know your real brother, and he ain't much of a man. Running a church that tortured young girls and what not. But I reckon he's good enough to still be your brother."

"He's blood. You . . . you ain't nothing."

His smile disappeared for a moment, and I knew I had wounded him.

"That's how you see it, huh?"

"That's how I see it."

"Well, I see it different. According to my way, you and me got an unshakable bond." The grin came back, just around the corners of his mouth, just enough so that I couldn't miss his delight. "I mean when it was time to bury your daddy, you didn't come to nobody else, now did you?"

I felt a wave of anger inching up out of me, building slow and powerful.

"I mean, I'll bet that cute little sex machine that's waiting inside don't even know how you knocked your daddy off that cliff, how he was all ablaze as he fell. Damn, many's a time I've reflected on how I wish I could have been there to see that spectacular fall. Like Satan himself falling from heaven, I'll bet." Now the grin was a full-fledged smile, and larger than ever. He was positively beaming.

The only thing that stopped me from hitting him was the way Goose was looking at me. He was sitting up, ears alert, body tense, and there was something in his eyes. I thought it might have been fear. I unclenched my fists and stepped back. I hadn't realized how close I'd gotten to Ronnie, how I was already within easy striking distance.

I took a deep breath. Goose wagged his tail, a tentative thump, as if he was encouraging me to take it easy.

"It'll have to wait until this afternoon, when Mary's gone."

"Of course. I wouldn't dream of interrupting your personal time, Earl."

"Tell me what you need," I said, and hated myself and the words even as I said them.

* * *

It was true that I'd killed my father, that I'd knocked him off a mountain, or rather, I'd knocked him *out of* a mountain. And it was also true that Ronnie was the only one who knew about it. He'd helped me bury my father's body. It wasn't one of my prouder moments.

When I went back into the house after watching Ronnie's jacked-up truck head down the mountain, Mary was sitting on the couch, fully dressed.

"That man ruins everything," I said.

She smiled. "What did he want?"

"He said he needed to hire me."

"For what?"

"He was a little unspecific about that. Said he needed an escort."

"Uh-oh."

"Right. He promised me that he wasn't doing anything criminal."

"You believe him?"

"No. But he seems to think we're friends. Maybe if I do this for him, he'll leave me alone for a while." I wasn't about to mention the real reason I was doing it: because part of me believed I did owe him something for the help he'd given me.

"Well, as long as it's legal, I'm glad you're helping him."

"Why are you so forgiving of him?"

She shrugged. "I know where he came from."

"What's that supposed to mean?"

"You of all people should know, Earl. He came from your father's church. His grandfather was your father's best friend. That church destroyed lives. All I'm saying is that maybe you two have more in common than you want to admit."

"Can we just talk about something else, please?"

"Sure," she said, and stood up. She walked over to me and kissed me hard. "I'll be back on Wednesday."

"I'm going to miss you," I said, dropping a hand to her ass and pulling her close. She moaned a little and kissed my neck again.

"I've got to go."

"I know."

"Hey, maybe we'll find another cave when I come back?"

"Yeah," I said. "Just one without the creepy factor."

She shrugged. "Teenagers, remember?"

"Maybe."

"Definitely. It was a toy skull. Bad guys hide real ones."

"Right," I said.

She kissed my neck, just the way I liked, and I closed my eyes, thinking how there must be some kind of law of physics that said nothing could ever be quite perfect. This was pretty damned close, and if I could breathe deep and make myself forget Ronnie Thrash was even alive, I could fool myself, at least for a little while.

5

I spent the rest of Tuesday morning and early afternoon cleaning the house, first the kitchen and then the two bedrooms in back, before finishing with the den, while I listened to Willie Nelson singing about blue skies and cowboys. Before moving back to these mountains, I'd been a poor housekeeper, preferring to go as long as possible until a visit from a friend became imminent. Only then would I do a mad cleaning, and generally it was just as bad a few days later. But here, in the mountains, I felt an obligation to keep things presentable. As Ronnie had so succinctly pointed out this morning, I didn't own the place. Which was one reason to take a little care, but far from the only reason. Another was that Mary did own it, and she'd insisted I stay there and absolutely refused to take any rent. The third, and most compelling reason had to do with the previous owner.

Her name was Arnette Lacey, and besides being one of the hardest-working women I'd ever known (which was why I felt a duty to continue her tradition of housekeeping), she was also—by far—the kindest and most empathetic one too. When things went bad between me and my father after the snake bit me, Arnette took me in. She also single-handedly showed me what it meant to care for another person unreservedly, without any hope of getting something in return. It wasn't long before I started calling her Granny. I lived with her for nearly three years before leaving in the middle of a windy autumn night with nothing but a change of underwear, an extra shirt, and the Bible my mother had given me a few years earlier. The shirt made it as far as Denver, Colorado, before I lost it somewhere in Rocky Mountain National Park while skinny-dipping with a girl I'd met earlier that morning. The underwear wore thin a few years later near Sault Ste. Marie in Michigan, and it was one of many items of clothing I simply left in the apartment I shared with three small-time drug dealers. I still had the Bible. It was tucked beneath the bed where I slept now, Granny's old bed. Despite still having it, I'd gotten very little use out of it. I kept it in memory of my mother because, like my brother Lester and me, she'd been a victim too. Unlike Lester and me, she was an adult and should have been able to fight back, or at least she should have made an attempt. She never did, and that was one of the reasons I only kept it and never opened it. Any book that my mother used to guide her life couldn't have much to say to me.

Or was I being too harsh? Sometimes I thought I was. Sometimes I thought about it lying under the bed, in the dark space, collecting dust, and wondered if there was some great insight or wisdom inside it that I sorely lacked.

Ironically, the person who'd come the closest to making me pick that book up was Granny. She'd been a believer, but her faith was nothing like the one I'd grown up with. Hers was a faith based on love and not judgment, acceptance and not rejection. They say Jesus saves. I wasn't sure about that. What I did know was that Arnette Lacey had saved me. And that was why I cared about keeping the house clean.

When I finished the den and sat down to eat a sandwich in the kitchen, I heard the familiar rumble of Ronnie's truck.

"Shit," I said around a mouthful of pimento cheese. I finished up, fed Goose, and holstered my 9mm. It was September and still too hot for it, but I pulled on my blue jean jacket to keep the gun hidden and then sat outside to wait on him.

He beeped twice at the top of the gravel drive, and I walked over. He grinned at me and cut the stereo up when I got inside. The music was fast and ragged. A woman screamed her lungs out. Ronnie drummed on the steering wheel and bobbed his head with each thunderous beat. I reached out and cut the volume all the way down.

"Well, Jesus, Earl. I would have turned it down. Wasn't no call to be rude."

"I need to know what we're doing. And don't think about not telling me. If I'm going to help you, I *have* to know."

He held his hands out, as if fending off an attack. "Easy there, tiger. I'm going to tell you. Shit. Impatient. You know you can trust me, buddy. We're kindred spirits, you and me. Brothers until the end."

"Cut the shit. Talk to me. What's going on?"

"Okay, so you may not know, but I'm a businessman. I've—"

"Forget it. I'm not getting involved in a drug deal."

"Now, that really hurts. You just like to take that proverbial knife and stick it in, don't you, Earl? I'm not a drug dealer. I run a siding business."

"Siding business?"

"That's right. Well, it's not the typical kind of siding business. It's based on something I invented. It's weather-resistant siding."

"You didn't invent that."

"Sure I did. I mean, I guess if you're going to get technical about it, there's some others out there that *claim* to be weatherproof, but mine really is. And for cheap too."

"Okay, even if I were to believe you, what's this got to do with me?"

"I've got an investor who owes me some money. They promised to invest and then reneged. I've got the contract and everything, but they know I won't take them to court because of my priors and whatnot. So, I need to go pick up the money myself."

"And I'm going along to . . . ?"

"As. You're going along *as* an insurance policy. I think it should be easy, but there's this fellow named Lane Jefferson, and if he's there, he'll make trouble. But if I've got a PI with me, an armed PI—you are packing, right?"

I nodded.

"Good, then it'll be easy."

“And that’s all it is?”

“Yep.” He cranked the truck.

It sounded like there was definitely some potential for trouble, but considering who I was with, I figured it could have easily been worse.

* * *

We were halfway down the mountain when Ronnie turned the music down again and offered me a cigarette.

“I don’t smoke.”

“Color me surprised. I always took you for a smoker.”

I shrugged. Honestly, I had no desire to engage in any more conversation with Ronnie than was necessary.

“You know when I started smoking?”

I shook my head.

“I was eight. Daddy had just got out on parole. I’d been staying with my granddaddy. You remember Old Billy, don’t you?”

I didn’t answer. He knew very well I remembered his grandfather. He’d been my father’s best friend and most trusted advisor for most of his life.

“Anyway, Grandpa told Daddy he couldn’t come inside the house until he promised to clean up his ways. I think he might have even wanted him to confess his sins before the Lord or some such bullshit. ’Course the only thing my daddy and his daddy ever had in common was their mule-headedness, and Daddy told Grandpa he’d be fucked before he confessed anything.” Ronnie took a drag off his cigarette and laughed at the memory. “Well, as you can imagine, that didn’t sit too well with Grandpa, and he took to swinging at Daddy right there on the porch. Pummeling him. Straight up beatdown. Daddy was as stubborn as Grandpa, but not half as tough.”

“Your grandfather was a vile man,” I said.

He laughed again. “You got that right. Anyway, my little sister, Wanda, she flipped out, went to crying her head off. I didn’t blame her much. She hadn’t seen her daddy in a good five years, she couldn’t have been more than eight at the time. Top of that, Grandpa had been giving us straight hell about getting our hearts and minds right with God—you know the drill."

"Yeah," I said. "I know that drill."

"Sure you do. My grandpa and your daddy were like two peas in a pod. Sort of like me and you."

I shook my head. "In the end, your grandfather and my father hated each other."

"What's that prove? Those two men hated everything, Earl. Don't you know that was their real power? It was why they held sway over so many people for so long. People want to be loved, not hated. And those two knew just how to hold that love back and when to give up a little bit to draw people in. And then once they had you, they'd pull it right back again, so that it was like a drug you had to have another hit off of."

He was right about all of this. I didn't like it, though, not just because it brought to mind so many bad memories but also because it only helped to strengthen the bond between the two of us. I'd let him charm me once before, and that had caused me to foolishly trust him with the biggest secret of my life.

"I thought this was about how you started smoking," I said.

"Oh, I'm getting there. Damn, patience, Earl, patience."

I said nothing, keeping my eyes focused on the winding road ahead. We were about to turn onto 52, and it occurred to me I didn't really know exactly where we were going.

"So, you got to picture this, Earl. Grandpa, sleeves rolled up on that starched white shirt he wore every day of his life, fists clenched, face red as a damned tomato, just *screaming* scripture at my daddy. Daddy's laid out on the front porch, bleeding from his nose, his mouth, his goddamn ears for all I know. Then you got Wanda crying like she's trying to wake up the dead. Me? I'm standing in the doorway with a lighter and a pack of cigarettes I stole from Herschel Knott. I'd been trying to be good, Earl. Grandpa had warned me about smoking. Said it was a devil's habit. Said it wasn't for someone trying to find the Lord. But I'd seen some of the older guys doing it, and I was ready to get older. I couldn't wait to get older, you hear what I'm saying, Earl? So, fuck. What do you think I did?"

"Smoked those cigarettes."

He slapped the steering wheel. "Damned right I did. And you know what else?"

"What?"

"I liked it. Sure, I coughed a little and felt some queasy, but I liked how when I ran off to the woods to do it by myself, I felt like a man. I felt like it took me away from the other shit. You ever have something like that?"

I leaned back in my seat. I didn't want to answer him. Or at least part of me didn't want to answer him. Another part of me wanted to talk because, like it or not, he did understand.

Before I could say anything, he sat on the horn. A small deer had run out into the road in front of us. It froze when it heard the horn, but Ronnie swerved quickly to avoid hitting it.

"What I wouldn't give for my hunting rifle right about now," he said, and the spell was broken. I closed my mouth and didn't speak again until I saw the cornfield.

* * *

It was about a twenty-minute drive around the Fingers, which was where Ronnie and I lived, to the narrow strip of flat land people called Corn Valley. Corn Valley was nestled in between the Fingers and Summer Mountain to the north. There wasn't much out here but trailer parks and flood plains. And corn, of course. Hell, there was a lot of that.

Eventually, we came to an old county road that looked to be used mostly by logging trucks. Ronnie turned right onto it. The road wound down through the valley, parting some woods and coming out into an open, sunny area, the cornfield on our left and scrub pines on our right.

In the distance, I saw the Blackclaw River.

"This here is Skull Keep," Ronnie said. "You ever been out this way?" He slowed the truck just as I saw the big farmhouse up ahead on the left.

"Can't say that I have. What kind of name is Skull Keep?"

He shrugged. "It's more of a nickname than anything else. This is unincorporated land. It's owned by that rich bastard over there." He pointed to the house on our left. "Lane Jefferson. He's fucked in the head. And"—Ronnie leaned forward, squinting at the house—"he's not home. Hot damn."

"What's that mean?"

"Means you can stay in the truck. Keep an eye out. If you see a sawed-off piece of shit with crazy fucking eyes drive up, stall his ass."

"Stall his ass?"

"Keep him outside."

"How am I supposed to do that?"

Ronnie pulled into the gravel drive and killed the engine. "You'll figure it out."

Before I could reply, he jumped out of the truck and slammed the door. I watched him jog up to the house and try the door. It was unlocked. He turned back to me, waved, and went inside.

6

I sat there for a few minutes, diddling with my smartphone. The service was too bad out here to do anything other than check my text messages, and there weren't any new ones anyway. I put the phone down on the seat and looked out the window.

The cornfield was really something. The stalks looked like great waves cresting as the wind bent them slightly. I couldn't help but wonder what it would be like to be hidden inside those giant stalks, to look up and see the sky through the corn silk and tassels and feel small and insignificant, but also a part of something larger.

My thoughts turned—as they often did—to my father. Wasn't that exactly what he'd wanted at first? To be a part of something larger, to touch the natural world and find out there was something divine there? I wanted that too, but so much about the idea of the divine troubled me. Jeb Walsh, for instance. How did a man like that become so powerful, so influential, if there was divinity in this world? Was it like my mother believed? That there was a perpetual war being waged between evil and good?

Maybe. I know I felt that within myself sometimes. That my own heart was a battlefield, a place scarred by the toil of casualties and the false promises of peace.

I sighed and turned my attention back to the house. Whoever owned it did have some money. Ronnie had been right about that. All brick and two spacious levels. I figured it set somebody back a pretty penny. The yard was a mess, but that was an easy enough fix. Clean up the trash, cut the grass, and weed-eat a little, and the place would be as—

Something caught my eye. A toy truck sitting near the front steps. One of those dump trucks, its bed filled with dirt. There was something else there too. A ragged old doll. It took me a minute to understand what that meant. Kids.

I was out of the truck and jogging to the door as soon as I realized how bad this could be. Ronnie Thrash trying to get money from someone with young kids around. Shit.

Shit.

Shit.

I was almost at the door when something moved in the cornfield.

I stopped cold. There had been a rustling in the plants, and now I heard a high-pitched whispering. I stepped toward the field for a better look, but there was no one there, only the massive stalks moving in a slight breeze, the corn silk floating out from the dark green husks, the widespread tassels waving against the blue sky like paper claws. And then in a flash, like the flicker of lightning, I saw someone step across one of the rows and disappear. I moved to see down the next row, but it was empty. The rows beyond that weren't really rows. They were jumbled with stalks, as if whoever had planted them had lacked the skill or patience to lay the seeds in straight lines.

An angry voice from the house broke my trance, and I remembered the urgency of the present situation. Whatever was in the cornfield would have to wait.

Once inside, what I saw made my face flush with anger. Ronnie stood over a woman, who held a small child in her lap. He wore a ski mask and held a gun aimed at the woman's face.

"Back away from her," I said.

Ronnie jumped, surprised by the sound of my voice.

"Jesus," the woman said. "What now?"

"Wait outside, Earl. This ain't what you think."

"You're waving a gun around in that woman's face. Not to mention the little boy in her lap."

"She owes me money, Earl. We talked about this."

"I ain't got no money to pay," the woman said. She seemed remarkably calm considering the situation. The child seemed calm too. He was watching Ronnie closely, his mouth opened in a look of deep fascination, but otherwise appeared unperturbed.

"Put your gun away, Ronnie. Then we can talk about this."

"Fuck you, Earl. I know you ain't gonna shoot me in front of these people. That ain't your style."

He was right. So instead of shooting him, I flipped my gun around and took three giant steps across the room. Ronnie understood what I meant to do on the second step and swung the gun around on me. I kept coming because I was pretty sure Ronnie didn't mean to shoot me either. On the third step, he tried to get his hands up to ward off my blow, but it was too late. I hit him in the forehead with the stock of my 9mm. He went down. I took his gun out of his hand and started to unload it. Empty. Jesus.

The woman laughed.

"What?" I said.

"It's just funny because he bragged about having you watching out for Lane. And now you come in and whip his ass."

"Momma?"

I turned and saw a girl no more than twelve standing behind me.

"What?" the woman said. "You finally decide to come in out of the cornfield?"

"What happened to Uncle Ronnie?"

"Wait," I said. "Uncle Ronnie?"

The woman sighed. "You wouldn't think a man would pull a gun on his own kin, now would you?" But that's just Ronnie. The boy ain't never been right. He thinks wearing that damn mask is going to fool the kids. Damn, you didn't have to hit him so hard."

Ronnie groaned in protest but was either too groggy or in too much pain to make any sense.

"So this has happened before?"

"Not in a while. Lane had put an end to most of it, but now Lane ain't home half the time, and Ronnie has been asking for money again."

"Is it true? About the investment?"

"Yeah, we promised we'd invest, but what can you do?" She nodded toward the girl standing by the door. "This one is eating us out of house and home, and now she wants to join every damn club at the school. They ain't cheap, none of them." She turned to me, putting her hands around her mouth, and whispered the next part. "It wouldn't be so bad if she wasn't so damned *weird*, you know?"

I shot her a sharp look. She shrugged. "It's true. Virginia's always been weird. Her daddy was a one-night stand. What can I say? She don't want for nothing."

Except respect, I thought, but didn't say anything. I figured I'd said and done enough already. It was time to get Ronnie out of there. I'd follow up with a call to Mary about getting these kids some help, but I wasn't counting on much. I'd seen situations worse than this one, where local authorities couldn't do a damned thing. It was maddening, but out of my control.

"Let's go," I said to Ronnie, reaching down to help him to his feet.

"Not without my money," he said.

"You aren't taking money from these people."

"She'll spend it on drugs if I don't. I was going to invest it for her. Give these kids a chance at college."

I pulled him to his feet and handed the empty gun back to him.

"Come back in a couple of weeks," his sister said, "and ask nicely, and I'll loan you a little."

"What about Lane?"

"We're quits. Caught him with one of them trailer park sluts. I'm just waiting until he comes back from out of town before leaving."

"Where are you going to go?" Ronnie asked.

"I've got a man up in the Fingers who'll take care of us."

"Shit, Wanda."

She shrugged as if to suggest it was all out of her control, that she was simply along for the ride.

"So where did he go?" Ronnie asked.

"Hell, if I know. Said he'd be back on Wednesday."

"Well, shit, I ain't coming in to work tonight, then."

"Work?" I said. I was so confused.

"Lane pays Ronnie to watch the cornfields," Wanda said.

"Watch them? Why?"

Ronnie glared at me and pulled the ski mask off. His forehead was bleeding a little, but I figured he deserved that much. "Don't worry about it."

Then he did something I hadn't expected, something that made me realize I'd stepped right into the middle of a family dynamic I'd probably never understand.

"Can I hold him?"

His sister looked at the child in her lap. "Briscoe, you want to go to your Uncle Ronnie?"

Briscoe grinned tentatively.

"Hey, big boy," Ronnie said.

Briscoe held out his arms and Ronnie took him.

It would have been sweet if it wasn't so completely fucked.

"I'll be in the truck," I said.

The girl, Virginia, was waiting for me outside.

"You're Earl Marcus," she said.

I smiled. "Yeah. How did you know?"

"I read the newspaper."

Her fast and completely serious answer disarmed me a little. In fact, nearly everything about her was disarming. She was a child, but her countenance was not that of a child's. Her face was serious, unrelentingly calm, and full of subtle expression, as if she were used to talking to adults instead of kids her own age.

"I want to hire you."

"Hire me? For what?"

She looked around, her eyes settling on the cornfield. "There's something in that cornfield, and it's hurting people."

"What do you mean? Have you seen it?"

"Once. From my window upstairs." She pointed up to the window on the second story of the old farmhouse.

Before she could say anything else, Ronnie came out. He was grinning, and I shook my head in disbelief. He was one deeply fucked individual.

"We ready, Earl?" Ronnie said. "Quit hitting on my niece. I know she's a little hottie, but she's too young for your old ass."

Virginia rolled her eyes. I turned on Ronnie. "Apologize."

"What the fuck?"

"Apologize to her. That was inappropriate, even for you."

"Fuck you, Earl. You need to apologize to me."

"Let it go," Virginia said. "Just remember what we talked about."

Ronnie climbed into the truck. "Come on, Earl. Time to get out of here."

I nodded at Virginia and got in the truck.

As soon as I shut the door, Ronnie said, "Thanks for nothing, asshole."

"It didn't look like you were getting very far," I said. "Do you really think she was going to give you the money?"

"Eventually," he said. "But now I'll have to get it somewhere else."

He was backing out of the driveway when another truck slowed down on the road and turned in.

"Oh no. Hell no."

"What?"

"It's Lane."

The pickup truck pulled up next Ronnie's. Of course, Ronnie's was so jacked up and tall, I was looking down on the driver.

"I better make nice," Ronnie said.

He killed the engine and climbed out.

I had a feeling things might not go well since Lane had obviously returned earlier than expected, so I climbed out too.

Lane Jefferson was built like a tree stump—short, compact, thick, and hard as pinewood. He wore a holstered pistol and a scowl as wide as his face.

"Hey, Lane," Ronnie said.

Lane looked at Ronnie and then at me. "Who's this?"

"I'm Earl Marcus," I said.

His scowl went away. "From the newspapers?"

"From Ring Mountain."

He laughed. "Modest. I get it. Hey, you still dating that cop from Atlanta?"

"Yeah."

"What's she like?"

It was a weird question. "She's nice."

"Really? I've always found women in positions of authority to be real bitches."

"She's not."

"Nah, she definitely is."

"Excuse me?"

"You heard me." And then he turned away and headed toward the house.

I followed him.

He stopped at the door. "Can I help you?"

"Yeah, take it back."

"Take what back?"

"What you said about Mary."

"Fuck you. You're standing on my property. I'll say what I like."

I clenched my fists, itching to use them, but I made myself breathe deep. Relax. What did it matter what this asshole thought?

"Sure," I said.

He laughed again and went inside.

* * *

"Let's go," Ronnie said.

"No. Not until I'm sure he's not going to hurt her or one of those kids."

Ronnie lit a cigarette, and we leaned against one of his big front tires, waiting.

The house was quiet. I was beginning to think maybe it was okay to leave, when the door was flung open, and a suitcase flew through the opening.

The suitcase was followed by some toys and some random articles of clothing and finally, Wanda, carrying Briscoe.

They both looked okay. "Virginia!" Wanda shouted. "Get your ass to the car!"

I walked over and helped them load up the car.

"Thanks," Wanda said. "And take care of Ronnie. He ain't so bad."

"You take care of these kids," I said.

"They'll be fine," she said, and pulled away.

I looked at the house and saw Lane Jefferson standing at the door, an almost imperceptible grin on his face, as if he were privy to a joke he'd never share.

* * *

I'd been dreaming about the black water off and on for nearly a year before I realized how it ended. The dream came in several variations, but certain details never changed: it was night; there was a train or at least the sound of a train in the distance; and I was always in the middle of a train trestle suspended over black water, a field of corn blowing darkly to my right and something (or someone) I could not quite make out coming from my left. Mary wasn't always in the dream with me, but the sense of her was. Sometimes she was below me, already in the water, and I knew I had to jump over the side to find her. Other times she stood right on the train trestle with me, her eyes wide with something like fear, but not quite. One way or the other, I always made the plunge into the black water. And it always rose to meet me, welcoming me inside its silky folds. Then came silence and total darkness. A sudden peace.

In the mornings, I woke up, feeling despair about the juxtaposition of the sensations in the dream. The panic of falling, the utter sense of impending doom seemed to contradict the peaceful resolution. I couldn't make sense of it.

Until this morning.

Last night I dreamed of Jefferson's cornfield. I was running through it, being pursued by someone or something I couldn't see. Mary ran in front of me, and I urged her forward as we slipped out of the cornfield and into the woods. I looked behind me to see what was chasing us but saw nothing except for the bright headlight of a train. We were running on train tracks now as a great gorge in the land opened before us. A wooden train trestle ran across a glistening expanse of water. The Blackclaw River.

And then I saw it was the same dream I'd been having. The only difference was that I knew this was a real place. The black water I'd been dreaming about was the Blackclaw River. The cornfield blowing in the wind was Jefferson's.

Mary slowed, but I told her to keep going. We'd beat the train and the invisible pursuer behind us.

Once out on the trestle, I felt it vibrating underfoot. We'd made it halfway across when I saw the dark figure waiting for us. It was a tall, faceless man, holding a knife. Mary stopped. The train bore down on us.

"Jump," I said.

The last thing I remember before waking was the black water of the river, rising to take us in.

But I woke up with a new understanding. Call it intuition, or maybe it was just the experience of interpreting my own lunatic dreams for so long, but I knew how the dream ended.

The peace was the knowledge that Mary was okay. The darkness was my own death.

7

My life could be divided pretty neatly into two parts: there was the time before the snake bit me and everything that came after. The world itself seemed to shift when I was seventeen years old and my father handed me the cottonmouth while I stood in front of the church. I had been hoping to feel something powerful, something supernatural and holy, but instead, I felt desperation and impotence. The snake, dead-eyed and alien, struck me in the side of the face. The scar is still there, but mostly hidden by the scruff of my increasingly graying beard. After the cottonmouth, I could no longer accept the beliefs of my father. I could no longer accept there was a plan, secret or otherwise, that I was simply too foolish or unenlightened to understand.

I stopped believing the bullshit about everything having a purpose, everything working out for the greater good.

Even the people I knew and loved looked different when viewed from opposite sides of this bellwether event. My father went from a man I had to please to a mystery I wanted to solve. My mother went from being the good wife I admired for all the reasons Daddy did—patience, meekness, and a kind of soft ignorance that I had once believed all women should possess—to a woman I had to struggle to think about kindly after realizing how fully she'd swallowed my father's duplicitous act.

Then there was Rufus. My impression of him pre-cottonmouth was not good. Even before I'd pulled fully away from the church, the seeds of bitterness were already there. He and his mother sat in the front row, taking in Daddy's words every Sunday without fail. Rufus was often the first person my father passed the serpents to when the time to handle them came. While in front of the church, Rufus's face showed nothing but an assuredness in every action, every moment. In short, he was sold out—not so much for the Lord, but for my father and his own twisted version of faith.

The next time I encountered him—nearly thirty years later—Rufus had changed as much—maybe more—more than I had. His journey had mirrored mine in many ways, though the specifics of his were vague to me. All I knew was that he'd been inspired by my departure, and shortly thereafter he'd left our little community by choice. He spent some indeterminate number of years wandering the area, living hand to mouth, trying to figure out what there was in life that was worth believing in. Somewhere along the way, he lost his eyesight but gained a moral clarity second to none. Rufus had never explained how he went blind, and I'd never asked.

Now, Rufus had become nearly the exact opposite of everything my father stood for. He was an avowed atheist who spent his time thinking about the big questions in life and trying to help the less fortunate. The irony being that Rufus, in his atheism, had actually become a better example of a Christian than my father ever was. Lately, his passion had been organizing a group to resist Jeb Walsh's influence in the area.

But the bite had changed me in other ways too, ways that worried me, that kept me open to the possibility of the divine in this life despite the deluge of anecdotal evidence that suggested the world was ruled less by providence than passion, less by absolutes than absurdities.

My dreams changed after the snakebite. There was a clarity to some of them, a vivid, movielike quality that allowed me to replay them scene by stuttering scene upon waking. The only saving grace was that the dreams were increasingly farther and fewer between. But when I did have one—and I always knew when it was a special dream compared to a normal one—it never failed to put me on edge, and it always made me remember the snakebite and all the many ways I'd never outlive my father's legacy.

Which was why I found myself nearly shaking whenever I visited Rufus's house. Okay, *house* wasn't really accurate. Rufus lived in the remains of an old church. And not just any old church. Rufus lived in *our* old church, *my father's* old church, the Holy Flame.

Not only that, Rufus's closest neighbor was none other than Ronnie Thrash, who had been squatting in the old moonshiner's shack across the creek from the church for the last couple of years. A year ago, the two had been at odds, but from what Rufus had told me lately, Ronnie had been keeping to himself most of the time, which was a welcome relief from the days when Ronnie and his buddies had spent their evenings in their pickup trucks, kicking up mud and grass and making a general nuisance of themselves.

Add it all up, and I had very little reason to visit Rufus, yet most days, I found myself heading over to his place anyway. Today was no exception. I told myself I was doing him a favor, checking in, making sure he hadn't fallen in the night, but truthfully, the chances were greater that I'd fall and hurt myself during the night than Rufus would. No, the truth of why I visited him was that he understood me in a way few others did.

As I pulled up to the old church, I checked the shack across the creek and saw Ronnie's truck parked outside. I figured he was still sleeping, and for that I was glad. There were two reasons I dreaded visiting Rufus at the church: first, I would probably never feel comfortable coming back to the place where I'd been bitten by the cottonmouth, and second I wanted to avoid Rufus's disdain when he realized Ronnie and I had become . . . what was the word exactly?

Friends? God, there had to be something else. *Acquaintances.* That was a term I could live with. Maybe. But either way, Rufus would not approve.

Rufus stood beside his fire pit, tossing trash into it with uncanny accuracy. When I stopped the truck, he turned to face me, almost as if he could see.

I walked over and helped him clean up. We worked in companionable silence until the fire had consumed all the trash. Then he offered me some whiskey, and I told him that sounded about right.

A few minutes later, he returned with an unopened bottle of Wild Turkey and sat beside me in one of the four cast iron chairs he kept near the fire pit. "Figured we could dispense with the glasses," he said. He nearly always said this when we drank. Oh yeah, that was the other reason Rufus and I got on so well. We both shared an abiding love for whiskey, and the outdoors. In fact, we tried to combine the two as much as possible. Nothing could be nicer than whiskey by the fire on an early fall day.

"Jeb Walsh," he grunted.

I nodded and took a sip. "Yeah. What the hell are we going to do about him?"

He frowned. "I been thinking on it some and came up with something. A way to at least make sure I'm heard at his book signing." He reached into one of his overall pockets and pulled out what looked like a tiny microphone. He held it out, and I took it.

"Where'd you get this?"

"I was walking up on the eastern ridge the other day, around those caves you and Mary are always trying to explore, and I felt something underneath my boot that wasn't grass or a rock. When I first picked it up, I couldn't figure out what it was, but then Nedra told me it was a mic." Nedra was Rufus's friend. It was unclear to Mary and me exactly how to define "friend" in this case. We suspected there might be a physical relationship, but the truth was, we really had no idea.

"You'll need an amplifier," I said.

"Got it already," Rufus said. "It's in my pocket. Hand it back, and I'll demonstrate."

I put the mic back in his hand, and he clipped it to his shirt, under one of the lapels of his blazer. He reached into his pocket and flipped a switch.

"Reckon this will be loud enough to get his attention?" he said, his voice booming.

I covered my ears. "Uh, yeah, that'll be loud enough."

There was a click as he turned the amplifier off.

"So you just carry this around in your overalls?"

He shrugged. "I like to talk to the asshole across the creek sometimes." He clicked the amplifier back on and held the mic up to his mouth. I covered my ears.

"Hey, asshole," he said, his voice booming out even louder than the first time. "Wake up. Day's a-wasting."

I looked over at Ronnie's place. It was silent, but I could just imagine him sprawled out on his couch, holding up two middle fingers before rolling back over and going to sleep.

"So, you're going to use this at his book talk?"

"Damn right, I am."

"They're gonna carry your ass out, you know."

"Maybe," he said, and reached back in his pocket to kill the mic. "But at least they'll be able to hear me when they do."

I drank some whiskey and thought about the look on Walsh's face when Rufus interrupted him and he couldn't just talk over him. I decided that alone would be worth whatever trouble Rufus's plan brought us.

"What are the chances?" Rufus said.

"Excuse me?"

"I've just been thinking. What are the chances that this area finally gets rid of one cult of personality, one demagogue, and then almost a year later, another one emerges that—hell, I'll just say it—seems even more dangerous than the first?"

He was talking about my father and now, Jeb Walsh. I didn't have an answer. Not a good one anyway.

"Maybe there was a vacuum? Had to be filled?" I offered.

He shook his head. "No, it's just a crazy coincidence. Like being struck by lightning. It just doesn't happen, except . . ."—he hesitated and opened his hands—"when it does, but even then, it doesn't feel right. It feels like the person was just a fool or maybe God was angry or something."

I cleared my throat. I *had* been struck by lightning.

"Shit," Rufus said. "I forgot about that. But you don't count. You've been bit by a snake in the face too. You break the mold, Earl."

"Thanks," I said.

He laughed. "But you follow what I'm saying, right?"

I thought it over. "Maybe. It's almost like the whole area is cursed or something."

"Could be," he said. "Which is why you and me can't ever get too complacent."

"You mean like we are today, sitting around and getting drunk?"

"That ain't what I'd call it."

"Well, what would call it?"

"I'd call it making a pact."

"A pact? What kind of pact?"

"The kind that says we don't let that asshole win."

"I'll drink to that," I said.

8

I stayed at Rufus's until about four, and then I spent the rest of the afternoon tying up some loose ends in a couple of cases and killing time until Mary's arrival Wednesday afternoon. Since the newspaper article detailing the downfall of my father's church, I'd been in high demand. Most of the cases were of the mundane variety—cheating spouses, workman's comp, and real estate squabbles—but I didn't mind the relative boredom. Being struck by lightning on a case will do that to a man.

That night, I was cleaning out my refrigerator, taking stock of what I needed to pick up before Mary came up the next day, when Goose began to bark. I closed the refrigerator door, walked over to the window, and pulled back the curtain. It was dark and windy, the early fall weather trying to settle in. Goose growled, and I tried to listen. I suddenly wished Rufus and I had consumed a little less whiskey. My head was beginning to hurt, and I was very tired. I waited, squinting out into the dark until I heard it.

The mountainside thrummed. There was a downshift, and then the engine grew even louder.

"You've got to be kidding me," I said, and grabbed a beer out of the fridge. I didn't bother with a glass, downing most of it in one swallow. I'd finished it off by the time his truck was close enough to shake the house, so I tossed it into the recycling bin and reached for another.

I'd managed to take the edge off my burgeoning hangover by the time I heard his truck door slam. I went to the door. Goose burst out, barking and snarling, only to stop the second he caught a whiff of Ronnie.

"Hey there, boy," Ronnie said, kneeling to scratch behind Goose's ears. Goose dropped to the ground and rolled over, showing Ronnie his belly. Ronnie patted it a few times and stood up.

"We need to talk," he said.

"About what?"

"Lane Jefferson."

"You gonna try to rob him again?"

"No. I want to see him behind bars."

"Come again?"

Ronnie stepped forward, and I saw he was wearing a tank top, sweats, and a pair of flip-flops. He had something in his fist that looked like leaves.

"Can we go inside?"

I just stared at him.

"Look, Earl, I'm sorry for that stuff the other day. I wasn't gonna hurt anybody. Hell, Wanda knew that. And I just wore the mask because of them kids. You might not believe it, but I love them two."

"Why don't we just talk out here?" I said.

"Fine." He held out his hand, turning it over and opening it up. Something dark and plant-like was in his palm.

"What's that?"

"It's good ole marijuana, Earl. We can roll it and smoke it later, if you want. But I brought it to prove what I'm about to tell you."

I waited, actually a little curious now, and not just because it had been a *long* time since I'd smoked any weed. I wanted to know where this was going.

"Lane Jefferson pissed you off the other day, didn't he?" Ronnie said.

"I'm not sure *pissed off* is the right term, but I don't respect the man. Anyone who would treat a woman and her kids like he did is a piece of shit."

"My thoughts exactly. Now, what if I told you that this here pot is from his cornfield, and that if you know where to look, you can find about two acres hidden in there. It's one of the reasons he hired me and some of the other boys, so we could guard it at night."

"Sounds like a reason to call the sheriff," I said.

Ronnie laughed. "You still think this damned sheriff is anything but corrupt? Hell no. Several folks have reported exactly what I just told you, but he hasn't done shit."

"So you want me to do it? I'm not a cop."

"But you sleep with one."

I started to argue but stopped. "What's your angle here? Why drive all the way up this mountain to get me to bust the man you work for?"

Ronnie lit a cigarette and stuck it between his lips, taking a long draw before exhaling and shrugging at the same time. "My angle is simple. I can't stand the motherfucker. He's a dick. It's bad enough that I had to put up with that sawed-off piece of dried-up shit as my boss, but then he starts fucking my sister. I hate him. I just want to see him get what's coming to him. So I'm asking as a favor—just go check it out."

Honestly, if Lane Jefferson hadn't come across as such an asshole the other day, I might have been tempted to let it go. What did I care about somebody growing pot in their cornfield? No business of mine. But if you're going to be an asshole who makes comments about my girlfriend, well, that's different.

Besides, I wanted to see for myself how Sheriff Patterson would react if I brought him actual photos of the plants, with Mary as a witness.

"If Mary comes, it'll have to be tomorrow night," I said.

"That's perfect. I'm working then. I can meet you out there and take you right to it."

"Where will we meet?"

"On the other side of the cornfield. You'll have to take Highway 18. When you see the old water tower on the left, pull over and park by the corn. I'll be waiting there."

"Water tower on Highway 18. I got it."

Ronnie took another drag on his cigarette. The orange flare from his cigarette revealed furrows of worry etched across his face.

"One more thing," he said in a voice that didn't sound like Ronnie at all. "Stick together. It's easy to get lost in that cornfield."

It wasn't until later that night, when I was lying in bed, counting the seconds between lightning strikes and the subsequent deep booms of thunder, that his words really hit home, and I realized there was something off about his last statement. *"Stick together. It's easy to get lost in that cornfield."*

But before I could reach any conclusions, my eyelids grew heavy, and I fell asleep.

9

The next time I dreamed about the river, it started on the train trestle, overlooking the Blackclaw. A train was coming. I felt the trestle vibrate with its power. I turned and saw the bright light of its locomotive cutting through high stalks of pale corn. I would have to run to make it to the other side before the train came. I started to do just that, when I realized that another train was coming from that direction. I was going to be sandwiched between the two freights.

Unless I jumped.

I looked down at the black water. In my dream it was pure glass, flecked with icelike rivulets where the water broke across the rocks. I tried to gauge the distance but felt vertigo and panic overtake me at once.

There weren't two trains. Only one. From my left. There was something else coming from my right. Like the train, it pounded the tracks and rattled my ears. The thunder and beat of furious footsteps.

Squinting into the shifting darkness, I saw a faceless figure advancing toward me. The figure appeared to wear a cowl over his head, and it made progress toward me in great strides.

I had to jump. I had to try.

For Mary. Because she was down there. It was the one thing I felt sure of.

I turned to do just that, when I realized I'd already made the leap. It wasn't so much that I was falling, but instead that the water, that black glass surface, *was rising.*

When I hit the sleek black river, I went through like a pin slipped into a felt pad. It was only when I reached the bottom, only when I was completely out of air, that I saw her tangled in river weeds, like chains. She struggled against the bonds, the fear large and unfettered in her eyes.

My lungs burned as I swam toward Mary. Her mouth moved soundlessly as she screamed at me.

And then a shadow fell over us both, a dark-winged bird plunging through the depths. I looked up and saw nothing but a darkness that was so total it felt like the last lingering moment before the deepest sleep.

* * *

The remnants of the dream dissipated as the day wore on. It was worrisome, sure, especially given my history with dreams, but I refused to let it ruin the time with Mary. When I'd told her about the cornfield, she'd seemed excited to go. Though diminutive in stature and reserved in demeanor, Mary relished an adventure as much as I did.

Goose and I sat in the yard that afternoon and waited for Mary to arrive. The previous night's rain had gone the way of my dream and been replaced by a clear, slightly cool afternoon. It would have been the perfect time for a beer, but I didn't dare risk comprising any of my faculties. While I'd mostly forgotten the dream by that point, I'd found myself returning to Ronnie's puzzling words again.

Why would he need to warn Mary and me to stick together if he was going to meet us before going into the cornfield?

It was a question for which I didn't have an answer, but my instinct told me something was up. Could Ronnie be setting me up? It didn't seem likely. If he was doing that, why go out of his way to tell us to stick together?

No, there had to be something else going on, something else I was missing.

Mary arrived a half hour later, all smiles and hugs and flirtatious kisses, and just like that, I felt myself letting go of all the doubts about Ronnie's strange admonition.

As she kissed me, I moved toward the house, nearly dragging her along with me.

"I thought we had to meet Ronnie," she said.

"There's plenty of time. He said to come at night. It's not even dark yet."

She kissed my mouth. I kissed her back and pulled away. "Hell, we've got time for two sessions."

She play-slapped my arm. It was an old joke between us. Once, when our relationship had still been new, I'd asked her if she was ready for another "session."

"What?"

"You know, another . . . session in bed?"

"Session?"

I shrugged.

"That is totally *not* a romantic term," she'd said, but I could tell she was teasing. And she'd never stopped teasing me about it, either.

She giggled and said, "Two sessions, huh? You are feeling full of yourself today. I'm always up for two, and you're always up for two . . ." Her eyes nearly danced with mischief. "Until the first 'session' is over, and then you suddenly want to sleep."

"Not this time," I said.

"*Every* time."

She was right of course. At fifty-one, sometimes my desire was greater than my abilities, and I often promised more than I could deliver.

We tumbled into the bed in Granny's old bedroom and found the closest thing to heaven that there can be on earth.

* * *

As Mary had predicted, session number two was beyond my abilities, but that didn't seem to bother her too much. She snuggled next to me, our bodies still intertwined, and purred softly in my ear.

"I'm happy."

I felt something in me shift. Of all the things women had ever said to me, I didn't believe I'd ever heard anything so perfect, so damned heartfelt.

"Me too," I said.

And the moment lingered, a blissful glow that made me think that maybe there was something closer to heaven on this earth than making love.

* * *

But despite the perfection of the moment, I still felt a growing anxiety on the inside. It was a familiar one, hard earned from years of disappointments and betrayals, and perhaps most prominently, my own knack for self-sabotage. It was the flat, dull feeling that crept around the edges of happiness, the one that whispered, *Something is about to go wrong. How can you be so happy?* There was almost a guilt in it, a sense that I didn't deserve anything resembling lasting joy.

You'd better wake up. Something is coming, the voice cajoled.

I tried to ignore the doubts, the pervading sense that something was about to go wrong, but it seemed the closer Mary and I got, the deeper our relationship grew, the more I sensed doom—like the black waters rising in my dream—on the periphery of it all.

By the time we were ready to leave for the cornfield, I was practically in despair, and Mary noticed.

"You okay?"

"Yeah," I said. "Just thinking how bad things would be without you."

"Why are you thinking that? That was a moment we just had. Don't borrow trouble."

"You're right. It was." But she couldn't mistake the pitiful note in my voice. I couldn't mistake it either, and I hated myself, not only for letting it show but for feeling it in the first place.

"Well, what's the problem?"

"Forget it," I said. "Just the venom making me crazy."

Another old joke. I'd long believed the snakebite I'd suffered at seventeen had changed me profoundly. It wasn't just the dreams; sometimes I saw things that couldn't be there. Mary—like any sane person—didn't believe in those kinds of things, so it had turned into a kind of joke between us. Except only one of us was really joking.

"That venom is why I love you," she said. "Makes you dangerous."

I laughed and leaned over to kiss her cheek.

* * *

We left at dusk in my truck. We both had flashlights and our firearms. Mary was excited, especially when I told her about what a jackass Lane Jefferson was.

"Sounds like he could be friends with Jeb Walsh."

"Problem is," I said, making the turn at the bottom of the mountain, "half the people in this damn county could be friends with Jeb Walsh, which is exactly why he's here."

"I like those odds," Mary said.

"What odds?"

"Well, you said half of the people would be friends with him, so that means half *wouldn't* be. In an even fight, I always like the odds of the people with decency and morals. We're gonna win."

"I hope you're right."

"I know I am. We're smarter. We care more. We're stronger because of it."

See? *That* was why I loved her so goddamn much.

We turned onto Highway 18 just before we hit downtown Riley, and headed north toward Summer Mountain. Corn Valley was essentially the narrow strip of land between Summer and the Fingers where I came up and live now. The joke was that Summer Mountain was named that because it got the best weather, and it got the best weather because that was where all the rich assholes lived.

Okay, so the joke didn't say *assholes*. I included that word, mostly because it was becoming increasingly difficult for me to use the word *rich* without—at least mentally—adding *asshole*. Was I bitter because of my lack of money? Maybe, but I believed it was more indignation than anything else. But then again, like most people, I was really good at lying to myself.

It didn't take long for the scenery to change dramatically as I drove through the valley. Not only was the land flat here, but there was also a real sense of being swallowed up by the mountains on either side, like we were traveling across the base of a murky, flat-bottomed bowl, and the starry sky above was more than a sky. It was a hint of a better world, if only we could squirm over the lip of the mountains and out into free space.

The fields on either side were dotted with the remnants of a past that had largely been forgotten: plantation homes and grape arbors grown over with every creeping vine until the dark night made them into the husks of previously sentient structures. It was hard to look at them and not imagine their stories like untold secrets tangled up among the spliced-together bits of man and nature. All of them seemed to suggest the same theme: nature wins.

The corn came suddenly, like great waves, and it was as if the bowl contained even a deeper chamber, and we'd entered it, enclosed now not only by the mountains but by the corn stalks with their silky husks and tassels that seemed to whisper in the late September wind.

Mary reached over and touched my arm lightly. I smiled at her, and she smiled back, but there was something under the smiles, something existential, something that made my heart ache the way a heart can ache sometimes when you're with the right person at the right moment and you realize just how fragile it all is, how time, despite the deceptive way in which it lulls us all, wins every race in the end.

"I've never seen corn so tall," Mary said. "You could hide a dozen pot fields in here."

"All we need to do is find one, and we can take him down."

We crossed some railroad tracks, and I looked down them both ways as we went over, amazed how they sliced through the cornfields clean, what it must be like for the engineers to see this ocean of corn between these mountains, and for a second I wished I could be one of them, bound by nothing but the way forward.

Because sometimes—no *all* the time—being bound to the land or to a person was a painful thing. When you thought about it, love—the true kind anyway—always ended in sadness.

"Earl?"

"Yeah?"

"I thought you were fading out for a minute. You're so damned quiet tonight."

"Sorry, just feeling my age." Before she could reply, I saw something rising out of the corn on my left. A water tower was situated about thirty yards from the shoulder of the road.

"Here we are," I said, and pulled over off the right side of the road, leaving just enough space on Mary's side, between the truck and the corn, to allow her to get out.

"I don't see Ronnie," I said.

"Do we really need him to look through a cornfield?" Mary asked.

"Maybe," I said.

She gave me a look. "Really? I think me and you will be okay, Earl."

I swallowed and realized I had been feeling more than my age. I was feeling something else, something terrifying, something that had come alive inside me and had lodged itself against my chest.

"We should wait for Ronnie," I said.

Mary—obviously on a different wavelength from me at the moment—leaned in for a kiss, and said, "Boring."

"We just need to wait, okay? He'll be here soon—"

Something flashed to my left. It was the briefest of lights, as if someone had flicked a lighter or maybe unlocked a smartphone. It seemed to have come from the water tower.

"Did you see that?" I said.

"See what?"

"A light." I jabbed my thumb at the water tower. "It came from up there."

She nodded at the road. Headlights were coming toward us. "You sure it wasn't the headlights?"

I considered the approaching car, glancing from it to the water tower. "No. It came from the water tower itself."

The car blew past us, its driver and possible passengers hidden by the night.

"Want to check it out?" Mary said.

I looked at the water tower again. It was one of the old ones, wooden legs, corrugated tin tank. In the dark of night, it looked like some ancient god, holding watch over the fields, awaiting some sacrifice to be poured into the depths of its belly.

I didn't want to check it out.

I'd never felt like this before. Normally, very little made me afraid. I relished conflict with the bad guys and actually wondered if my lack of fear might be a personality defect. But looking at that tower beside this dark cornfield frightened me like I'd never been frightened before.

It was the dream. I didn't want to admit it, but that was what was behind my fear, my hesitation, and I hated myself for it. I didn't want to be the kind of man who believed his own visions. My father was that kind of man, and I believed it was this trait, this inability to see through his own delusions that had ultimately led to his downfall.

I couldn't let myself end up like him.

I needed to just face it, and it would go away, I'd return to normal, be fearless again.

"Okay," I said. "Stay put."

"No way," Mary said. "I'm coming too."

We both exited the truck. I was halfway across the road when Mary hissed at me. "Over here," she said.

I turned and saw her pointing into the cornfield, just past the truck. A light bobbed through the stalks like a firefly, flickering mysteriously.

"Wait," I said, but Mary was already gone, gun raised, through the wall of stalks.

10

I entered the cornfield and was immediately disoriented. I'd heard military veterans talk about something called the fog of war, during which they become confused and unable to determine the best course of action. I felt that now. In fact, I stopped almost as soon as I entered, trying to figure out where I was and what had happened to the road and the water tower. They were gone. It was all gone, replaced by the looming stalks and the claws of their tassels, which seemed to scrape the bottom of the starry sky.

I moved my flashlight slowly, tracing a wall of plants clustered so tightly they could have easily been mistaken for a single, impenetrable barrier.

These stalks hadn't been planted in neat rows like most of the cornfields I'd visited. These were tossed haphazard and thick across the land, so that it was difficult to see a way forward.

"Come on," Mary said. "Stay close."

I heard her voice but didn't see her. I moved my flashlight slowly as I turned around, trying to locate the source of her seemingly disembodied voice.

"You just passed me," she said.

I moved the light back, blinking into the dimness, and saw the edge of her and then all of her. How many times had I passed the light over where she stood and not seen her?

And then she was gone again.

I followed, coming to my senses gradually as my eyes became

accustomed to the blinding presence of the stalks. Picking up my pace, I reached for her and slid my hand from her shoulder down her arm and grasped her hand.

She squeezed and let go. "It'll slow us down."

"Okay," I said, but the words in my mind were Ronnie's: *"Stick together."*

"We need to slow down," I said.

She stopped. "What's going on with you?"

I decided to come clean. "Bad dreams. A feeling something is about to go wrong. Something Ronnie said that didn't sit right with me."

"What did he say?"

"That we should—"

There was a clattering of stalks just behind Mary. It sounded like some wild beast was barreling through the corn.

She turned, gun raised. Something pushed against the stalks near Mary, bending them forward, like a piece of buckled wood, before straightening again, leaving the stalks wagging, their tassels dripping corn silk into Mary's hair.

"Who's there?" I said.

There was no answer. But it was clear that whatever it was that had caused the damage to the stalks was still there. The night had fallen into an uneasy silence. A waiting.

"Ronnie?" I said. "What the fuck is going on?"

Then something happened that would stay with me for a very long time. Someone laughed. It came from behind the wall of stalks, an eerie tinkling of laughter that penetrated the wall of stalks like a sharp blade.

Mary stepped back.

"Show yourself, or I'll shoot."

I meant it. I had my 9mm out, had it aimed steady at the place in the thick stalks, had it leveled at the place I guessed a man's heart might be.

The stalks whispered. The sounds moved away.

The night let out the breath it had been holding.

"Shit," Mary said.

"Let's go back to the road. I think we've been set up."

"Either that or somebody's trying to play a trick."

"Hell of a trick," I said.

"I know this question is going to sound crazy, but was that . . ."

"A person?"

"Yeah."

"I think so. Just a person trying to scare us, I think."

"Why?"

"Hell if I know. Come on." When I reached for her hand this time, she grasped mine tightly and held on. After a few false starts, we found a path that led us back to the road.

Once there, Mary walked to the truck and leaned against it, her gun still in hand. "Something's bothering me too," she said.

I walked over and leaned against beside her. I had to piss, but that could wait until Mary had had her say.

"My first thought when I heard that thing was of Jeb Walsh."

"Jeb Walsh? You think he's running through the cornfield, spooking folks?"

"No . . ." She shook her head. "I can't quite explain it. It was the way he looked at me that day. It was . . . I don't know . . . more than a threatening look. I could actually see the . . . I guess I'd call it *calculation*."

"You mean he was thinking of how to hurt you?"

Mary nodded.

I put my hand on her shoulder and squeezed gently. "Whatever that was—inside that corn—it had nothing to do with Jeb Walsh. Walsh might wish he could hurt you, but he can't."

She nodded.

"You okay?"

"Yeah, I guess we both got a little spooked."

"Yeah," I said. "I'm going to take a piss, and then I'm taking you to the house. Fuck Ronnie Thrash and his pot field." I started toward the corn and had my pants unzipped, meaning to take care of business fast when I heard her groan.

"I gotta go too."

"Grab a stalk," I said.

"Easy for you to say."

I closed my eyes as the piss started to flow. Daddy used to say a good piss was better than good sex, and though that made me question whether he'd ever even had good sex before, I did enjoy a good piss.

"You okay?" I said, craning my head to see where Mary was. "Mary?"

"Over here," she said.

"You didn't go back in the cornfield?"

"Just a little. I'm not peeing out in the open where a car could come by and—"

She stopped abruptly.

"Mary?"

No answer.

A drop of panic hit me. Just a tiny drop. I felt it somewhere in my neck as it spread, warming my face, tingling my scalp.

"Mary?" I said, raising my voice as loud as I could without screaming.

I cut my piss off midstream, wincing at the pain. Zipping my pants as I turned, I realized I'd put my 9mm on the truck, and now I had to go back for it.

In my hurry to grab the gun, I knocked it across the roof to the other side of the truck. It hit the ground with a thunk.

"Say something, Mary. Say something for me, please!"

But the only sound was the wind, a high and lonesome keening through the stalks.

Mary was gone.

11

I barreled into the stalks like a drunk, falling and getting back up and then falling again. Sharp husks cut my arms and hands. I dropped my flashlight. Picked it up and remembered I'd never retrieved my gun. I crashed back out and grabbed it. It was only then when I remembered my phone. I tried to call Mary only to find that I had no signal.

I plunged into the corn again, trying to find a path, but there was something dizzying about the strange silence that greeted me. I broke it, calling Mary's name.

My voice fell flat, a dead bird crashing into another wall of stalks. I aimed my flashlight ahead of me, but its glow seemed to be swallowed alive by the layers of dark so thick there was no end to them.

I reached out to steady myself on the cornstalks, and my hands touched corn silk like spiderwebs, woven by the relentless September wind.

The moon was a thick thumbnail in the pearl black sky.

As I moved deeper into the cornfield, I tried to keep the moon on my right, so that I knew I was heading in the direction I hoped I'd find Mary. Or Ronnie. Just thinking the name filled me with anger. Why had he not met us?

This was his fault. His motherfuck—

Relax. Just take it easy. She's okay. You're panicking.

But why hadn't he shown up to meet us? I couldn't think of one adequate explanation.

After a time, the wind picked up, bending cornstalks until they were nearly parallel to the ground. Voices rode the tail of the wind, soft, hurried. They were off to my right, and I immediately changed directions, even though there was a part of me that worried about getting too far away from "ground zero" so to speak. But I had to see what it was, who it was.

When I heard the voices again, they sounded like they were coming from my left. I stopped to listen, but then either the wind shifted or I'd been confused, because now the sounds were directly in front of me. I plunged forward, breaking stalks as I barreled blindly into the dark, desperate to find a way forward, a path.

A shadow passed overhead, and when I looked up, I saw it rising through the sky, a dark kite. Bats, hundreds of them, eclipsing the cold moon shard and then vanishing into the empty spaces between the stars.

I slowed down again, tried to think.

I attempted a second call to Mary. This time I had service, but it went straight to her voicemail. Which meant her phone was dead or didn't have service. We were way out, and I was a little surprised I'd even been able to get through. I tried one more time to be sure, but when I got the same result, I put my phone away and focused on getting my bearings.

Gradually, I realized my eyes had adjusted and I could see better. The problem was the stalks again. It was almost as if someone had flown an airplane over this patch of land and dropped the seeds, scattering them to the wind, letting them land randomly, in a maze-like pattern instead of in the neat rows one usually imagined when thinking of a cornfield.

Sometime later, still moving doggedly deeper into the cornfield, I saw a series of lights dancing in the small cracks between the stalks. I parted them with my hands, and glimpsed three men standing in a clearing with flashlights.

One of the flashlights jumped. There was a shout, and then the light bobbed toward me.

"Don't move!" a voice said, and the flashlight was bright in my eyes.

I covered my face with the arm holding the flashlight. "Where is she?"

"Hold it, boys. I know this man."

The voice belonged to Ronnie Thrash. The light moved out of my eyes. I blinked several times, trying to get my bearings.

"I'm sorry about this," Ronnie said.

My eyes locked on Ronnie. He was standing about ten yards away, holding a shotgun pointed at the ground. I looked at the other two men. One held the large flashlight, and the other a rifle trained on my head.

"You set this up?"

"It wasn't like that."

"What was it like then?" Despite the rifle that was a muscle twitch from putting a bullet in my head, I stepped forward, too angry to care.

"Can we talk about this somewhere else?" he said, holding his hands up.

I moved closer.

"Stay back," the man with the rifle said.

"Don't shoot him." Ronnie had dropped his own shotgun.

"I don't take orders from you," the man with the rifle said. He fired and I hit the ground, belly first. I reached for my gun.

"That was a warning," he said. "Put your gun down, or the next one will be in your mouth."

I let go of my 9mm and held my hands up.

"This is Earl Marcus," Ronnie said. "The one whose daddy was RJ?"

Both men were silent.

"Hell, you sure was excited when I told you about him the other day."

"What's he doing here?" the man holding the light said.

Before Ronnie could answer, I rose to my knees. "I'm looking for my girlfriend."

“She a black girl?” the man with the rifle said.

“Yes.”

“Johnny’s done taken her to Mr. Jefferson’s.”

I looked at Ronnie. “What the fuck is going on?”

“I can explain.” Ronnie held a hand out to his friend with the rifle. “If you’ll just lower that, Justin.”

Justin lowered the gun.

“Goddamn, you want to shoot somebody, don’t you?” Ronnie said. He walked over, holding out his hand as if to make an apology. I waited until he was very close before throwing the punch. It hit him square in the jaw, and if I didn’t know better, I’d say it lifted him off the ground. Either way, he crumpled like a piece of loose leaf paper. The man holding the flashlight whistled appreciatively. For a second, I didn’t think Ronnie was going to get back up, but then he lifted an unsteady hand.

“I reckon I deserved that, but Jesus, Earl, did you have to make it so damned hard?”

I reached down and grabbed him under his arm, dragging him back to his feet. “You’re going to take me to her right now.”

“Sure, sure . . .” He tried to put an arm around me, but I shrugged him off. “She’s fine, Earl. I promise you that. I made him promise me he wouldn’t hurt her. He just wanted to scare her.”

I almost hit him again and would have if I didn’t need him to take me to Mary.

“Let’s go,” I said.

“Okay, okay. Boys,” he said, turning to the other two men, “pray for me.”

* * *

“He told me if I didn’t get both of you here, he was going to hurt Virginia.”

“Who?”

“Virginia, my niece.”

“*Who* was going to hurt her?”

"Lane. He would do it too. Hell, he probably already has. He's a real piece of shit. The only reason Wanda ever got hooked up with him was because of his money. And the access to drugs. But, I told him I'd only do it if he promised not to hurt her."

"Do you even hear yourself?" I said. "You're not making a lick of damned sense."

"I know it looks bad, but it's going to be okay. We'll just head up to the house and . . ."

"What does he want with Mary?"

"I'm not sure, but he promised he wasn't going to hurt her. He said he just wanted to teach her a lesson."

I was beyond bewildered. First, why in the hell would Ronnie believe that Lane Jefferson wasn't going to hurt Mary? And second, how did this asshole even know Mary or anything about her?

I was about to ask him one of these when Ronnie pointed at a fork in the corn ahead. "Stay left," he said. "Here's the deal. Lane ain't got no pot fields. At least none that I know about. He has me and some other boys watch the corn at night to make sure nobody comes snooping around. He said he wanted us to get Mary and take her to him. He was going to embarrass her and then let her go. He knew she was a cop. He was going to try to make it a story or something about her snooping around, looking for pot. Hell, I don't know. It sounded like it was a stupid-ass plan to me, so I figured my best choice was to go along."

"You're so dumb it makes my head hurt," I said. "None of that even makes sense."

He stopped. "Look, I know you think I'm a degenerate, pothead, whatever. And maybe that's true. I won't argue with it. But I care about those damn kids. And Lane threatened Virginia. I did what I had to do."

"You care about them so much, you tried to rob their mother."

"Shit, Earl, she owed me that money."

"You're a piece of shit, and you had better hope Mary's okay. If she's not, I may kill you."

That made him go quiet. It made me quiet too. The scary part wasn't that I'd said it. The scary part was that I meant it.

We worked our way through the thick corn in silence. It was a torturously slow journey. On more than one occasion, Ronnie led us down a path only to realize it was a dead end. Two other times, he stopped, admitting he was confused. Eventually, we found a relatively wide path and followed it for a while.

"How much farther?" I asked.

"Once we get out of the cornfield, it's like a mile or so."

"Shit. Walk faster."

"Let me get a smoke. Hold on." He stopped and pulled out a cigarette.

I slapped the cigarette out of his hand. "Forget the damned smoke. Walk."

"I ain't never seen you like this, Earl," Ronnie said. "Jesus. You must really love that girl."

"Just get me there."

"Sure, but I don't see why a cigarette is gonna hurt."

I glared at him, and he got moving again.

"You should come by the house for a barbeque some time, so we could hang out when things ain't so tense. I got a new grill and some really nice pot."

"That's not gonna happen, Ronnie. You lied to me. You put Mary in danger. Can't you see that?"

"Can't you see that I didn't have no choice?"

I didn't know what to say. Even if it was true that he had no choice, I was too angry at the moment to care.

"'Cause it ain't like we don't go way back, you know? Hell, me and you've shared secrets I'll bet you ain't told nobody before."

I let that go and was pleased to see trees up ahead instead of more corn.

The ground sloped gradually upward as we walked, and I realized we'd walked so far that we were getting close to the base of Summer Mountain.

From somewhere on my left, I heard the distant shriek of a train whistle.

"What's he trying to protect anyway?" I asked.

"Who?"

"Jefferson. You said he'd hired you to watch the cornfield. What's to protect? Is he expecting somebody to steal the corn?"

"Hell if I know. He just pays by the head."

"By the head?"

"Two hundred for whites, four hundred for blacks."

I stopped. "What did you say?"

"You heard me."

"He pays more for blacks? Why?"

"Earl, you ain't ever been hard up for work, have you?"

"Sure I have."

"Maybe you *think* you have, but when you're *really* hard up for work, you don't ask but one question: How much? That's all I know: two hundred for whites, four hundred for blacks."

"How many have you caught? Before Mary."

He shook his head. "We ain't been at it very long. This is just the third night we've been out. We almost caught a kid last night, but the little fucker was fast."

I still didn't quite follow the logic of paying more for blacks, but I decided to let it go. Hell, one way or another, Sheriff Patterson would be hearing about this. Lane Jefferson might not be growing pot, but he was doing something out here that wasn't legal. I was sure of it.

We kept moving, reaching the tracks just in time to see the tail end of the freight train blasting by, breaking the night into slabs of hot air and dense sound.

Once it was gone, we stepped across the tracks, and Ronnie pointed at a little trail I would have certainly missed without him. It was overgrown and took us into the heart of the deep woods.

We walked for another ten or fifteen minutes on the trail, before the trees fell away and I saw the farmhouse, dark and huge against the starry sky. A smaller garden to the right of the house rippled in the breeze, and beyond them both, a silent highway made a snaking scar across the landscape. Far away, I saw headlights moving along the road. I looked around. To the right were the Fingers, where I lived. To my left, I saw the lights of what had to be Sommerville Chase, high atop Summer Mountain.

"Is anybody home?" I said.

"I ain't sure," Ronnie said.

"I swear, if he's not here, if *Mary's* not here, I'm going to . . ." I trailed off. The fact was, I wasn't going to do anything except fall into despair. My anger was already fading away. Ronnie was stupid, sure, but I honestly believed this hadn't been malicious.

"Let's go knock on the door," he said.

We stood on the covered porch and rang the bell. I couldn't help but remember how, a few days ago, Lane had thrown Wanda and her kids' belongings into the yard.

"Look," Ronnie said.

"What?"

He nodded at the hardwood floor of the porch. A cigarette butt lay near the welcome mat. "That's Johnny's. He's been here."

"Ring it again," I said.

Ronnie rang the bell, and I banged hard on it with my fist.

We waited. No one came.

I tried the door handle, but it was locked.

"Where else would he take her? Was there a plan B if this guy isn't home?"

Ronnie shrugged. "Maybe out to the road?"

I looked around. The road was empty. Somewhere, far away, a car downshifted, and it sounded like a lonely groan at the end of the world.

"I'm calling the sheriff," I said.

"Hold your horses, now, Earl. That ain't necessary. You know I got priors."

"Fuck your priors." I turned on my phone and dialed the

number. It rang once before my phone died. "Oh, you've got to be kidding me."

"What?"

"It died. Let me use yours."

"Left it in my truck. It don't get no service out here. Where you going?"

I'd stepped off the porch and was looking around the yard. "I need a brick or a stick or something."

"Why?"

"Going to break a window and get to a phone."

"Shit, Earl. I need this job."

I ignored him and ranged out across the backyard, looking for something I could use. When I didn't find anything, I walked back toward the woods we'd come from, with the intention of breaking a branch off, but something stopped me.

There on the ground, still hot, was another cigarette butt.

I waved Ronnie off the porch. "Another cigarette."

He came over and stood beside me. "That's his," he said. "And look at this. There's a little trail here. God knows, I wouldn't have ever seen it."

I didn't respond. I was already following the trail, moving sideways through the thick tree limbs before breaking into a run.

12

Ronnie saw him before I did. In fact, in my hurry, I'd already run beyond where he lay beside the little stream, his body sprawled out, one boot in the running water, the other propped up on a moss-covered rock.

"It's Johnny," Ronnie said.

I knelt beside him, trying to determine if he was dead. I put the back of my hand under his nose and felt the heat of his breath. "Alive."

"What should we do?"

"Get a little water from the stream," I said. "Pour it on his face."

Ronnie cupped his hands in the stream and leaned over, letting the cold water slip out of his hands. It hit Johnny's face, and the man stirred slightly. "Again," I said, reaching for my 9mm.

The second dose of water made him groan and open his eyes. I pressed the gun against the side of his head.

"Oh," he said. "Who are—Ronnie?"

Ronnie shrugged at him as if to apologize.

"Where is she?" I said, pressing the gun against his temple.

"I . . ." He looked around, genuinely confused. I felt the panic rising again. This wasn't good. "Old Nathaniel," he said.

"What? Who is Old Nathaniel?"

"He took her."

"Which way?"

He tried to sit up, gasped, and lay his head back on the ground.

I saw now that he'd been hit pretty hard. Blood had pooled on the ground around his head. "Help me up?" he said.

Ronnie gave him a hand, helping him to his feet. That was when I saw what had been lying under his leg.

Mary's gun.

Ronnie reached for it.

"Don't," I said.

"Why?"

"Prints."

He nodded and stepped back. "Cool."

Johnny—a dumpy man who wore shorts and a windbreaker—steadied himself against a nearby tree.

"I need you to tell me what happened," I said. The words came out of my mouth, but it didn't even feel like I was speaking them. My head buzzed with the images from my vision. The black water from the dream, rising to meet me. Mary, struggling in the water below me.

"Earl?"

"Huh?"

Ronnie shook me a little. "You with us?"

"Yeah. I'm fine." I looked around. Johnny was staring at me. "Tell me," I said.

"I was trying to, but—"

"Start over."

He nodded. "Me and Eldridge were watching the south end of the cornfield. It's the spot we like because it ain't so dense." He wiped at the back of his head and looked at his bloody hand. "Jesus."

"You're fine. Tiny wound."

He nodded, maybe too concussed to disbelieve me.

"We saw her coming, and, well, Mr. Jefferson said the ones we're supposed to be looking out for are probably young and black, and she looked young and black, so Eldridge took out his gun and told her to stop. She said she was a cop and she was lost. That she'd gotten confused in the corn. I kind of believed her. I mean, she seemed like she was telling the truth, but I also figured she could be lying, so I told her to give me her gun, and she did. Then I took her to Mr. Jefferson's house. Eldridge stayed behind."

"And then what?"

"He wasn't home. So I called him, and he said he'd meet me over on County 7. Said to bring her through the woods and he'd be there soon. She barely seemed scared at all, so that made me think she really was a cop."

"What happened then?"

"Then we walked for a while along this trail. It's the quickest way to 7. Wasn't long before I started hearing something. She heard it too. We both thought somebody might be following us. At first I figured it was one of the boys playing a prank, but then I wondered why they'd waste their time, you know? I heard the noise again, and I turned around, and I saw something move behind a tree. That was when I panicked."

"Why?"

"You never heard of Old Nathaniel?"

I searched my memory. The name seemed distantly familiar. Where had I heard of him, and why did it feel recent? It also felt connected to Mary somehow. "I don't know, maybe."

"Old Nathaniel, the Hide-Behind Man? You can only see him out of the corner of your eye. Until it's too late."

"What are you talking about?"

"I thought it was just a legend too. But I saw him. Just like the old story said. At the last minute. Right before he hit me. I saw him."

"What did he look like?"

Johnny looked afraid now. His face was drawn and his lips twitched. He touched the top of his head again, wiping away blood. "He had a mask on. A . . . I don't know . . . a burlap sack. It was tied around his neck. He hit me with a . . . shit . . . I don't know what it was. It was hard and heavy, like a tire rod or something."

"And where was Mary when he hit you?"

"She was right beside me."

"Do you remember anything else?"

He shook his head.

"Let me have your phone."

He reached into his pocket and his hand came back empty.

"It's gone."

"Shit," I said. "What about your gun? Where's that?"

He looked around, feeling his waist. "I had it in my hand."

"There," Ronnie said, pointing. It was near the stream.

Johnny started for it.

"Nope," I said. "Leave it too. Both guns better be in the same place when I come back."

"Where you going?" Ronnie said.

"To find her. Is this the way to the road?"

"Yeah," Johnny said. "Keep on the trail."

That was exactly what I did until I made it to the road five or ten minutes later. Once there, I knelt on the shoulder and caught my breath.

Mary was gone. The knowledge of it opened up something inside of me. It felt like a lightning storm in the pit of my stomach. I rubbed my face and collapsed onto the ground. My fears had come true, and now I felt more afraid, more vulnerable than ever.

13

At the road, I managed to flag down an eighteen-wheeler. The sleepy trucker let me borrow his phone, and I called the sheriff's office directly.

A deputy said somebody would be out as soon as possible. I gave the trucker his phone back and watched his taillights fade into the darkness.

I sat down on the side of the road to wait.

Trying to think was nearly impossible. The heaviness I felt inside my chest mingled with the hope I kept telling myself I needed to be feeling, and made the night around me seem surreal, like something from a film I was watching. I tried to make myself believe that Mary had simply escaped in the struggle, that she wasn't too far away at this very moment. It was even possible, I tried to convince myself, that she'd come walking out of those trees at any moment.

One nagging doubt kept me from buying into this particular fantasy.

The gun. Mary's gun. If she'd been able to escape, wouldn't she have taken her gun? It was possible she'd taken off before Johnny had dropped the gun, but why hadn't she come back for it? It was what I would have done, and any survival instinct I had, I felt sure Mary would have too.

And what about Old Nathaniel? On the surface it seemed utterly ridiculous. The Hide-Behind Man? Horseshit. There was something else happening here. It infuriated me that I couldn't figure out where I'd heard the name Old Nathaniel before.

Then it hit me. The fake skull in the cave. Someone had written "Old Nathaniel" on the wall of the cave. They'd written something else too. "AOC."

I stood when I saw the police car approaching and waved my hands. It was one of the Tahoe's, which meant Coulee County Sheriff's department. A female deputy got out of the vehicle and nodded at me.

"I'm Deputy Clark," she said. "Did you call?"

"Yeah. My girlfriend is missing."

"And someone is injured?"

I nodded. "Yes. I can take you there."

She pulled a two-way radio from her hip. "This is Deputy Clark. I need another unit and a medic." She looked at me. "You're the detective. The one from the newspaper."

"Yeah. And my girlfriend is Mary Hawkins. She's a homicide detective from Atlanta. She used to work for Coulee County, as a matter of fact."

This got her moving. "Okay, take me to the injured party. You can tell me on the way."

* * *

I was worried that one or both of the men would be gone when we arrived, but was pleased to see them sitting on a big rock beside the stream. Both guns were still untouched where they lay.

I'd explained everything to Clark as we'd walked there, and she went over now to interview Johnny.

I covered my face, hating the waiting, the slowness of it all.

"I'm going back to Jefferson's," I said.

"I don't advise that," Clark said. "You need to wait on the sheriff. He'll be here soon."

"You can't just expect me to wait around and do nothing."

"Sure I can. Sit tight. I'm sure your friend can take care of herself."

She was right. Mary could take care of herself, but as much as that thought should have made me feel calmer, it didn't. Mary *could* take care of herself, which somehow made her disappearance even more disturbing. Mary wasn't one to get lost. Even if she had run away, she would have circled back for the gun. Yet it still lay there, untouched. I walked the area, trying to alleviate some of the nervous energy I felt.

An eternity seemed to drag by. Ronnie loaned me his flashlight, and I held mine in the other hand, creating two large swaths of light. I walked back and forth, shining them over the forest floor. Pine needles, leaves, and grass blended together to create a dense cover over the ground. I kicked at it and shone the lights at the exposed ground, growing angrier and less patient by the minute.

Something caught the light. I knelt, moving away some fallen leaves, and saw a small black snakelike wire. I picked it up and realized it was longer and thicker than I'd first imagined. On one end was a tiny microphone, like the one Rufus had showed us the other day. I wound the line up and stuck the mic in my pocket, wondering why or how it had gotten here. Was it a clue or just a random artifact, perhaps blown by a storm far away from where it had originally been lost? And how much should I read into Rufus finding another one just like this near the caves? The same caves where "Old Nathaniel" had been scrawled across the back wall?

I was about to say something to the deputy about it, when her radio crackled. She answered it, and the voice on the other end wanted to know where she was.

"In the woods, near a little stream. Probably feeds into the Blackclaw. There's a little trail. Follow it. You'll see us."

"Can I go?" Ronnie said.

"No," Deputy Clark said. "You can't."

"Shit. I need a smoke, and Earl made me lose my last one."

"Me too," Johnny said.

"You need a medic. But never mind that. Nobody leaves until the sheriff talks to you."

I opened my mouth to tell the deputy about the mic I'd found, but at the last minute decided not to. I wasn't sure why. Maybe I was already fearing being shut out of things. Maybe I still had a bad taste in my mouth from the last sheriff, a good friend of my father's and just as corrupt. Either way, I decided to just hold it. It probably wouldn't ever amount to anything anyway. But it made me feel like I was making some progress nonetheless.

A few minutes later, Patterson showed up with a holder filled with four cups of coffee. He handed one to Clark first and then passed out the rest to Ronnie, Johnny, and me. When Patterson handed the coffee to Ronnie, I couldn't help but notice a barely concealed disdain on his face. Apparently, the two men had already been introduced.

"Thank you," I said, and drank quietly until, gradually, the world seemed to come back into focus.

"I've already spoken to Lane Jefferson. Called him on the way over. His story checks out. He was visiting a friend. Says he took a call about a woman from one of his men guarding the cornfield. He told him to take her to the road and he'd come by. He said he never saw them, and when he tried to call back, he couldn't get his guy on the phone."

"Where is he now?" I asked.

He shrugged. "Back at his house, I suppose. Can you tell me exactly how you and Detective Hawkins ended up in the cornfield tonight?"

I glanced at Ronnie. "He set us up."

"Explain," Patterson said, eyeing Ronnie suspiciously.

"Shit, Earl. It wasn't like that," Ronnie said.

"I'll be the judge of that," Patterson said.

I told him everything, starting with my first run-in with Jefferson a day or two earlier. When I got to the part about Mary and I arriving and not finding Ronnie, Patterson interrupted me.

"I think I get the picture."

"I want to talk to Jefferson," I said. "He's the one behind this."

"Nope," Patterson said. "This isn't the first time I've dealt with issues between these two men. Ronnie here hates Lane Jefferson because his sister decided to date him. It's as simple as that. In my mind, he's done this as some kind of elaborate way to frame Lane Jefferson."

"Bullshit," Ronnie said.

"Doesn't anybody care to hear what really happened?" Johnny said.

"I'll get to you in a minute," Patterson said. "I want to hear what Mr. Thrash has to say for himself."

"I say bullshit on all of it. Lane threatened to hurt my niece. I'll admit to lying to Earl to get him and his girlfriend out here, but . . . shit, I didn't know she was going to go missing."

Patterson looked at me. "You believe that?"

The crazy thing was that I did. "Yeah."

Patterson laughed. "I misjudged you. Thought you had basic walking-around sense."

"Never claimed to be smart, but sometimes a man just knows."

"That right? Well, fine, let's see if we can get to the bottom of this," Patterson said. "I think we can." He turned to his deputy. "Take Mr. Thrash's statement. Ronnie, you better get your story straight because I got a feeling it's going to show up in court one day."

"Fuck you," Ronnie said. "Why don't you go score some more weed for your wife?"

Patterson's face stayed blank, but even in the dark I could see his jaw twitch reflexively at Ronnie's words.

He let his gaze linger on Ronnie a little longer before turning to Johnny.

Johnny told it just like he told it to me and Ronnie.

When he finished, Patterson was silent. He turned around, surveying the scene. "Old Nathaniel, huh?"

"That's right. Wore a mask and all."

Patterson paced over to the gun again, peering down at it. He looked back at Ronnie.

"I think what we have here are a couple of dumbasses who thought they could pull off a kidnapping of a police officer."

"I didn't kidnap nobody," Ronnie said. "You need to talk to Lane Jefferson. He's the one who told me to get them out here."

"I've already talked to him," Patterson shot back.

"Talk to him again," Ronnie said. "Hell, none of us would be here if he hadn't threatened my niece."

Patterson groaned, as if Ronnie's deceitfulness truly pained him. "Cuff them both," he said to Clark.

"What?" Johnny said. "Why me?"

"I think you two worked together. I'm going to guess one of your friends has the officer somewhere. The sooner you tell me where, the easier the DA will go on you two boys."

Clark came over and slapped handcuffs on Johnny's wrist first. Johnny tried to jerk away before she got the other one, but Clark just shook her head and nodded toward Ronnie.

"Shit," Ronnie said. "Earl, can't you do something?"

I shook my head. I honestly didn't know if I wanted to. Even though I did believe Ronnie, I couldn't help but think he was getting what he deserved for bringing me and Mary into this mess to start with.

"Read them their rights," Patterson said, "and keep them here until I get back." He nodded at me. "Take a walk with me, Mr. Marcus."

I followed him back toward the road. When we were out of ear-shot of the others, he said, "Lane Jefferson told me something else."

"What?"

"He said Johnny's an ex-con. I checked and it's legit. Want to guess what he did time for?"

I shrugged. It still felt like we were wasting time.

"Rape. The victim was a thirty-something black woman. A real looker."

That caught my attention. "Jesus. We've got to find her."

"That we do, but I don't think there was a third man involved."

"You said—"

"I know what I said, but it was just—I don't know—a floater, to gauge their reaction. Neither man seemed to take the bait. I feel like this was all Johnny. He must have offered Ronnie something to help him, and they decided they could blame it on Jefferson."

I nodded. What he was saying wasn't without logic, but if there wasn't a third man, where was Mary? I asked him that very question.

"I think she hit Johnny over the head and took off. My guess is she's probably already out at the road, walking for help, or maybe she's already been picked up by a trucker."

"She left her gun."

"*She* didn't leave it. Remember, Johnny had it. He probably just dropped it when she hit him."

"What did she hit him with?"

"I'm guessing a rock. Probably asked to stop at the stream for a drink. When she bent down to drink, she got her hand on a rock and hit him hard. He's probably been lying there trying to figure out some story to tell ever since. Old Nathaniel? What the hell is that?"

"I admit it sounds far-fetched, but remember the other day when you came up to the cave?"

He nodded. "Yep. Old Nathaniel was on the cave wall. I remember."

"You don't see a connection?"

"Why should I?"

"That day, you said someone had sprayed the same thing on a missing black kid's trailer."

This seemed to give him pause. He hesitated for a beat longer than usual before answering. "These things come and go. It's the trend right now. I guarantee Johnny heard about it from some other thugs and decided to capitalize on it."

"So, you're dismissing the possibility of a masked attacker, somebody pretending to be Old Nathaniel?"

Patterson stopped walking. "Look, I know you cracked a real humdinger when you took down your Daddy's church. Real fantastical shit. Lightning and pits full of snakes?"

"I had a lot of help from—"

"I'll bet you did. My point is, Mr. Marcus, that might have predisposed you to believing some . . . I don't know . . . for lack of a better term, *wild shit*. Old Nathaniel. A fucking burlap sack? You're kidding me, right? Simplest explanation is the best. And we got two simple explanations—either one of their Neanderthal friends has her right now because they're working together, and the injury was self-inflicted, so to speak, or Mary hit him, and she's lost in these woods."

"I hear you," I said. "I really do. Old Nathaniel sounds ridiculous. No argument there. But I'm also not ready to condemn Johnny yet. I talked to him and didn't get the feeling that he was lying. And to be honest, I'm pretty damned certain that Ronnie's not lying."

Patterson fixed me with a piteous look. "That's probably because they're both so good at it." We stepped out of the woods, and the empty highway came into view.

"So what's the plan?" I asked.

"I made a call to Atlanta, and they're coming up tomorrow in force. We'll get some dogs in the cornfield and woods, and in the meantime we'll put pressure on Johnny and Ronnie. One of them will crack."

"I want to help."

He nodded. "I figured you would. Just obey the law, and let me know if you find anything." He held out his hand, and I took it. "Remember," he said. "Only two possibilities, and they both end with Johnny and Ronnie."

His words were probably supposed to make me feel better, but I knew he was wrong. There were way more than two possibilities, and while they all might start with Ronnie and Johnny, I honestly had no idea where they'd lead from there.

14

I waited for Jefferson to pull away before walking back through the woods toward Lane Jefferson's house. I felt sure he was behind this, and I didn't want to waste any time in confronting him.

As I walked, I tried to go through the possibilities. Patterson wanted me to swallow something that I just couldn't: Ronnie being involved. It felt strange to be in a position where I was defending Ronnie's moral character, but as vile and reprehensible as he could be sometimes, he didn't seem like the kind of man to plan a crime like this. He *did* strike me as a man that would do a hell of a lot to save his own ass. Desperation: that was Ronnie's downfall. That and a kind of lecherous immaturity that he seemed incapable of not inflicting on others. His story lined up with the kind of person I knew him to be. He acted out of desperation to get Mary and me to the cornfield. He did it to help his niece, an act that almost made me admire him.

I wasn't as sure about Johnny. I'd been a PI for a long time, long enough to be on both sides of the intuition argument. When I'd first started out, I'd relied on my intuition a lot. After a year or two of near-death experiences, I'd decided to rethink that strategy and spent the next several years steadfastly ignoring my gut—at least until I found some hard evidence to back it up—but I had faired only marginally better. In the end, experience taught me to take my intuition the way an old man might take his erectile dysfunction meds—with care, and only when the moment was just right.

The moment felt right with Johnny. I'd seen him waking up. If he'd concocted the Old Nathaniel story in that brief amount of time, he truly was a gifted liar.

So where did that leave me?

I parted the trees and stepped off the trail into Lane Jefferson's backyard. His truck was parked in the driveway. I knew as I stepped toward his house, this had the potential to go sideways very quickly because I was still angry, but I also understood that time was extremely important in these kinds of cases. The longer Mary was missing, the more likely I'd never see her again.

That thought didn't do anything to calm me down. In fact, it did just the opposite.

* * *

I slammed the side of my fist into Lane Jefferson's door hard enough to shake the frame.

A light came on upstairs. I banged again, this time harder—so much so, the skin around my knuckles split and started to bleed. Wincing, I pulled my hand away and touched my 9mm hidden inside my blue jean jacket.

I heard footsteps coming to the door. The door opened a crack. "Who is it?"

"Earl Marcus. We need to talk."

Jefferson opened the door wider. He wore a pair of boxer shorts and a muscle shirt that revealed chiseled arms and tattooed shoulders. He held a .45 in his right hand.

"Hey, it's the detective. What brings you over?"

"I came to talk about you calling my girlfriend a bitch."

I allowed him just enough time for his face to register confusion before I did my damnedest to knock him out.

He dropped his gun as he fell, and I kicked it down the hall, deeper into the large house.

"You're going to regret that," he sputtered, bubbles of blood forming as he spoke.

"Where is she?" I said, through gritted teeth as I dropped to a knee and drew back my fist.

"Ask your boy Ronnie," he spat, cringing and holding his hands up to block the blow.

"I already asked him. He said you set all this up, threatening his niece."

Jefferson shook his head. "I didn't threaten nobody. You don't know me too well. I don't make threats. I make promises."

I stood up and kicked him in the stomach. He gasped and beat his fist against the floor.

I knelt until my face was a few inches from his. "You want to get kicked again?"

He gasped. "No."

"Then tell me where she is."

"I don't fucking know where she is."

I was about to kick him again, when I heard a voice behind me.

"Mr. Marcus," Sheriff Patterson said, standing in the open doorway, "I think that's enough."

Lane sat up, still trying to catch his breath. His mouth was bleeding badly, and his face looked discolored, like he might be about to throw up.

I stepped away from Lane and held up my hands. Patterson wasn't holding his firearm, but I wanted to make it clear that I was finished.

"Arrest his ass," Lane said, coughing.

"I'll take care of my end, Lane. You just take care that you hire a higher quality of worker."

"I'll fucking talk to my daddy if you don't arrest him," Lane sputtered. He sounded like a middle school kid. His daddy?

"Do what you have to do, okay? I'm going to handle things the way I see fit."

Lane scrambled to his feet and glared at me. "If I ever see you again, old man," he said, "I'll kill you."

Patterson groaned. "You know what? One more word out of

either of you, and I'm arresting you both. Then you can talk to Daddy your own self when he comes and bails your ass out."

He looked from Lane back to me. Neither of us spoke.

"Let's go, Earl."

"I'd like to ask him some questions."

"You already had a chance to do that. Now, we're going to talk."

I didn't protest. If anything, I was angry at myself now. I'd let my rage get in the way of getting some answers about Mary.

I followed Patterson out. Behind us, I heard Lane Jefferson muttering to himself. I couldn't make out the words, but the tone was clear: I'd made an enemy.

* * *

I'd always been a man in conflict with himself. Even from childhood, I remembered being of two minds about my father and his religion. On the one hand, I wanted it more than I wanted anything. On the other hand, I felt repulsed and frightened by the stifling words and songs and thoughts of heaven and hell.

Later, after my time spent with Granny, I became a great believer in peaceful solutions. I didn't support war, believed in gun control, and condemned our nation's jingoistic tendency to become embroiled in conflicts that could easily be avoided if we'd focus more on trying to get along with other countries instead of trying to take advantage of them. Yet, despite all of this, I had a hard time not resorting to violence myself. As a young man, I fought early and often, winning more than my fair share and learning from the losses. When I left Georgia, I lived hard, on the road, mostly taking jobs at local bars as the guy you'd call in to whip the ass of some drunk asshole. Even though I always felt bad about these actions the next day, I always justified them in the moment. For a while, I fooled myself into thinking the beatdowns I participated in were actually moral because the guys had it coming. We're talking about racists and rapists and pedophiles and all manner of vermin. It was only later, when I'd lived with myself after the outbursts long enough, that I understood the real reason I engaged in violence. The real reason was that the violence was already inside me, and letting it out felt good. It was like an addiction. A drug, the kind you're always quitting with good intentions, only to return to it a few weeks later, to satisfy a craving so deep and wide, all you can think about is filling it.

Even though I'd come a long way since those days, the urge was still there. I could control it better and sometimes even direct it for good, but I was always susceptible to losing my shit. I'd gotten to the point where I understood the urge would never completely go away. I suppose I could blame it on my father and get away with it. Most everybody I knew had been horrified by my father and the way he treated me, but that was another way in which I felt conflicted. I knew that these things affected people. Take Ronnie for instance, and his story about how he started smoking. Hell, after a story like that, I could see exactly how Ronnie had become the man he was now.

But I couldn't—or wouldn't—cut myself the same slack. I had to do better. I had to win the war inside myself or die trying.

And now it wasn't just my ass on the line. It was Mary's too.

15

"Who's his daddy?" I asked after we'd climbed into the sheriff's cruiser.

"You're kidding, right?"

"No."

Patterson gave me a look as if he thought I was playing an elaborate prank on him. "Mayor Keith."

"What?"

"Yeah. After the divorce, Lane took his mother's name. But he and the mayor are real close." Patterson crossed his fingers and held them up. "More like friends these days than anything else."

I nodded, trying to understand how this news affected . . . well, everything. "Are you going to arrest me?"

Patterson shook his head. "I'm going under the assumption that Lane started it. And if that's not what happened, I don't want to hear about it." He reached over and touched my jaw lightly. "Yep, he gave you a good blow there. Might be broken. Go get it looked at."

I nodded. "Thanks."

"I'm serious. Go get it looked at. Make sure there's a medical record in case he tries to push things."

"Sure," I said, even though as soon as I'd said the word, I realized it wasn't going to happen. *Nothing* was going to happen besides trying to find Mary.

All at once the realization that she was really gone hit me hard. Maybe it was because, in that moment, there was no one to fight, no one to blame, nothing, really, for me to do at all, other than face the reality of the situation.

Mary Hawkins was missing.

"You okay?"

"No," I said. "I love her."

Patterson nodded. "That's why I'm letting this thing go with Lane. His daddy knows he's a hothead, so he'll buy that you two were talking and he threw the first punch." Patterson made the turn onto County Road 18 to take me to my truck. "At least I hope he will."

"Where was Jefferson?" I asked. "You said he was at a friend's? Who was the friend?"

Patterson looked over at me warily. "Why, you going to go kick his ass too?"

"No, of course not. Look, that's not normally how I work. It's just . . . I had to do something, you know?"

"Yeah, I know. And that's why I'm cutting you a little slack." He slowed the cruiser as my truck came into view. "This time."

I felt like I was at the end of a short rope, hanging on with one hand while the wind blew like crazy. Below me was the black water, and even though I could hang on for a long time, it wouldn't matter because the water was rising, and there was nothing I could do about that.

He stopped the cruiser. "Get some sleep. Like I said earlier, she's either out there somewhere, or one of Ronnie's friends has her. Either way, we'll find her."

"You never answered my question."

"What question?"

"Who was Lane with?"

"I don't think you know him."

"Try me."

Patterson sighed. "His name is Tag Monroe. He lives up on Summer Mountain."

I nodded. "So, he's respectable."

"Excuse me?"

"It just seems like that would be the only reason you'd add the part about where he lived."

"Come again?"

"It's a subtle way of saying he's rich as fuck and therefore reliable. It's okay. You probably didn't even realize it."

"I don't know what you want from me, Earl. I'm just following protocol. He's got a solid alibi. Now, if you want to argue that he masterminded the whole thing . . ."

"That's exactly what I want to argue. He *told* Ronnie to get me and Mary to the cornfield tonight."

"That's according to Ronnie. Do you know he's been calling the office for the last three months trying to get Lane arrested for something?"

"Maybe you should have listened."

"We did. Before I understood their dynamic, before I understood Ronnie, we looked into it all. There wasn't shit there. Mind if I ask you a question?"

I shrugged.

"How'd you even get hooked up with a man like Ronnie anyway?"

I laughed. It was a good question. I surprised myself with my response. "He's not what you think."

"Yeah? What is he then?"

For some reason I thought of my mother. Her theory about evil jumping from one person to the next. I thought of my own daddy and Ronnie's grandfather, who'd been my father's best friend. Maybe *jump* wasn't the word I was looking for, but there had definitely been some kind of transfer there, some kind of throttling of innocence from a young age, and neither of us had quite recovered since.

"He's just a man," I said, and got out of the car.

16

I didn't sleep that night. Instead, I sat in the yard outside the house, near the ridgeline, looking over the town of Riley. I was trying to think, trying to decide how to proceed once the morning came.

Goose lay beside me, his nostrils flaring in the early fall wind. Sometimes I wondered what it would be like to be a dog on a night like this, a night where the wind carried all the secrets in the world, if you just could read them. Goose read them all, his head still, his ears alert, his nose sucking in the wind and the world in silent anticipation.

I needed to be like Goose, I decided. I needed to somehow get into the world out there, to invite it inside me, and then live there for a moment. I tried to go back to the crime scene, to imagine what must have happened.

Johnny would have had a gun on Mary, and either someone approached him from behind and hit him over the head or Mary somehow did. Accepting the former meant strongly considering that Johnny had been hit by a man wearing a burlap sack as a mask. Accepting the latter meant dealing with why Mary had not recovered either gun. And why she hadn't turned up yet.

Could there be a third option?

I tried to think of something but drew a blank. Instead, I recalled something else I'd forgotten. When I'd gone to the road to call the sheriff, I'd left Ronnie and Johnny alone. They could have easily split if they'd had something to hide, but neither did. Didn't sound like the behavior of most guilty men I'd known.

The wind picked up again, and Goose growled at something he must have smelled on it. I looked at my watch. It was almost four in the morning. I decided to get started.

I fed Goose and gave him some water, filling several bowls because I wasn't sure how long it might be before I was able to check on him again. Then I took a quick shower, ate some sausage and half a hard biscuit leftover from Mary's visit. I thought about coffee but decided to go with a couple of shots of whiskey instead, to take the edge off.

After the shower and the whiskey, I felt better. I put on my Braves hat and tucked my 9mm into my waistband and put on a long-sleeved shirt that hung low and loose enough over my ass to cover the weapon.

I drove to Rufus's first, pulling up to the old church just as the sun was coming up. It looked more ominous somehow in the half-light, and I wondered again why a man would choose to live in the place of his first misery, but Rufus was not like most men.

As if to illustrate my point, I found him awake, tottering around the little graveyard where my mother was buried. He wore a pair of black overalls and some old high-top tennis shoes. He wasn't wearing the dark shades that he usually wore to keep people from getting spooked by his glassy eyes and the attendant scarring.

I parked the truck and killed the engine. Rufus put down the rake and started toward me as I got out. He knew it was me. He could always tell by the sound of my truck.

"I don't feel the sun up," he said. "Which means something's wrong."

"Yeah," I said. "Something is very wrong."

"Want to sit down?"

"No time. I just wanted you to know Mary is missing."

"Missing?"

"Yeah." I explained as briefly as I could what had happened the night before. Rufus listened patiently, barely moving.

When I finished, he shook his head. "Ronnie fucking Thrash."

"I know," I said. "You lay down with dogs . . ."

"But from what I'm hearing, you don't think it was him or Johnny behind it?"

"No. I think Lane Jefferson is."

Rufus nodded. "You know who his daddy's big buddy is, don't you?"

"You mean Mayor Keith?"

"Yeah."

"No idea."

"The one and only Jeb Walsh. Thick as thieves, those two."

"So, Keith is likely a racist?"

"That'd be a fair conclusion."

"What do you know about the son?"

"Not a lot. People say he's fucked in the head. That he's into drugs and guns and conspiracy theories. Shit like that."

"What kind of conspiracy theories?"

"Hell if I know. Talk to Susan at the library. She knows the mayor and hears stories."

"Okay," I said. "I've got another question."

"Shoot."

"Who's Old Nathaniel?"

Rufus seemed taken aback by the question. He was silent for a moment, and I tried to read his expression.

"You know who Old Nathaniel is."

"I do?"

"Of course you do. You sure you don't want to have a seat? I got some coffee on inside. I'll bring us a couple of cups."

"No. I need to get moving."

"Where are you going to go? It's not even six in the morning yet."

He had a point. I didn't really have any place in mind other than the cornfield and the woods behind it.

"Okay," I said, and sat down, hating the wait but knowing there wasn't much I could do until I had something to go on besides stumbling through the woods and fields by Jefferson's house.

Rufus ambled toward the church, avoiding a tree easily and navigating a rise just like he had seen it coming. Rufus amazed me with his ability to always know just where he was in the world.

It was an ability that was even easier for me to admire after the disorientation I'd felt in the cornfield. From beneath those stalks, the world seemed to shrink. Without the ability to see over them, it was hard to get any context for where you were in the—

I remembered something else then, something that *would* give me something to do. The water tower. Before Mary and I had heard the sounds in the cornfield, I'd seen a light coming from the water tower. Was it possible someone had been inside, watching us, waiting until my attention was elsewhere before giving the okay to abduct Mary?

It seemed unlikely, but I couldn't rule out anything at this point. I'd go to the water tower first and see if I could get inside.

Rufus came back out, carrying two coffee mugs. I met him halfway to take one of them and help guide him to his seat.

Once seated, he took a sip and nodded in my direction. "Put a little whiskey in them."

"Thanks."

"I got to say, I don't like that Old Nathaniel reference."

"Why?"

"I can't believe you don't remember. I'm sure your mother told you the same stories my mother told me. He was just some boogeyman, made up to keep kids out of the valley, where the blacks lived."

"I do remember both my parents warning me about the valley, but nothing about Old Nathaniel. Daddy just said the people there weren't our kind."

"Yep, that sounds like your daddy. He probably didn't want to give any credence to the stories because he didn't come up with them. Your daddy could be amazingly rational when it came to other people's bullshit. When it came to his own? Well, that shit was inarguable."

I almost laughed. Rufus knew my father almost as well as I did. "True. But what about Old Nathaniel?"

"I'm getting there. The point you should understand is that the stories about Old Nathaniel were told to me for the same reason your daddy told you to stay out of the valley."

"Because that's where the blacks lived?"

"Way back, before you would remember, they called it the Valley of the Devil or the Devil's Valley."

"Sounds ominous."

"Yeah, that was the point. It fed into a larger narrative, that people of color were Satan's own, and the good white folks like me and you shouldn't mix with them."

"So where does Old Nathaniel fit in?" I couldn't help but feel like Rufus was taking his time. I needed to already be gone from here, making progress toward finding Mary.

"Well, the real story—the one the blacks down in the valley grew up hearing—is that Old Nathaniel *only* killed blacks. Over the years I've had the opportunity to meet some folks that came up in the valley. They all said Old Nathaniel was supposed to be like an old white farmer. Apparently, he was angered by the presence of blacks near his land, blacks that were free, and he decided to move his family into the mountains."

"You mean the Fingers?"

"That's right. Or maybe Summer Mountain. These legends ain't an exact science."

"Sure, but it sounds like this one mirrors reality, because, other than Lane Jefferson, all the whites live in the mountains or in Riley, and all the blacks live in the valley."

"Right, legends always mirror reality. It's why they resonate so much."

I considered this and decided it made a lot of sense. But what I couldn't get my head around was how Old Nathaniel could still have any power today.

"Does 'AOC' mean anything to you?"

"*A* what?"

"'OC.' It's something Mary and I found on a cave wall. 'Old Nathaniel' was spray-painted right next to it."

Rufus shook his head. "AOC." He said each letter slowly. "Don't know that one. Did you try the Google on it yet?"

"Not yet. It's all come at me so fast, I can't even figure out what to do first."

"I'd drop by the library. Susan knows a good bit about the history of this area. If this AOC is a real thing, she'll know about it."

"Thanks."

"So, what's the plan?"

I told him about the water tower.

"Want some company?"

"Don't you have protest stuff to do?"

"Not until Walsh's book thing. Then I'm going to wear the mic and have my say. If they carry me out, then they carry me out."

"I'll be there," I said.

"No, don't worry about it. You'll be busy looking for Mary."

That hit me like a gut punch. "No," I said. "She'll be back by then."

Rufus said nothing. He wasn't the kind of man to believe in false hope, or to give it. Usually it was something I appreciated about him, but just then I hated him for it.

17

We arrived at the water tower right as they were letting the dogs loose into the cornfield. I watched as a police officer from Atlanta held a jacket that must belong to Mary in front of the dogs. They bayed loudly, and the handler let them go.

We parked behind Sheriff Patterson's squad car, but he was nowhere to be found. Instead, a big, bearded deputy came over.

"Help you boys?"

I held out my hand. "Earl Marcus. Mary's my girlfriend."

He didn't look impressed. "This is an active police investigation. You're going to have to move on."

"I'm a private investigator." I resisted the urge to add, *Maybe you've read about me*, and it was a good thing too. *That* would have probably sealed our fate. Instead, I pulled out my state-issued badge. "Can you call Sheriff Patterson? I think he'll say it's fine that I'm here."

The bearded deputy—Nichols, according to his breastplate—pressed a button on his two-way. "Sheriff? Come in, Sheriff."

"Yep," Patterson replied.

"You know an Earl Marcus?"

It was barely audible, but it sounded like Patterson cursed softly.

"Sheriff?"

"Yeah, I know him."

"Okay for him to be snooping around?"

"It's okay. Just keep an eye on him, all right?"

"Will do. Over."

The deputy shrugged. "You heard him. I'll be watching."

* * *

Because of Deputy Nichols's watchful eye, Rufus and I decided to drive back down the road and park out of sight. Then we worked our way up through the scattered stalks on the left side of the road, unobserved by Nichols. We stopped when we reached the underside of the water tower. I stared up at its large corrugated belly about ten yards above our heads. There was a large tear in the bottom of the basin, but I didn't see a way to reach it short of a ladder, which we didn't have.

"Well?" Rufus said.

"There doesn't appear to be any way up."

"That's bullshit. There's got to be a ladder."

"I'm sure there was at some point, but it's gone now. Based on the hole in the bottom of this thing, it hasn't been in use for years."

But Rufus wasn't listening. Instead, he had his hands out in front of him, feeling for the nearest leg of the tower.

"A little to your left," I said.

He clutched it and felt the length of it, obviously looking for notches or footholds. I followed his example and did the same with the one across from it.

On the second leg, I found something I would have overlooked if not for Rufus. There was a thin cord someone had nailed to the wooden leg. I yanked on it, trying to pull the nail out, but it held fast, and I realized it had been nailed in multiple places.

"Be right back," I said. "Going to the truck."

I opened the toolbox I kept in the bed of my truck and glanced around to make sure Nichols hadn't wandered this way. The road was still clear, so I grabbed the hammer and jogged back over to the tower.

Rufus was leaning against one of the legs. "Haven't heard much out them dogs," he said. "Not sure that's a good sign. Usually the louder they are, the more they're on the scent."

I ignored him and went straight to the wooden leg with the cord and pulled the nails out. Once I had them out, I gave it a good tug and something clattered inside the tower. I pulled harder and heard it sliding across the metal floor of the tower. A little more . . .

Water dripped out of the opening, followed by something solid. A rope ladder unfurled itself right beside me.

"What was that?" Rufus asked.

"Our way up."

I climbed up first and then leaned over the opening to direct Rufus to the ladder. Once we were both safely inside, I looked around. My suspicions about the place were confirmed. Carved into the corrugated tank was a small window. A stool sat by the window, and beside that, a table and some chairs. A pair of binoculars lay on the stool.

"Watch yourself," I said to Rufus. "There's a gap right in the middle of the floor."

"I know *that*," he said, impatiently. "Why don't you tell me what else is here?"

Before I could, my cell phone rang.

"Shit," I said, looking at it. "This is a sheriff's office number."

"Better answer it."

"Okay, just . . . step back, okay? You're worrying me."

"I'm fine. Answer."

I answered, and in one phone call, everything changed.

18

"It's Patterson," the voice said.

"What's the word?" I found myself hopeful. Maybe the dogs had already found her.

"A bit of good news and . . . some bad," he said. "The bad news is that the dogs haven't found anything yet. We'll keep them out here, but they're just circling the same damned area over and over, and there's nothing there. We've even had a helicopter up this morning because there's places in the cornfield where it's flat out hard to get to, but they didn't see anything either. We'll keep them out here until either they give us something definitive or they wear themselves out, but generally by this point they would have found a scent if they were going to."

"And the good news?" I had no idea what he could possibly say that was going to be good if Mary hadn't been found.

"We got a confession today."

"A confession? From who?"

"Johnny Waters. He confessed the whole thing to one of my deputies. Got it all on tape. It's compelling."

"So, what did he do with her?"

"Well, that's the thing. She knocked him over the head with a rock, and now it's just a matter of finding her."

"That doesn't make sense. You just said the dogs weren't getting anywhere."

"Well, that doesn't mean she's not out there somewhere. Their handler says the cornfield confuses them. She could have very easily gone the other direction, up Summer Mountain and gotten lost in those woods. We'll find her."

I was silent, trying to make sense of it.

"Earl?"

"Yeah?"

"This is good news. It means she's out there. We've just got to find her."

"Did he say anything about Ronnie?"

"He said Ronnie wasn't involved."

"What about Jefferson?"

"It was Johnny from the beginning. Just Johnny."

"That doesn't make sense. Why would Ronnie make up that story about Jefferson?"

"I already explained it to you once. Ronnie has been out to get Jefferson for some time."

"Doesn't add up."

"It's a confession. And a strong one. He goes into some detail about the whole thing. Calling Jefferson was part of the ruse. He was going to say she escaped at the stream. He won't say what he was going to do to her because . . . well, why would he confess to something he didn't ever get a chance to do? But you can figure it out for yourself. A stream is a good place to wash up afterward."

"It doesn't make sense."

"Sure it does."

It felt like anything but good news to me. I couldn't get my head around Johnny confessing.

"You still there, Earl?"

"Yeah. Has Johnny had any visitors?"

"Not that I'm aware of."

"Can you check?"

"Sure. I'll check. You think somebody talked him into it?"

"Or threatened him."

"Okay," Patterson said. "I'll keep it in mind. My deputy said you were snooping around the cornfield earlier. Find anything?"

I was about to tell him about the water tower and the binoculars, but suddenly it felt wisest to just keep it to myself. Maybe it was learning about Johnny's suspicious and sudden confession, or maybe it was just my gut, but I couldn't escape the feeling that the fewer people who knew about this, the better.

"Nothing of any interest."

* * *

After I told Rufus the news, he agreed I'd done the right thing about keeping the info from the sheriff.

"I can't help but think he was threatened," I said.

"Well, you should be able to check the surveillance footage at the jail. If Patterson tells you nobody signed in, push the issue. Ask to see the footage."

"Okay." I picked up the binoculars and leaned against the corrugated side of the water tower, pressing them to the opening.

I moved them slowly, taking in the detail of the corn but also wondering how they were really helpful. Sure, they gave the viewer a close-up, but only of the corn stalks, which were too dense to reveal anything useful. I lifted the binoculars, searching for something on the horizon. I saw the train tracks and followed them until they disappeared inside thick trees.

I couldn't figure out why anyone would want to use binoculars from here. They were essentially useless.

"You see anything?" Rufus asked.

"Kernels of damn corn," I said. "And leaves. There's nothing to see. The water tower isn't tall enough to see what's actually inside the field, under the stalks."

"There's got to be a reason this stuff is here," Rufus said.

"I agree, but damned if I know what it is."

I picked the binoculars up again and made another sweep, this time focusing on the cornfield, taking it slow to see if there was something hidden in the details. Talk about not being able to see the forest for the trees.

I put the binoculars down and pressed my face against the opening, to see if I would fare any better without them. Now I could see Patterson standing near Deputy Nichols. They were talking about something. Nichols glanced toward the water tower. I ducked back quickly.

"Let's get out of here," I said.

19

I took Rufus home and went by to check on Goose before heading to the sheriff's office. I wanted to talk to Ronnie and check to see if anyone had been to visit Johnny Waters.

The deputy on duty was Deputy Clark, the same one who'd arrested both Ronnie and Johnny a few hours earlier. She led me to Ronnie's cell, where he was leaned up against the wall, snoring loudly.

"Johnny's two cells down. I wouldn't talk too loud unless you want him to overhear." She looked inside Ronnie's cell and shook her head. "The way this one is sleeping tells me something."

"Yeah? What does it tell you?"

"He's either innocent or doesn't have a conscience."

I nodded and watched him snore. I hoped it was the former. Otherwise, I'd read this whole situation wrong.

"Want a chair?" she said.

"No thanks, I'll stand. Shouldn't he be cut loose?"

"Not until the sheriff says so."

"Right."

"Coffee?"

"I'm good."

"At least one of us is. I'm ready for this shift to be over." Just before walking away, she took out her baton and clanged it against the bars.

Ronnie sat up, sucking a line of drool back into his mouth and looking around. When he saw me, he smiled.

"You're a damned sight for sore eyes. You come to bail me out?"

"No, I came to talk."

"You know this is bullshit, don't you? I didn't do nothing to your girlfriend."

"I'm pretty sure it's bullshit."

"Pretty sure? Why only *pretty* sure?"

"Well, you did set me up. It's hard to trust a man that would do that."

"Yeah, well, I told you why I done it. I didn't have a choice."

I leaned against the bars. "There's always a choice."

He spat onto the floor in disgust. "That's what people say who've always had one. One of these days, you'll understand. Sometimes there ain't a right or wrong. Sometimes there's just two wrongs and it's all a matter of priorities."

"Priorities, huh?"

"That's right. And, I don't mind saying I put the safety of my little niece before yours and your girlfriend's."

"If you would have just come clean in the beginning," I said, "I could have helped with the little girl."

"No, you couldn't. See, this is what you don't understand. Lane does what he wants. You couldn't have stopped him then, and you won't be able to stop him now. I'm surprised a smart guy like you ain't already figured that one out. I'll bet you didn't sleep last night, did you? And I'll bet you're frustrated because there's not any leads. You know why? Because it's Lane Jefferson. He's un-fucking-touchable."

I gripped the cell bars so hard I felt the skin around my knuckles stretching. "Nobody's untouchable."

Ronnie stood up and walked over to where I stood. "He's smarter than you think."

"I'm smart too."

Ronnie smiled. "You ain't smart, Earl. You're just determined."

I shrugged. "Maybe that's better."

Ronnie laughed. "Nah, it's not, but if you can get me out of here, I could help you."

I looked at him closely, trying to decide what the best approach was. He obviously didn't know about Johnny's confession yet. And because of that, I had one more question I needed to ask. And I didn't care nearly as much about his answer as I did his reaction when I asked it.

"Did they tell you about Johnny confessing?"

He looked confused. But not scared. Confused *and* scared would have been a bad combination. Confusion by itself was probably good.

"He did?"

"Yeah." I waited, wanting to see how much he knew.

"Well, fuck. I don't understand." He kept shaking his head in disbelief. All at once he stopped. "Oh shit, he and Lane were in it together, weren't they?"

I shrugged. "It's a possibility, but that's not what he's claiming. He says it was just him."

Ronnie shook his head. "Somebody got to him."

"That's what I thought too. You seen any visitors?"

"I been asleep the whole time."

"I wanted to ask you something else."

"Hit me."

"You ever heard of Old Nathaniel or the AOC?"

"The first one. I knew a guy who had that tattooed on his chest."

"Old Nathaniel?"

"Yeah. Wasn't just the name either. He had this real grim reaper–like shit right below it."

"Grim reaper–like?"

Ronnie shrugged. "Sort of. Maybe like if you mixed the grim reaper with a scarecrow. It was fucking creepy. Come to think of it, the guy was fucking creepy too."

"This friend have any contact with Lane Jefferson?"

"Yeah, he worked with us in the cornfield once or twice, but mostly he was up on Summer Mountain."

"Doing what?"

"Security."

"What was he securing?"

"Hell if I know. There was some warehouse up there. He told me people came and people went. As long as they had the little sticker in their window, they got let in. If they didn't, he sent them packing. Easiest job I ever heard of."

Just then the admitting door opened. Patterson came in. He looked irritated as he approached Ronnie's cell.

"You're free to go, Mr. Thrash," he said. He reached for a key and unlocked the cell.

Ronnie grinned. "About fucking time."

Patterson looked at me. "If someone had just opened a jail cell to let me go free, I think I'd show a little respect. How about you?"

"I'm right fucking here," Ronnie said. "Why don't you look at me? Why don't you talk to me?"

Patterson swung around quickly, his face twisted with a sudden rage. "Want me to talk to you? I'll talk to you." He pushed his face into Ronnie's until their noses almost touched. "Just give me one damn reason, and I'll stick every charge I can think of so far up your asshole you won't be able shit for the rest of your life. Do you understand me, you pompous fuck?"

Ronnie's eyes lit up. He smiled. I realized then that he'd won, that Ronnie always won when he got under another person's skin. It was a silly game, a vindictive game, but just like me, Sheriff Patterson had found himself playing it, and just like me, he'd lost.

"I will make a note of that, Sheriff. Thank you for making your intentions regarding my freedom and my asshole perfectly clear." Ronnie extended his hand comically. "I respect that in a man."

Patterson was furious at this point, but somehow he kept it in check and walked away. Ronnie shot me a victorious grin and literally skipped to the door.

Patterson turned to me. "What are you doing here?"

"I want to talk to Johnny, and I want to know if he had any visitors."

He sighed. "So you really think he was threatened?"

"I'm not ruling it out. Are you?"

"Of course not."

I followed Patterson to Johnny's cell. Johnny was sprawled out on his cot in nothing but a pair of soiled briefs.

Patterson frowned. "Put some clothes on. We need to talk."

Johnny looked at me but otherwise didn't move. "Why's he here?"

"He wants to talk to you."

"You ain't going to let him hit me, are you?"

Patterson chuckled. "I don't do that kind of shit."

"You sure?"

"Just get some clothes on. Goddamn, when's the last time you changed your underwear?"

Johnny shrugged. "A few days ago." With that, he stood and collected his blue jeans from the other side of the cell. He slid them on slowly and went back over to the bed to lie down.

"You had a visitor today," Patterson said.

"So?" Johnny said. "What, did he forget to sign in?"

"No, he signed in. Used the name Preston Argent. Claimed he was your counsel."

"That's right." Johnny lifted his right leg and twisted his torso a little and then farted loudly. "Can I have something to eat?"

"This guy, this Preston fellow—he's not a lawyer."

"Says who?"

"Says me. I know the lawyers in this town. He's not one of them."

"He's from out of town."

"This is bullshit," I said. "It's obvious this visitor coerced him to confess."

Patterson held up his hand. "Why did you confess, Johnny?"

Johnny sat up and looked at me as he answered. "I was advised to confess because it would be in my best interest." He sounded like he was repeating a canned line.

"He's full of shit," I said.

"I don't know, Earl. It's a confession. We can't just assume he's lying. I mean, as much as I don't like the visitor, I don't know why he'd agree to confess."

"Because he's being threatened."

"I don't know what to tell you."

"Just promise me you'll keep the investigation open."

"We'll keep looking, but as far as I'm concerned, we know what happened. We're not looking for any more criminal angles."

I stepped toward Johnny and gripped the bars in my fists, shaking the cell. "If you'll tell me the truth, we can get the people who really did this, and you'll be safe, Johnny."

He looked at me, studying my face, as if trying to determine if I was the kind of person he could trust. Slowly, he shook his head. "I already told you the truth."

20

Patterson led me to a little room that was no bigger than a closet and sat down in front of a large computer monitor. He opened a program and surveyed a long list of files. He shook his head and pulled out his two-way. "Martha?" he said.

"Yes, sir?"

"What was the approximate time of Mr. Waters's visitor?"

"About ten or so. Maybe ten thirty."

"Over."

He selected a file, and a view of the front doors of the sheriff's department came up. He pressed a key, and the footage sped up. He stopped it a second later and reversed, going slowly this time. A man moved backward toward the main entrance. Patterson stopped the video and played it forward at normal speed.

The man walked toward the desk, his head down, but I didn't need to see his face to know who it was.

The feathered hair, the faux-Southern gangster style. It was Walsh's thug, the man who'd accompanied him to the library a few days ago.

* * *

I argued with Patterson until my voice was nearly gone. He just kept shaking his head and telling me it was out of his control. "I'd be a fool to ignore this confession."

"How do you explain Preston Argent's visit?"

"I'm going to get to the bottom of this," he said and picked his two-way off the desk. He clicked the button again.

"Martha, can you run a search on a Preston Argent?"

"Yes, sir."

"Print me anything relevant, and bring it to the closet, okay?"

"Give me a minute."

He put the two-way down. "Happy?"

"Maybe. Depends on what she finds."

While we waited, I tried to explain Jeb Walsh to him. That was part of the problem. Patterson didn't understand why I considered Jeb so vile. All he seemed to know about him was that he was an author and good friends with the mayor.

When I finished telling him about his book and the hateful rhetoric inside, he sighed. "I get your concerns. I really do. And because of that, I'm going to keep an open mind about this. But, I have to tell you"—he looked at his watch—"I feel like we've wasted nearly an hour talking about the part we already have the answers to when we could be out there looking for her."

I understood his point. In his view, she was missing, alone, maybe injured. In my view, someone had her. And until I figured out who, nothing else mattered.

Martha came in with a file a few minutes later. She handed it to Patterson, smiled at me, and walked out.

Patterson looked it over and nodded. "You ain't going to like this."

"What?"

"He's a lawyer, all right. Or at least was in Alabama. He's fairly clean too. There's something in here about assault and battery, but he was a minor, and the charges were ultimately dropped. Since then, not even a speeding ticket." He closed the file. "I think we just need to keep looking for her."

I wished he was right, but every instinct I had told me he wasn't.

21

I drove out to the cornfield that afternoon. I parked my truck in the same place I'd parked it the night I'd lost Mary. Then I walked over to where I'd last seen her.

She'd had to pee and had walked into the corn. I did that now, immediately feeling a sense of dislocation as I entered the high stalks. From here, there was no telling where she'd gone or how she'd gotten turned around.

I looked up at the perfectly blue afternoon sky. It was the kind of day that I'd taken for granted before Mary went missing, the kind of day that used to mean something to me. The kind of day that made me think maybe, just maybe, everything was going to be all right in this godforsaken world. That feeling was gone now, replaced by a longing so deep I felt hollowed out inside. I tried to breath in the fresh air, the smell of the corn and the red clay, but there was nothing sustaining in it. I remained an empty vessel.

I closed my eyes and tried to remember something good.

It wasn't too difficult. In my front yard, near the ridge, Mary and I had once shared a bottle of wine and danced to the music of the wind chimes she'd hung around the house, both of us deliriously drunk. Later, we'd made love against and on top of Granny's ancient cast iron table, oblivious to the way the iron latticework gripped and twisted our bare skin. We ended up in a heap on the grass and fell asleep. Sometime later I awoke in the cooling dark of that summer night and looked over at her sleeping, her face content and bathed in the light of a rising half moon. Crickets and cicadas and other summer sounds throbbed in the night. It was a moment of profound contentment that I had not experienced before, and I realized that in many ways, I had held on to that moment, carrying it with me. But now, even that was gone, like a lost coin that had fallen out of my pocket somewhere along the way.

I hadn't realized just how much I'd needed her. Now I did. It was like hunger, like slow starvation, but worse.

I sat down and buried my face in my hands. I didn't look up again for a long time.

* * *

When I did get moving, dusk was fast approaching, and a partial moon loomed high above the fields, surrounded by stars as far as the eye could see.

I walked through the corn for a long time, moving in the direction I imagined Johnny and Mary would have taken. It was ridiculously easy to become disoriented and confused, but I kept at it, plunging through the places where the stalks grew so closely together that they formed wall-like barriers. At some point, I heard a train coming from up ahead on my right, and that helped me get my bearings. A half hour after that, I emerged from the corn and into the woods. They looked vaguely familiar, and I thought I must be getting close to the spot where we'd found Johnny. I kept walking until I reached the train tracks. I stepped onto the tracks and turned left.

I walked long enough to see the Blackclaw River and the lights glittering on the other side. It looked like a small community over there, possibly a trailer park. I picked up my pace, deciding suddenly to cross the river and see if I could find anyone in the community who might know something.

I'd gone no more than a few hundred yards when I realized I was living my dream. The black water of the dream was the Blackclaw River. The train trestle was right in front of me now. I slowed as I neared it.

Something was on the trestle. I stopped, squinting into the dusk. A girl sat halfway across the long trestle, her legs dangling lazily off the side.

She turned and saw me. I stepped forward, holding up a hand in greeting. She lifted her hand in return, and I took that as implicit permission to continue out onto the trestle.

By the time I reached the halfway point, where she sat, I had no doubt that this was the setting of my dream. I moved carefully, aware that a misstep could result in a fall that would make the dream come true.

"Hello," I called.

The girl said nothing, watching me draw near. The moon above the river washed everything in a pale gold, and I wondered briefly if this wasn't just a different version of the same dream, and all of this would be only half-remembered later in my waking hours.

But then the girl spoke, and something about her voice seemed more solid than a dream, and I knew then that I was awake. There was still a sense that I'd moved across a threshold, that I'd found a place where the regular rules of the road—and the world—might not apply.

"You a cop?" she said.

"No, were you expecting a cop?" I asked, stopping a few feet from where she sat, trying to steady myself against a sudden rush of vertigo. "Mind if I sit?"

She looked at me closely. "Free country. But don't get too close." She held up her hand, and I saw darkly lacquered long nails. "I scratch."

I nodded and sat down, leaving a good three feet between us. "This okay?"

She looked at the gap between us. "I guess."

She was about fifteen or sixteen, wearing torn blue jeans and a tank top. Her hair was short and curly. The most distinctive thing about her though were her earrings. She had a hoop hanging from each ear that looked big enough to shove a small bowling ball through. Her expression was guarded.

"You're not a cop?"

"No." I held up my hands. "I swear."

"You must be a drug dealer or something then."

I shook my head. "Why do I have to be either a cop or a drug dealer?"

"Because I've lived in this trailer park my entire life, and the only white men I've ever seen here are cops or drug dealers. One man was both."

I nodded. "Well, I'm neither. So take a good look. I'm here because I'm looking for somebody."

"Okay. If he ain't black, he ain't here. So . . ."

"It's she. And she's black."

"Well, I still think you might be confused. There's only eleven women in the trailer park, and I'm pretty sure none of them are interested in being found by you."

"The person I'm looking for is named Mary Hawkins. She disappeared on the other side of the tracks a couple of days ago. Have the police not been out to talk to anyone over here?"

"I saw some the other day, but they didn't talk to me. I'm just a kid. Most of them deputies don't even look at me, or they look at me the wrong way. You understand what I'm saying?"

"I think so. Well, I'd like to ask you some questions, if it's okay?"

She shrugged. "I guess, but make it quick. I've only got an hour and a half before the next train comes."

"It's good that you know when it's coming because this doesn't seem like a safe place to sit."

She grinned, but there was no joy in it, only a rueful kind of exasperation. "You think there's any safe places in the world to sit? Maybe for men like you, but not for me. So, I stopped worrying about safe. I only think about the places that matter to me—safe or not safe, it ain't even about that."

I nodded. "I can appreciate that. What is it about this place, this bridge, that you like?"

"You blind or dumb?" she said.

"I . . . uh . . ."

" 'Cause you'd have to be to ask a question like that. Look around you. There ain't no other place in the world better than this right here. Especially when the moon is out like tonight. God, I can feel the moon pulling my insides up against my skin. I figure it's how it must feel to be a werewolf. Sometimes I wish I was one of those. Think about that. When that moon is up, you get to slip out of this world and go into another one, go wild, and when the moon goes down and you come back to yourself, you can't remember none of it, but you feel . . . I don't know . . . you feel relieved, like the demons are gone."

It was a strange analogy from a strange girl, but I had to admit it made perfect sense to me. When she put it like that, I wished I could be a werewolf too. But wishes were easy things. Reality was always more difficult.

"Best part is when the next train comes along, I can feel the tracks beginning to vibrate." She shrugged. "I like thinking about the train, where it is, what it's passing by."

"Okay," I said. "Sounds nice."

"Most people think it's stupid."

I shook my head. "It's definitely not stupid. Everybody else who lives out here and *doesn't* come out here to sit is stupid."

She smirked. "Don't do that."

"What?"

"That thing. Patronize me."

I shook my head. "I'm not. I promise."

She looked me over closely. "What's a white man looking for a black woman for?"

"She's my girlfriend."

"Now I know you're full of shit."

I smiled and held out my hand. "That is probably true. Earl Marcus. And Mary really is my girlfriend."

She took my hand and said, "I'm not really supposed to talk to strangers, but as you may have noticed, I don't put a lot of stock in *supposed-tos*. My name's Deja." She pumped my hand once and let go. "Just make sure you keep your distance, Earl."

I tipped my hat to her. "I promise."

"Well," she said, "ask me something."

"Okay," I said. "Have you really not heard about the missing police officer?"

"I heard about it."

"Well, that's Mary."

"I figured that."

"Do you know anything about it?"

"I heard Old Nathaniel got her."

"Old Nathaniel? You know the story?"

"Everybody in the trailer park knows the story. My brother even saw him back in the summer."

"Your brother?"

"Gone."

"What do you mean, 'gone'?"

"I mean he's been missing since July."

"Wait a minute. Start over. Where did your brother see Nathaniel?"

"In the cornfield. He used to sit with me on the tracks sometimes at night. One night we were sitting out here, and over there in the cornfield"—she pointed across the river where I could just make out the darks stalks bending in the breeze at the edge of the cornfield—"we saw lights."

"Lights?"

"Yeah. Brighter than flashlights. Two or three of them. Wayne—that's my brother—wanted to go look, and he tried to get me to come with him. I told him to forget it. Was he crazy? Mama had raised both of us to stay on this side of the bridge, but Wayne didn't care'. He said he was fourteen and not scared of some old story. He wanted to see.

"So he went on over on his own. I sat right here and watched him disappear into the corn. He was gone maybe ten minutes or so, just long enough for me to get worried about him. I started across to look for him, when he came tearing out of the woods, running like his pants were on fire. He got to the bridge and shouted at me to go home, so I ran too. It wasn't until we were both back home that he told me he'd seen Old Nathaniel."

"Can you tell me exactly what he saw, how he described Old Nathaniel to you?"

"Well," Deja said, "he didn't really describe him to me. But he didn't have to. Everybody around here knows what Old Nathaniel looks like. He's tall and wears like a sack with eyeholes over his face. And below that it's like a gray Confederate soldier's uniform."

"Okay," I said. "Did he ever say what the lights were about?"

She shook her head. "No. He said he couldn't find them and he was walking along in the corn, getting confused, when he heard a sound behind him. He turned to look, and there was nothing there. That was when he realized that it might be him, 'cause you know, he's the Hide-Behind Man, right? A few minutes later, he heard it again, but this time he ran, and when he started running, he heard someone chasing him. He looked back and saw it was Old Nathaniel. He thought he was going to die then because that's what the story tells you. Once you see him, it's too late, but Wayne has always been fast, and I guess he was too fast for Old Nathaniel."

I shook my head. "Do you really believe he saw Old Nathaniel? I mean seriously? It's not something that sounds realistic."

"I know. But . . . I've never seen him so afraid. He didn't want to leave the trailer for days. Then Mama sent him to the gas station to get some milk and . . ." She shook her head.

"He never came back?"

"Never."

"Do you have to go through the cornfield to get to the gas station?"

She shrugged. "It's shorter to go that way, but I don't think it matters. I heard they'll catch you on the road and take you to Old Nathaniel."

"Who'll catch you on the road?"

"Some white men."

"Where did you hear that?"

"There's stories all over the trailer park."

"Did you call the sheriff? When your brother didn't come home?"

"Of course. Mama called and called. He came out several times, and they looked all over. But in the end, he said Wayne was at that age where he would be "feeling his oats," whatever that means, and we had to consider that he just took off. We told him that wasn't like Wayne, and we told him about Old Nathaniel, but the sheriff didn't want to hear that."

I just shook my head. I had no words for the anger I felt upon hearing Deja's story and realizing that this was the second person to go missing in the last several months.

The second *black* person.

And they both had ties to Old Nathaniel.

And what were the lights about? Brighter than flashlights? Deja was looking at me closely.

"Sorry. Just thinking."

"About how my brother went missing and your girlfriend went missing around the same area?"

"Something like that."

"Were you also thinking that maybe Old Nathaniel had something to do with her disappearance too?"

"I don't really believe in Old Nathaniel, but yeah, I think someone out there is using Old Nathaniel as a way to do some very bad things."

"I didn't really believe it either. But then Wayne told me what he saw, and I know Wayne. He wasn't lying."

I watched her carefully in the light of the moon. The river below us hummed, a steady rush of time sliding by. Somewhere below it all there was the insistent tick of a clock inside my own skin that was marking time against the moment when I'd either find Mary or admit to myself that I wasn't going to.

"Look," she said, pointing across the train trestle, toward the dark edge of the cornfield. Her voice was a whisper. A gasp.

I looked but didn't see anything. "What am I looking at?"

"Right by the edge of the field. It's him."

I scanned the edge of the cornfield slowly, looking for a disturbance in the solid wall. I was almost to the place where the stalks ended and were replaced by trees, when something caught my eye. It was just an irregularity, a misshapen stalk. Or it was a scarecrow, leaning with hook-limbed dexterity on its stake. Or it was a man, wearing a bag over his head, standing out against the corn because he was unmoved by the wind while all the stalks bent and swayed and whispered a song in the tongues of reapers.

And then the figure—be it man or scarecrow or misshapen stalk—dissolved, melting back into the endless and haphazard rows.

"Did you see?" she asked, her voice like a slow breeze.

"Yeah," I said. "I did."

* * *

When I made it back to my truck, it was nearly eight o'clock. For the first time since Mary had been missing, I found myself worried about someone else. Maybe it was the time spent with Deja, or the story about her brother, but whatever the reason, I found my thoughts returning to Wanda's kids, Virginia and Briscoe, and what Ronnie had said about Lane Jefferson threatening Virginia.

I climbed into the truck and glanced up at the water tower. No signs of life, just a dark relic of the past, one more object for the wind and the weather to wear down and turn to ruin.

I put the truck in gear and drove well over the speed limit up to Ronnie's place.

I found Ronnie smoking a joint and watching porn on his laptop. His place, which had once housed a still and the men who used it to make moonshine, was no larger than a shotgun shack. It had two rooms. One of them was the den, where Ronnie was seated on the couch, the computer in his lap, and the other served as a kitchen, with a small table and a large cooler. He had a generator in the middle of the floor, but it was off at the moment. There was an outhouse about twenty yards from the shack, though from what I could tell, Ronnie preferred to do his business in the great outdoors.

"You got to see this, Earl. This girl is truly gifted," he said, without looking up from the computer.

"Cut that shit off. I'm here because we need to talk."

"I can talk and watch."

I walked over and slammed the lid of the laptop. "You fucking owe me," I said.

It wasn't planned. In fact, it was the opposite of my plan, which had been to come over and try to appeal to the part of Ronnie that had always wanted to be my friend.

Shit. Now, I'd have to improvise.

"I owe you? That's interesting. Seems to me, when the chips were down not too long ago, you needed Old Ronnie to help you take care of some shit and keep his damned mouth closed about it, which I'd like to point out, Old Ronnie has done."

"Like that's been hard. Considering your priors, you'd go to prison for the rest of your life if you spilled the beans, so don't act like you're doing something noble."

He held out his hands. "Fine, it's not noble, but you know what was?"

I waited, hoping he would say something that would piss me off enough to hit him.

"Getting you and Mary to the cornfield to save my niece."

"That was just stupid. There were so many ways around that."

"Yeah, like going to the police? How would that have worked? Or going to you? Do you think that you would be able to save my niece?"

"I think I could."

"Of course you could. How could I forget the all mighty savior, Christ our Lord, Earl Marcus?"

"Fuck off. If you're really concerned about those kids, you'll go with me right now to find them."

"Find them? Why?"

"You said Lane threatened Virginia. I just talked to a girl—a girl whose brother disappeared back in the summer. I think Lane Jefferson had something to do with it. The point is, he's not above hurting kids."

"Well, shit, that's what I've been trying to tell you. He's a piece of garbage, makes regular criminals look like decent human beings."

"We can't let him hurt one of those kids."

"How are you going to stop it?"

I sat down beside him on the couch. I put my face in my hands. All I wanted was Mary. But it seemed like there was always one more thing to keep me from her.

"Let's ride out to wherever your sister is staying and check on the family. On the way, you can tell me who can help me find some dirt on Lane Jefferson. You do know where's she's staying, right?"

"I got some ideas."

* * *

On the way, he told me again about the man with the Old Nathaniel tattoo, the one who'd worked security at the warehouse on Summer Mountain.

"Name's Timmy Lambert. His daddy was in the KKK and raised Timmy to hate everybody that wasn't white. Timmy was good at that. The thing was, Timmy wound up hating most whites too. Timmy was just a hateful kind of guy."

"You say *was*."

"Well, Timmy's back in prison. This time he ain't coming out. He sicced his pit bull on his girlfriend and her little boy. Waited until they were in the bedroom and let the dog in the room with them. That pit hated that little boy. Mama died trying to keep the dog off him."

"Jesus."

"That's right. Jesus is the only one that can forgive Timmy Lambert."

"And he has the tattoo?"

"Sure does. And he worked for Lane. To be honest, he was probably a lot closer to him than I was. Doesn't mean he knows anything, but it would be worth a drive up."

"Hays?"

"Yep. Hey, ain't that where your brother and my grandfather are?"

"Yeah," I said. "You know that."

He grinned. "I suppose we'll have to pay them a visit if we go."

"Yeah," I said, though I already felt myself dreading it.

22

My heart broke when I saw where Wanda was staying with the kids. The house was little more than a shell, burned out and overgrown with kudzu vines. When we pulled up, Virginia was standing on a bucket, trying to pull the vines away from the windows. The boy, Briscoe, was sitting in a bare patch of dirt, sucking his thumb and pushing his dump truck around. All of this despite it being after nine o'clock at night. By any decent standard, both those kids should have been getting ready for bed and school the next day.

Briscoe grinned when he saw Ronnie and me get out of the truck. Virginia glanced at us and kept working.

"Where's your mama?" Rufus said.

"Gone," Virginia said.

"Gone where?"

Virginia shrugged and pulled some more kudzu off the low-hanging roof.

"Why didn't she take the car?" Ronnie asked.

"It's out of gas."

"How long has she been gone?" I winced, fearing the answer.

"Since sometime last night."

"Jesus Christ, what is wrong with that woman?" Ronnie said. He balled up his fist and punched the front door of the house. I grabbed his arm.

"Take it easy," I said. "These kids don't need to see you freaking out." Oddly enough, seeing Ronnie freak out had calmed me down some. I would listen to my own advice. Getting angry about their idiot mother might feel good, but it didn't do a lot to help them.

"We've got to call the sheriff and get these kids some help," I said.

"No," Ronnie said. "I promised Wanda I wouldn't do that. I'll take them to my place."

"Hell no," I said. I honestly thought they'd be better off alone than with Ronnie. "We call the sheriff. He'll get them some help."

"I won't let you do it. I owe it to Wanda."

"You *owe* it to her? The woman who left her kids to go look for . . ." I started to say *drugs*, because really, was there anything else she would have left for, but noticed that both kids were watching me closely.

"You can say it," Virginia said. "I know about the drugs, and Briscoe's too young to understand."

I swallowed. Briscoe's mouth hung open, and he stared at me expectantly, and I wondered if maybe Briscoe understood more than they knew.

"I just don't get it," I said. "Why do you owe her?"

Ronnie had wandered off to the other side of the house. When he turned around, I saw he was upset. "Wanda stood by me when I was on the needle bad," he said. "I thought I was going to die, and I would have too if she hadn't reported me for the B and E. They put me in lock-up and I was forced to get off the stuff. Saved my life. Now, she's got the same problem. I want to help her. So she can have her kids back. I know it don't seem like it, but she loves them kids."

I sighed. Normally, this would have been where I would have called Mary. She would have known just what to do, would have given me the soundest advice. Now I was alone to figure it out myself.

"For now, let's get them out of here and find them something to eat."

"McDonald's," Briscoe said. "McDonald's."

"He don't know too many words," Ronnie said, "but he sure as shit knows him some Mickey D's."

"Mickey D's!" Briscoe shouted, standing up and lifting his arms to the sky.

I walked over, smiling despite everything, and picked him up.

"I don't have a car seat or anything," I said.

Ronnie gave me a look like he thought I was making a joke. "Briscoe ain't never sat in one, so he won't know the difference."

Virginia looked at my truck warily. Something told me she'd come by that caution honestly. "Where are we going?"

"It's going to be fine, Virginia. Uncle Ronnie is going to take care of you."

She gave him an odd look, one that seemed to suggest she wasn't quite sure Ronnie could take care of himself, much less two kids. I had to agree with her on that one, though the more I hung around Ronnie, the more I was starting to believe he *did* care about them, and the whole holding up his sister thing had been more about trying to get some of Lane Jefferson's money than anything else.

"Is there something you want to get from inside first?" I said.

She shook her head. "Briscoe's gonna want his truck."

I nodded and walked over to pick it up, shaking the dirt off it.

"I did have some books," Virginia said, her voice not much more than a whisper, "but Mama loaded them all up in the car and took them to the thrift store. She got seven dollars for all of them."

"Your mama's doing the best she can, Virginia," Ronnie said.

I shook my head. No, she wasn't. Not even close, but I kept my mouth shut and made a mental promise that if I did nothing else, I'd get the girl some books.

We all crammed inside the truck, Ronnie in back with Briscoe, and Virginia up front with me. Ronnie, who'd been in tears just moments before, looked as happy as I'd ever seen him as we pulled away from the shack and drove to McDonald's.

23

After some hamburgers, we drove back up Ghost Creek Mountain toward Ronnie's. I wasn't sure if he believed I was going to let the kids stay with him or not. The truth was, I was planning on asking Rufus if the kids and me could crash with him for a night.

When I pulled up to the church, Ronnie grunted. "You don't think I can take care of these kids?"

"You don't have enough room even if you wanted to. Besides, they'll just be next door. Now, I know you and Rufus have had your differences, but you know he's a good man."

"I don't know shit about him being a good man. Only thing I know is that he creeps me out. Fucker moves like a panther and doesn't need eyes to judge me. What's that about? You'd think living next to a blind man would be the best thing for a man who's been judged on sight for his whole life, but no. This is the one blind man who can just *sense* that I'm a loser. Hell no, I don't want them staying with him."

"I want to stay in the church," Virginia said. "It's . . ." She shook her head, staring at it in the oncoming dusk. "Creepy."

"You got that right," Ronnie said.

He put his hands in his face for a minute. "Fine," he said. "They can stay with the blind bastard."

With that, he opened the backdoor of my truck and slid out. He walked quickly toward the creek, hands stuffed in his pockets. He crossed it and broke into a jog, heading for his house. Just before going in, he turned, and said, "What about tomorrow?"

"We'll go early," I said. "I think I've got a place they can stay tomorrow."

He nodded and went inside.

I turned back to my truck. Virginia was standing near it, holding Briscoe. "Let's meet Rufus," I said.

* * *

I never had any doubt that Rufus would let the kids stay. Rufus loved kids. Which was odd because he scared the shit out of them, at least at first.

Virginia warmed up to him when he made her a cup of hot chocolate over propane heat and told her stories about the wolves he heard sometimes when the moon was full. In reality, they were coyotes, but Rufus knew how to work an audience.

Briscoe fell asleep on one of the padded pews Rufus had kept, and seeing him sleeping peacefully in the place that had caused me so much pain over the years made me feel good, at least briefly. Then I remembered that Mary was still gone, and I was no closer to finding her than I'd been the moment we found Johnny lying on the ground by the stream. Hell, if anything, I was farther away after his bogus confession.

I checked my phone, hoping against hope there was a message from Mary, or at least something good from Patterson, but no one had called or texted me. I tried Mary's phone for the hundredth time and waited while it went straight to voicemail. I hung up before I heard her voice. It was too painful. Too soon.

I called Susan Monroe next. She answered on the second ring.

"Earl Marcus?"

"Hey, Susan."

"I'm so sorry."

"Don't be," I said, but my voice was breaking as I spoke the words. "She's going to be okay."

"Yeah, this is your thing, right? Finding people?"

"Yeah, but even if I don't find her, she'll be okay. Mary's tough."

"Is there anything I can do?" she said, and she sounded sincere. I'd always liked Susan because she was a genuinely nice person. Some people could fake it well—like Ronnie's grandfather, Billy. He'd been my father's right-hand man and best friend for most of his life, and he'd fooled me for a long time with the bright, optimistic persona he projected, but in the end I'd realized it had been nothing but a projection all along. Susan wasn't like that. Susan truly wanted to help, and though it was a small thing, at that moment, it felt like a big one.

"Would you be willing to let a couple of kids stay with you?"

"Kids?"

I explained the situation the best way I knew how. When I finished, I said, "I'm just not going to be able to watch them, and, well, Rufus could, but people think he's creepy, and it might come across weird if he did."

"Say no more. I'll definitely do it. The only issue is that I have to work tomorrow."

"The girl loves to read," I said. "And she's responsible. Would it be okay if they sort of hung out with you?" I felt like I was pushing it now, but what could I do? These kids needed somebody.

"That's a great idea," she said. "We can let the little one play in the children's room, and the older one can keep an eye on him while she reads. I'm delighted she's a reader."

"Yeah, I think somehow she overcame her family genetics."

"We all have to do that in one way or the other."

"Yeah," I said, wondering if she understood just how close to home those words hit. "I think that's true. Listen, I've got an early morning tomorrow."

"Don't worry about it. Tell Rufus I'll come by and get them on the way to work."

"Thanks so much, Susan."

"It's not a problem, Earl. I know what you're going through right now. When I lost Ed, I was devastated. Lost."

I didn't respond. Mostly because I had no idea how to.

"I'm sorry, that was terrible. I didn't mean to compare the two.

Mary's not dead. It was stupid, Earl. I was just trying to let you know . . . well, if you ever need to talk, I'm here."

"No, it was fine, Susan. And I really do appreciate it."

When I hung up, I turned and saw that Rufus had fallen asleep too on his own pew. He was snoring softly, his face drawn and worried in the flickering candlelight. Virginia sat beside him, her legs crossed, her face far too serious for a twelve-year-old. She was looking right at me.

"What?" I said.

"I know what happened to her."

My mind didn't process her words. Maybe I was too afraid to.

"What?"

"I know what happened to her."

"To Mary?"

She nodded solemnly.

"Go on."

"Old Nathaniel. He has her."

"How do you know that?"

"I've seen him."

"When?"

"At night, from my old bedroom window at Mr. Lane's place."

"Who is he?"

She looked confused. "He's Old Nathaniel."

"But Old Nathaniel isn't real. It had to be someone dressed up like him. Was it Lane?"

"Lane's too short."

"What?"

"Old Nathaniel is tall and strong. And fast."

"Did you see him often?"

She shook her head. "Mostly during the full moon. It makes the cornfield look like an ocean of gold. It lights up everything." She shrugged. "Maybe he's there every night and I just can't see him. But in the moonlight, you can see a lot, even the paths in the cornfield."

I tried to think when the next full moon was, but the truth was, I had no idea.

"So, what do you think Old Nathaniel wants with her?"

"He hates black people. He wants her to suffer. That's what I heard from my friend."

"What friend?"

"Addie. She lives in the trailer park across the river. Sometimes, I cross the river and play with her. She never comes to my side. She knows better."

"Smart kid."

"Sometimes I would sneak Lane's phone to my room if he left it lying around, and I'd text Addie when I saw the lights."

"The lights?"

"Yeah, the times I saw Old Nathaniel, I also saw lights in the cornfield. Bright lights. I asked Lane about it, and he made me start sleeping on the couch. It didn't matter—I'd still sneak up there at night and watch."

"How often did you see the lights?"

"Not a lot. Just sometimes. But whenever I did, I always looked for Old Nathaniel. Sometimes he was there and sometimes he wasn't."

"What about Lane? Did he ever leave the house at night and go into the cornfield?"

"I don't know. Maybe. He always said he was going to his friend's house, Mr. Tag." She made a face.

"What? You didn't like Mr. Tag?"

"He was creepy, but not in a good way like your friend. Creepy in a bad way. A really bad way."

Mr. Tag. I'd heard *that* name somewhere before too. Then it hit me. Tag was the name of the man Lane had been visiting on Summer Mountain.

"Is there anything else you can tell me about Old Nathaniel?"

She shook her head. "He's real. That's the truth."

"Do you know what pot is? Marijuana?"

She laughed. "Are you kidding? Of course I know what it is."

"I'm sorry. I'm not used to kids. I don't know how much to . . . expect . . ." I trailed off. "Sorry."

"It's okay. But yeah, I've known about pot since I can remember. I know about all the drugs. Coke, meth, LSD, OxyContin." She shrugged. "Ronnie said never to do drugs because he almost died. I wouldn't have tried them anyway because . . . well, look at Mama."

My heart broke again. I wanted to hug her, to wrap her up in the kind of hug that would let her know somebody cared about her, but I stayed put. I wasn't sure how she would take it. What kind of hugs she might have already experienced from men who had different motivations.

Instead, I pressed ahead. "Do you know if Lane grows pot?"

"That's what everybody says."

"But you haven't seen it?"

"No." She lay down on her pew.

"Sleepy?"

"Yeah."

"Me too."

I yawned, realizing just how sleepy I really was. I needed sleep. I was going on forty hours without it. I was already starting to feel the cracks in my thinking, my reasoning. I leaned back on my pew and closed my eyes.

"We'll talk more in the morning," I said.

"Okay," she said.

I was asleep when I heard her voice again. I don't know how much time had passed—maybe just a minute or two or maybe several hours. Her voice came from a great distance, as if she were calling from the bottom of a deep well, and there was a strong possibility I dreamed the entire thing: she said something about mirrors, something I didn't remember the next morning, but somehow the seed slipped inside my mind because my dreams that night were of great mirrors in the sky, reflecting my falling body as I tumbled into the black water of a river that was beginning to feel more and more like my destiny.

24

The next morning, a snarling prison guard led Ronnie and me to a large concrete room with several tables and chairs. It was empty except for what appeared to be some parents making a heartfelt visit to their distraught son. The guard looked at his clipboard as we entered the room. "Jesus, you guys sure do have a lot of friends in prison. Who the hell do you want to see first?"

"Lester," I said. The guard's eyes widened, and his snarl dissipated a little. "Hey, I read about you. You put your brother here, didn't you?"

"No," I said. "Lester was a victim."

The guard laughed. "Right. Sit wherever you want. He'll be out in a minute."

Hoping to avoid the drama playing out in the rear of the large room, we sat as far from the other family as possible. Still, I couldn't help sneaking glances. The kid couldn't have been more than twenty-five, and seeing him with his parents, in tears like that, made him look even younger. The mother reached across the table and put her arms around his neck, pulling his head toward her shoulder. He began to sob.

Ronnie chuckled. "Fucking pathetic."

"Shut up," I said. "Have some decency."

"Now you're a family man, huh? You're a real piece of work, Earl. Must be nice to go with whichever way the wind blows."

"What's that supposed to mean?"

"It means here you are feeling all misty-eyed over family shit.

Your family never did nothing for you or Lester. And the thing is, you know it."

I was about to point out that he'd done some things for his family over the past few days, but before I could, the door in the back of the room swung open, and Lester appeared. My breath stopped, and I looked away, not wanting to meet his gaze. Not like this.

Lester looked broken. Not just on the outside either. Sure, his shoulders were slumped, and he'd gone totally bald, and there were new dark spots on his face that looked serious enough to see a doctor about, but there was a deeper brokenness there too. The kind that was unmistakable. The kind that resided in the eyes and was always searching for something to latch on to, the kind that was always seeking help without the hope it would ever come.

I forced my eyes back up to meet his. I was surprised when I didn't see any anger there. That too seemed to have been broken. I stood up and reached out for him. He embraced me limply. I didn't want to let go. My brother was a ghost, and I couldn't help but feel responsible for his death.

He nodded at Ronnie, and I noted that he didn't seem surprised to see him with me.

"Hey," I said. "How are you making it?"

He sat down across from us and clasped his hands beneath his chin in a prayerful gesture. "I'm alive."

I swallowed hard. "Lester, I'm sorry it's taken me so—"

He waved me off. "Don't. Please. Let's just be brothers for a few seconds," he said. "With none of the damage."

"Okay."

Ronnie cleared his throat. "You had any trouble in here?"

He shook his head. "Nah."

"Good for you. I had a friend who was sent up on a five-year stint. When he came out, he told me the first week was brutal. Said every swinging dick in the place got a piece of him. They turned him out. Was fucking terrible."

"Ronnie," I said. "Jesus. Take it easy."

"It's okay, Earl. I've seen that happen to others. But I was lucky."

I was curious now. "How so?"

He looked at me with something like pride, and I saw that he wasn't completely finished yet. There was a still a small spark left inside of him, even if it was from the wrong kind of fire. "Daddy."

"Daddy?"

He nodded. "He's a legend, Earl. I never realized how much so, but when me and Billy got here, word was already going around that my daddy had risen again. That me and Billy still talked to him, and that if you knew what was what, you'd leave us alone." He shrugged. "And they pretty much did."

He leaned in, searching my face. "Did you ever find him, Earl?"

Ronnie shifted in his seat and cleared his throat. I thought he was going to let it all out of the bag, but Lester wasn't paying any attention to Ronnie anymore. His eyes were on me, and me alone.

I considered telling Lester about my final encounter with Daddy. Hell, if anybody deserved to know, it was him, but the time didn't feel right. He was obviously still haunted by the man. I realized now that what I had misread as prison "breaking" him had, in fact, been the same thing that had always dogged him—our father. Somehow, he was still obsessed with the man, and I didn't think telling him I'd killed him and buried his body in the mountains was a wise idea just now.

"No," I said. "I didn't find him. He never overcame death, Lester. He was just a man."

Miraculously, this seemed to cheer him up a little. He reached out for me and hugged me again. "Thanks, Earl."

"You're welcome," I said, even though I wasn't completely sure what I'd done other than lie to him. But maybe his thankfulness was a sign. I'd done the right thing.

When Lester pulled away, he looked over at Ronnie. "Would you mind giving us a minute?"

Ronnie raised his eyebrows and tried to appear offended, but Lester didn't notice, and I was used to his histrionics and said nothing. He sighed, seeing neither of us was going to take the bait, and stood up. "I'll just see if they sell smokes around here."

Lester and I watched him walk over to the guard window and ask to be let out. When the door closed behind him, Lester turned and looked me over.

"What?" I said.

"I'm just trying to understand it," he said.

"Understand what?"

Lester shook his head. "You always did like to push the boundaries."

"What in the hell are you talking about, Lester?"

He glanced back at the door before turning to me. "Ronnie Thrash. He's a loser, Earl. Why would you bring him here?"

Now it was my turn to sigh. I should have known it would be about Ronnie. Seemed like everybody I cared about was telling me to stay the hell away from him. I might have listened to them too, but I didn't have that luxury anymore. And as much as I hated to admit it, the Ronnie thing had gone beyond just needing him to keep his mouth shut about what had happened between me and my father. I really did need him now. He was my ticket to a world I couldn't access otherwise. Not to mention, now that I'd helped his niece and nephew, we'd become even more inextricably bound.

"Look, Ronnie's not perfect, Lester, but none of us are."

"He's a thug, Earl. You know that. He has no plan for his life other than getting high and getting drunk."

I felt myself growing angry. I didn't want that. I'd spent my life trying to reconcile with my brother and then ended up indirectly being responsible for him going to prison. Add to that my failure to visit him for over a year. No, I simply couldn't live with myself if I lost my temper now.

I'd keep my damned mouth shut. Change the subject. "So," I said, "any news from your lawyer?"

"I'm serious, Earl. As your brother, I'm telling you, don't let this guy into your life. He's a loser."

"Damn it, Lester. Let it go."

"Are you using drugs, Earl?"

I slammed my fist on the table. "You're being awfully self-righteous for a man whose great plan in life was pastoring a church that did far more harm than good," I said.

"Earl," Lester said, reaching across the table and touching my hand softly, as if he wished to calm me, "you know I was oblivious to all that. I only wanted to do good. It's like I said when I testified, my sins are ones of omission. Sure, I was in charge, but those things that happened don't reflect who I am." He patted the back of my hand again, and I felt the desperation in his touch. He badly wanted me to agree, to forgive him and clear his conscience.

But I wasn't about to do any such thing. "That's your problem, Lester. You're oblivious to everything. You never could see the way Daddy was tearing you apart. And when I saw it and left, you doubled-down on the fundamentalism, didn't you? Hell, you can't ever figure out the right side to be on, can you?"

"Not everybody can be as smart as Earl Marcus. Have a little humility, Earl. You've made a hell of a lot of mistakes in your life too." He withdrew his hand from mine and curled his fingers into a fist.

My ears were hot, and my head felt like it might explode at any minute. I was past the point of thinking clearly, and that was why I said what I did.

"The only mistake I ever made was not taking Maggie out of the mountains sooner."

Maggie. The very mention of her name changed the air in the room. The family at the other table fell silent, sensing it too.

Lester sat back in his chair, twisting his face up into a scowl. "There he is, ladies and gentlemen! The real Earl Marcus in all of his asshole glory." He stood up. "Don't bother coming to see me again, okay?"

He waved at the guard, who came in and escorted him out.

And just like that, I'd undone any goodwill I'd built between the two of us during my brief visit.

25

"Who's Maggie?" Ronnie asked while we waited for Timmy Lambert to come out.

"What? You were listening?"

"Hell, that door ain't that thick. Was hard not to."

"That was a shitty thing to do," I said.

"Well, I just want to say I appreciate you defending me."

"I wasn't doing that."

"Well, that ain't what I heard."

I was tempted to keep arguing, but to what end? Letting it go seemed like the wisest choice.

"Oh, I remember," he said. "Maggie. She was that girl that killed herself and blamed it on you."

"That wasn't what happened."

He shrugged. "Nothing like a pretty girl to split two brothers apart. It seems like ya'll could move on by now, though."

"Don't ever listen in on my conversations again."

"Sure, Earl. Sorry about that. Oh, here he comes."

I looked up in time to see the door swing open. A mountain of a man stepped inside. He wore a long beard and longer hair that was streaked with gray. The sleeves of his jumpsuit were rolled up far enough to show off massive tattooed biceps. He looked like an older version of Hulk Hogan if he'd been arrested as a young man and spent most of his life in prison.

The contrast between Timmy Lambert and my brother could not

have been more stark. Everything about Lambert screamed confidence. Where Lester looked broken by prison, Lambert appeared to be bolstered by his environment, like a king finally returned to his kingdom.

He saw Ronnie and nodded. Ronnie stood up and the two men embraced, patting each other on the back. Lambert dwarfed Ronnie, causing the smaller man to look like a child hugging his daddy. The embrace ended.

"Hell," Lambert said. "This is a nice treat. Only been in a week and already got visitors."

"Got somebody who wants to ask you some questions," Ronnie said.

Lambert nodded at me suspiciously and then looked back at Ronnie. "You vouching for this guy? I smell po-po all over him."

Ronnie laughed. "This here is Earl Marcus, Timmy. You remember how me and my daddy used to talk about the kid that stood up to Brother RJ?"

Lambert's eyes moved from me back to Ronnie. His face showed no expression. He either didn't remember or didn't care, it appeared. Then all at once, he nodded. "Yeah. That's him?"

"The one and fucking only."

Lambert sat down across from me. "I'm Timmy," he said.

"Earl."

He didn't extend a hand, so I kept mine under the table and waited.

"I got nothing but love for Ronnie, and I heard about you when I was a kid. I used to like that story about how you stood up to your Daddy a lot, so that's why I'm going to give you the benefit of the doubt and talk to you, understand?"

Ordinarily, I would have told him to fuck off. I didn't deal well with people who made it clear they were doing me a favor to speak to me. But I couldn't afford to ruin this opportunity.

"Got it," I said.

He reached out a monster-sized hand, and I let it engulf mine.

"Now what's this about?"

I looked at Ronnie, who'd taken a seat beside Lambert. Ronnie held his hands out as if to say, *"It's your show."*

"Do you know a man named Lane Jefferson?"

Lambert leaned back in his chair, his eyes narrowing. I couldn't tell if he was angry or just surprised by the question.

"Yeah," he said. "I know him. What about him?"

I hesitated, trying to decide how to best phrase my next question. The problem was, I didn't know just how much Lambert might be willing to protect Lane. Were they close friends? Was there loyalty there? Or did Lambert even give a shit?

At the last minute, I decided to go in a different direction. "I was wondering if you know anything about any white supremacy groups in Coulee County."

"White supremacy? What makes you think I'd know about that?"

I looked at Ronnie. Ronnie nodded. "Yeah, um, I remembered you were sort of . . . you know, *racist.*"

For a minute I thought Lambert was going to break Ronnie in half, but just about the time I was going to call for the guard, Lambert let out a crazed laugh. "Scared you, didn't I?"

Ronnie breathed a sigh of relief. "Oh shit, don't do that, Timmy."

"Yeah, I used to be. I'm trying to take a broader view these days. You know after what happened with my dog and all." He shrugged as if it were all water under the bridge. "I'm trying to judge every man on how he treats me. If you're black and you treat me like shit, I'm going to call you out. If you're black and you treat me with respect, I'll do the same for you." He turned to look at me. "You trying to join up or something?"

I considered lying, but something told me he'd know, so I shook my head instead. "No. I just have some questions. Do you know a man named Jeb Walsh or Preston Argent, by any chance?"

Timmy stuck out his lower lip, considering. "Don't think so. Maybe they go by something else? Sometimes dudes have handles. I used to be called Pit, back when I gave a damn. Now, Timmy is good enough because I don't fucking care who knows how I live. You know what I'm saying?"

"I hear you," I said, even though I didn't really understand what he was talking about. "Let's go back to Lane Jefferson. Did you do any work for him?"

"Sure. So did Ronnie. And if you're wondering if Lane is a white—what did you call it? Supremacist?—I'd say yes, but not like most men I know. He's got all these theories and shit. Says he doesn't hate black people, just wants to see them returned to Africa."

"Anything else you can think of?"

"He belongs to this group. I can't remember what they're called, but it's a bunch of white dudes who meet and talk about blacks and Jews and how they're ruining the fucking world."

"Do you know anyone else in the group?"

"Yeah, maybe."

"Maybe?"

He shrugged. "I went to his house once up on Summer Mountain. I don't remember his name, but I got the feeling he and Lane were close. Lane liked me. Not enough to invite me into his inner circle or nothing, but I think that's where it was heading. This party, up on Summer Mountain, was something to see. Shit, there were women there that could make the Pope get hard. And these assholes are telling me to watch a movie. I think they were disappointed when I didn't give a damn about the movie."

I had so many questions, I didn't know exactly where to begin. I decided to start with the basics.

"What was the man's name? Who threw the party?"

"See, that's where it gets fuzzy. I remember he had a weird name. Like a kid's game or something. Hell, I ain't never been that good with names. Faces? Faces, I can do, but names just kind of go in and come right back out."

"Okay," I said. "What was the movie about?"

"So, this dude—the one who's name I can't remember—is apparently some movie director. It was his movie, and best I could tell it was about this old man who lived way out in the country. Early in the movie, he falls out in the field and breaks his leg. Has to drag himself back to the house and take care of it because his car won't start. Some dudes wearing black masks show up and try to break into his house. He starts killing them. I stopped watching after a while. Too much pussy there to worry with a stupid movie."

He rubbed his face, and I got a glimpse of a tattoo on the back of his upper arm, near his elbow. It was a deep yellow circle, outlined in black. In the middle of the circle were what appeared to be two axe handles. And in the middle of those was a skull.

He saw me looking and moved his arm closer for a better view. "That's from the warehouse," he said.

"What do you mean?"

"I mean, I saw it on the cars that would come in and out. It was a sticker. That was where I worked for Lane mostly. Up on Summer Mountain, guarding that fucking warehouse."

"Told you," Ronnie said.

"I thought it looked badass," Lambert said, ignoring Ronnie, "so I got my tattoo artist buddy to do it for me. Hell, he worked the warehouse too when he wasn't giving tattoos. Dude made bank on the tattoos."

"Mind if I take a photo?"

"Suit yourself. I don't give a fuck."

After taking a couple of shots, I asked him if he could give me directions to the warehouse.

"I don't think so."

"Why not?"

"There was something serious going on in there. I ain't stupid. I talk, but I don't blab."

"I don't understand."

"I don't give a fuck whether you understand or not. I ain't giving you directions. Next question."

I glanced at Ronnie. He raised his eyebrows slightly but otherwise kept his expression neutral, which told me a lot. Ronnie *never* kept his expression neutral. I decided it would be a good idea to move on.

"I heard you have another tattoo?" I said. "One of a local legend?"

"Oh, Old Nathaniel." He grinned. "Gotta take my shirt off to show you that one. Probably not a good idea. These guards already don't like me."

"It's fine. I'm curious, though, why you would choose an old legend like Old Nathaniel?"

"Legend? Shit, he ain't no legend."

"Excuse me?"

"I've seen him."

I glanced at Ronnie. He raised his eyebrows at me but said nothing. "You've seen him?"

"Yep. Earlier this summer, right about the time my girl and my pit bull got tangled up. I was working one night for Lane, and there was a full moon. I remember that because it already had me spooked. Full moons make the cornfield different." He looked at Ronnie. "You know what I mean, right?"

Ronnie nodded. I couldn't tell if he was just going along or if he really believed it.

"Anyway, I was up on the north end, near the train trestle and the river. And that cornfield—shit—it ain't got no rhyme or reason to it, but occasionally there's a path, almost like somebody was trying to make a way to get around in it but wanted to keep it a secret from everybody else. I was taking a piss, right by one of those long paths and, way down on the other end, I saw the bastard walk by."

"Wait, it was dark, and you saw him 'way down on the other end?' "

Lambert shot me a look of pure irritation. It wasn't hard to imagine that he'd make the leap quickly from irritation to violence.

"The fucking moon," he said. "I already told you it makes everything different."

"Okay," I said. "What did he look like?"

"Tall. Walked with big strides. Wore a mask. Shit, let me just show you." He lifted his orange top on one side, revealing a large, smooth gut and hairy nipples. Just above his left nipple was a detailed color tattoo of Old Nathaniel. He was depicted as standing in the middle of a row of cornstalks, holding a long, slightly curved knife. He wore gray clothes and a brown burlap sack with holes cut out for his eyes. His eyes were bright yellow and seemed to be alive with a supernatural power.

"That's some fucking detail," Ronnie said. "Who did it?"

"That's the thing. This is how I know I didn't imagine it. Had it done down at the crossing, over by Small Mountain. The only tattoo artist I ever met who didn't have a single tattoo. Like I said, I don't do good with names, but he knows me. Everybody knows Pit. But here's the thing. I came in and he says, 'What do you want?' and I says, 'You ever hear of Old Nathaniel?' He says he has. I tell him I saw the bastard, and I want it to look just like he *really* looks. At this point, I'm expecting him to laugh and ask me what I really want, but he just gets out a sheet of paper and sketches out pretty much exactly what you see here.

"Which means, he's seen him too. So, I didn't imagine it."

I looked at the tattoo closely. "Do you have any idea who it is?"

"Who what is?"

"The man wearing the costume?"

"What the fuck are you talking about? The man wearing the costume is Old Nathaniel."

"You really believe this is some phantom that's been stalking the cornfield since the 1800s?"

Lambert nodded. "Okay, I see how it sounds when you put it like that. I only know what I saw. And it looked pretty real to me."

I nodded. "Okay, can you think of anything else? Anything at all about Lane Jefferson or Old Nathaniel or even this man on Summer Mountain?"

"I told you everything I know. Like I said, Lane wanted to get me in the inner circle. I think they wanted, you know, like, some young blood in their group, but then I think his friend was disappointed I didn't dig the movie. Who knows, maybe I'd be there now if I hadn't gotten pissed at Julie and her kid."

I let that go. Being reminded of exactly what kind of a man I was talking to made me feel a little sick to my stomach. It was time to wrap this up.

"Thanks for meeting with us," I said.

Timmy Lambert shook his head. "Any time. I enjoy talking. Hell, prison ain't so bad. Lots of people say it is, but I do all right. Still, it's nice to have visitors. Ya'll come back, sometime, okay?"

He stood, and Ronnie hugged him again. Timmy turned to nod at me and then walked out of the room.

26

As much as I'd dreaded visiting with Lester, just thinking about the man who'd enter the room next made my skin crawl. Billy Thrash had been my father's closest advisor and best friend for years. After Lester took over the reigns of the Holy Flame, Billy had used his influence to torture young girls he viewed as promiscuous. The fact that he genuinely believed he was doing them a favor said something about the depth of his depravity.

"Maybe I should leave you two alone," I said.

"What? Hell no. I want you to see this."

"See what?"

Ronnie smiled slyly. "You'll see."

"If you're planning on making a big scene, I think I'll pass."

"Well, that's no fun. Just hang around. As a friend."

There it was. Whenever Ronnie said that last bit—"as a friend"—I knew where things were heading. If I continued to argue, he'd say he'd been there when I needed a friend. After that, if I still didn't give him what he wanted, I'd never hear the end of how he'd helped me bury my father, a reality I'd rather not continue to dwell on.

I hated him for the hold he had on me. Hated him even while I found myself sympathizing with him. It was a weird, disorienting combination. He'd learned to hold me emotionally hostage in order to get me to like him, which made me dislike him even more. Yet, there was a huge part of me that believed maybe he had a point. After all, he really *had* been there for me. And somehow, despite it all, I found myself developing something that almost felt like positive feelings for him.

A few minutes later, the door opened for the third time, and Billy Thrash—smiling Billy Thrash—walked into the room. The guard who led him in was smiling too, and it was clear Billy had been talking to him, and in an instant I saw how it was for Billy here. Not so different than how it had been for Billy on the outside. He had a magnetic personality, the kind that drew people to him and made you think, *Wow, what a nice man.* For years and years, I'd been perplexed by his close relationship with my father, because he was always so happy and friendly, while my father was a dour, angry man who saw only the worst in human nature.

It took me nearly half a century to understand what Billy Thrash really was: an actor. He hid depravity under a veneer of joy, and even now, even knowing what I knew about him, I found myself reacting subconsciously to his shtick. He was that good.

"There he is," he called from across the room. I wasn't sure if he meant me or Ronnie, but when he bypassed Ronnie and headed straight for me, arms extended for a big bear hug, I knew.

I wasn't sure why I stood to greet him or why I allowed myself to be wrapped up in his arms. It was just his power, I think. Or maybe for me it was the path of least resistance. I'd had a long day, and I was anxious to be back on the road, my mind focused on how to find Mary. Seeing Billy Thrash again was honestly something I'd never expected would happen.

Ronnie snorted at our hug as his grandfather pounded me on the back. So much for him being angry at me for busting up his little child torture scheme.

"I want to thank you, Earl," he said. "You've truly proven that God can use any man, regardless of his faith. You opened my eyes. I see now, what I was doing was wrong. Those girls may have been lost, but I wasn't helping them any. I should have spent that time on bended knee, in prayer, and saved us all a lot of misery."

He let go of me and for the first time seemed to notice Ronnie. “Hello, Ronald.”

I was shocked when I looked at Ronnie and saw all of his confident swagger had vanished. He looked like an angry little boy.

Billy stepped to the other side of the table and held out his arms. Ronnie looked for a second like he was about to say something, something mean, but then he shook his head and looked away from his grandfather.

Billy smiled at me. “Young ones hold resentments sometimes. It’s the way of the world. Sometimes it takes a lifetime to come back around to what’s right.” He said all of this without a trace of irony. It was as if he believed we were the criminals and he was still a faultless preacher. Like my father, his capacity to deceive himself was unfettered by any sense of reality or common decency.

We sat down, and I watched Ronnie, waiting for him to do whatever it was he planned on doing.

“Well,” Billy said, “I want to thank you two for visiting an old man like me. Jesus said, ‘Naked, and ye clothed me: I was sick, and ye visited me: I was in prison, and ye came unto me.’ Whether you two know it or not, you’re doing the Lord’s work.”

Neither Ronnie nor I spoke. I felt like it was Ronnie’s show, but he wasn’t saying anything.

“I heard the church has undergone a troubling transformation,” Billy said. “That saddens me.”

“Why?” Ronnie said. “It couldn’t get no worse than when you tried to run it.” He spoke the words so quickly, they were almost unintelligible, but I could tell from Billy’s face he got the message.

“Please, Ronald, do not put my sin on the entire church. Those people were God’s flock. I pray for them daily. I just fear that my transgression has led them astray, and now they are falling victim to a new, enticing form of Godless Christianity. The kind that does not acknowledge hell or the devil.”

“So, you still believe in the supernatural?” I asked him.

"Of course. How could I not? I've seen miracles with my own eyes, Earl. I've seen evil too."

"What about Old Nathaniel?" I said. I figured I might as well pick his brain too. If anybody had been around long enough to know the history, it would be Billy."

"Nathaniel? Sure, I remember those stories. I guess I'm showing my age because I remember when folks just called him Nathaniel. But I suppose even monsters can grow old."

"So you believe he's real?"

"Oh, without question. See, that's the problem with our world today. People have forgotten the power and majesty of the world our Lord created. Demons have always walked this earth. Angels too." His face twisted into a sly smile. "The real question, of course, is which one is Nathaniel? A demon or an angel?"

Ronnie muttered something under his breath.

"Sorry, did you say something, Ronald?"

"I said, 'Fuck you.' "

Billy shook his head. "I still pray for you, boy. Just like I prayed for your father."

"Yeah," Ronnie said, breathing heavily as if he'd just finished a long run. "That did a lot of good."

"My son and your father was a reprobate, Ronald. He denied all the help I tried to offer him. Believe me, I prayed for him more than I prayed for anybody else."

"You're a piece of shit," Ronnie said. It was quiet, meek almost.

I decided to try to steer the conversation back to something useful. "Did you ever see him?"

"Who? Nathaniel? Oh no. But I know a man who might have."

"Who's that?"

"Name was Cedrick Vaughn. Cedrick used to own all that land out there in the valley—well, excepting the parts where the blacks live, but honestly, that land's not fit for owning. Anyway, he was obsessed with the idea that Nathaniel existed and wanted to corral him. So, he went to work cultivating that cornfield, planting it just so, in the hopes that Nathaniel would be forced toward the trap he'd laid for him."

"Did it work?"

Billy laughed. "No, the only thing Cedrick succeeded in doing was confusing himself. The problem was he couldn't see the cornfield, not like he needed to. It was like creating a maze while you were inside it."

"He needed an aerial view?" I said, thinking of the binoculars in the water tower, and how I couldn't really make anything out because I wasn't high enough.

"That's right," Billy said. "It's funny too because, just before he died, he told me how he'd solved the problem. It was really ingenious and simple at the same time. You know Summer Mountain is nearby, right? It's closer to the cornfield than any other mountain."

Billy stopped and glanced over at Ronnie, who was muttering something.

"What did you say?"

"I said I fucking hate you. That you're going to hell and that Jesus ain't real." Ronnie was practically growling the words now, and as much as I understood his need for rebellion, it was the worst possible time for it to happen. Billy had just been about to tell me something important.

"Take it easy, Ronnie," I said. "Go on, Billy."

But it was too late. Billy's attention was now fully focused on his grandson. "I'm sorry you continue to fight the Lord, Ronnie." He turned back to me. "And how about you, Earl? Do you still fight the Lord?"

"I'm not a traditional believer," I said, and instantly regretted even engaging. "Can we go back to the Old Nathaniel thing?"

"Well, there's a lot of us out there, Earl, who have differences on some of the minor details. Baptism by immersion or baptism by other means. Some among us even believe that the handling of snakes is an outdated mode of worship. What I'm saying is, I understand your past. I understand what you've been through, and I want you to know, there's still room for you in God's kingdom."

I'd honestly believed that my father's faith held no more surprises for me. I was sure I'd already run the gauntlet of trying to be saved by people from the Holy Flame. Hell, the Holy Flame didn't exist anymore, and its last surviving remnants—my brother and Billy here—were serving out multiple-year sentences in a maximum-security prison. Yet here I was, listening to another conversion spiel. It never ended with these people. Why did it not surprise me that the one time Billy Thrash was about to be helpful, he interrupted himself to try to save me, yet again?

Billy—seemingly oblivious to my resistance, as he'd always been—kept right on talking about the kingdom of God and how he'd learned to lean on Him even more while in prison, and how the Lord had showed him a day, after he was released from these bonds, when he'd rebuild his church. Meanwhile, I was aware of Ronnie across the table from me. He was growing increasingly more agitated. It started with a small facial tic, blinking his left eye repeatedly, but soon grew into the curling and uncurling of his fingers and the tensing of his entire body.

"I really wanted to hear about your friend," I said.

"Oh, forgive me," Billy said. "I get carried away when I talk about the Lord and His blessings. Now, where was I? Oh, yes. Cedrick designed a great—"

I never heard the rest.

I lunged across the table just in time to impede the swing. It went wide, grazing the old man's earlobe. But Ronnie wasn't done. He leaned in again, despite the hold I had on him, and tried another swing. Billy stumbled out of his chair and to his feet.

I held Ronnie down. It took everything I had to do it. He was so angry, his body bucked beneath mine, shaking the table.

"I think I understand what this was all about now," Billy said. "You want information, and Ronald wants a fight. Well, you'll get neither from me. And to think, I was willing to trust that you two had godly motivations today."

Ronnie lunged again, and I decided to just let him go. From the expression on his face and the speed at which he moved, I was pretty sure he meant to kill the old man. Lucky for both of us, a guard stepped into the room right then, his revolver drawn.

"Easy there," he said.

Ronnie stopped and held his hands up.

We waited, watching as they escorted Billy out, but not before he told me he was still praying for me. He didn't say anything to Ronnie.

27

"You should have let me," Ronnie said as we made the drive back to Coulee County. "I don't care if they would have arrested me. Would have been worth it. Why'd you stop me? I thought you hated him too."

I squeezed the steering wheel tightly. "I tried to stop you because he was about to tell me something that would have helped me find Mary. That was a stupid ass thing to do."

Ronnie looked crushed. "Sorry, Earl."

I sighed and focused on the road. I *did* feel badly for Ronnie. It was obvious to me now where most of his issues stemmed from. It wasn't so much that his grandfather had wanted to save him but more that he seemed indifferent to Ronnie, instead focusing all his attention on me. It was a shitty way for a grown man to behave, but I wouldn't have expected anything else from Billy Thrash.

"Billy's full of shit anyway. Whatever he was going to tell you wouldn't have been true."

"Maybe you're right."

"Hell, I know I am."

I was silent. I saw his point but didn't think it applied in this situation. Billy didn't even know that Mary was missing. For all he knew, I was just curious.

"You still want me to help you out?" Ronnie said.

"Yeah," I said.

"I figured you might be done with me."

"Well," I said, "there's many that would be, that's for sure."

"But not you?"

I sighed. "Not me."

Ronnie didn't say anything, but I snuck a glance at him and saw that he was smiling—not *grinning*. Ronnie grinned all the time, and there was a manic kind of joy in that grin, the kind of joy that delighted in seeing the world burn. This wasn't a grin. It was a smile, and I thought there was something real in it, maybe even hopeful.

"What now?" he said.

"What do you mean?"

"I mean since we're still working together. What do we do now?"

"I got plans this afternoon, but tomorrow I'd like to visit the tattoo artist Lambert talked about. The one who has seen Old Nathaniel. You know where we can find him?"

"I'll figure it out. Can you pick me up?"

"Sure."

"What time?"

"Early."

"Most of these joints don't open early. Think noon to seven."

"Okay, I'll call you in the morning. Don't get wasted. Tomorrow is important. I want to see if this guy can help get us find the hidden warehouse on Summer Mountain."

"Got it. No problem."

"Can I ask you something?"

He was still smiling. "Sure thing."

"What were you thinking the other day? When you tried to rob your sister?"

"Heh. I wasn't really robbing her. I was robbing Lane. She ain't got no money. That's why she takes up with men like Lane. She's a good-looking woman. Hell, she's my sister, but that don't make me blind to what's going on. She does what a man like Lane Jefferson wants, and in return he feeds the kids and supplies her drugs. I just thought maybe I could get a little of his money because, well, I ain't too proud to admit it, Earl, the damned siding business is for shit these days."

I didn't bother arguing with him about his "siding business" again. Instead, I just drove, trying to concentrate on the new information I'd learned from Lambert. I replayed our conversation in my mind, trying to make sense of it. I felt like I'd begun to gather the pieces, and if I could just twist them around some, I'd begin to see how some of them might fit together.

Like the film director who lived on Summer Mountain. The one who's name reminded Lambert of a kid's game . . .

Tag. Tag Monroe. That was the man Lane Jefferson was supposedly visiting on the night Mary disappeared.

I looked over at Ronnie. "Tag Monroe. That's the movie director. You know anything about him?"

He shook his head. "No. But Lane used to work in movies. I do know that."

"How'd you find that out?"

"Wanda told me. Said he built sets out in Hollywood for a while. Probably how they know each other."

"Yeah, that makes sense. Did Wanda ever tell you anything else about Lane?"

"She hated the bastard. He was abusive and mean and she was afraid he'd hit Virginia."

"Jesus. Why didn't she leave—?"

I stopped myself. I knew exactly why. The drugs. It occurred to me that drug addiction was the kind of evil my mother had believed in, the kind that got inside you. Except, when it finally ended you, it ended too.

Or did it? Wasn't I forgetting a huge component of the addiction? It wouldn't end when Wanda was gone. Those kids would bear the brunt of that evil for the rest of their lives, and eventually they'd love someone enough to pass it on.

I felt sick suddenly at the hopelessness of it all. Finding Mary consumed me, but finding her would be only a single good thing in a vast sea of evil.

"Yo, Earl," Ronnie said. "You missed the turn."

I shook my head, slowing my truck and made a U-turn, heading back toward Riley, my mind as unsettled as it had been since I was young and dealing with the fallout of learning that none of the stuff my father had taught me about God was true.

Now a new question plagued me: What if my mother had been right about evil all along?

* * *

I got Ronnie home just in time to take Rufus to the library. He tried to talk me out of it, telling me I needed to be looking for Mary. I explained that this *was* looking for Mary.

"I want to confront Jeb Walsh about his little bootlicker lawyer."

"Okay then," Rufus said, "that sounds like a plan."

Rufus and I made it to the library just in time to slip inside the auditorium before they closed the doors. It was standing room only at that point, and I marveled at the people who sat eagerly in the chairs, holding copies of Walsh's book that they hoped to get signed. The small stage was empty when we came in, save for a table with a stack of Walsh's books and a microphone lying beside them.

"How big is the crowd?" Rufus asked.

"Big. We're going to have to stand."

"No problem. Anybody else here for the same reasons we are, or are they all buying his shit?"

I looked around, scanning the faces, checking for books or T-shirts that made each person's affiliation clear. "Let's just say it looks like we're in the minority."

Rufus nodded. "'Bout what I expected."

"Where's Susan and Nedra?"

"Nedra said she would be here. Susan's probably running around trying to do something for Mayor Keith. She says he treats her like his personal secretary."

A cheer went up from the crowd as Walsh stepped onto the stage. He was dressed much as he had been the other day—slacks, golf shirt, and a clean shave. He was carrying a few note cards, which he put on the table before picking up the microphone.

"Thank you," he said. "Thanks to all of you. You are the heart and soul of this country, and don't let nobody tell you any different."

The crowd cheered again, and Walsh pointed at someone in the back of the auditorium. An image was projected on the screen behind him. He stepped aside to give everyone a better view. It was a shot of a Confederate flag. Another round of applause rose up from the crowd, and Walsh smiled.

"I feared it might not show up. The library director here resents my presence. Luckily, you have a fine mayor in Riley, who is willing to step in and use his authority in an effort to save free speech."

"Jesus," Rufus said, "they're buying it, aren't they?"

"I think so."

"What's on the screen?"

"You don't want to know."

"Tell me."

"Confederate flag."

Rufus's countenance changed then. He looked pained and angry, but mostly he looked scary, like some kind of twisted angel, with a single mission. I wasn't sure exactly what that mission was, but I thought it had something to do with justice and stopping Jeb Walsh.

"This is a symbol," Walsh said, pointing at the flag. "Symbols are—get this, folks—symbolic and therefore open to interpretation."

The crowd murmured as if this was some great insight. As much as I hated it, it was easy to see why they were enamored with Walsh. He had the whole handsome, trim, and healthy thing down cold. He was charismatic and smart enough to fool anyone who was already predisposed to his views or was looking for easy answers.

"So," he continued, "by definition, the flag itself can't be racist.

It's an inanimate object. It can no more be racist than a tree, or a rock. It's only what a person brings to it that creates that symbol. For me, I see Southern pride, heritage, a sense of roots, and where I come from, maybe even glimpses of Lynrd Skynrd." The auditorium laughed as Walsh pretended to play an air guitar. "Somebody else might see something else. That's what a symbol is. It's a mirror, really."

Out of the corner of my eye, I saw something that I should have known was coming: Rufus raised his hand.

Walsh looked up at him, and his face changed a little. Maybe not so smug as before. His eyes flicked back to the rest of the audience.

"He see me yet?"

"He definitely saw you."

"Excuse me," Rufus said, his voice booming out over the auditorium. Apparently, Rufus had turned on his mic. There was no way Walsh would be able to ignore it.

"Yes, sir, in the back," Walsh said. "You have a question."

"He's talking to you," I whispered to Rufus.

He nodded. "You don't remember me, Mr. Walsh?"

Walsh pretended to squint up at Rufus. "I don't know, sir. I meet a lot of people."

"You're lying. I can always hear it in your voice when you lie. It's one of the advantages of being blind. You get attuned to sound the way other people aren't. Then again, you lie nearly every time you open your mouth, so there's that."

There was some grumbling in the crowd. They were catching on that Rufus was going to be hostile. But it was just grumbling. I could tell from the low volume that most of them were interested enough in a potential conflict to let Rufus have his say. Maybe it was the microphone. It made Rufus's voice so commanding it was hard not to be interested in what he had to say.

"I think I do remember you now. You and your buddy there are trying to stifle free speech."

Rufus spread out his hands. "No, sir. You are speaking now. I'm here to listen and to respond."

"Well, maybe you can respond when I'm finishe—"

"No, sir," Rufus said. "I'm responding now. You're way off base here."

Walsh leaned against the table, grinning. "Okay, you want to debate, old man? I'll debate. How am I so far off base?"

"Well, the Confederate flag is more than a symbol."

"Okay . . ."

"It's also a flag."

Walsh gave the crowd a conspiratorial look. "That's what mathematicians would call a 'given.' Next point?"

Someone laughed. But I thought it was a nervous kind of laugh, and the tone inside the auditorium had changed markedly. Everyone was listening, waiting for Rufus to explain himself. A thought struck me then: What if they'd all just been waiting for someone to have the guts to speak out against Walsh's bullshit, to articulate an opposing view. God, I hoped that was the case.

"You make light of my point," Rufus said, "but you shouldn't. Before it was a symbol in the metaphorical sense, as you seem so intent on belaboring, it was also a symbol in the literal sense. It literally symbolized the Confederacy."

"Well, of course, but—"

"Would you mind shutting up while I make my point?" Rufus said. "Or is this one of them safe spaces where only the assholes get to talk?"

The auditorium grumbled at little at this, but I thought I heard a few laughs too. Walsh suddenly looked a lot less comfortable than he had just minutes earlier. Every eye was now turned, watching Rufus closely.

"So, the Confederacy was essentially a grouping of states that wanted to be their own nation so they could do what?"

No one spoke.

Walsh sighed, trying to regain some of his bluster.

"You can answer me now," Rufus said.

"Oh, I'm allowed to speak at my own event now? That's good to know. Well, to answer your question—"

"I changed my mind," Rufus said, and though both men had microphones, Rufus's voice was still somehow louder, more authoritative than Walsh's, and the author stopped. "Besides, I know what you're going to say. The Confederacy was about preserving a way of life and states' rights and federalism and all that bullshit. Save it for the racists, okay? Because I don't believe a word of it." He held up a hand and rubbed his fingers against the fat of his thumb. "Money. Power. That's what the Confederacy was about. The money came from free labor. The power came from feeling like they were the privileged class. African American slaves gave the whites of that era someone they thought they were superior to. So, I reject your answer. The correct answer to my question was that the Confederacy was essentially a grouping of states that wanted to be their own nation so they *could continue the unfettered practice of slavery.*"

The auditorium was silent. Rufus leaned back against the wall, relaxing a little. I wondered if he realized every eye in the place was on him.

Walsh cleared his throat. "Thank you, Mr. . . ."

"You can call me Mr. Fuck You," Rufus said.

This was so unexpected and well-timed, a section of the auditorium exploded in laughter, whooping and hollering. To be fair there was a large contingent who booed or scowled at Rufus. Walsh pounded a hand against the table, but something had gripped the place, and the noise—both cheering and booing—went on.

It took some time, nearly a full minute, before Walsh was able to continue. When it was finally quiet, he clicked the next slide over to what looked like a crude and racist sketch of a slave. Cheers and boos went up in almost equal number. Walsh frowned and clicked to the next slide without comment.

Rufus was quiet for the rest of the talk, and when it came time for people to get their books signed, there weren't as many in line as I'd expected. I elbowed Rufus. "You did a good thing. I really think some people turned on him because of you."

He nodded. "Let's get in line."

28

The line moved swiftly, and soon Rufus and I were standing in front of Walsh.

He looked up at us and cursed softly. He motioned to someone standing offstage. Preston Argent stepped out and strode quickly over to the table.

"Get these two out of here."

"If you touch me, I swear I'll scream," Rufus said.

Argent started forward, reaching for me first. I let him grab me, and I grabbed him back, pulling our faces together. "What did you say to Johnny Waters?"

Argent's face turned to a smile. His eyes widened, and he began to chuckle. "Now why would I want to talk to a rapist like that?"

"I saw the video of you at the sheriff's office, asshole."

Argent laughed. "You didn't know I was a lawyer, did you, Marcus?"

"What you did was a mistake," I said. "It points the finger right back at you"—I nodded my head toward Jeb Walsh, who was standing behind the table now, trying to keep his distance from the scuffle and, mostly likely, Rufus—"and him."

Walsh locked his eyes on me. "What did you just accuse me of, you son of a . . ." He stopped, seeming to remember that there were other people around.

"Get them both out of here," Walsh said.

Argent and I were still locked in a tight embrace, and at Walsh's urging, Argent shoved me back into the people standing behind us. A woman screamed. I kept my balance and reversed my momentum, bearing down on him. "Who has Mary Hawkins?" I said. "Tell me."

"I don't know any Mary Hawkins." He pushed me again.

"You're a liar," I said, and took a swing at him.

He side-stepped the punch, laughing. "You bleeding hearts are all the same. All bark, no bite."

I was about to prove him wrong, when a voice boomed through the auditorium. "Please clear the room." I looked and saw Susan Monroe holding the microphone. "The police have been called."

Argent was still laughing. "Hey, maybe we'll meet again somewhere out there."

"Maybe," I said.

He leaned in close, and for a second, I tensed up because I thought he was going to grab me, but he stopped short of touching me, his face inches from mine.

"You want to know who has your pretty nigger girlfriend? His name is Nathaniel. And he don't like uppity ghetto bitches excepting and until they're dead."

I raised my fist, determined to make this one count.

"Earl!" the voice from the microphone boomed, stopping me before I swung. I looked up. Susan was looking right at me.

I nodded at her and put my fist down. I bumped Argent as I pushed past him to go get Rufus and help him get out.

* * *

Susan took Rufus and me back to her office, where Briscoe and Virginia were watching a movie on a computer at Susan's desk. She told us to wait while she dealt with the police. "And don't worry—I'll keep your names out of it."

When she came back a few minutes later, the library was officially closed, and all the lights were off except for the two lamps in her office.

She looked worn out, and I wondered if I was asking too much of her to take care of the kids on her own.

"Wow," she said, as she sat down across from us. "I'm so glad you two showed up."

"Really," I said. "I figured you'd be angry at me."

"No way. You two were the only ones standing up to him—to them. I appreciate what you did. *And* I appreciate you not letting it get out of control. If you had hit him . . ."

I nodded. "Yeah, sometimes I forget about the consequences."

"It's okay. I'm not a violent person, but those two . . ."

"Those two would make Gandhi want to punch them in the face," Rufus finished.

That made Susan giggle, which in turn caused Briscoe to turn around, his eyes big and round and full of surprise. He watched her for a second before bursting into a giggling fit of his own. That sound must have touched something in Rufus because he smiled bigger than I think I'd ever seen him smile, his lips stretching ear to ear, while the rest of his face looked relaxed and peaceful.

As much as it would have felt good to laugh, I didn't have it in me.

I wasn't sure, at that moment, I'd ever have laughter or joy in me again, at least not until I knew Mary was okay.

"I can't get over the way that Jeb Walsh looks at me," Susan said. "I told Mayor Keith I didn't want to work tonight, but he said I should get over it."

"Keith is a shitty mayor and a shittier man," Rufus said.

"Yeah, I agree," Susan said. "But the fact that I had to come in tonight meant I had to deal with Walsh. The city paid him to do this, and it was my job to hand him the check and make sure he signed for it.

"Jesus," I said. "I'm sorry."

"I'm okay, but . . ." She shook her head. "What he said . . . it's just disturbing."

Rufus and I were silent.

"I went up to him and handed him the check. He took it and opened it right in front of me, like he was making a big show of checking that we weren't ripping him off. After that, he looked at me with that same look—you all saw it the other day—and asked me if I wanted to go to dinner with him. Ordinarily, I'm flattered when a man asks me out. Even if it's a man I'm not interested it, I still take it as a compliment. Twenty-five years of marriage makes you appreciate being appreciated. Oh, that came out wrong. Anyway, what I mean is that somehow, his asking me out seemed threatening. I told him no. Firmly. Do you know what he did?"

"I'm afraid to ask," Rufus said.

"He said he could tell I really wanted to go with him, that I didn't 'know' myself as well as he did. He addressed me as 'girl.' I told him I was a woman and knew myself much better than he did because he didn't know me at all.

"He laughed and said I'd find out about the world someday, and when I did, he'd be waiting.

I asked him what that meant and he said I could figure it out. And the worst part was that he kept referring to me as 'girl.' "

"He needs an ass-whipping," Rufus said.

I was thinking the same thing but didn't say it. Sometimes saying it out loud made it sound like a threat. It felt more like a promise to me right now.

"Please," Susan said, "I don't want either one of you messing around with him on my behalf."

"It won't just be on your behalf," I said. "It'll be on behalf of the entire human race."

"Well, thank you," she said. "But please, don't be rash."

"We'll try not to be," Rufus said. "But Earl ain't got much talent in the ways of not being rash."

She laughed a little and met my eyes. I looked away.

"Rufus told me you know something about Old Nathaniel?"

She nodded. "I've been studying him ever since I started seeing the stickers."

"The stickers?"

"Yeah. They're little yellow stickers on the bottom right-hand side of people's windshields. I kept seeing them and wondering what they were, so I did the librarian thing: research."

"What did the stickers look like?" I asked, thinking of Timmy Lambert's tattoo and how he'd told me he had gotten the design from the cars coming to the warehouse he was guarding. Remembering that, I pulled out my phone. "Anything like this?"

I passed it over to her. She looked at it and immediately nodded her head. "That's it exactly," she said.

"Someone want to tell me what it looks like?" Rufus said.

"Two axes, a skull in the middle," I said.

"What does it mean?"

"You ever heard of Skull Keep?"

"Yeah," I said, remembering that Ronnie had referred to Lane Jefferson's cornfield as Skull Keep the day I'd gone with him to rob Wanda.

"I'm surprised. Most people around here haven't. At least most *white* people. Black people, though? They know all about Skull Keep."

I shook my head, thankful for Susan. "Go on."

"Well, you asked about Old Nathaniel. The legend originally had him killing kids in the mountains. Way, way back, he was called the Hide-Behind Man. He was known for only being seen out of the corner of your eye unless he was close enough to kill you. When you saw him full on, it would already be too late. This Hide-Behind Man killed anybody he could catch alone in the woods. The story existed for nearly a century, unchanged. Then around the turn of the century, sometime before the First World War, the area saw its first and only serial killer. His name was Nathaniel Vaughn. He was a white man who exclusively killed black people. There's some debate as to whether he was motivated by racism or obsession, but either way, it was a frightening time to be black in these mountains. With Reconstruction and Jim Crow getting going, they had enough to worry about, but then throw in a serial killer?"

Rufus grunted in agreement. "I got a feeling I know where this is going."

I had a feeling I did too.

"Sometime in the twenties or thirties, long after the real Nathaniel had been apprehended and put to death, the Hide-Behind Man legend got mixed together with the true story of Coulee County's first and only serial killer. Old Nathaniel—a black-hating, skull-collecting legend—was born."

Rufus grunted. "He was supposed to roam the woods in the valley, to keep out any blacks who had a notion to climb into the mountains where the good white folks were."

Susan nodded. "Exactly. But it wasn't just perpetuated by whites. Black parents told their kids about him for the same reason. They feared a kid wandering up from the valley and into the mountains. This was the time of lynchings and cross burnings. Old Nathaniel may not have been real, but the danger certainly was."

The room fell silent. Rufus shifted in his seat. I thought about what it must have been like to live in the valley. What it was like even now. As long as there were people like Lane Jefferson and Jeb Walsh out there, living in the valley was a bad proposition, even if you didn't take into consideration the poverty of the area.

"So, the people using these stickers," I said. "Do you know anything about them?"

"That's where I hit a dead end. I tried to ask a few people, but either the people I asked didn't know, or they knew and weren't willing to talk. The only way I realized it was connected to Old Nathaniel was through a newspaper article I came across from the 1970s. It's in my drawer there, if you want to read it."

I slid away from the desk so she could come over and open the drawer. She pulled out a photo copy from the *Riley Reporter*, a now-defunct newspaper. "It's short but interesting. Read it out loud."

I cleared my throat. "The headline says 'Mysterious Bunker Found in Field.'"

"That sounds ominous," Rufus said.

"Yeah. It's by Mark Dillion. Dated August 4, 1977."

Rufus nodded. "Go on."

A local man claims to have found a bunker in the woods near the old Vaughn place. After exploring the concrete bunker, Lawrence Wharton said he found six human skulls inside. That wasn't even the strangest part. According to Mr. Wharton someone had painted symbols on the walls of the bunker.

Wharton said, "Some of them looked like swastikas, but some of the others I'd never seen before. There was one of them that had two axe handles with a skull in the middle. Whoever done them was a good artist."

Wharton explained that he didn't touch anything inside the bunker, but instead climbed back out and went to the police immediately. He brought Sheriff Hank Shaw back with him the next day, and the men were unable to find anything.

Wharton said, "I can't explain why I wasn't able to find the bunker again. Maybe because it was overcast and dark that day. Sheriff Shaw got frustrated . . . I know he's a busy man and all, but I think if he'd let me go back out . . ."

But neither Wharton—nor anyone else—has been allowed back out. The area has recently been fenced off by order of the county commission. According to County Commissioner Steve Wallace, the area is popular "among criminals and blacks. It's in everyone's best interest to stay away."

"Jesus," Rufus said. "Criminals and blacks. Wow. Talk about blatant racism."

"Have you tried to find Wharton?" I asked.

"He's dead."

"Shit."

"But that's not the end of it. Though there weren't any more articles written about it, the story lingered in the collective memories of the people in Coulee County. Before long, Old Nathaniel was the curator of Skull Keep—that was what the bunker came to be known as."

I shook my head, trying to make sense of it. "It's almost as if Old Nathaniel is being dredged back up to coincide with Walsh coming to town and the more overt racism that came with him. Maybe it's the same as when white supremacists hang out their Confederate flags to remind black people that they'd better stay in line."

"That would make sense when you consider the rally earlier in the summer," Susan said.

"What rally?"

"The one to remove the mural in the courthouse. You've seen it, haven't you, Earl?" Rufus asked.

"I don't think so."

"It's got a lot of bad shit in it. A cross burning, some white men wearing white hoods, slaves picking cotton. But its defenders say it's supposed to represent Riley's history, good and bad." He shrugged. "Easy for them to say when they've only been on the good side of history."

"Yep," Susan said. "It's a subtle reminder of the way things used to be. It's a way of saying, 'You've got your place, don't you dare try to reach for any more.' It doesn't matter that *their* place is The Devil's Valley, where the only piece of good land is owned by a white man. They aren't just relegated to the valley; they're relegated to a flood plain that basically makes their homes uninsurable and their land a swamp."

I sighed loudly and rubbed my face.

"What?" Susan said.

"I think this has something to do with Mary. Think about it. Johnny's original story was that he was attacked by Old Nathaniel. Then Walsh's thug, Preston Argent, paid him a visit at the jail, and now Waters has suddenly found Jesus."

"You think Walsh is behind it?" Rufus asked.

"I don't know. Maybe. Hell, would you put it past him?"

"No," Susan said before Rufus could answer. I could tell from the expression on her face that she was remembering the way he'd looked at Mary the other day in front of the library.

"I agree," Rufus said. "But how do we find out for sure?"

"Well, I think we could start by paying Jeb a visit. See if we can make him talk."

Rufus shook his head. "That's just the anger talking, Earl. It's not going to do any good to beat him down. Well, it might do your soul some good, but he's still not going to talk, and you'll only get in trouble with the police."

I sighed. "I don't really care. I'd love to be alone with him for just ten minutes. That's all it would take. I wouldn't even need a weapon. By the time I was finished, I'd know for sure if he was involved."

Susan stood and walked over to where Virginia and Briscoe sat, still engrossed in their movie. She whispered something to Virginia, who nodded and picked Briscoe up. He started to protest, but Susan grabbed the laptop and carried it along beside them so he could continue to watch.

She led them out of the office and into the stacks, where she put the laptop down. Virginia sat down in front of it, holding Briscoe in her lap.

When Susan came back in, she shut the door. "I didn't want them to hear what I'm going to say next."

Rufus looked confused.

"She took the kids out of the office," I said.

He nodded.

"Earlier today, when they were in the children's library, I went in to check on them and found a strange man talking to Virginia. When he saw me, he left in a hurry."

"Did you ask Virginia who it was?" I said.

"I did. She said it was one of the men who worked with Lane Jefferson."

"What did he want?"

"She said he was asking her where her uncle was."

"Shit," I said. "Lane's going to go after Ronnie for trying to pin the kidnapping on him."

"Sounds like it to me," Susan said. "Which is why I'm going to tell you how you can find Jeb Walsh tonight."

"How?" I said.

"When I was giving him the check, he was talking to Argent about their plans afterward. It sounded like they were heading to Jessamine's for some drinks."

Before I could say anything, Rufus spoke first. "You already got a history there, Earl."

"I just want to talk to him," I said, but Rufus knew I was lying. Hell, I wasn't even sure why I bothered. The truth was, I knew going to confront Jeb Walsh at Jessamine's wasn't going to end well, but I hardly cared. Mary was still missing. That simple fact eclipsed all other concerns.

"Want me to take you home first?" I said.

"Hell no," Rufus answered. "You're going to need somebody to keep your ass out of jail."

29

Jessamine's was a bar and diner situated just outside of downtown Riley, in a small strip mall that consisted of two other stores, both long closed. Only Jessamine's remained, and from the looks of the parking lot as Rufus and I pulled up, it was doing better business than it had in years. I had to park in the grass lot in back.

Jessamine's was the rare place that was actually two distinct establishments, depending on the time of day. Weekday lunch was populated by the working man—loggers, clergy, cops, and workers from the lime plant a few miles away. Most came for the lunch specials, which that day included baked chicken with your choice of three sides. At lunch, parents would feel fine bringing in their kids to eat here. At night, most responsible parents would keep their kids as far away as possible.

By night, Jessamine's became a honky-tonk that was as good a place to get drunk and into a fight as any place in the county—hell, maybe the state. In fact, the last time I'd been here at night, I'd managed to get into a fight with a sheriff's deputy, which was still in the back of my mind as I opened the door and surveyed the bar.

People stood three deep at the bar, and nearly every table in the place was full. A band played on a makeshift stage in the corner of the room. It was a band I'd heard before and liked, named Ghost Bells. They played scary folk blended seamlessly with bluegrass and old-time country, and they played it like their lives depended on every beautiful goddamn note. They were a three-piece: a tiny, redheaded girl played guitar and sang, backed by two scraggly men, both bearded and solemn-eyed, on the drums and the bass.

They were in the middle of a slow, lurching rendition of Roy Orbison's "Blue Bayou," and most of the crowd was mesmerized. Only one table seemed oblivious to the sounds, and that was Jeb Walsh's table, over in one corner of the bar. Walsh sat with Preston Argent and six other men. I looked closely at each man, trying to determine if there was anyone else I recognized.

Only one: Mayor Keith.

They all ranged in age from their sixties (Keith and Walsh) to their thirties (Preston Argent) and even younger (there were two men who looked to be little more than boys, wearing pastel-colored polos and sporting haircuts with severe parts and lots of hair gel).

I didn't see Lane Jefferson.

"Point me toward the bar?" Rufus said.

I touched his shoulder and guided him lightly through a throng of people, who parted as he approached. Most only glanced at him before quickly looking away. In fact, because of this phenomenon, Rufus had no trouble getting straight to the bar. He leaned against it, his mouth crooked into a half smile, and waited. A twenty-something kid with a ponytail came over, a worried look in his eyes.

"What can I get you?"

"Two double shots of bourbon," he said. "Wild Turkey, if you've got it."

The bartender returned with the drinks, and Rufus held one out to me. "What's your plan?"

"Wait. Watch."

"That don't sound like much of a plan."

The band finished "Blue Bayou," and the place erupted in cheers. They went straight into a hillbilly version of "Stand by Me."

The truth was, I actually did have more of a plan that that, but I didn't want to tell Rufus because I knew he wouldn't approve. "Just give me some time," I said, sipping the whiskey. I was watching Jeb's table closely. Mayor Keith seemed to be telling a story. Everyone at the table was listening closely except Walsh and Argent, who seemed to be having their own animated conversation.

I just needed to wait.

A few minutes later, what I'd been waiting for finally happened. One of the younger kids in a pale blue polo stood up and headed for the restroom. I swallowed the rest of my double shot in one smooth motion, steadied myself against the bar until I felt the liquor hit my belly and spread out to the rest of me, a warm trickling. I squeezed my fists together, testing the muscles and liking the way my knuckles felt hard and solid and almost numb, like concrete hammers.

I pushed through the crowd, my eyes locked on the bathroom door.

The kid was pissing in one of the urinals when I walked in. I checked the door for a lock, but there wasn't one. I'd have to make it quick and hope no one came in.

"Hey," I said.

The kid turned his head slightly but said nothing.

"Hey," I said, "I'm talking to you."

He ignored me. I pulled out my gun and racked the slide. It wasn't necessary because I knew it was loaded, but I wanted him to hear it so he'd stop ignoring me and understand that I meant business. A single round hit the floor, and I kicked it away.

His hands went up at the sound. "I don't have any cash," he said.

"I don't want cash. I want to talk. Don't turn around. We can talk just like this."

"Can I at least zip up my pants?"

"Nope. Don't even move."

"What do you want?"

"I want you to tell me about the men you're sitting with."

He shook his head and scoffed. "What do you mean? It's the fucking mayor and some of his friends."

"Why would you and your little polo-wearing twin be sitting at the mayor's table?"

"We're friends."

"What's your name, pencil dick?"

"Jason."

"Jason what?"

"Man, who are you?"

"I like that. 'Man.' Think of me as *the* man who is going to bust up your little group. Now tell me your last name."

"You ain't going to shoot me," Jason said.

He was right about that, and it pissed me off that this damn kid had swung the situation to his advantage so quickly. I stepped forward—on instinct more than anything else—grabbed the back of his neck with my hand, and slammed him forward against the wall. His forehead struck the drywall with a sickening crack.

He groaned as I pushed him again, this time sideways into the outside of a nearby stall. His shoulder took the brunt of the impact, and he tried to regain his balance and get off a punch, but I was ready for that and sent a short jab into his gut before he could finish his wind-up. He crumpled and fell over onto the bathroom floor.

I knelt down to finally get some information out of him, when I heard the bathroom door swing open. Someone whistled happily as he came around the corner.

"Well, would you look at this?" It was Jeb Walsh, accompanied by a whistling Preston Argent.

I held the gun up, pointing it at both of them.

Walsh laughed. "You don't impress me as the kind of man to go on a shooting spree in a bar bathroom."

"Don't be so sure," I said.

"Oh, I'm very sure. Let me tell you a couple of things . . ." He turned to Argent. "Press, watch the door, okay? I don't want anyone else to hear what I'm about to say."

Argent, still whistling the same tune—maybe "Satan, Your Kingdom Will Come Down"?—said he'd be honored and disappeared behind the edge of the barrier separating the door from the urinals.

Walsh was grinning now, looking like a kid on his birthday. "You're in over your head, okay? I see what you're doing. You think I'm responsible for your girlfriend's disappearance. And I'm not going to say that I didn't have anything to do with it because, frankly, that's irrelevant. She's gone. You'll never see her again, so a word to the wise: stop while you're ahead. This ain't your daddy's town anymore, Mr. Marcus. It's mine. And though I am a man who believes in the admonitions of Jesus Christ, I'm not above hurting a child to make sure his kingdom can be advanced. Like that whore Wanda's little brats. The other—"

I raised my gun with every intention of shooting him. It would have been a sacrifice, a move that would have helped the world, not so different from the idea of killing a tyrant. Sure there were moral complexities to this sort of thing, but I had no time to consider them. Instead, I had been gripped by such an overwhelming rage and hatred that I was going to do it. I was going to pull the trigger.

Walsh saw it too. The confidence that seemed to be a part of his physical makeup disappeared in an instant. He put his hands up.

"I didn't mean that—I . . ."

I took a deep breath and felt my finger tensing on the trigger.

Then—without warning—I felt myself falling again toward the black water. But something was different this time. There was a shape ahead of me falling too. It was Mary.

My finger slipped off the trigger. The vision went away, replaced by the kid—Jason's—fist.

All that wind-up paid off this time. I dropped the gun as I went down.

"Stay at the door," Walsh said. He walked over to me and put his foot on top of my jaw. Gradually, he shifted his weight until my jaw was taking most of it. I groaned.

"I want you to remember this moment when I'm in Congress, Marcus. You had a chance to kill me, but you let it slip right through your damned fingers. You won't get another one." He removed his foot, and I thought that was going to be the end of it, but then he kicked me right in the mouth. I felt a tooth come loose and ricochet off the back of my throat. I coughed it up and spat it out on the floor. My lip began to bleed and swell.

"And before you get a notion to go calling that sheriff, just remember, the mayor himself saw you following Jason in here. Jason?"

"Sir?"

"What did this man do to you?"

"He pulled a gun on me and threatened me."

"And?"

"He slammed my head into the wall."

"And?"

Jason looked confused.

"I thought you said he attacked you while you were taking a piss and caused you to get piss all over the damned place?"

"That's right. But I was pretty much done piss—"

"No," Walsh said. "Remember? It got everywhere?"

"Yeah, that's right," Jason said. He sounded uncertain, as if he couldn't decide which one of us was being ridiculed.

"Damn right, it got everywhere," Walsh said. "Though to be fair, most of it got on the asshole that attacked you, right?" I heard Walsh unzip his pants.

"No," I said.

Argent laughed from the door.

There was a pause during which I slid back against the wall, trying to escape the inevitable, but Jason kicked me in the stomach, and all of my focus went from trying to avoid the piss to trying to breathe.

The stream of piss hit the side of my face. It was hot and smelled worse than anything I'd ever smelled in my life. The smell was so extreme, it made the pain I felt in my face and stomach seem small. Small enough to get me moving. I clambered to my feet, shaking the piss off my face, but Jason grabbed me from behind and tried to jerk me back down. I turned on him and punched him hard in the mouth. He staggered back, hitting the stall for a second time.

The piss was coming up my leg now, toward my ass and lower back. I tried to turn around, but not before someone took a hold of the back of my neck and slammed it hard into the stall.

I didn't remember anything else until I heard Rufus's voice coming from above me, and the smell of old piss invading my nostrils from every side.

30

Rufus helped me wash most of the piss and blood off my face, but there was nothing I could do about my blue jeans and shirt, which were also soaked through.

"What the hell happened?" he said.

"I got jumped by Walsh, Argent, and some kid."

"Did you piss yourself?"

"No, Walsh pissed on me."

"Sweet Jesus."

I looked in the mirror. My Braves hat had even been darkened on one side by piss. My nose looked crooked and hurt with every beat of my heart. My lip was so swollen, it looked like roses were growing out of it.

"He also threatened those kids if I didn't stop trying to find Mary."

"Fuck him. He's got to go down."

"Yeah, but I don't think we can count on much support from Patterson."

"I thought you said he was a good man."

"He's not crooked like Hank Shaw was, but he's still comprised. The mayor is tight with Walsh." I splashed some water on my face. "I need some pain meds."

"I got whiskey at my place. Tons of it."

I shook my head. "I need to go to Susan's."

"Why Susan's?"

"That's where the kids are. I've got to make sure they're all right."

"Makes sense," Rufus said. "Then what?"

I closed my eyes and tried to think. There was the tattoo artist who did Lambert's tattoo. I'd already planned to pay him a visit with Ronnie the next day. There was also the warehouse that both Lambert and Ronnie had guarded for Lane Jefferson. There seemed like more, but I couldn't think of anything else.

"I got some places to check out tomorrow, but I'm going to need Ronnie," I said. "You're welcome to come along . . . but maybe you need to work on protest stuff."

He nodded. "I'm available if I can help."

"I know."

"And I'd like to think I'm more useful than that asshole."

"You are . . . in most cases, but the things I need to do tomorrow . . . well, one of them is going to be illegal."

"Shit, let's get you to bed. You ain't thinking straight."

Leaving the bar that night would normally have been beyond embarrassing, but I was still too pissed about Walsh all but admitting he'd masterminded taking Mary, not to mention his threat toward Virginia and Briscoe, to give a good goddamn.

People cleared a path for us as we came through, probably as much due to the smell of piss as the way we looked, which I'm sure was ghoulish at best and downright horrific at worst.

At the door, I turned around and saw Jeb Walsh back at the table with his friends, including Mayor Keith. He raised his glass at me and smiled.

31

I noticed the moon as I drove to Susan's place. It wasn't full—not yet—but in a few days it would be. I remembered what Lambert had said about seeing Old Nathaniel in the full moon, how the cornfield became a different place under the light of a full moon. Virginia had said the same thing, and I wondered if it was possible that this talk of full moons mattered in a way I was missing.

Each breath I took through my nostrils, felt like a windstorm of pain, and my gut felt like it was bleeding on the inside, so maybe I wasn't even thinking right, but the moon suddenly seemed important.

"Was there anything in the legend about Old Nathaniel and the moon?" I asked Rufus as I made the turn into Riley's nicest neighborhood, a quaint little area called Tumble Brook.

"Not that I know of, but nothing would surprise me. Could be he got conflated with the werewolf myth. Why do you ask?"

"I was just noticing the moon. And the people who claim to have seen Old Nathaniel all mentioned that they could see him clearly because of the full moon. Apparently, the cornfield comes alive when the moon is full."

Rufus grunted but didn't offer anything else.

Despite the pain, I kept glancing at the moon, trying to estimate how many days until it was full again. Three? Maybe.

The GPS on my phone told me Susan's house was up on the right. I'd called earlier, and she'd said Rufus and I were both more than welcome to stay, as long as one of us didn't mind sleeping on the couch.

I pulled into the driveway and stopped the engine. "When you open the car door," I said, "the walkway will be right there. It'll get you to the steps of her porch."

"You ain't coming?"

"I need to think for a minute."

"Sure," he said. "I've got to get some sleep, so that's going to put you on the couch. Good with that?"

"Yeah," I said.

He got out of the car, and I watched as he navigated his way slowly to her front door.

I opened my smartphone and searched for *moon phases, Georgia*. I clicked the first link that appeared, and a chart showed up, detailing the moon cycle in this area for the entire year. I zoomed in and found October. The first full moon was on October 5. It was listed as the Harvest Moon. I went back to the home screen and saw that today was Saturday, September 30. The 5th would be on Thursday. As soon as I realized that, I was struck by the overwhelming sense that something else was happening on Thursday, something that I needed to remember.

Something that hadn't made a lot of sense when I'd first heard about it . . .

Of course. Walsh's rally for traditional values was Thursday, something that had struck me as a strange time to plan an event that he clearly hoped would be big. Unless, of course, part of the point of the event was to make sure everyone was distracted . . .

But from what? That's where my full moon theory fell apart. Even if my gut told me the full moon was important, and that Walsh's rally was a ruse, I still had no idea what either one of those two things meant.

I sighed and started to get out of the truck. Then I stopped. It had been several days since I'd tried it. Might as well give it a shot. I unlocked my phone and dialed Mary's cell.

It rang three times, just as it had always done and then went to voicemail.

"This is Mary. I promise I'll call you back. Just leave a message and tell me who you are and what you want!"

There was a long beep, which I knew signified her voicemail box was almost full. When the beep ended, I began to speak.

"It's Earl. I love you. I—I'm going to find you. Wherever you are, I'm going to be there too. Just give me a little more—" The line beeped, signaling that there was no more room on her voicemail.

"—time," I said into the silent phone.

* * *

After a shower, Susan plied me with Percocet, and I fell asleep on the couch, feeling nothing for the first time since Mary had vanished. I knew it was a risk because every second wasted seemed like it took me further away from ever seeing Mary again, but I also knew that pushing my body too hard would lessen the chance of me ever finding her.

So I slept and didn't wake up until nearly ten, when Briscoe began tugging on my beard and giggling. Despite feeling like I'd been kicked in the mouth and pissed on the night before, I couldn't help but laugh too. He was so damned cute.

I sat up, realizing I had not dreamed of the black water rising, or if I had, it was lost to me now in the fog of the Percocet. I heard voices coming from the kitchen, and then Virginia stepped in.

"There you are. Leave Mr. Earl alone."

Briscoe giggled and toddled away as if he was being chased.

"It's okay," I said. "I need to get up."

"Ms. Susan made breakfast."

"I smell it," I said.

Virginia went back into the kitchen, and I sat there for a moment, trying to think. I couldn't afford to linger over breakfast. I'd have to grab something and get out the door.

When I walked into the kitchen, Rufus had Briscoe in his lap and was letting the boy play with his jowls. I laughed at that, mostly because Briscoe didn't seem to be the least bit intimidated by Rufus or the outsized shades he wore.

"How do you feel?" Susan asked.

"Perfect," I lied.

"I doubt that."

"It's true."

"What's the plan for today?" Rufus said as I sat down.

"You don't want to know."

"Ah," Rufus said, "you're breaking the law with Ronnie."

"We're not breaking the law. We're just going to hit up a tattoo parlor where somebody has supposedly seen Old Nathaniel." I didn't mention that we hoped to find out where the warehouse was on Summer Mountain, so we could break into it.

"Should I just hang here?" Rufus asked.

"Do you mind?"

"Are you kidding? Susan's a great cook, and"—he grinned—"these kids are damned fine company."

32

Before going to Ronnie's, I went by my place to check on Goose. He was beside himself when he saw me, and it made me feel guilty about leaving him here by himself. I decided that when I had a chance, I'd see how Susan felt about a dog joining them.

I plugged my phone in to charge and called Ronnie while Goose continued to paw my leg to get me to pet him.

About an hour later, I pulled up to Ronnie's place.

He met me outside and nodded toward his truck. "I'll drive."

"I'll pass."

"You want this to look legit, right?"

"Yeah."

"Then let me drive."

Maybe he had a point. My truck was standard issue, no frills, the kind of truck a man drove who didn't have tattoos all over his body. Ronnie's jacked-up piece of shit would lend an air of legitimacy to our visit. Reluctantly, I shut my truck off and walked over.

He lit a cigarette as he pulled across the creek and past the old church cemetery, toward the road. "Can I ask you something?" I said.

"I reckon you can do most anything your heart desires, Earl."

"Why the jacked-up truck?"

"You're kidding, right? That is a fine, fine piece of machinery. It's a Ram body with Big O tires and a salvaged hemi that makes six hundred horsepower. I can't even measure the damn torque. Hell, that truck will crush anything else on the road, and I do mean crush. As in roll over it. Damn, I get all evangelical just talking about it."

"I'll bet it's a damn fuel hog," I said.

"Hey, grizzly bears are food hogs, but that don't make them any less fearsome. You gotta feed the beast."

"But . . . I guess. How practical is it anyway? You've got to use a step stool to get inside. Either that or strain your back, and with you needing money all the time . . ."

He looked at me blankly, and I realized his feelings about that truck went beyond reason. Trying to get him to think rationally about that truck was akin to trying to make my father think rationally about his faith. It wasn't going to happen.

After a quick stop at McDonald's for some biscuits, we arrived twenty minutes later at the base of Small Mountain, where a trailer park I recognized was positioned on the side of the hill.

One of the trailers had a sign on top that said "Tatoo's Here." In the yard, another sign read, "Drank Machines for sell."

Ronnie pointed at that one and giggled. I shook my head, not so much at the poor grammar as at the thought of someone actually coming out here to purchase a drink machine.

We climbed down from the truck and walked up the hill. I couldn't help but glance over at the trailer I'd visited with Mary over a year ago. Inside, we'd found two people grieving the loss of a young girl who'd committed suicide years earlier. They'd acted angry at first and then shocked when they realized that Mary and I actually cared about them and the girl who'd killed herself. It was a good reminder as we approached the tattoo parlor: the people in this community were tough on the outside, but just as vulnerable as the rest of us underneath.

"You been here before?" I asked Ronnie.

"I get mine over in Chatsworth. I used to fuck a girl there. But you want to find out about Old Nathaniel, right?"

I nodded. "And how to get to the warehouse."

"Follow my lead then. You can act, right?"

"Yeah, of course."

"Can you act like a piece of shit?"

"Yeah, I think so."

"Good."

He pushed open the door slowly. It looked like a regular trailer. There was a dingy couch sitting on top of dingy carpet in front of an old television. The TV was tuned to a local station, and Judge Judy was on, talking about her lack of patience for people who didn't respect authority. Seated on the couch was a teenage girl wearing a tank top that revealed detailed and colorful ink on her shoulders and arms. She had a sucker in her mouth and seemed transfixed by Judge Judy's monologue.

"Hey," Ronnie said. "I need a tattoo."

The girl didn't turn around. She just pointed toward another doorway, which appeared to lead into the kitchen.

"Thanks," I said.

She gave no indication that she heard me.

I followed Ronnie into the kitchen, where a man sat at a table, eating lunch. He was probably in his forties but took care of himself. He was as thin as Lambert described him, but not without a layer of roped muscle revealed by a loose tank top. Even though Lambert, had told us he didn't have tattoos, it was still surprising to see his skin unmarred by ink. He nodded at Ronnie and me and put down his fork.

"One or both?" he asked.

"One," Ronnie said. "Me."

I didn't realize Ronnie had been planning to actually get another tattoo, but I was glad for it now. This guy didn't look like a man who would take kindly to questions or having his time wasted.

The man at the table glanced at me and then back at Ronnie. "What's he—your daddy?"

"No, he's my ride. Truck's in the shop."

The man at the table studied me carefully, as if there was something about me that he didn't like. I tried to assume the role of a racist asshole and sat down across from him. "I don't have long," I said.

"That truck outside belongs to you?" he said.

"Yeah. You like it?"

"What kind of hemi does it have?"

I tried hard to remember what Ronnie had said, but had to guess. "Seven hundred."

It must have been reasonable because the man nodded, satisfied.

"I work at my own pace," the tattoo artist said. "If either of you are going to rush me, fuck off. Leave now."

"Fine," I said, pretending to be pissed at Ronnie for wasting my time.

Ronnie sat down. "I'm Ronnie," he said. "This is Earl."

The tattoo artist nodded. "I'm Anton. It's Russian." He looked at Ronnie. "Got something in mind?"

"Yeah. I want Old Nathaniel."

"What do you know about Old Nathaniel?"

"I know he kills darkies," Ronnie answered without missing a beat. He was convincing.

Anton looked at me, smiling slightly. "You two are into killing coons, huh?"

I nodded.

"Let me ask you," he said. "How many coons have you killed?"

Ronnie cracked his knuckles. "This some kind of requirement to get a tattoo?"

"Just conversation," Anton said, and that was the first time I picked up the very slight tinge of a Russian accent. He hadn't been born in these mountains, but he'd been here long enough to replace the Russian accent with hillbilly. Mostly.

"I killed one last year," Ronnie said. He sounded damn confident, so confident I wondered if maybe he had.

Anton turned to me. "And you?"

I swallowed. "I ain't killed any, but I've killed a white man."

Anton smiled. "A queer, I hope?"

I shook my head. "No, just an asshole."

This seemed to satisfy Anton. "Okay," he said. "To the parlor."

He led us to a room off the kitchen where he'd set up a cot and his tattoo instruments.

"Where?" he said.

Ronnie lifted his shirt. "On my back."

"Lie down."

Ronnie, shirt still up, lay down on the cot.

Anton looked at me.

"So many people these days are wanting Old Nathaniel. It's like he's alive and well. Where did you boys hear about him?"

"Online," I said. "And we know a guy who saw him. Said he got his tattoo from you. That's why we came."

"What guy is this?"

Ronnie spoke up. "Dude goes by the name of Pit. We go way back. Went to visit him at Hays the other day, and he spoke highly of your skills."

"I remember the guy. Fucking lunatic," Anton said, but the way he said it made it seem like a compliment.

"He said you could tell us how to get to a place we need to find." I lied, figuring it was worth a shot.

Anton nodded, ignoring my last statement. "I've seen him too."

I decided I could circle back to the warehouse later. "What's he like?"

"He's like . . ." Anton seemed to consider his words carefully. "He's like an avenging angel, come down to set the world right. He's like a white man who's had enough, you know? So, he puts on a mask and only then can he become what he truly is, which is more than a man. He becomes a god."

"When did you see him?" I asked.

"Back in the summer. Me and some buddies heard he likes to hunt on the full moon, so we went out to the cornfield. You know the cornfield, right?"

"Yeah," I said. "Lane Jefferson's place."

"Right. We went to Lane Jefferson's cornfield. We didn't know what we were doing, so we just parked and stumbled in. We were there five minutes when I decided we'd never find him. It was a maze inside there. You think there's going to be rows, but there's no rows, just stalks everywhere you turn.

"I told the boys we needed to start trying to find our way out, but one of them—I think it was Drew—pointed at a light moving in the distance."

"Light?"

"Yeah, I don't know. It was the only part that didn't make sense. The moon was so full . . . the corn was like on fire, you know? It was like being in a fire. But the light was there, and that was when we saw the long, clean row. And he was standing at the very end of it, a long way away. Some of the other guys took off running, but Drew and I stayed put. Why should I be afraid? I wasn't black. So we waited and he moved forward, taking his time, big steps. He held a long knife, and you could see the full moon on it. You know, reflected.

"We stood there for a long time. The light seemed to follow him."

"That doesn't make any sense," I said.

Anton looked at me as if remembering suddenly that I was there. He shook his head. "I don't care if it makes sense; it happened. Why are you so curious about Old Nathaniel anyway?"

"I want to see him. Me and Ronnie are thinking of heading out there one night."

Anton nodded slowly, his face set, guarded. "Make sure there's a full moon." He picked up his tattoo gun and inserted a fresh needle. He turned it on and leaned over Ronnie's bare back.

"We were going to hit the warehouse on Summer Mountain pretty soon. You know it?"

"I might. Why you going there?"

I waited to see if Ronnie might answer, but he was silent. "Um, Pit left something up there and wanted us to get it for him."

Anton nodded. "What, drugs or something? You going to smuggle it in to him?"

"Yeah," I said. "That's the plan."

"How much is he paying you?"

"A couple of grand," Ronnie said before I could answer.

Anton whistled. "Well, shit. Why are you wasting time getting fucking tattoos? I'd already been up there and grabbed that shit."

"Well," I said, "that's sort of our problem. We don't know exactly how to find the warehouse."

"You don't? Why didn't Pit just tell you?"

"He ain't so good with directions," Ronnie said. "All he could tell us was Summer Mountain, and hell, we already knew that."

"So," I said, "we been asking everybody we can. Figure we'd eventually stumble onto somebody that knows the place. And it looks like we finally did."

"Here's the thing, boys," Anton said. "I don't mind helping you out, but it seems like I should get a little cut for my services."

I pretended to be pissed. "Shit. How much do you want?"

"Five hundred."

"You get it after we get ours, not before," Ronnie said.

"Of course," Anton said. "But here's the other part of it. I don't finish the tattoo until I get my five hundred dollars."

"Shit," Ronnie said. "That's harsh."

"Deal or no deal?" Anton said, holding the needle close to Ronnie's skin.

"Deal," I said.

Ronnie groaned, but I couldn't tell if it was out of pain as the needle broke the skin, or frustration, or both.

Anton didn't speak again until he was finished and Old Nathaniel, from the waist up, stared at us from beneath a full moon.

33

We went back to Ronnie's to grab something to eat and trade trucks. Anton had drawn us a pretty detailed map, and Ronnie spread it out over his cooler in the kitchen while we ate ham sandwiches on moldy bread and chased them down with light beers.

"What exactly are you hoping to find here, Earl?"

"Not sure. But there's got to be a reason Lane wanted to have security there."

"You think maybe that's where Mary is?"

It had definitely crossed my mind, though I'd purposefully chosen not to dwell on the idea. I didn't need to set myself up for any more disappointment.

"Maybe," I said. "But even if she's not, there's bound to be something there that can help us find her." At least that was what I had been telling myself.

"Well," Ronnie said, plucking off a piece of mold from his bread. "Either way, I'm your man. I ain't going to let you down, Earl."

I nodded, hoping it was a promise he would be able to stick to.

* * *

We waited as long as I could tolerate sitting still before heading out. It was a little after nine when we loaded up. Ideally, we would have gone even later, but all there was to do at Ronnie's was drink, and after four beers, I decided that one more might be a bad idea.

Twenty minutes later, I came to the turn that would lead us up

Summer Mountain and slowed the truck under dark boughs heavy with unfallen leaves. When the wind swept down off the mountain, they'd all rattle and fall. Any minute now, I thought, autumn would arrive, and the dregs of summer would float away in a haze. Now was the in-between time, the season of change, and I hoped (or maybe it was just a wish) that among the changes would be finding Mary, and returning to the tentative peace that had been mine just a few days ago.

A sign was positioned next to the turn. It read "Sommerville Chase—North Georgia's Most Exclusive Community." Below that was another smaller sign that said:

"Sommerville Chase Town Square—2 miles
Community Gates—3 miles
Jumper's View—5 miles
Top o' the World—6 miles"

"Why do they spell it different?" Ronnie said.

"What's that?" I said. I was focused on the words *Community Gates* and thinking about how, within those gates, I'd find both Jeb Walsh and Tag Monroe.

"Sommerville Chase. Why use the *o*? It's just confusing?"

"I don't know. Rich fuckers like these guys like to make things complicated. It makes it easier for them to feel superior."

Ronnie nodded. In the dim light of the truck's cab, his face looked drawn and contemplative. "Me and a buddy have been meaning to get up here and see about taking some shit from some of these rich pricks."

"That ain't something I really feel comfortable hearing about," I said as I made the turn and started up the steep curve.

"Well, why not? Damn, you ain't exactly a saint yourself, Earl."

He had a point there. "Look," I said. "I'm not trying to judge you. I just would feel better if I didn't know."

Ronnie leaned back in his seat and blew out a long sigh. "Shit,

I probably wasn't going to do it anyway. I can't deal with prison again. I think I'd kill myself before I did hard time again."

"How old were you?" I asked.

"Went to the federal penitentiary as a twenty-one-year-old. This was when I was living in Kentucky. Bet you didn't know I lived in Kentucky, did you?"

I shook my head.

"Yep. Got me for breaking and entering, illegal possession of a firearm, and terroristic threats." He shook his head. "The last one was utter bullshit."

"Who'd you threaten?"

"The woman who lived in the house."

"Jesus, Ronnie."

"*Threaten* is a strong word," he said. "*Terroristic* is just plain wrong. I suggested she let me go without calling the police."

"And she didn't like that suggestion?"

"Yeah. And when she didn't like it, I told her I was going to make her regret calling. Hell, she must not have taken me seriously because she called right after that."

"Why didn't you run?"

He chuckled. "Bitch managed to lock me in her cellar. I couldn't go anywhere or hurt anybody even if I'd wanted to."

"Can you look at the map?" I asked.

He unfolded the paper and turned the overhead light on. "Be looking for a little road on our right," he said. "He wrote on here that it's pretty hidden, and you'll probably miss it. If you come to the gas station, you went too far."

He was right. I went right past the road and would have continued too, if Ronnie hadn't whistled and pointed at the gas station.

I turned around at the gas station and headed back in the other direction more slowly. "There," Ronnie said.

"I don't see it."

"Right there. Just between those trees."

"Oh hell, that can't be it."

"Turn. You'll see."

I turned, easing the truck between two trees and their low hanging branches. The branches scraped my windshield and the sides of my truck.

"Keep on," Ronnie said.

I kept on, and eventually the branches snapped back into place, and I had room—just barely—to drive.

The road was dirty gravel and hardly there at all. Thick undergrowth wove a rug across much of it. In the glare of my headlights, fine lengths of spiderwebs hung across the road. I took that for a good sign, that it had been a long time since anybody had been this way.

* * *

"That's probably where the guards stood," Ronnie said, pointing at a little shed near the entrance of the dirt lot. The warehouse loomed behind the shed and lot, dwarfing them both in size and presence. Windowless and low-slung, the brick structure seemed to be almost crouching in the darkness, waiting on our arrival.

I pulled past the small shed and into the empty lot, looking for a way in. "Probably on the other side," Ronnie said. "And I'll be shocked if it isn't locked."

I pointed to my back window and the truck bed behind it. "That's why I keep a sledgehammer and some bolt cutters in my truck at all times."

"Well, look at you being all criminal and shit." Ronnie rubbed his hands together excitedly. "Let's do this."

Ronnie carried the bolt cutters, leaving me to drag the heavy sledgehammer around the side of the building. We stood before an aluminum door. "Try it," I said.

Ronnie wiggled the handle, but the door didn't open.

"Bolted," he said.

I hoisted the sledgehammer high and brought it down into the center of the door. There was a loud clang, and the sledgehammer put a dent in the aluminum but didn't break through.

Ronnie shook his head and held out his hands for the sledgehammer. "Let me show you."

I handed it to him. He lifted it with surprising ease and stepped back. He swung smoothly, knocking the door handle right off the door. Then, using the other side of the sledgehammer like a pool stick, he pushed it into the hole where the handle had been. Twice he did this, and then a third time, with great force. Something popped and fell to the concrete floor on the other side of the door.

I watched, impressed, as he stuck three of his fingers into the hole and grimaced, repositioning his body so that he could stretch his fingers as far as they would stretch. Next came the satisfying sound of the bolt turning. He grinned and withdrew his fingers, holding them up for my inspection.

"Long fingers," he said. "You fucking know what they say about men with big hands, don't you?"

I ignored him and pushed the door open. The darkness inside was absolute.

A click and a hiss. Ronnie's lighter coming on. He waved it toward the wall until I saw a light switch. I flicked it up and the lights above us hummed and gradually came to life.

The space was mostly bare, but on one side there was what appeared to be some film equipment. Not only was there an old boom mic stand, I also saw a pile of dusty cables and a stand of lights looming over it all.

Ronnie and I moved closer as the lights made it up to full strength. There was also some rough-looking furniture haphazardly tossed around the back corner. It wasn't too difficult to imagine this being an actual film set at some point.

Ronnie asked the question I was thinking. "Do you think they were filming pornos?"

I stepped through some of the furniture and picked up a clipboard with a sheet of paper on it.

"What's that?" he asked.

"Maybe the thing that will tell us what they were filming."

The paper contained some lines from a script.

Man: Because you don't know what's across that river.
Girl: I know more than you think.
Man: You don't know nothing about the world.
Girl: He's going to protect me.
Man: I'm going to protect you from him.
Girl looks at the window. Rain is coming down. She shivers quietly.
Girl: I'm not afraid.
Man: You aren't yet, but you will be.

It ended there. The page with the rest of the lines had been torn off. I handed it to Ronnie and waited while he read it.

He looked up. "So they were filming a damned movie in here all that time?"

I shrugged. "Looks like somebody was."

"But why keep it so secret and shit? This don't sound like nothing from any porno I've ever seen."

"Me either," I said. "But there's something ominous about it. Something I don't like."

Ronnie handed the clipboard back and I looked at it again, trying to put my finger on what didn't sit right. My eyes fell on the parts—man and girl. Did these characters not have names?

Then it hit me. Man and girl. That sounded like some of the bullshit from my father's church. Men were men, but all the women—at least the pretty ones—would always be girls. I was so used to this kind of casual misogyny I'd almost completely missed it on the first read, but now, as I read it again, I noted the details that made me uneasy.

"He's going to protect me."

"I'm going to protect you from him."

"You don't know nothing about the world."

Where had I heard that last line before?

Susan. She'd relayed the encounter she'd had with Jeb Walsh, and it sounded eerily similar to this script.

Did that mean Jeb Walsh had written the script? That seemed highly improbable. Did it mean he or his followers had been involved with this film? That seemed more likely.

It wasn't much of a leap to say Lane Jefferson and Taggart Monroe were involved. And if that was the case, it meant Jeb Walsh probably was too.

But I still didn't get the secrecy, the stickers, hiring a guard, the whole—

Then it hit me—it hit me hard. Too hard. I moved toward the back wall to brace myself.

"What?" Ronnie said.

"What if they were doing a snuff film?"

"Come again?

"You know, filming somebody dying."

"Like them *Faces of Death* movies?"

"No, those weren't real. I'm thinking maybe they were doing the real thing here."

"You mean killing somebody?" Ronnie looked around, as if seeing the place in a new light. "I don't know, I don't see any blood or nothing."

"They could have contained the blood."

He shook his head. "Maybe."

"It's just a theory," I said, "but it would explain the secrecy."

"So would porn."

"Right, but this doesn't seem like a porn script."

"Well, it don't really seem like the kind of script that would be in a snuff film neither."

He had a point. I'd never actually seen a snuff film, nor would I want to, but, like Ronnie, I wouldn't have imagined any of them having much of a script.

"You hear that?" Ronnie said.

"Wha—" I stopped. I *did* hear it. It sounded like a vehicle approaching.

"Shit," Ronnie said. "What do we do?"

I pulled the 9mm out of my waistband. "Look for a place to hide."

"Should I cut the lights?" Ronnie said.

"No, they already know we broke in. Shit." I looked around frantically for some route of escape or at least a place to hide. The only thing I saw was the couch. There was room for both me and Ronnie to hide behind it.

I grabbed his arm and pulled him over to it. We crouched behind it, waiting. A long, tense silence followed, long enough for me to wonder if the sound had just been a passing car.

But then there were voices outside. We heard them speaking in hushed tones.

Ronnie stood up. "What are you doing?" I hissed.

"Got an idea. Trust me."

I wasn't really sure that I trusted him, but I didn't have many options, so I stayed down, peering just over the back of the old sofa.

I watched as Ronnie lit a cigarette. He turned back to me and said, "You'll find me, right?"

"Yeah," I said, because what else do you say when some asks you that?

He nodded and sauntered over to the door we'd busted. He stood there, smoking, waiting.

I had no idea what he was planning.

He inched closer to the open door, standing right at the threshold. Voices came closer, and I could make out something about "running plates," and that was all I needed to hear to know that they were sheriff's deputies and whatever Ronnie was planning wasn't going to work.

Two things happened almost instantaneously then: two deputies rounded the corner of the warehouse, guns drawn. At the same time, Ronnie barreled through the open door, splitting the deputies. In their panic, both fired. One shot hit the wall behind me. I wasn't sure what happened to the other shot. I came up, 9mm in hand, ready to fire, but both deputies were gone, giving chase to Ronnie.

Sprinting to the door, I leaned out, saw the dark downward slope of the mountain, and heard the deputies cursing as they tried to pull out their flashlights and catch up with Ronnie.

"Goddamn," I said, not believing what had just happened. It was foolish, probably more than foolish, but it was also a damn selfless thing to do. I realized I didn't have much time before the frustrated cops came back up the hill to look for me. After all, my truck was parked outside the warehouse, and there was a strong chance they'd already run my plates.

Which left me in a quandary. If I left, taking the truck, the deputies would pick me up tomorrow. Basically, if they came back and my truck was gone, it would prove I'd been in the warehouse with Ronnie. But what if they came back and found my truck was still there? They'd assume Ronnie had stolen it and broken into the warehouse on his own.

Which meant he'd probably do hard time.

There had to be some other solution.

I could only think of one, and it was filled with its own kinds of pitfalls, but at least it gave me an opportunity to keep looking for Mary, and it wouldn't mean hanging Ronnie out to dry.

I sprinted back into the warehouse and found the clipboard with the scene on it. I looked around once more for something that might make this whole debacle worth it, but I didn't see anything.

As I was walking toward the door, I flipped the clipboard over and saw a yellow sticker on the back. I stopped, looking closer. Two axes. A skull in the middle.

I stuck the clipboard under my arm and jogged to my truck. I fired it up and crushed the gas as I made my way back to the main road.

34

I couldn't help but think of my conversation with Ronnie when he'd been in jail. Hadn't he told me that sometimes there wasn't a good choice? In this moment, driving down Summer Mountain, I felt that. People always tell you to make the right choice. But what if there isn't a "right" choice? What if both choices are equally fucked? What then?

My answer was simple. I would make the choice that was best for Mary Hawkins. Just like Ronnie had made the choice that was best for Virginia.

I drove around the mountain on County Road 7, looking for Ronnie. I slowed the truck when I neared my best estimate of the area where I suspected he might come out. That was, *if* the deputies hadn't caught him. Or worse, if they hadn't shot him.

Once I reached the other side of the mountain, I turned around and made another pass, slower than before, my thoughts turning darker. What if the choice I'd made had led to his death? How would I live with that?

And then, almost as if *that* thought had opened the door, another slipped out. And it was the worst one of all.

What if the choice I'd made last Wednesday night to ignore all the ominous feelings I was having and bring Mary to the cornfield had caused her death?

Because I had to face that, right?

With each passing day, the likelihood of her being alive decreased.

Why take her at all if not to kill her? Unless the reason was ransom, but there had been no request, so why else? Torture? I shivered at the thought.

An eighteen-wheeler downshifted on the highway somewhere far behind me. How long should I drive around looking for him?

As long as it took, I decided. I owed him that much.

If not a lot more.

In typical Ronnie fashion, he wasn't visible until I'd almost run him over. One minute, the road was clear, and the next, there he was, waving his arms and grinning like a fool directly in front of my truck. I hit the brakes and cut the wheel, narrowly avoiding killing him.

He didn't seem to mind. He rushed over to the passenger's side, cigarette in hand and climbed in. He whooped loudly, pounding the dash with the hand that wasn't holding the cigarette. "Goddamn that felt good! Makes my nuts tingle, Earl! Makes me fucking hard. Let's go find some pussy. You and me. Whoo!" He stuck the cigarette in his mouth and drummed on the dash with both hands.

"I appreciate what you—"

"Uh, Earl, you better go. Them boys ain't far behind."

I nodded and slammed my foot on the gas.

* * *

"I need to hide the truck," I said. "You know a place?"

He'd calmed down a lot and now sat smoking, his head tilted back into the open passenger side window, the wind pushing his hair up into a wild tangle.

"Shit," he said, "I just realized me and you are going to be wanted men."

I nodded. "Yeah. And we've got to get out of this truck."

"Fuck," he said. "I got priors."

"Yeah, listen. What you did took some guts. I'm going to stick with you through this. If I can find Mary . . . if *we* can find Mary, Patterson will go light on the other shit. But if we don't, we're fucked.

So, the first thing is we need to ditch the truck and find a place to lay low."

"I got a friend, name of Martin. He lives next to an old salvage place south of Riley, not too far from here. We could dump your truck in there and hide out at his place for a while."

"Sounds good for you, but I've got another place in mind for me."

"Shit, the first place they'll look is at the old blind bastard's church."

"I know. I'm thinking somewhere else. I don't need to be too far away from the cornfield. Besides, I think this person will let me use her car."

"*Her?* Damn, Earl, you ain't wasting no time."

"It's not like that," I said.

"Sure it ain't. It wouldn't be that pretty little library girl, would it?"

"She's not a girl, and you should be thanking her. She's keeping your niece and nephew."

That made Ronnie go quiet. He seemed sad suddenly, and I wondered if it was guilt because he wasn't the one taking care of them. Because he, like his sister, was *incapable* of taking care of them.

"Easy, Earl. I didn't mean nothing by it."

I nodded and let out a breath. Nothing felt right in the world anymore. It had only been a few days since I'd been so thankful for how perfect everything had seemed, but now trials seemed to be coming at me from every direction.

"Which way is best to get to Martin's?" I said.

* * *

We made it to the little salvage yard a little before eleven. Ronnie pointed at a line of old vehicles. "Squeeze in there."

It took some doing and Ronnie's help, but I managed to get my truck in between a Chrysler Oldsmobile and a rusted-out Chevy Blazer. The only problem was that that now I had no way to get out because I couldn't open either door.

"Climb through the back window," Ronnie said.

Five minutes later, I'd managed to squeeze through the window and into the truck bed. I checked my pocket for my phone. It was there. My 9mm was in the back of my blue jeans, and my other Braves cap—the one Jeb Walsh hadn't pissed on—was on my head.

"Come on—you need to meet Martin. He's a trip. And he can break into anything. Don't matter if it's got an alarm or not." He reached a hand out for me and helped me down. "He's got a little bit of a drug problem, though, so just be aware."

"Drug problem? We talking hard stuff?"

Ronnie shrugged. "He likes coke, but he's cool with it. Hell, I think he needs it. If he's not tweaking, he's pretty much dead, you know. Like I've never known a more laid-back motherfucker."

I checked my phone for a signal, but it was out of range. I knew I should probably wait until the morning to call Susan anyway, but that meant spending a couple hours at Martin's place. If he had a computer and Internet service, I could at least make the time count. The visit to the warehouse and the idea that somebody—most likely Lane Jefferson and Tag Monroe—might be using it to make snuff films had given me plenty of avenues to explore, but I'd definitely need to get online to explore them.

We rounded a pile of scrap, and there was Martin's trailer, sitting up on some cinder blocks. A dog woofed loudly at our approach and then shifted to a deep suspicious growl. A voice called out from inside the trailer. "Who's there?"

"It's Ronnie. And Earl Marcus. Can we come up?"

"Shit, Ronnie. You ain't never heard of a phone?"

"We're in a bad way," Ronnie said.

"Hold on. Wait right there. I got a girl. Need to get her dressed."

I looked at my phone again. Maybe I would go ahead and call Susan tonight if I could catch a signal out here.

A few minutes later, Martin shouted for us to come on up. "Move slow, but with a purpose. Don't fucking creep. Huckleberry hates that, and he will tear your fucking balls off."

I looked at Ronnie. "Huckleberry?"

The dog—Huckleberry—growled again.

"He's okay. I been here a bunch, and he only bit me once."

"That's not very reassuring."

A light came on outside the trailer. "Easy, boy," Martin said. "These are friends."

The dog continued to growl.

"I think the problem," Martin said, "is that he don't know your friend."

"Why don't you just put him on a leash or in the backroom or something?" I said.

Martin scoffed. "Huck don't like leashes, and the last time I tried to put him in a room, he nearly chewed through the fucking wall."

"Nice," I said.

"Hey, if you don't like it, go the fuck somewhere else."

He had a point. "I'm planning to do just that," I said. "But I can't get service out here. You got a landline I can use? Even better, a computer with Internet?"

"Got both. But you ain't using shit out there. You've got to make it to the trailer. You keep acting nervous like you're doing, and Huckleberry will be munching on your nuts soon. Mark my words on that one."

"Come on," Ronnie said. "Just walk normal. Hell, you know what I did the first few times I came over? I pretended he was one of them snakes Billy made me hold when I was a kid. It relaxed me some. I figured if I could hold a cottonmouth and not get bit, I could walk by a damn dog and not get . . . oh, shit. I'm sorry, Earl."

I just shook my head and kept walking.

Huckleberry kept growling.

When we got close enough to see him, I focused on Mary. How I had made very little progress, but how I also felt like going to the warehouse tonight had been crucial, not only because it somehow solidified Ronnie and me as . . . well, for lack of a better term, partners in crime but also how it seemed to be important in a way I couldn't quite name yet.

And just a few feet away from the growling, tense, teeth-baring pit bull named Huckleberry, it hit me.

And I felt like an idiot.

The mic. I'd found it right after Mary disappeared, near where Johnny Waters lay. Was it possible that someone had filmed the whole thing?

And—better question—what if Mary had actually been taken *for* some kind of snuff film? I was horrified at the thought of someone planning to kill her on film. But it might mean she was still alive, at least until the moment of filming. And I might still be able to find her in time.

"You made it," Martin said.

I looked around and realized I was standing just inside his trailer, Huckleberry behind me, growling low and steady, but not viciously like he had been.

Martin was about my height and skinnier than any man had a right to be. His face looked like God had decided to try an experiment in human extremes—his skin was stretched close over his chin and jaw bones and drawn to a shiny tightness across his harried eyes. He wore a five-o'clock shadow and a big cowboy hat tilted high so no man would miss the skeletal definition of his gaunt face.

"Computer?" I said.

"Nice to meet you too," he said. "In the kitchen. Don't step on Shelia. She had a line or three too many tonight."

I slid past him and stepped into the nearly dark den. Shelia was on the floor, a blanket pulled up to her neck. Her dark hair formed a pillow around her pale face, and for a moment I was sure she was dead, but then she opened her eyes and looked at me groggily. "Who. Are. You?"

"Just a friend. Take it easy and get some rest, okay?"

Her lips flexed into something like a smile. "M'kay," she said. Her eyes fluttered and shut again.

I found the computer and sat down and moved the mouse to wake it up. I went online and opened up a search window.

Ronnie and Martin sat down on the couch behind where Shelia lay and passed a joint back and forth.

Thankful I'd had a good night's sleep the night before, I leaned in and got to work.

35

The first thing I did was search for Old Nathaniel. I was surprised when I got a few hits.

One was from a site that collected Appalachian folk tales. The site verified what Susan had said about the legend's origins. There was no mention of using Old Nathaniel as a racist symbol, though.

The next hit was from a message board called White Strikes Back. A poster who went by the screen name rightpower33 asked if anyone had ever seen Old Nathaniel.

There were three replies. The first one was just a question mark and emoji of a face looking confused.

The second said, "I am Old Nathaniel."

The third, from screen name nogeorgiaaoc, said, "Dude, you are an idiot. Only the n$ggers see Old Nathaniel, and that's right before they die . . . hahahaha! Film on the dark web."

I studied that response for a long time, trying to make sense of it. First, the screen name. Nogeorgiaaoc. North Georgia AOC. AOC was what had been written on the wall in the cave. I still had no idea what it stood for. And what did it mean that there was a "film on the dark web"?

I'd heard of the dark *net*—could this dark *web* be the same thing? It almost had to be. From what I understood, accessing the dark net was a secret thing, and I didn't have the first idea how to do it.

I opened a separate tab and searched for *AOC*. Several businesses came up that used those initials, but none were located in or even near Georgia. I tried *North Georgia AOC* and found something called the Atlanta Outdoor Club that looked benign enough. I kept paging, looking deeper and deeper into the results until, seven pages in, something caught my eye.

AOC Productions.

I clicked the link and it took me to the homepage for a 1999 film called *Angels of Depravity*. I clicked on the trailer, but the link was broken. A brief summary of the film gave away little, just that it was set in rural Georgia and was a "visionary horror masterpiece" directed by "the cult auteur, Taggart." A screenshot showed a man standing on the edge of a country road as headlights crested the hill and bore down on him. He wore overalls and big boots. In his hand was a large kitchen knife, streaked with blood.

Taggart.

Jackpot. I opened yet another tab and searched *Taggart Monroe, Director.* An IMDb page came up as the first result. I clicked on it and read the short bio.

> Taggart Monroe directed his first feature film in 1979. *Living to Die*, a thriller about a man whose suicide attempts keep being thwarted by people of color brought him instant recognition as one of Hollywood's top young filmmakers, despite the objections of many critics who praised the film as "beautifully shot" but found the script and overall theme of the film racist and xenophobic. Other critics—as well as the filmgoers who helped make *Living to Die* an underground hit—argued that it was a comment on racism, and that if the film had a flaw, it was an overabundance of subtlety, which served to obfuscate the commentary on the racist culture of the South at the time.
>
> Monroe's follow-up left little doubt as to his intentions. The 1985 film *The Killer* stands as one of the most controversial

films ever made by a large studio. It was pulled from theaters only three days after its release because of protests and bad publicity, prompting Warner Brothers to release a statement disassociating themselves from Taggart Monroe and the film. *The Killer* was a critical and financial flop. Worse, it made it impossible for Monroe to work in Hollywood again.

Monroe's film career appeared to be over, but then in 1999, he emerged with a straight-to-DVD release called *Angels of Depravity*. For this film, he dropped his last name, most likely in an effort to rebrand himself and reboot his career. But the reboot was short-lived. Taggart went on to make two more films, *Rando* and *Ivory War*, both of which lost money and are now out of circulation.

Monroe's final film came in 2005. *Utter Destiny* was his first release from his own Georgia studio called Skull Productions. He is credited as the director under the name Tag Monroe.

When one surveys the whole of Monroe's work, some curious themes arise. Besides rampant racism and misogyny, the director seems obsessed with numerology and moon phases. All Monroe films feature a climatic sequence that involves three scenes of increasing impact. In each film, Monroe seemed to focus on a different moon phase—new, first quarter, full, etc., and the climatic scenes are always washed in moonlight. Perhaps, if he hadn't also washed his films in intolerant ideals and a vile worldview, critics might have spent more time delving into his other fascinating idiosyncrasies.

So, Lane's alibi for the night Mary went missing was verified by a washed-up racist director. I wondered if Patterson even knew Monroe's history. This guy checked all the boxes as being involved with Mary's disappearance: racist, eccentric—hell, he even named his film company Skull Productions.

Not to mention his other company—AOC Productions. Old

Nathaniel, AOC, skulls. Tag Monroe brought them all together in one neat little package. And he was Lane Jefferson's alibi.

I decided to dig a little deeper and searched his other films. The first two returned the most hits. The third, *Utter Destiny* seemed to barely exist at all. The only mention of it I could find was a single landing page for a website that was apparently never finished. The page showed a white woman wearing a black dress, kneeling beside a pond. The tagline read, "There is one thing none of us can escape."

Living to Die was far more interesting. According to some obscure fan forums, many film buffs still saw it as one of the most well-made films of all time. I found posts where fans spent paragraphs discussing how Tag (as they referred to him) had staged and filmed the shots. If someone did bring up the racist elements of the film, they were basically told to shut up because it was old news.

"We're discussing technique," one rabid fan commented in response to another one who'd said *Living to Die* sickened her. "Go somewhere else for your liberal snowflake rant." Snowflake. I'd first encountered the term when someone had called Rufus a "snowflake," which still made me laugh, thinking about it. Sure, I could see how Rufus could be considered a liberal, but I *definitely* couldn't see how anyone might mistake Rufus for a snowflake. Serial killer with a streak of asshole, yeah, but snowflake, no. So, whenever I saw this term being used disparagingly, I immediately judged the person using the phrase as an idiot.

I clicked on the avatar of the fan who'd said this—his screen name was ifTHEsouthDONTrise. Clicking the avatar took me to his profile page, where he listed his presence on some other sites. He had a blog and something called Tumblr. I clicked on both only to find pages of racist and anti-Semitic screeds.

One of his posts was about Taggart Monroe's films. I clicked and read a mind-numbing essay about the "underappreciated genius" of Monroe and the laughable assertion that "all great minds are by definition racist." The reasoning behind the last statement was that most normal people or "normies," according to the author, didn't possess the intellectual abilities or honesty to see the world for what it was, one in which color *did* matter. Dark-skinned people were lower on the scale of humanity than lighter-skinned people.

I felt sick even reading this kind of thing, but I pushed on to the end of the essay anyway, simply because I owed it to Mary to exhaust every avenue. I was glad I did because the ending did not disappoint and made me understand exactly why Lane Jefferson might have targeted Mary.

> The very worst thing a person of any race can do is try to break out of the natural order. This is why I hate white people who will not affirm their divine rights as the keepers and rulers of this earth. It's why I hate colored people who try to take on positions of authority that should by right go to whites. Black women are the worst and most smug of all who commit these grievances. A black woman is God's lowest creature—

I stopped. There was more, but I just couldn't bring myself to read it. How could someone be so vile, so evil? Were people born like that, or had our world been so corrupted that they were altered as they grew older? Was it even possible that someone like this had once been a cute, innocent kid like Briscoe?

I knew it was, and that knowledge gutted me. I wanted to find the source of this evil. Find it and shut it off at the valve.

But no matter how badly I wanted that, I knew it was an impossibility. The best thing I could do for Briscoe and Virginia and all the kids like them was also the best thing I could do for myself, and that was finding Mary, a person whose light shone brighter than any I'd ever known in a world that always seemed to be getting darker.

When I looked up from the computer again, it was well after midnight, and the house was quiet. I glanced over at Shelia, still lying on the floor. She was so relaxed, so zoned out. Part of me envied her. Oh, to be in a place where I just didn't give a damn about anything. Even for a little while.

Of course, that was the kind of thinking that had created some of the worst moments I'd ever known. It was the addict's mentality, and I'd fought against it for most of my life.

Was I an addict?

Maybe. No, *probably*. But, for much of my life, I'd kept it right on the edge, able to alternate between long stretches of functionality and short, rapid-fire bursts of substance-induced forgetting.

Luckily, I'd managed to stay away from hard drugs, but I probably owed that more to my love affair with whiskey than to any kind of good decision-making on my part. Hell, right now, I wanted nothing more than some quick shots and a couple of beers. Then I'd be relaxed. Then I could let things go.

At least that was what I told myself. Sometimes the biggest lies we tell ourselves are when we think we are being brutally honest.

"You find anything?" Ronnie asked from the couch. I was surprised he was awake.

"I found enough to understand we're dealing with real depravity."

Martin, who was sitting beside Ronnie, with a glazed look in his eye, twitched suddenly.

"Sorry about your girlfriend," he said, and then leaned his head back and began to snore.

"Yeah, me too," I said, and left the kitchen to lie down on the floor beside Shelia and sleep.

36

The dream was more vivid than it had ever been. This time it began on the train trestle. I was standing there, holding Mary's hand while a train bore down on us from one side, and on the other side was Old Nathaniel, carrying a burning cross. Old Nathaniel seemed as much an apparition as a physical thing, and didn't walk or run toward us, but instead *floated*. The cross trailed long tongues of fire behind him. It was unclear which would reach us first, Old Nathaniel or the train, but there could be no mistaking that if we stayed put, we were trapped.

"We've got to jump," I said to Mary.

"No," she said. "The children."

"What children?" The words were no more out of my mouth when I saw them. Briscoe and Virginia both sat a few feet to my right, their legs dangling over the side of the train trestle just as Deja had dangled hers.

I sat up with a start and sucked in a deep breath, coughing it back out.

For a moment I didn't know where I was at all. Then Shelia spoke. "Can you feed Huckleberry?"

I stood up, stretching my sore muscles. I was far too old to spend the night swinging sledgehammers, hiding behind sofas, and—I cracked my back—crawling through fucking truck windows. Not to mention sleeping on the floor and experiencing dreams like that one. Jesus, I could still feel the panic surging through me when I'd seen Briscoe and Virginia on the train trestle.

I dug my phone out of my pocket. Dead.

"What time is it?" I asked the room. Ronnie and Martin didn't move from their spots sitting on the couch. Only Shelia raised her head.

"Hell if I know. You've got the phone."

"It just died. I need to make a call."

"Phone's by the computer," she said. I walked over, gradually becoming aware that Huckleberry was barking outside.

"He's hungry," Shelia said. "You going to feed him?"

"Give me a second," I said.

I picked up the phone and dialed Susan's number. It rang for a long time before she answered. "Hello?" Her voice sounded unsure.

"It's Earl."

"Oh, thank God. I've been trying to call you most of the night."

"What's wrong?"

"Someone came to the house last night. They knocked on the door. Loudly. I looked out the window, but the person was . . ."

"What? Tell me."

"The person was wearing a burlap sack over his head. Whoever it was was dressed like Old Nathaniel. I was going to call the police, but at that moment a rock came through the window. It nearly hit Rufus. Attached to the rock was a note."

"Jesus Christ."

"It said . . . hold on—I'll go get it."

A moment passed during which I closed my eyes and tried not to have a panic attack. How would I be able to find Mary *and* take care of Susan and those two kids?

"I've got it here. It says, 'This is just a warning. Call the police and the girl dies. If your boyfriend continues messing in our business, they both die.' "

"Okay," I said. "Can you bring the kids and pick me up? I'm in a little trouble right now."

"Sure, but what about last night? What should I do? Rufus said to talk to you, but I've been calling since three in the morning."

"I'm sorry. I was sleeping."

"Where are you?"

"With one of Ronnie's friends. I'll get you the address. Hang on."

Shelia managed to give me the address, which I relayed to Susan. "Look, I'm going to figure this out. Just come as soon as you can."

"Okay. Are you sure?"

"Positive. Can you put Rufus on?"

"Just a second."

About a minute later, Rufus said, "This is getting serious."

"You don't know the half of it. I spent most of the night following up on some leads, and it looks like Lane's friend Taggart Monroe is involved in some vile shit."

"What kind of vile shit?"

I took a deep breath. "I've got a hunch."

"Okay, let's hear it."

"Well, Ronnie and I broke into a warehouse last night that looked like it had been used to film movies. We even found some of an old script on a clipboard. This was the place Lane Jefferson used to pay his friend Pit to do security for. Anyway, someone obviously knew we were there because they called the cops. We got away, barely, but I'm thinking that was why the move was made on Susan and the kids."

"Could be."

"There's more."

"All right."

I swallowed, dreading Rufus's reaction. He always favored the most rational and logical approach to any situation, which was why I *really* dreaded telling him this next part.

"I think it's a possibility that Mary was taken for a snuff film."

He said nothing, but I could still hear his incredulity about the theory loud and clear. The phone line pretty much buzzed with disdain.

"Hear me out," I said.

"I ain't said a word."

"I know. But I also know you can speak without saying a word."

Again he said nothing.

"So, I found a microphone on the ground near Johnny that night. Near the place he claimed he was attacked by Old Nathaniel. And you found one too near the cave where Mary and I first saw Old Nathaniel and AOC written on the wall. And now the film warehouse. There's just too much to ignore."

He was still silent. It was killing me. But I knew I had to get the whole theory out. Because, despite Rufus's obvious skepticism *and* the fact that saying it out loud made it sound even sillier than it had been in my mind, it was the only damn thing I had. It represented a path forward. Sure it might peter out or lead me to a dead end, but at least it was somewhere to go. I'd been standing still for so long.

"What if someone was filming when Mary and Johnny were attacked? And what if that's just one scene and they're filming the rest later? You know how I mentioned doing some research last night? This Taggart guy is known for three things: making movies that are racist trash, being obsessed with moon cycles, and using three climaxes in his scenes."

Rufus was still silent, but this time I meant to wait him out. After a moment he said, "You've lost me."

"Okay. I guess I can see that. So, here it is. Working backward. The three climaxes. A fourteen-year-old boy has been missing since July. He's from the trailer park right next to the cornfield. His sister thinks Old Nathaniel got him, and I tend to agree, based on what she told me. That's one."

"One what?"

"One climax. Pay attention."

"Okay, I'm trying. You said there were three."

"Mary being taken. That could be another one."

"And the third?"

"Maybe it hasn't happened yet. Maybe that one will involve Mary too."

"Still not following. Even if I concede that Monroe and Jefferson are behind this, how could it involve her, if they already have her?"

"They have her, but I don't think they've killed her yet."

Silence.

"Shit, okay, maybe it's more wishful thinking than anything, but based on the moon cycle—that's Taggart's other obsession, remember—the next full moon is Thursday. If he was going to do the third and most explosive climax, wouldn't it make sense to do it on a full moon?"

"A lot of assumptions there, Earl—"

"I've got more."

"Okay . . ."

"The rally. What night is it?"

"Thursday."

"The night of the full moon. I think it was planned that way. If the rally is Thursday, all of the attention will be focused on downtown Riley. Taggart and Jefferson will have free reign to do as they see fit."

I paused to catch my breath. My heart was pounding in my chest. It was a stretch. I knew that. But after saying it out loud, it felt more plausible somehow. I waited while Rufus took his sweet time to respond.

He cleared his throat. "I think it's a pretty wild hunch, but it does have some interesting components. You need to disprove it so you can go to the next one."

That was actually way more support than I'd expected from Rufus. I let out the breath I'd been holding. "My thoughts exactly."

Now I just needed to figure out how to disprove it.

"Earl," he said, "what are we going to do about Susan and these kids?"

"I've got an idea about that."

"You want to share it?"

I looked over at Shelia. She was awake. "Not right now, but soon."

"Roger that. Earl?"

"Yeah?"

"When you find out about this hunch, I want you to know I'll be there to help you however I can."

"I know."

"I'm always willing and ready to talk. The only thing on my schedule is to protest Jeb Walsh on Thursday night."

"Got it," I said, and hung up the phone.

I couldn't help but feel a little worse after talking to him than I had before I'd called. Without coming out and saying it, I could tell Rufus was already thinking what I feared: that Mary was dead.

Why else all the stuff about wanting to be there for me? *I'm always ready and willing to talk.* It sounded like what you told a person who'd just lost a loved one.

"You know who you need to talk to?"

The voice surprised me. I looked up and saw that it was Shelia. She'd obviously been paying attention to the entire conversation.

"Who?"

"My ex. One of the reasons I left him was because he was into some dark shit."

I walked over to the chair I'd slept in and sat down. "Dark shit?"

"Yeah, he didn't really know when to stop. Like most people have a little thing inside them that says something's too far. You know, like it's okay to do drugs . . ." She smiled sheepishly. "But selling them? That's too far for me. I'm allowed to fuck up my own life, just not anybody else's. Well, Frank—that's my ex—he sold drugs and he did . . . other things . . . I couldn't tolerate."

"Like what?"

"I don't even want to say, but if anybody knows about snuff films, it's him. I'll bet he's seen his fair share."

"Does this ex have a last name?"

She nodded. "Bentley. Frank Bentley."

"Where can I find him?"

I suppose I was expecting to be given the address of some kind of out-of-the-way trailer or drug shanty kind of like this one, which explained why my mouth fell open when she answered my question.

"He's in Sommerville Chase."

37

Susan showed up at a little after ten. I shook Ronnie awake. "I wrote down Martin's number. I'll be in touch."

He nodded at me, then stood up to give me a hug. "Thanks," he said.

"For what? You're the one who saved my ass."

"For coming back for me. You didn't have to do that."

"Sure I did. Friends don't abandon their friends."

I never thought I'd live to see Ronnie Thrash cry, but that was exactly what I saw. A single tear wet the corner of his eye, and he nodded at me, patting my back.

"Well," I said, "let's see if Huck will let me by."

Luckily for me, Huck seemed to be elsewhere, and I jogged over to Susan's Honda Accord.

Rufus was in the back with the two kids, laughing at something. I climbed into the passenger seat, and Susan immediately put her hand on my arm. "We are *so* glad to see you. When I couldn't get you last night, I thought something had happened, and I panicked. I don't think I can do this without—" She stopped, suddenly aware that everyone—kids included—was listening to her.

She patted my arm. "I'm just glad you're okay."

"Me too," I said.

I turned around. "And how are you guys?"

Briscoe giggled and shouted something that sounded an awful

lot like "Earl." Virginia, ever calm, nodded slowly. "I think we're causing you problems."

"Nope," I said, probably a little more harshly than I intended. "You guys are doing the opposite of that. You guys are reminding me how important it is that I deal with my problems, and those don't have anything to do with you guys."

"You're just being nice," Virginia said. "I'm not stupid. If we were back with Mom, you'd be free to find your girlfriend."

I didn't have a good response for that, so I changed the subject. "You kids ever been to church?"

"Church!" Briscoe shouted.

Virginia rolled her eyes. "Mom sent us to church once. I didn't like it."

"Yeah, I had the same experience, but sometimes, in the right situation, churches can be good."

"What in the hell are you going on about, Earl?" Rufus said.

"I know where we can take the kids."

* * *

The Church of the Holy Flame was established in 1970 by my father. The original building, of course, now belonged to Rufus. Squatters rights, or maybe just the rights you get when most people are too freaked out to come near you. The next building was a hell of an upgrade. Situated on the affluent east side of Riley, the church featured a sanctuary that could hold over a thousand congregants. There was a gym, an assembly center, an outdoor amphitheater, and a separate day school. The view from the sanctuary's large windows was named by a local magazine as one of the top ten views in the state. What other church could claim such a thing?

Yes, my father had created a megachurch. His son—my brother, Lester—had kept it going, and now that Daddy was dead and Lester was in prison, I was hoping that a lot had changed and one thing had not.

With any luck, it would be a less fundamental place and a more Christian one. And hopefully, the Marcus name still carried some weight.

I was encouraged on the first point when I got out of the car and walked toward the main entrance. The orange flames that had covered the space above the doorway when my brother had been the minister were gone, replaced by four words: Love—Joy—Family—God. If there had been four words hanging on Daddy's version of the Holy Flame, they would have been Hell—Sin—Fornication—Damnation. At least if you wanted to go by the things he preached about the most.

I pulled the door open and immediately saw a familiar face: Stephanie Walton. At one time she'd been my father's personal assistant.

She tensed up when she saw me coming. Surely she wasn't still brainwashed enough to think I was somehow an agent of the devil? But as I drew closer, I saw that I might have read her reaction wrong. She stood up and came from behind the desk to embrace me.

Was she crying?

"Oh," she said. "I've spent the last year praying for you every day. I have never felt such conviction about anything in my life than I have about the way our whole community treated you."

"It's okay," I said. "Really. I'm here because . . . well, are you interested in making it up to me?"

"Absolutely."

"Wait here."

* * *

An hour later, Stephanie had made the necessary arrangements to ensure that Susan and the kids could stay in one of the preschool rooms. She called the current minister, a man named Art Stebbins, who I gathered had been hired as much due to his outsider status as his theology. Stebbins said he'd bring by some cots and blankets when he came up later in the day, and some food too.

The only problem was Rufus. I'd purposefully told him to wait in the car because Rufus carried all the same baggage I did without the Marcus name to help ease the judgment. And let's be honest. Rufus knew how to piss people off, especially the unenlightened, like he would assume these people were.

"I've got one more favor to ask," I said.

"Okay. Name it."

"There's a blind man I know . . ."

"Oh no."

"Yeah, he needs a place to stay too."

She raised an eyebrow. "His name wouldn't happen to be Rufus, would it?"

"Yeah. You remember him?"

"How could I forget? He's not the kind of man to keep his nose out of anything. Do you know he was the only person who showed up to protest the new wing we built under Brother Stebbins? Oh no, I don't think that is going to fly with our members."

"Here's the thing, Stephanie. The members don't have to know. What if I promise Rufus will behave? That he'll keep a low profile?"

"I don't know," she said.

"It can be our secret. No need to even tell the pastor."

"I don't understand why he has to come too. He should be able to take care of himself."

"He's blind. But that's not the reason I want him to come. He can take care of himself. I want him to be here to help Susan take care of the kids."

Susan, who'd been very quiet through all of this, cleared her throat. "I'm sorry, but I've got to wonder about a church that picks and chooses who it helps. I don't remember Jesus refusing the leper because he wasn't good enough."

Susan had a kind of sternness that seemed to be the province of teachers and librarians. When she made a point, she made it clearly and firmly, and it was very difficult to argue with. Stephanie shrugged. "Fine, but Brother Stebbins can't find out."

38

Rufus didn't like it very much when I told him where we were. He liked it even less when I told him he needed to be invisible and most of all keep his mouth shut. But in the end, Rufus knew it wasn't about him. It was about those two kids and Susan. So, he went inside begrudgingly, leaving me with Susan's car and the rest of the afternoon to look for Mary.

I drove back to my house and charged my phone while I fed Goose and made myself a large meal. I stared at the whiskey for a very long time before the beep from my phone finally broke my trance. I looked at my phone and saw I had eleven messages. Ten of them were from Rufus or Susan from the night before.

The other one was from the sheriff's office.

I listened to the voicemail, expecting to hear something about the warehouse or even the fight in the bathroom with Jeb Walsh.

"Earl, this is Sheriff Patterson. Hell. I don't know where to start exactly. First off, you need to turn yourself in for whatever that shit was last night. We've got your truck at the scene of a break-in at the old warehouse on Summer Mountain. I've showed all the patience I can with you. Go ahead and just turn yourself in, and I'll talk to the DA about making it easy on you. Nothing I'll be able to do for Ronnie Thrash, though. His antics caused one of my deputies to tear a damn ligament chasing him down the mountain. But—shit—forget that. It's all minor compared to what I'm about to tell you."

He was silent for a moment, and I panicked, thinking my voicemail had become too full and cut him off. But then his voice came back.

"Johnny is gone. We found his cell empty yesterday afternoon." Another pause. "We don't know how he got out. The deputy on duty stepped away from her post for a few minutes, and we think that's when it happened. But that ain't even the real news."

Another pause. I felt my hand tightening around the phone.

"The real news is what one of my deputies found over near the cornfield. It was a human skull. Well, it was a head, but a lot of the skull was exposed. Shit, it looked like the face had been ripped clean off. It's going to be a bit before forensics can get back to us, but I have to tell you it look—"

The phone beeped and a female voice said, "End of messages."

I dropped my phone and tried to breathe.

I'd never had a panic attack in my life until the night Mary went missing. This was my second one. I couldn't breathe. No matter how hard I tried.

I sat down at my kitchen table and put my face in my hands. I tried to be very still. I fell into sleep quickly, and the dream came in brilliant flashing images, like a film played against the back of my eyelids.

When I woke up again, I wasn't sure how much time had passed, but my breathing was normal. I sat there, swimming in the broken images of the dream, trying to recall the moments that had made me sweat and shake and gnash my teeth just moments earlier.

The train was coming in the dream, the sound of it shaking the whole dark world. I looked up and saw the moon, full and bright in the sky. I was in the cornfield, surrounded by the tall stalks. Corn silk blew down like ragged threads from some tantalizing thought I could not quite grasp. The train trestle appeared, and I ran toward it, as if it were salvation, but like so many of the things that we expect to save us, I knew it was really the thing that would kill me. I kept running toward it anyway.

And then the train was coming at me so fast and hard that I had no choice but to jump. As I fell, I saw Mary in the water below, waiting to catch me.

* * *

When I got moving again, I drove to the hardware store in Riley and bought an exacto knife and some superglue. Back out at the Accord, I took the clipboard, turned it over, and went to work scraping the yellow sticker with the skull and axe handles off the back. It was an arduous task that required extreme patience. I needed to peel off the thin top layer of the sticker while keeping it intact. After thirty minutes, carefully chipping away at it with the exacto knife, I had it off with only a minor tear.

I went to the front of the car and found a clean spot on the Accord's windshield on the passenger's side. I squeezed out a tiny amount of superglue and then pressed the thin sticker onto it. I held it in place for nearly five minutes without moving. When I let go, the sticker seemed firmly in place, though the real test would be when I drove.

I waited for another hour, as the sun set, before cranking up the Accord and heading for Summer Mountain and Frank Bentley's house.

* * *

I wasn't too familiar with Summer Mountain. Other than the trip I'd made the night before with Ronnie, I wasn't sure if I'd ever been here before. I'd certainly never been inside Sommerville Chase before. Hell, nothing like that even existed when I'd been a kid, but things were definitely changing.

When I'd come up in these mountains over thirty years ago, the racism and misogyny had had as much to do with ignorance and poor education as it had with pure hatred. Sure, it was still vile, and men like my father who perpetuated it and capitalized on it were beyond reprehensible. Yet, what seemed to be happening now with Jeb Walsh—and all the people who put these yellow Skull Keep stickers on their vehicles—felt meaner, more despicable somehow, as if it were an extension—or maybe a better word was a *symptom*—of the corrosion of goodwill and basic decency that seemed to be pervading so many parts of our country.

Of course, there were some who would always follow a persuasive leader, but I couldn't help but draw a distinction between folks who didn't have the worldly experience and education to know better and those that did. The latter seemed unspeakably vile to me, and try as I might to focus on what was ahead of me, my mind kept turning back to the skull they'd found in the woods near the cornfield and the idea that somehow, behind it all, Jeb Walsh was responsible.

I was forced to finally abandon my obsessive thoughts about what the deputy had found in the woods, and Walsh's guilt, when I finally reached the town square in the heart of Sommerville Chase. I slowed down, taking in the newly built area, which, in short, was everything that Ghost Creek Mountain, where I'd grown up, was not.

As nice as downtown Riley had become, this little area put it to shame. Everything was new and shiny, but somehow also retro and classic, as if it were a hidden pearl that had been on this mountain forever but had only just been discovered. There was an ice cream shop called Sweet Dreams, where young parents with strollers stood in line behind retirees holding hands. Across the street from Sweet Dreams was a steakhouse called Steak Masters, and next to that was the Sommerville Mountain Brew House.

The road veered sharply to the right around a spectacular fountain that launched plumes of glowing water into the night sky. There were at least fifteen people gathered around the fountain, mostly teenagers, talking and watching the water as it exploded up and out, only to come back down in thick, colorless globs that splattered on the pavement and sometimes on the bystanders (much to their delight). Once around the fountain, the road began to rise again. At the top of this rise, there was a library and post office, both closed. According to the GPS on my phone, I was three miles from Frank Bentley's place.

It was full dark, save the three-quarters moon, when the car in front of me pulled up to the gates of Sommerville. I rolled the Accord's window down to hear what the guy driving said to the guard who controlled the gate, but the wind was blowing too hard to catch anything.

The guard flipped through some pages on a clipboard and nodded at the driver. I eased up next, and the guard greeted me with a nod. He was somewhere north of fifty and wore a mustache over his downturned lips.

"Hello," I said. "Heading up to Frank Bentley's place." As I said it, I pointed at the sticker on Susan's windshield.

He squinted out at the Accord, which was in good shape and well-cared for, but despite that, was still a major step down from the kind of vehicle that would normally come through these gates.

"It's my daughter's," I said, and immediately regretted it when he gave me a funny look. Over-explaining was a surefire way to draw unwanted attention. I needed to get my game face on and quick.

"Your name?" he said.

"Bob Jenkins. I doubt it's on your list. Frank told me the sticker should be enough."

He scanned the list anyway, wetting his thumb before flipping each page. I waited, the night air growing heavy, my heart beginning to pound against my chest.

"Yeah, I don't see it on here."

"Well, I didn't think you would," I said, keeping my voice lazy, nonchalant.

"You say you got some sticker or something?" He leaned over, craning his neck at my windshield.

"Yeah, hell. I didn't know this was going to be such a pain in the ass."

"Just hold on. It's only my third night. Let me call my supervisor. I ain't never seen a place with so many damned exceptions in my life. I'm sure it's good enough to get you through. Hell, they might as well just open these damned gates with all the exceptions they make.

This damned list ain't worth a flip." He tossed it down inside the guardhouse and picked up the phone. I watched him make the call. He talked for a minute, shaking his head and then hung up the phone. He seemed angry. I didn't know if that was good or bad.

He stepped out of the guardhouse with a flashlight and walked around to the other side of the Accord and shined the light at the sticker.

He flipped the light off and came back to the window. "Go on. But my boss said you need to go ahead and get Mr. Bentley to put you on the list. We ain't supposed to let nobody in based on the sticker no more, he said. I told him you didn't look like trouble, though, and he figured if you were going to Bentley's, it would make sense you weren't on the list because he's always forgetting to put folks on and then raising hell when we don't let them in."

I tipped my hat at him. "Sounds just like Frank. Have a good one, my friend."

He raised the gate, and I eased the Honda through into the most spectacularly obscene neighborhood I'd ever laid eyes on.

* * *

The entire area was well lit with street lamps, and many of the residents were taking advantage, strolling along the sidewalks, lounging on porches, around stone fire pits, and in some cases just standing in the well-manicured lawns, drinking cans of beer. I couldn't help but notice that all the people I saw looked like they belonged. Which was to say, they were white, attractive, and somehow oozed a sense of money and privilege like I had rarely encountered.

Against all odds, the houses grew larger and larger as the elevation rose. By the time I reached another fountain—this one less colorful than the previous one—and stayed right, as the GPS instructed, the houses were so large, I began to wonder if perhaps they were apartment homes made to look like houses, but I knew better. There could be no apartments in an area like this.

I parked a few houses down from the one that the GPS told me was Bentley's. Now came the hard part. Waiting, hoping he'd leave the house. Short of that, waiting until I had the nerve to knock on the door.

I let the window down, and the breeze came in. The summer felt like it was officially gone, replaced at long last by what I knew would be an all-too-brief fall. In the South, especially the mountains, fall was the very best time of the year, but like all the best things, it lasted only a short time, crowded out on one side by a stifling summer and on the other by the cold, dry winter.

I watched the house and saw a man through one of the large windows. He was holding a remote and pointing it at a gigantic television. He didn't look like he planned on going anywhere tonight.

Fuck it.

I climbed out of the Accord, leaving it unlocked and taking a moment to make sure my 9mm was tucked safely into the back of my jeans, before walking up to his house and knocking on the door.

A couple of minutes later, there was a beep and a voice came out of a speaker above me.

"Yes?"

"I'm here from the neighborhood association. I need to talk to you about a complaint."

"Say that again?"

"Complaint. Two of your neighbors have filed them against you. I'm here to deliver the official citation."

"Is this some kind of joke?" the voice said.

"No, sir."

"Chrissake. What's the complaint about?"

"It's all on the citation, Mr. Bentley."

"Fuck. Hold on."

I couldn't believe it had been so easy. I'd actually had a backup plan, which included mentioning the sticker if he didn't buy the complaint angle.

The door swung open, and a small man stood before me. He was barefoot and wore a pair of gold gym shorts and a tank top. He looked like he worked out, but he was small compared to me, and I was pretty sure if it came to a fight, I'd be all right.

"Well," he said, "where is it?"

I reached for the gun. "Right here."

He stepped back, his hands in the air.

"Is anyone else home?" I asked.

"I live by myself. What is this about? How did you get through the gates?"

"I told the guy I was coming to whip your ass and he let me right in." I stepped inside and closed the door.

"Who are you?"

"Think of me as your preacher. You a religious man?"

"No—"

"Well, it's time you find the Lord, Frank. The first thing a new Christian has to do is confess his sins. So that's what I want you to do. Right now."

"Is this about the election, the thing with the underage girls? Because that was dropped in court. It's old news. I can't be—"

"This isn't about that."

"Oh . . . okay." He seemed relieved in the way only a guilty man could. I decided not to cut him any breaks.

"It's about your film collection."

He shook his head. "I don't—"

I rushed him, slamming the tip of my 9mm against his forehead. He stiffened, growing perfectly still, even as a line of drool ran down the side of his face.

"Don't fucking lie to me, okay?"

He nodded.

"Because I already know everything I need to know about your sins. Remember, I'm your preacher. You live in these mountains and you didn't know preachers knew everything?"

"I didn't know," he said, gasping the words.

"Well, now you do. So, tell me about your film collection. The *snuff* films."

"Oh, shit. Okay. Is that what this is about? Jesus, yeah, I've watched a few. Look, I'm not a bad guy. I'm just interested in the extremes of human behavior. The way—"

"Shut up. I need to know where you get them."

"What?"

"Where do you purchase them, asshole?"

"Oh, okay. I understand. There's a place over in The Fingers where—"

"The Fingers? Which mountain?"

"Uh, I think it's Ring. Yeah, Ring Mountain. It's a little pawnshop in a trailer. Dude sells them there."

"Okay, I think I know the place. Now, think really hard about this next question, okay, Frankie?"

"Sure. I'll answer it. Whatever, man. I got nothing to hide."

"Do you know of anyone around here who films them?"

"Films what?"

I kicked him in the knee. Hard enough to double him over. He moaned, grasping his leg. I put my palm on the top of his head and pushed him over until he was lying on his back. I put a foot on either side of his chest, straddling him and pointing my gun straight down at his face.

"Do you know of anyone around here who makes snuff films?"

He shook his head. "No."

"I don't believe you."

He started to cry then. "I wish I did. I swear, I wish I did. The only thing . . . the only thing is that I've heard somebody's making one."

"Who did you hear it from?" I leaned forward, putting both hands on the gun, as if bracing for a shot.

"Just some guy at a bar. I don't even know his name."

"What bar?"

"The brewery down the road."

"So a rich dude?"

"Yeah, I guess."

"Who did he say was making it?"

"He didn't say. He just said it was going to be about Old Nathaniel killing some black kids."

"And what did you say?"

He held up his hands. "I told him that it sounded good and asked him how I could get a copy."

"I ought to shoot you right now," I said, and I meant it too. I couldn't remember the last time I'd felt so angry, so out of control. What kind of a man was I dealing with here?

"No, no. I'm not a bad guy, okay? I just . . . I just like to watch. That's all."

I took a deep breath and nodded. "Okay, this is the way we're going to do the last question."

"I've been honest," he said. "So honest."

"Just listen. I'm going to ask the last question, and you are going to tell me the truth or I'm going to shoot you."

"What? What if I tell you the truth and you think I'm lying?"

"Too bad."

"No, please!"

"Just don't lie," I said. "If I was going to leave here and go see someone who *would* know about this snuff film, who should I go visit?"

He stared at me, and I could tell he knew. He was trying to think of a way he could lie, or maybe he was trying to determine just how crazy I was. If it was the latter, it meant whoever he knew was pretty damned scary too. I didn't doubt it.

"I need an answer," I said.

He nodded. "Okay. There's a little house down in the valley."

"The valley? Which valley?"

"The Devil's Valley. Corn Valley, whatever. Where the blacks live. Except this house is on the other side of the cornfield. If you go there, you'll find what you're looking for."

"What will I find? Be more specific."

"You'll find the man you're looking for. He's the one that can get you the movies."

"Like he got them for you?"

"I don't own nothing. He showed it to me there. At his house."

"What's his name?"

"Hell if I know. He's a scary dude. Tall. Tattoos."

"Tell me how to get there."

"It's . . . shit. Go like you're going to the cornfield, but instead of turning left on the road with the old water tower, stay straight. It looks like just woods, but those go away after a while, and you'll see the cornfield again. Keep going until you see a little unnamed road. It'll take you right to it."

"If I get there and don't find anything helpful or it's some kind of trap, I'm coming back, Frank. Do you understand?"

"Sure. Yeah. How did you find out about . . . Who are you?"

"I already told you. I'm the Preacher, Frank. Don't forget. Preachers always know."

"I understand. You won't be disappointed."

"I'm disappointed just looking at you," I said.

He shook his head. "I'm not a bad guy, not like him. Like I said, I'm a just watcher. I can't get too close to the real action. I have to keep my hands clean. See, I'm not so—"

He was probably going to say *bad* but I slapped him with the back of my hand, and whatever he meant to say turned into a groan. I got off him and walked out of his house, knowing I didn't have much time to get out of the neighborhood before I wouldn't be able to get out at all.

39

I stayed straight instead of turning on the road that would take me to the water tower. The landscape was just as Bentley had described. It looked like I was going into a deep forest, but the dense trees didn't last too long before they scattered and gave way to long, rolling fields. I drove another mile before spotting a gravel road on my left. It ran between scrub pines on one side and a winding creek on the other. I made the turn, creeping along the gravel road, gripping the wheel tightly, hunched forward, alert and tense.

It was a trap. I knew that almost as soon as Bentley had mentioned the place, but I didn't care. I was willing to take my chances with a trap. I'd survived them before, and I figured knowing was half the battle anyway.

Holding the wheel steady with my knee, I withdrew my 9mm and double-checked to make sure it was loaded. I took the safety off and laid it on the passenger's seat next to me.

On my left, the creek had wandered away and been replaced by the ruins of old homes, some wrapped in kudzu vines and others roofless and burned to husks.

On my right, the scrub pines vanished, and now scattered cornstalks stood in their place. As I eased forward, the road became rougher, and tiny pieces of gravel pinged off the undercarriage of the Honda. The cornstalks grew more dense like a gathering storm, assembling its wrath, slowly, methodically, and I felt a chill opening up inside me as I realized where we were. This really was just the other side of the cornfield. The best I could tell, we were on the opposite end, as far away from the Blackclaw River and Deja's trailer park as possible, just as Bentley had described it.

The gravel road turned to dirt and then to just tire ruts. Ahead was a tiny house with a light on inside. It was in much better shape than the ruins I'd passed earlier, but it still didn't exactly look like a place suitable for living. Pieces of the roof were missing, and the shutters near the front windows had been torn off, most likely by a storm.

There was a Corolla parked in front of the house. Several lights were on inside and there were no blinds. I saw a kitchen and what looked like a den.

I scanned the area again before getting out of the truck. Other than the car, I didn't see anything. I decided to stay put anyway. That was when I saw someone in the kitchen, a man, standing in front of an open refrigerator, peering inside.

The yard was deserted. The cornfield was on my right. It waved silently, as if in greeting. From where I sat inside my truck, it appeared to stretch around the corner of the house and into the backyard. I looked left and saw only open space, the land dipping and rising before a line of darkly outlined pines like bottlebrush cleaners stood against the shredded wreckage of fading silver clouds.

I slipped out of the truck, gun in hand, and started toward the house. I could still see the man—he looked on the young side—through the window. He was drinking from a can now, unaware of me, or at least pretending to be. A bristling sound came from the cornfield on my right, and I spun, clutching the gun with both hands, ready to fire, but the sound was gone, and the cornfield stood unmoving. Gradually I lowered the weapon and stepped toward the door.

It was cracked—a sign that he was expecting me? A sign that I could literally be walking into a trap, but I couldn't stop myself. It seemed like Mary had been gone for months instead of days, and for the first time since she'd been missing, I felt close, really close, to finding out what had happened and where she was.

The door groaned as I pushed it open, and I stepped into a darkened room. I reached for the light switch, but when I flipped it, nothing happened. Burned out.

"Knock-knock," I said.

No reply, just the wind picking up in the cornfield.

"Hey," I said. "I'm coming in."

I heard footsteps in the next room, and then a door opened, and he was in the hallway. He didn't turn to face me; instead, he walked down the corridor and made a right, disappearing into another room.

"Come out of there. I'd like to talk to you," I said, but in the silence of the house my voice sounded weak and impotent. He wasn't coming out. I knew I should leave.

In fact, this sudden urge to leave was nearly overwhelming, and I recognized it as originating from the same place my prophetic dreams came from—the snake venom, the life-changing moment of being struck down by a serpent, the poison still swimming somewhere in my bloodstream.

The black water, still rising . . .

But even as I recognized the source of the feeling and realized the urgency of it, I chose to ignore it. I was too close.

Too close to turn back.

I made it to the end of the hallway and saw that, again, he'd left the bedroom door ajar, an invitation . . . there was no other way to interpret it.

I pushed it open and saw that the room was nearly dark, but not quite. A single bare bulb burned dimly from a bedside lamp. A stripped mattress lay on the floor. On top of the mattress was a calendar and some faded yellow papers.

But as much as I wanted to look at those, my eyes were drawn to the other side of the room, where a door leading to the backyard had been left open. The wind blew slightly, causing it to creak and open far enough to reveal the man, standing beside a picnic table in the backyard, his face lit momentarily by the orange flare of his cigarette as he took a drag.

I recognized him. He was the kid from the bathroom at Jessamine's, the one I'd been in the process of beating down before Jeb Walsh and Preston Argent had come in.

He was looking at me and waved me out to join him with a quick, casual gesture.

"Remember me?"

"Yeah."

I opened the door all the way and stepped into the backyard. There wasn't much of it. Just some weeds surrounding the picnic table, an old shed, and behind it all, the giant stalks that I knew stretched on for miles, all the way over to the train tracks and the trestle, where I was becoming increasingly sure I might die, assuming I survived tonight, that is.

A single floodlight illuminated most of the backyard and a swath of the cornfield, turning the husks and tassels to pale flames that flickered endlessly.

"We didn't really get properly introduced in the bathroom," he said. "I'm Jason."

"I was told to come here. I want to know about the snuff films."

Jason laughed. "You do? Well, shit." He put a knee up on the picnic bench and watched me. He smiled around his cigarette and gestured at my gun. "Why don't you put that away? You said you wanted to talk. You don't need a gun for that."

I circled him and the table until I was on the other side, my back to the cornfield, but I didn't lower the gun.

"I'll hold on to it, thanks," I said.

He shrugged. "Okay. Have a seat." He sat down on the picnic bench across from me, reached into his shirt pocket, and pulled out another cigarette. "Want one?"

I shook my head.

He returned the cigarette to his pocket and continued to smoke, seemingly relaxed, taking his time, watching the smoke rise into the night air and dissipate out over the cornfield.

"You wanted to talk?" he said. He glanced at me. "Still with the gun? Jesus, man. Put it down. You and me both know you're not going to shoot me. Right? I mean, you didn't shoot me that night in the bathroom, did you? Shit, you didn't even hit me all that hard. Mr. Walsh has a term for men like you."

"And what's that?"

"Limp-dicked liberal," he said, giggling.

I put the gun on the table between us.

It was a trap, right?

Fine, I thought. *Bring it on.*

I sat down on the opposite bench. He leaned forward, smiling. "Ask me anything."

"Where's Mary?"

He cocked his head to one side as if he hadn't heard me. "Who?"

"Mary," I said, "my girlfriend."

"Ohhh, you mean the negress."

"Excuse me?"

"You don't like that term?"

"No," I said, and my mouth felt sour and dry with anger and something else aching inside of me, rumbling.

"Well, it won't matter in a few days now, will it?"

"Where are they keeping her?"

He laughed. "I heard they had her right in the belly of the beast."

"What's that mean? The belly of the—"

"Skull Keep. It's the place where he puts all the skulls. It's a bunker somewhere out there." He motioned nonchalantly toward the vast cornfield behind me. It's well hidden they say, which is probably why they're keeping her there."

"Jeb told you this?"

He shrugged. "I heard it from lots of people. Important people. People who actually see potential in me."

"You said *they* put her there. Who is *they*?"

He leaned across the table, as if he was about to share something confidential with me. "Can I ask you something? Just between you and me?"

I held my breath. Made no movement at all other than my fingers flexing involuntarily toward the gun that lay between us.

"You know what they say about black men, you know big dicks and all? I was wondering if there was anything special about the women. You know, maybe like they're—"

I picked up the gun and swung it at his head in what amounted to one smooth—and ferocious—motion, clipping him across the temple with a dull thunk. He sat up straight, his mouth still moving but saying nothing.

His mouth snapped shut and his hand moved to the wound the gun had left on his temple.

"What did you do?!" he said. I was on my way around the table, to beat the information out of him, when a cornstalk snapped behind me.

I spun around, gun raised, as the wind drifted out of the field and cooled the sweat on my brow. The three-quarters moon hung low over the cornstalks. The breeze died against my skin, and a hush fell over the backyard and the furrows of corn that stretched away as far as the eye could see.

Another sound, this one a rattling. One of the stalks, a few rows deep, moved, bending sideways, as something seemed to slide into its place, a walking scarecrow, now still and silent, blending into the field. It sounded like what Mary and I had heard moments before she disappeared.

And now, there was more than hearing. I'd *seen* something too. The sliding into place. The stalk or scarecrow or man. Right there, pulsing ever so slowly with every beat of the field.

Or was it just a trick of the eye, so many stalks sweeping their tassels against the dark canvas of the night that I was bound to see something else?

I lifted the gun again, aiming it directly at the strange stalklike man and squeezed off a shot.

The night cracked open. Bats burst free of the field, leaving gossamer strands of corn silk floating across the swollen moon.

The cornstalk did not move. Just a trick of the eye, I decided, and was about to turn back around to deal with Jason, when I suddenly realized he had gone strangely quiet.

He led with his shoulder, crashing into my side and knocking the wind out of me. My legs went weak, and I fell to the ground.

The gun.

It came free from my hand. I patted the ground for it but found nothing, my hands landing hard on the dry, dusty ground.

Jason loomed over me, and I was about to reach for his leg to pull him down with me, when he suddenly stepped away. Something was really coming through the corn. There could be no denying it now.

I turned, still trying to catch my breath, and saw a tall figure striding through the stalks. The man—or woman because it was impossible to tell which—stood at the edge of the cornfield, holding a large, curved knife. The reason I couldn't determine if the figure was male or female was because there was a burlap sack over the person's face. Eyeholes had been cut into the sack, and the bag had been cinched tight around the neck with a thin rope. The remainder of the outfit was a gray uniform, like one that a confederate soldier might have worn a hundred and fifty years ago.

"Shit," Jason said. "Took you long enough."

My breath came back all at once, and I rolled away from the masked figure, scrambling to my feet.

"Who are you?" I said. "Take off the damned mask." I didn't expect an answer; I was only trying to buy some time in order to locate my gun, so when the male voice responded, I gasped.

"You can call me Nathaniel."

Old Nathaniel lunged at me, leading with the knife. I dove to the right—not daring a dive into the cornfield, where I felt certain I'd never come out alive—and collided with Jason. We both went down, tangled together.

Old Nathaniel loomed over us, and despite my best efforts, I wasn't able to extract myself from Jason, who was now on top of me.

Old Nathaniel brought the knife down, and I heard Jason gasp. I pushed him off me and slid away.

"Why?" Jason said, as blood ran out of his back into the grass, pooling quickly.

Old Nathaniel didn't answer. He only brought the knife down again, this time burying it in the boy's neck.

When he turned his attention back to me, I was already in the air.

I'd launched myself with everything I had into Old Nathaniel's midsection, taking my cue from what Jason had done to me just minutes before.

I knocked him back, but not down. Something cold and then hot seared my hip, and I knew he'd cut me. I reached up for his mask and got a hand on it, wrenching it with all my might. The thin rope that kept it tied in place came loose, and the mask twisted in my hand, revealing a patch of flesh just below the assailant's ear. The neck that revealed itself in the floodlight was thick and patched with five o'clock shadow. I glimpsed a dark tattoo in the shape of a strawberry and then my fingers lost their grip on the burlap and the mask fell back over the man's face, covering it fully.

He swung the knife again, this time nicking my side, shredding the hem of my shirt. I reached in again, risking another cut from the knife, and grabbed the sack a second time. He sliced down, meaning to cut my arm clear off, but I twisted and rolled out of the way of the knife, still holding the burlap sack, but not for long. My fingers burned as the rough sack slipped free again.

I fell back onto my gun. Later, I'd wonder if that little piece of luck had been the thing that saved my life. Sometimes it seemed as if survival, like evil, was random and unthinking, that there was little a man could do to make his life go right, to find happiness, that sometimes he just had to hope he fell in the right spot.

And even luck guaranteed nothing.

My first shot missed.

Before I could get my next shot aimed and fired, Old Nathaniel, who was at least six feet from the edge of the cornfield, covered the entire distance, vanishing into the waves of tassels, husks, and corn as if he'd never been there at all.

My second shot seemed on target as I got it off, but the sounds of the cornstalks, snapping, bending, and rustling, told me I'd missed.

Briefly, I considered following him, but I felt like I was damned lucky to still be alive after our encounter *outside* the cornfield, and going in after him would be suicide.

40

My hip was worse than I'd originally thought. Not only would it not stop bleeding, it also hurt like hell. I rummaged through the drawers in the bedroom of the old house and found a dirty pair of sweatpants, which I tied as tightly as I could around my hip. The blood soaked through the sweatpants within minutes.

I went through several kitchen drawers until I found some duct tape. I untied the sweatpants, dropped my jeans and my blood-stained boxers and wiped at the wound with paper towels. I stuck a thick wad of paper towels on my hip and pressed my bare ass hard against the refrigerator to keep it in place while I worked some of the duct tape free with my hands. Once I had the tape ready, I stood up straight and pulled the wad of paper towels out of the cut. As soon as I did, I placed the duct tape directly on the wound, pressing it flat. I followed the first piece with several others, and pulled my jeans back up, sans underwear. I ran some water over the underwear, and used them to wipe the blood off the refrigerator and floor.

Unfortunately, there wasn't a phone in the house to call the sheriff, and I didn't want to use mine. Using mine meant he'd know I'd been here, and at this point, that was just unacceptable. Hell, I'd be the number-one suspect in the kid's murder. And explaining why I was here would only force me to talk about how I'd held Frank Bentley at gunpoint. While I really wanted to believe that Patterson was one of the good guys, I also understood that being a good guy meant arresting men like me who went around the law out of desperation.

I walked back outside and searched Jason's pockets until I found his phone. Just in case, I picked it up with a kitchen towel to keep my prints off it. I carried it back inside and laid it on the kitchen counter. My hip felt like it was melting from the inside out. I could really use some whiskey, but it would have to wait.

I found a pencil on the kitchen counter and pressed the phone's home button with the eraser end. Passcode required. Shit.

Using the pencil, I selected "emergency" and the phone connected me to 911.

I reported the crime anonymously, being sure to mention the burlap sack and the fact that the killer had emerged from the cornfield. When the operator asked for an address, I didn't know what to tell her.

"Can you track the phone?"

"You'll have to stay on the line."

"Sure," I said. "I'll do that."

I laid the phone on the kitchen counter and started to limp out, when something caught my eye. It was hanging on the refrigerator, an invitation.

Neal, You're invited to a cast party, it read. *10/4 at Tag's place. Party starts at 9 and runs until the sun comes up . . .*

There was an address and a gate code. I pulled out my phone and took a photo before continuing to limp to Susan's car. Once inside, I tossed the bloody underwear in the backseat, and eased down onto the injured hip. A new, sick kind of pain broke out, one that radiated up from the hip, through my stomach, and into my neck.

I gritted my teeth until it eased a little and then cranked the car and started back down the primitive road.

* * *

By the time I reached Riley, I was starting to feel like I might not make it. I'd blacked out once already, only to be jolted awake when an oncoming vehicle blasted its horn at me as the Honda drifted into the wrong lane. I righted it and focused on staying awake, which, I reasoned, had become the same thing as staying alive.

Focus on living, Earl. Not the pain. Or, hell, focus on the pain if it helps you stay alive. Awake. Alive. Both.

A tree was suddenly in my path. I swerved just in time to avoid it, but the sudden turn caused me to run off the road. The car died. I looked around. I wasn't far from the Holy Flame now.

If I could get there, I could give in to the pain, just go ahead and pass out. The church would almost certainly have a first aid kit, and Susan could put a real bandage on it, give me something to ease the pain . . .

I laid my head against the steering wheel.

When I lifted it again, it was only because of the blood. It was pooling in my seat, soaking through my jeans, warm against my ass and crotch.

I cranked the Accord again and pulled back out onto the road like a drunk, weaving and running up against the curb. Everything felt dark, darker than usual, and I turned on my brights. An oncoming car flashed brights back at me, angrily. I saw the sign ahead.

The Church of the Holy Flame.

I never imagined it being a place of salvation, but that was exactly what it was for me tonight.

I made the turn and then pointed the Honda at the awning near the front entrance. The car came to a stop when it hit the brick wall of the church. I opened the door to get out, but instead of stepping to the ground, I stumbled and fell, landing hard in the parking lot. I struggled to my feet, somehow understanding even in the deep fog of pain that my life might depend on getting to the door. That and somebody waking up soon enough to help me.

I made it to the awning, stumbled, and fell right at the double glass doors. I lay there for a moment before looking up, as if hoping I could get someone to help me just by using my eyes.

There was no one there. Not at first.

Then, gradually, I saw a shape behind the glass. One of the doors moved slightly, trembling, as it opened wider. A man stepped out, wearing my father's old boots.

At first, I couldn't get beyond the boots. They were Daddy's all right. He'd always had a thing for flashy boots. The rest of him was hard and grim and unrelentingly stoic, but he favored boots with intricate stitchwork done over bright brown, almost orange, leather. His most treasured pair had been handmade by one of his favorite members, a woman named Myrtle, who was so smitten with him, it was hard to imagine they hadn't carried on an affair at one time or another during their long relationship. These were the boots Myrtle had made. She'd stitched three snakes on each one, their forked tongues stretching and growing into flames that ran around to the front of the boots and licked the area where Daddy's toes would have been.

Slowly, I lifted my eyes from the boots up to his face.

"Look at you, coming home when you need the Lord," he said. "That's about right, though. I gave you all the chances in the world, and what did you do with it? Ran after some mulatto bitch and killed your own flesh and blood. Made sure to get the only other kin you had left locked away over in Hays. Here you go, Earl. Look around. This is what you earned in this life. You gonna bleed out right here on the damned steps of the house I built for you."

I shook my head at him. "No, not yet. I've still got to meet the black water. That snake you handed me gave me one more thing I never wanted."

"You never wanted anything but pussy anyway," this foul-mouthed ghost version of my father said. "What kind of man lives some fifty-odd years and leaves a legacy like that?"

"A better man than you," I said, but I was losing consciousness, and I wasn't sure how much I said or didn't say out loud. In fact, I wasn't sure of very much at all. Was there really someone standing over me? Was I even still alive?

I felt something inside me crack, and a great whooshing pain filled my lungs. That was all I needed. I was alive. The pain was the memory of Mary, the thought of dying right here. The wind inside me brought something else too, a flash of her face, stricken with fear, or . . . no, not fear. It was concern. Her face was stricken with concern for me.

She was standing over me now. Daddy was gone. Just Mary and me, and her mouth was moving, but I couldn't hear her or read her lips. My ears felt like they'd been filled with a long, slow crashing sound, or maybe it was the sound of water sloshing back and forth, in and out of my ear canals.

Her face disappeared, eclipsed by the night sky, filled with countless stars, none of which could come close to alleviating the dark pain that had entered me because Daddy was right: I had needed saving all along. Just not by his God.

41

Tuesday passed in a blur. My memory of it was like a deck of scattered cards, each one holding a poorly sketched image of a moment that might or might not have really occurred.

Mary's face came and went, the look of concern predominant, but sometimes she smiled, and once she whispered to me, telling me secrets that made me clench my fists and try so hard to hold onto her words that when I finally came to my senses, I had cut my palms with my fingernails. But all the trying in the world didn't help. I couldn't remember what she'd said.

I remembered Deja. Briefly she stood over me and told me that she had seen her brother's ghost once, that he was headless and carried his skull in his arms when he came to her, and that the skull had spoken with her brother's voice while his body stood very still and did not move at all. I asked her what the skull said, but she only shook her head at me, looking at me with the saddest eyes.

I also remembered Virginia. She kept grabbing my arm and shaking me awake every time I would go to sleep. I was angry at her and told her so, but she kept doing it anyway. Finally, I sat up, screaming as the pain in my hip hit me. "What?" I said.

"You forgot the mirrors," she said.

Finally, there was Daddy. He was back, laughing at me from the corner of the sanctuary where they'd laid me. Once he stood behind the lectern and preached a profanity-filled sermon that would have made Satan himself walk out in anger.

The sermon was directed solely at me. Fortunately, I was unable to remember any of the exact lines, though the tone and timbre of the sermon would likely stay with me forever, filed away right next to the time he had kicked me in the face after I'd just awakened after a five-day coma. What little conscious thought I could muster during this time was unfortunately devoted to the sense that I was already dead, and Daddy was my welcoming committee in hell.

But I wasn't dead. And sometime Tuesday night or early Wednesday morning, I sat up, fully conscious for the first time in twenty-four hours. My very first thought was of Mary. My second, that I'd wasted too much time. I struggled to my feet, wincing at the pain in my hip. I nearly fell right back down but managed to brace myself on a chair. I looked around in the darkened space, blinking my eyes hard, trying to make them adjust.

I wasn't in the sanctuary like I'd thought. Instead, I was in a children's room. Sunday school class for the little ones. I heard snoring. Rufus was asleep in the corner, covers pulled up to his chin. There was movement behind me. "Mr. Earl?"

It was Virginia.

"Hey," I said. "How long have I been asleep?"

"A long time." She glanced over at Susan, who slept on the floor by Briscoe. "She took care of you. Stopped the bleeding. Mr. Rufus wouldn't let her take you to the hospital. He said, 'If he ain't dying, he don't go.' "

I smiled. Good old Rufus. Thank God for him. He understood that going to the hospital would alert Patterson to my whereabouts, which would mean I might be arrested.

"I'm going to go now," I whispered. "Take care of your brother and Ms. Susan."

"What about Rufus?"

"Him too."

"Mr. Earl?"

"Yeah?"

"The full moon is coming."

"Why would you say that?"

Virginia shrugged. "It was just something that seemed important. The only time I ever saw him was during the full moon."

I didn't have to ask who she had seen any more than she'd had to ask me what I meant to do when I left there.

It was only when I was trying to find Susan's keys that she woke up. "Earl?"

"Shh," I said. "Go back to sleep. I just need the car one more time."

"I will not. You aren't leaving in your condition."

"Susan," I said, hoping against hope she didn't become indignant and wake up Rufus. "Please. Just let me borrow the car one more time."

"Do you even know how much blood you lost?"

"A lot," I said.

"A lot? Ha! That's like saying the Pacific Ocean has 'a lot' of water in it." She was standing up now, both hands on my arm. "I'll hold on if I have to."

"Let him go," Rufus said.

"I won't do it."

"Susan," I said, "Mary's life might depend on it."

She let go of my arm then and put her hands over her face.

"Hey," I said, putting an arm over her shoulder, "what's wrong?"

She shook her head, still not removing her hands. "I had a dream."

"A dream?"

She nodded. "You . . ."

"Just let him go," Rufus said.

". . . You died."

"Earl don't put stock in dreams, do you, Earl?" Rufus said, his voice tinged with the barest hint of sarcasm.

"No," I lied. "I don't believe in that. And you shouldn't either. I've got to go. You took good care of me, but I'm fine now. I've got to get to the cornfield. Try to find her before Thursday night."

"You do know that it's Wednesday morning now, don't you?" Rufus said.

"I guessed it was something like that."

"Where are you going to go?" Rufus asked. "What's the plan? And what the hell happened anyway?"

"Long story. But I'll put it like this. Old Nathaniel did this to me. And he killed someone else, so I was lucky. I'm heading back to the cornfield. I feel like something is going to happen on Thursday night. That's tomorrow. Today, I need to head back out to the cornfield, and tonight I'm going to a party."

"A party?" Rufus and Susan said at the same time.

"Yeah. At Taggart Monroe's house."

"You sure that's a good idea?" Rufus said. "Sounds like they've already got you pegged. You go poking around that party, you're liable to get yourself killed."

"I'll be all right."

"Jesus Christ," Susan said. "You're going to die."

How could I reply? That I didn't even care about that anymore? Somehow, I'd become obsessed with one thing only: finding Mary. Now that the kids were safe, there wasn't anything else to keep me from achieving the goal. Nothing, except fear. And I wouldn't even think of letting that stop me. I was close. So close.

"Please," Susan said. "At least consider resting for a few more hours."

"I can't. I'll rest when I've found her. Not until then."

I turned back to the others. Briscoe still slept soundly, wrapped up in three thick blankets on the floor.

"Give them hell at the rally, Rufus."

He nodded. "You do the same at the party, but do it on the sly. Getting yourself killed isn't going to bring Mary back."

I thought of the dream, of falling into the black water below the train trestle. "It might."

I turned to Virginia. "Take care of your brother."

Her solemn eyes just watched me. Finally, she nodded very slowly. "Of course I will."

With that, I turned and walked out of the room and my family's church. I couldn't help but sense I wouldn't ever be coming back.

42

The sun was already high in the sky as I left the church parking lot. My mind was jumping from one image to the next, trying to make sense of the dreams and visions I'd experienced the day before.

The one thing I kept coming back to was Virginia. "*You forgot about the mirrors.*"

She was right. I had no idea what she was talking about. I searched my mind until it hurt, but I couldn't remember any mirrors. Except that wasn't quite true was it? I had a vague recollection of hearing about mirrors once, but it was like seeing a face and not remembering a person's name. I knew that I should remember more, but the memory still wasn't there.

I stopped thinking about it, focusing instead on the drive ahead of me. I was going to go to the cornfield and see if I could find this place Jason had talked about—Skull Keep—where they were keeping her. This was a method I'd used many times in the past. It was time for intuition instead of logic, and intuition always failed if you tried to force it. But if I focused on something else, it might come to me naturally.

So, I tried to imagine Skull Keep. The old newspaper article had said it was a bunker, which didn't make a lot of sense. Why would there be a bunker out in the middle of rural Georgia? I supposed there might be reasonable explanations, but none of them occurred to me. Was it out in the middle of the cornfield somewhere? And if so, wouldn't it be nice to see the cornfield from above, an aerial view . . .

Shit. It came to me then. Mirrors. I still didn't know where I'd heard about them the first time, but it hardly mattered. When we'd visited Billy Thrash in prison, he had been telling me a story just before Ronnie hit him. A story about the previous owner of the cornfield and what he'd done to see the cornfield from above.

He'd put something up on Summer Mountain. It had to be a mirror.

The realization made me nearly giddy with newfound energy. I jerked the wheel, made a U-turn, and floored it. I'd have to go by the house first, but after that, I'd be able to test my theory.

* * *

The road was deserted when I pulled up alongside the water tower. I parked in the same place Mary and I had parked several nights before, and once again I was flooded with memories from that evening: the sounds in the corn, the light we saw in the water tower, the moment I let her out of my sight.

I crossed the road with the hammer I'd grabbed at my house in hand. Once beneath the water tower, I found the leg with the cord and pried the nails free. I dropped the rope ladder and climbed up and inside. A quick scan of the basin revealed that little had changed since Rufus and I had come in the last time.

I skirted the hole in the bottom and walked over and picked up the binoculars. I raised them to my eyes and leaned against the side of the tower, inserting them in the small open space. This time, I didn't even try to look at the cornfield, but instead pointed the binoculars up toward the peak of Summer Mountain. I moved them slowly along the ridgeline, noting several large houses and a row of blackberry bushes. Just past the blackberry bushes, everything changed. Suddenly, I was seeing the cornfield, except from above. It didn't seem possible. It was as if the world had flipped over on itself.

Looking without the binoculars, I saw exactly what I'd suspected. Near the top of Summer Mountain were several large concave mirrors. To the naked eye, they could have been satellite dishes or windows, but with the high-powered binoculars, they revealed what amounted to an aerial view of the cornfield.

Lifting the binoculars back to my eyes, I held them steady on one of the mirrors. It was disorienting at first, making it difficult to determine anything about the cornfield, but the more I looked, the more my brain seemed to adjust to what I was seeing and make sense out of it.

What had seemed disordered while I was inside the cornfield was actually a complex, intricate design. I counted five straight paths, or spokes, that branched out from the center of the cornfield. In the center was a wide, circular clearing, so the effect taken as a whole appeared to be a great bicycle wheel. To make it to the center, you'd have to find one of the spokes, which in theory seemed like it would be easy, but they were so far apart, you'd almost have to be lucky to find one. Of course, as you journeyed closer to the center of the field, toward the hub of the wheel, so to speak, the spokes drew closer together.

Amazed by this discovery, I studied it for as long as I could before my arm began to shake from holding the binoculars. I put them down and called Sheriff Patterson's direct line. This was the answer. I'd get him to look at the field with the binoculars, and then we'd go out together—with some deputies—for a better look at what was in the center. That could be where the bunker was. Once he saw that, I could tell him about Jeb Walsh in the bathroom, and the mayor, and everything else. He'd have to look into it, and he'd see that I'd been right all along.

* * *

"Earl Marcus," he said. "I figured you must have skipped town."

"Why would I do that?"

"Oh let's see . . . where should I start? You and Ronnie broke into a warehouse up on Summer Mountain. You apparently attacked Frank Bentley in his home, which I might have found hard to believe if, well, I hadn't already walked in on you doing the same thing to Lane Jefferson. And—ain't this a hell of a note?—apparently, you *pissed* on a kid we later found dead out near the cornfield."

"I didn't piss on anybody."

Patterson laughed. "*That's* all you've got to say for yourself?"

"Pretty much, but I do have something I want to show you."

He sighed. "I hope it's not somebody else you've assaulted."

"It's something that might help us find Mary. I'm at the cornfield. The old water tower across the road. Do you know it?"

"I know it."

"Good. Meet me here, but come alone, and leave your gun in the car."

"Earl . . ."

"Do you want to solve this case, Sheriff?"

"Well, of course I do."

"Then you're gonna want to see this."

He was silent for a moment.

"You there?"

"I'm here. Just thinking."

"About what?"

"How some people just don't stop."

"Why would I stop?"

He was silent.

"Sheriff?"

"I'll be there in an hour."

I closed my eyes and gritted my teeth.

"Remember," I said, "come alone. Leave your weapon in the car. Any shenanigans, and I'm gone."

"I got it. Jesus."

43

I spent the next thirty minutes looking at the cornfield, trying to estimate the place where we should enter once he saw the field and understood it had been designed so most people would get lost while a select few would know their way around. From there, I'd explain about the films and the rally. And the full moon. Which was tomorrow night. He'd agree to go in with some deputies today. He'd have to.

When I climbed down from the water tower, I walked straight for Susan's Accord and turned on the engine. I put my pistol on the passenger's seat beside me and waited.

I looked up at the cloudless sky. So different from a year before when I'd confronted another great evil: my father. Rain, thunder, and lightning. High winds. Storms compared to this . . . peace. That was the only word that made sense. It was peaceful out, but somewhere beneath the peace was an evil, growing a little bolder every day. And now that it had taken Mary, the peace had become barren and false, like one of those old movie sets where everything just looked real until you got close enough to see the truth.

The truth for me was that I'd believed I'd turned a corner after my father's death. I had believed I'd never have to face a monster like him again. But now I saw that the world never ran out of monsters. They were relentless and inventive, and sometimes the worst thing about them was that you couldn't reliably tell the difference between a monster and a man. Maybe there wasn't any difference after all.

Maybe we were all just vessels, waiting to be filled with something, be it good or evil, whichever found us first.

Looking at the clear sky made me think of something else. Something curious. Something that raised the hackles on the back of my neck.

After Mary had first gone missing, Sheriff Patterson told me they'd flown a helicopter over the cornfield in hopes of spotting Mary. Surely, he already knew of the wheel and spokes then. Or was it possible whoever had been in the helicopter didn't notice it?

That seemed unlikely.

Or maybe no one from the helicopter had relayed the information to him?

My thoughts were cut short when I checked the rearview and saw Patterson's cruiser coming down the road. He pulled over onto the left shoulder and parked. I eased the gearshift into drive, ready to punch it if he made any move to arrest me, but he stepped out of the vehicle, holding his hands up in the air.

"No guns, nobody but me," I heard him say through my closed window. I opened the window enough to hear him talk.

"Good."

He started over, but I shook my head. "Just stay there. We can talk like this."

He stopped. "Fine. What you got?"

"Well, while I was sitting here waiting on you, I remembered you probably already know all about it."

"All about what?"

"The cornfield. What it looks like from above."

He glanced to his left and then to his right, as if he were thinking of crossing the road, but he stayed put.

"What are you talking about, Marcus?"

"Didn't you tell me you took the helicopter up?"

"Sure. Well, I wasn't in it. But I had a deputy ride along."

"And that deputy didn't say nothing about the design in the cornfield?"

"Design?"

He looked to his left again, out at the cornfield on my side of the road. I followed his eyes. Just corn, blowing in the dry breeze. In my mind, I saw a match being struck and tossed out into the field. I saw the fire roll across the land, disintegrating everything in its path to ashes. Except the corn silk. That would rise and dive after the fire was gone. When it was reborn, it would have Mary's shape, and she'd walk with me again, the corn maiden lost and finally found.

Patterson spat on the road, breaking the daydream. He was still waiting for my response. I studied him carefully, trying to read something that might or might not be there.

"Hell, it's shaped like a damned wheel." "Spokes and all," I said, "but surely you already know this."

He made a face. It was a curious expression, one I'd seen before. A half smile with no involvement from the eyes, it was the expression of a man who knew more than you did but didn't want you to know it. I'd seen him wear that expression before. I was sure of it. I just couldn't place when or what it had been about.

His eyes darted to the field again, where the wind seemed to be rippling the tassels more violently, and lower still there was an undertow of something—or someone—moving in this direction. I picked up my gun and turned back to Patterson.

He wasn't there.

And then I had the memory, cold and bright, and it felt like a knife, sharper and more painful than the one that had cut a slice out of my hip. The face was the same face he'd made just before tossing the skull off the ridge on the first day I'd met him, the day Mary and I had found the cave not too far from my home and called him out to have a look.

He'd never let me hold the skull. Just showed it to me before tossing it casually over the ridge.

He was back in his car now, and I watched him, my hand flexing, ready to aim and shoot if he went for a weapon, but to my surprise, he cranked the cruiser and floored it, fishtailing into the road.

Shocked by his behavior, I was about to follow him when something flew from the field on my right.

At first, I thought it was a bat. Then I was sure it was an owl, big and gray.

When it hit the windshield, and a hand reached through the crack in my driver's side window and grabbed my face, I knew it was something different.

The thing on my windshield, the thing trying to gouge out my eyeballs was a man. Or at least I had once believed it was.

Now, I wasn't sure what to believe. What kind of man hurled himself at a car with such abandon? What kind of man wore a mask like that?

I got the gun up and fired a wild shot that shattered glass. He still had his huge hand over my face, and I fired again and again before he finally let go. I blinked hard, trying to focus, and the first thing I saw the knife hooking in a short arc through the still open driver's side window. The knife sliced through the seatback, but missed me. I remembered—almost too late—that I was in a car and the engine was running, and threw it in drive. Just as I did, Old Nathaniel slammed the knife at me again and plunged it through the collar of my shirt, pinning it to the seatback. I shoved his shoulders hard, and he flew back, taking the knife with him. I stomped on the brakes, and put the Accord in reverse, cutting the wheel. Once I had the car pointing at him, I pushed the gearshift into drive and floored it.

Old Nathaniel was too quick. He sidestepped the car at the last second. I blew past him, and that's when I saw something else I'd missed before—a man, stationed in the corn, holding a camera. I tried to make out who he was, but it was no use. He'd already disappeared back into the corn.

That was when I heard the gunfire behind me.

It was Old Nathaniel, standing in the middle of the road, holding what looked like a .45. A bullet blew out Susan's back windshield, and I decided it was time to get out while I still could.

I pushed the Honda as fast it would go, back toward Riley. I only looked in the rearview once, and what I saw didn't surprise me in the least. The road was empty, almost as if I'd dreamed the whole encounter.

44

But I hadn't dreamed it. All of it had been real. There was a shock and frustration in that realization. Patterson. Hell, how had I been so easily fooled? Suddenly, I remembered what Ronnie had told me a week ago, standing in my yard: *"The new sheriff ain't no better than the last."*

He'd seen it, but I'd missed it. Why? Maybe I just couldn't accept that the world was that far gone. Sure, one crooked sheriff seemed like just a bad guy, a rotten apple, but two? And two in a row? That was the kind of thing that could make a man disappointed in the world. The kind of thing that could make a man lose what little faith he had.

I called Rufus. He answered on the second ring.

"Any news?" he said.

"Don't trust Patterson," I said.

"What?"

"He's a part of it. He just set me up."

"Are you sure?"

"Hell, yes, I'm sure. I nearly died because of that bastard. Does he know where you or the kids are?"

"I don't think so."

"Good. Stay put. This should be over soon."

"You know I got the counterprotest tomorrow night."

"Maybe you should think about taking a pass on this one."

"I've got to be there. I've got to stand up to these assholes."

"I get that, but seriously, it's not a good idea."

"Well, I'm going anyway," he said, his voice blunt and his tone almost daring me to argue with him.

"That's a fool thing to do," I said.

"Well, I reckon you'd know all about why some folks do foolish things, wouldn't you?"

I didn't know what to say to that. He was right. Of course he was.

"Okay," I said. "I'm going to a party tonight at the filmmaker's house. I'll check in with you after that. If you don't hear from me . . ." I took a deep breath and saw the black water rising toward me as I fell. "If you don't hear from me tonight, you've got to get in touch with somebody who can help, somebody outside of this county."

"I'll do it, but you're going to call tonight."

"I hope you're right," I said. Then, shaking my head so hard it hurt, I added, "What's wrong with this place, Rufus? How can one little county in the mountains be so crooked?"

"Well," Rufus said, "your daddy would have blamed it on the devil in the valley."

"Come again?"

"That was his way, you know. If he was in the mountains, that was where God must be too. That meant anything that went wrong was because of the devil down in the valley."

"That's the way a lot of folks think, isn't it?"

"I'm afraid it is."

I was silent for a minute. I wiped my face with the back of my hand, and flecks of glass fell from my beard. "If the devil's not in the valley," I said, "where is he?"

Rufus laughed. "He's in us. Every last one of us. Most of all, the ones who think they're free of him."

It makes sense to me, I thought long after I'd ended the call. *The devil is in us all, and some people are able to control it and some aren't.* But that didn't take into account what I'd seen back there in the cornfield. *That* made me think somehow the devil had gotten loose.

* * *

I went home, slowing down as I climbed the mountain, to keep my eyes peeled for someone who might be following me or—worse—lying in ambush for me. I made it home without incident, showered, checked my hip, and was pleased to see it didn't look infected and was no longer bleeding. I pressed the bandage back in place and grabbed some heavy-duty duct tape to hold it tight. After that, I stood naked in front of my closet, wishing, probably for the first time in my adult life, I'd paid more attention to fashion. I settled on the nicest clothing I owned, a pair of brown slacks and a button-down shirt Mary said made me look "hip." I left my Braves hat on the kitchen table and made a frozen pizza. I ate it at the table, with my yellow notepad, while Goose watched me closely.

I waited until nine fifteen before saying goodbye to Goose and heading to the Accord. Shit, the broken windows weren't going to help me get in. I'd definitely need to come up with an explanation for that.

I grabbed a broom and some cleaning supplies and worked for half an hour or more sweeping out glass and scrubbing dried blood from the seats and floorboards before heading out. As I started down the mountain, I glanced in the rearview mirror in hopes of seeing Goose. He wasn't there. Instead, I could have sworn I saw my father, standing just outside the house, holding a serpent in his hands.

The devil had made it to the mountains after all. Hell, he'd been here for years.

45

I was relieved to see that the guard was not the same one from a couple of nights earlier. This was an older, white-haired man, likely the one who'd been on the other end of the call about the sticker. He'd told the younger guard that entry with a sticker wasn't an option anymore. I'd have to do a hell of an acting job to get in this time.

"Evening," I said, trying to sound cheerful. "Heading up for Taggart Monroe's party."

The old man looked at me through thick glasses, frowning.

"What happened to your car?"

"Oh, this?" I smiled brightly, trying to be everything I wasn't—effusive, charismatic, the kind of man that could make you believe the world was about to end and still sell you a front row seat to watch it all go down. "It's our stunt car."

"What's that?"

"Stunt car. You know. I'm an actor. We're having a cast party tonight. I thought Tag would get a kick if I showed up in it."

He rolled his eyes and cleared his throat, which told me he had bought it.

"Name?"

"Neal. Should be on the list."

He scanned the list slowly. I waited, the night air growing heavy, my heart beginning to pound against my chest.

"Last name?"

Shit, the invitation didn't have a last name on it.

"Uh, I don't really use a last name."

The guard frowned. "Say again?"

"I'm not into the whole last name thing. You know, it's just Neal. Like Madonna or Prince."

"Are you serious?"

"Yes," I said. "Serious as a heart attack."

He looked at me for a long time, as if trying to determine if I was pulling one over on him. I kept a straight face and waited. Finally, he looked back at his list. "I don't see a plain Neal on here," he said.

"Damn it," I said. "I've got the code. I unlocked my phone and pulled up the photo. "You ready?"

He still looked a little stunned. "Ready."

I called out the five-digit number. He nodded. "That's it. I reckon you can go on in."

The gate opened. I nodded at the guard and drove through.

I breathed a sigh of relief as I eased by the same houses I'd passed the other night, drawing some looks from a couple of men standing in their yards with beers.

I came to Frank Bentley's place, and I remembered standing over him in his foyer, pointing the gun at his head.

The GPS told me to keep on going.

I crested a hill, and my headlights illuminated a house that dwarfed even Bentley's. But more impressive than the size was the location. It sat up on a ridge, positioned so that the front of the house was looking off the sheer side of the mountain while the back of the house overlooked a long, sloping hill that appeared as if it went on forever down the other side.

A sign appeared, telling me to turn right for the Villas Monroe or continue straight to The Top o' Mountain.

I turned right and followed the winding road to a leveled parking lot that was close to full. I drove around a bit and finally found a spot I could squeeze into. What kind of private home had a parking lot? The kind that threw a lot of parties, I decided.

Once out of the car, I saw another sign hanging from a tree. It told me to follow the arrows to the front entrance.

Forget that. There was no way I was going in the front door. Instead, I walked in the opposite direction, toward the sloping back woods. I stepped off the asphalt and onto the grass, nearly losing my balance on an unexpected root.

Not so far away, I heard the sounds of the party. Laughing, bits of conversation that merged into a monotonous murmur, and the tinkle of music—light jazz, I thought. I crept along a ridgeline, trying to find a way to the party, but it was dark, and the dense trees hid the light of the moon. I pulled out my penlight and shined it out in front of me. That was when I realized I wasn't just walking along a ridge; I was actually on a path. It rose sharply before me, and someone had placed a metal handgrip in the side of one of the big trees. I reached for it and pulled myself up and over the steep rise. What greeted me was both marvelous and somehow terrifying.

The trees parted here to reveal the view on the north side of the mountain, all of it illuminated by soft light from an almost full moon. Acres of forestland stretched out from the base of the mountain for miles before shifting suddenly into a golden field of moonlit corn. This too stretched and stretched, defying all common sense, before—in the far, far distance—I could just make out a dark scar of the highway cutting through the gold like an infection marring an otherwise healthy body.

And farthest away of all, I could just make out a tiny house, a single light burning on the second story. I wondered if Lane Jefferson was sitting up, watching television, waiting for another victim to wander onto his land.

Or maybe he had the Old Nathaniel outfit on already, peering at his reflection in the mirror through the narrow eye slits.

But what if it wasn't Jefferson? What if he was the cameraman? Honestly, Old Nathaniel had seemed taller than Jefferson. And there was the dark, strawberry-shaped tattoo on his neck. I didn't remember

Jefferson having one of those. Of course, Jefferson didn't really look like the man I'd seen holding the camera near the water tower today either. Not that I'd gotten enough of a look at him to really be sure.

I tried to remember the voice I'd heard behind the small house just before Jason had been killed. The problem was, I'd almost need to hear it again and to compare it in real time to Jefferson's—or anyone's for that matter—to draw any kind of conclusion.

I shook my head. It didn't matter. What mattered, I told myself, was what was right in front of my face. Proximity. The fact that Tag Monroe's home was so close to the cornfield was one more tiny nail in the coffin. This was wide-ranging and deep. I wasn't just trying to take down Old Nathaniel—I was trying to take down the whole apparatus that made it possible for him to exist.

I couldn't stop looking at the view. It was truly spectacular and truly sad, especially when I realized—one way or another, dead or alive—Mary was out there somewhere, between where I stood right now and Lane Jefferson's house.

She had to be alive, right? Because otherwise why plan the rally on a Thursday, which just happened to coincide with a full moon?

"Nice view, isn't it?"

I turned and saw a man standing a few feet behind me. I couldn't be sure, but something told me it was Monroe. You can usually determine who a party's host is if you're paying attention. They're nearly always the most relaxed person in the room. This man was certainly the most relaxed person on this ridge.

He was a small man with dark hair and a quick smile. I immediately compared him to Old Nathaniel. Far too small. But that didn't surprise me too much. He was the director, not the star. Tag wasn't conventionally handsome, but he had a certain kind of pugnacity that, along with his obvious financial means, probably made him attractive to certain kinds of women. And confidence too. He fairly oozed it.

"I'm not sure we know each other," he said, stepping forward, holding out a small, thick hand. "Tag Monroe."

"Bob Jenkins." It just came out, and thank god it did, because telling him my real name would have been just about the most natural—and the most foolish—thing I could have done. The same went for telling him I was Neal. Hell, that might have even been worse.

"I'm going to call you Bobby. That okay?"

"Sure," I said, trying to feel out the role I should play.

He still had not let go of my hand, and I wasn't sure what that was about—some kind of overcompensation strategy? Or maybe he was just that enthusiastic about meeting new people.

"You live down on Fern Lane?" he said, and I could tell he was perplexed by my presence. He wasn't used to finding people at his parties he didn't recognize.

My mind spun, trying to think of how to best play it. "Actually, I'm the head brewer down at the Brew House. I hope it's all right that I stopped by. I've been hearing about your parties."

"Absolutely. Everyone in the community is welcome, my friend. Especially someone who brews the drink of the gods!" He finally let go of my hand but immediately started patting me on the shoulder. "I love your Mountain Vine IPA. What kind of hops are those?"

I reached back in my memory for something I'd heard recently. "Citra," I said, hoping to God that was a real thing.

"That's it? Single hop? Oh shit, man, you are a genius. Any plans to bottle or can any of the beers? I also really like the Mountain Honey. I think honey and lagers always work."

"We're working on the licensing now. We'll can the Mountain Vine first."

"Cannot wait. I've got some of it at the house in growlers right now. Let's head down for a drink."

"Sure," I said, deciding if worse came to worst, I could bolt at any time.

He led me back down the path, and I decided to take advantage of his friendliness because I knew it wasn't going to last. "So, who owns all that corn?" I asked.

"I'm surprised you don't know already."

"Why would I?"

He laughed, seemingly pleased by my challenge. "Well, it's been in the news a bit lately. A woman went missing." He laughed. "Supposedly they found her head. Gruesome stuff."

"Oh, wow, didn't hear that. You said, *supposedly*. Does that mean you don't believe they did?"

"Well, they found something, but it's sort of like the old saying about how all the coloreds look alike"—he ribbed me with his elbow—"skulls are the same way. They won't know for sure until they run tests." He shrugged. "You know, you should name a beer after the legend that's regaining popularity these days. It's from the same valley. Have you heard of Old Nathaniel? I think that would be a perfect name for a high-alcohol barley wine. Actually, that's the name of my next film. Perhaps we could do a collaboration?"

"You make movies?"

He stopped and looked at me curiously. "You really didn't know that?"

I saw instantly that I'd tried to play a little too dumb. Now he was suspicious.

"I'm sorry. I'm not always up on things. You know, I'm either brewing beer or drinking it."

He clapped me on the back again. "That's the life, I guess."

"It's what I love."

"Well, you need to come over more often. I'll have you up for a screening sometime." He leaned in conspiratorially. "I've got some movies that you'll never see anywhere else. I do private screenings you know. Private for a reason."

"You mean like porn or something?"

He grinned. "Something like that."

"Sure," I said. "How about tonight?"

He shook his head. "Tonight," he said, "we party."

We walked on, the sounds from the party closer now.

"World is changing, you know?"

"How so?"

He stopped at the bottom of the path. I could see the lights from the party just a couple of hundred yards away. "You really don't keep up with much, do you?"

"No, I guess not."

"Look, you're at my house, so I'm not going to pull punches. That okay with you?"

"Sure."

"Once, our country was great, but three things happened that created our current situation of utter decay."

"Three?"

"Three." He held up one finger. "Number one, white people started feeling sorry for the blacks. It started in the sixties and it's only gotten worse. Two, women decided they wanted another role other than mother. It's unnatural and unhealthy. Kids need their mothers in the home. And three, immigration has gotten out of control, especially among those that worship Allah and believe that Westerners are the devil. Any questions?"

I didn't have questions. I wanted to punch him in the face, but instead I simply shook my head. "Right on."

He smiled. "Good, a white man who doesn't let guilt run his life. Let me introduce you to some people."

He led me across the woods and through an opening in the hedges. Here was the party. Dozens of nice-looking people standing around with drinks, probably talking about how white privilege didn't exist. I swallowed down the bile creeping up the back of my throat and decided to do the thing that would help Mary the most: pretend to be one of them.

46

Taggart introduced me to several people—a drunk, middle-aged actress named Mercy; another director named Kurt something or other, who Tag claimed was nothing short of "visionary"; and his wife, a petite beauty at least twenty-five years his junior—but when I saw Jeb Walsh across the courtyard, I excused myself, asking for the restroom.

"Just inside the kitchen," Taggart said. "There's probably a line, though. Go upstairs. Use that one if you want." He leaned in. "I wouldn't open any doors though. You never know what you'll find." He patted my back and cackled loudly as I walked away.

There actually wasn't a line at the kitchen bathroom, but I wanted to explore as much as possible while I was here. But before I could even make it to the steps, a snippet of conversation stopped me cold.

From somewhere to my right I heard ". . . he's already released the early scenes."

"But not the actual hunt?"

"Nah, that'll only be available in the final version."

Now, that word *hunt* certainly wasn't unheard of in the South. In fact, even when I turned around to look, I wouldn't have been surprised if I'd misheard the first stuff about "early scenes" and they were just two good old boys talking about hunting deer.

They sure fit the stereotypical profile. They were both broad-shouldered young men and looked about the right age to be heading out to the woods early and often to hunt deer, but there was something else about them that made me think it was more likely they were talking about a different, darker kind of hunt. Maybe it was their hair. I'd never seen any good old boys—rich or poor—with their hair parted so severely and gelled up like theirs was. They also wore hipster suits. Their ties were too broad and too bright, and their pants a little too skinny. I moved toward the refrigerator, pretending to look inside for something to eat.

They continued to talk for a while, but from what I could tell, they'd shifted the conversation to complaining about how lazy their wives were.

I decided to take a chance. I turned, smiling at them. "Did I hear you boys talking hunting a minute ago?"

They both fell silent and looked at me suspiciously. Finally, the one with the bright red tie spoke. "We don't hunt. You must have heard wrong."

"No, I'm quite sure. I heard one of you say something about 'the hunt.'"

"Do you even live in Sommerville Chase?" Blue Tie said.

"No, I'm the head brewer at the brewhouse." I hoped to hell neither of them spent enough time there to know I was full of shit.

"Well, I think you're in the wrong fucking place. This is for residents and invited guests only." Red Tie stepped forward, like he wanted to make this physical. I would have honestly loved nothing more, but I couldn't afford to get kicked out yet.

"Sorry then," I said, and stepped away quickly around the corner. Once clear, I sprinted toward the steps. A woman in a long evening gown was coming down them, so I slowed up and pretended to laugh at myself as if drunk. She rolled her eyes and slipped past me. I started up the steps, keeping my eyes peeled for Walsh coming inside, but I didn't see him anywhere. I made it to the top of the stairs and found a huge loft-like landing that overlooked the kitchen. Here was the jazz band—all white, of course—playing some kind of sanitized version of the real thing. Some people were dancing while others sat in plush leather furniture, watching. I slipped behind the couches, heading for the next set of steps, a spiral staircase leading up to the third floor.

The third floor consisted of a common room where the party continued. A long hallway ran from either side of the common room. I tried both directions, pretending to look for a bathroom. I counted three bathrooms and six bedrooms, but nothing unusual.

I decided to sit down and try to listen a bit. There was an open spot on one of the couches beside a woman with short red hair and a dress barely long enough to cover her breasts and ass at the same time. She kept pulling it up and down, trying to get the coverage just right.

I smiled at her and she smiled back.

"You been to many of these parties?" I asked.

"A few."

"Let me guess," I said. "You're an actress?"

She giggled, and I realized she was either a little drunk or high. Just a little, but enough to lower her inhibitions. She uncrossed her legs slowly, offering me a telling peak at what she wore—or didn't wear, as was the case—underneath. She smiled, crossing her legs again.

"I'm Tag's secretary," she said. "I would *like* to be an actress." She giggled again. The man sitting beside her turned and glared at her.

"Are you flirting with this man?" he said.

"And so what if I am?" she said.

The man sighed and looked at me. He was probably thirty, well dressed, handsome in a well-heeled, polished sort of way. "Trust me," he said, as he stood, "you don't want any part of this. The pleasure isn't worth the pain."

"Fuck you," the redhead said. She turned back to me. "That's my boyfriend, but I swear sometimes it feels more like I'm dating my dad."

I waited until he walked away and replied, "He's got a damn stick up his ass. If I had a girl like you, I'd let you play." I gave her my best crooked smile, hoping she was adventurous enough to want to go into one of the bedrooms with me. Not because I wanted to have sex with her, but because if she was willing to do that, she'd also be willing to tell me more. Like where I could find the videos Taggart had already filmed. "*The early scenes,*" as Red Tie had called them.

"I like you," she said. "I'm Lilac."

"I like you too, Lilac. Is that like the flower?"

"It is. You didn't tell me your name."

"Bob," I said.

She bit her lip, suggestively. "You look like a country boy, Bobby."

I nodded. "I tend to think of myself as a hillbilly."

She giggled. "I'll bet hillbillies know a thing or two that city boys don't."

"Maybe we do."

She leaned forward, showing me some cleavage and a little more. "Like what?"

"Oh, I don't know. Us hillbillies, well, we tend to be a little more basic. A little more—shit—*primal*, I reckon."

"Ooh, say that again."

"Which part?"

"Primal."

"We're more primal," I said, in my lowest, deepest growl. I didn't know much about fashion or what to wear to attract women, but over the years, I'd learned that I had one damn good weapon: my deep voice.

"Oh, I like you," she said. "Does that primal stuff include, you know, the best way to fuck a lady?"

I shrugged. "I haven't had any complaints."

A couple sitting on a nearby couch got up and glared at us as they walked away.

"So, why don't you act in one of Taggart's films?" I asked.

"Are you kidding? I want to be a real actress. Nobody sees his stuff anyway except for, like, mentally deranged, stalker dudes and Klansmen."

I cocked my head to one side, feigning confusion. "Why's that?"

"You've never seen one of his movies before?"

I shook my head. "I'm just a poor hillbilly."

She laughed and picked up her glass from the table. It was half filled with what looked like bourbon. She took a sip and held it out to me. "Want some?"

I took two swallows and handed it back. It was the first alcohol I'd had in a while, and I immediately wanted more.

"Does he have a place where he keeps his movies here in the house?"

She gave me an odd look. "Are you serious?"

"About what?"

"Seems like you want to see one."

"Well . . ."

"I think they're sick."

"Then why do you work for him?"

She gave me a little half smile, half snarl. "Seriously? Look around you. I get to live here. He doesn't touch me, which is probably only because I heard he was secretly gay, but whatever. There's always booze and drugs, and honestly, the job isn't that hard, especially considering Hollywood ain't calling anytime soon."

"So, where does he get all his money?" I asked.

"You ask a lot of questions for a hillbilly who ain't never heard one of the women he fucked complain. Maybe if you would shut up asking questions, you might have heard them complaining."

I laughed. I needed to slow down a little. Work the situation more. "You are really sexy," I said. "Where are you from?"

"Nevada," she said.

"How'd you end up in these mountains?"

She shook her head, the way people do when they're frustrated with their decisions. "I came because my options out there were limited to working the casinos or stripping. My brother lives out here. He told me there was a filmmaker who was looking for a discreet secretary he could trust."

I nodded. "And your brother? What's he do?"

"He's an actor, supposedly. But working for Tag is a dead end. At least that's what I tell him." She shrugged. "He doesn't listen to me. Even if I am the kind of secretary Tag thinks he can trust."

"Little Miss Trustworthy," I said.

She smiled, eating up the flirting. "I'm not *that* trustworthy," she said.

"For instance?"

"For instance, I know where he keeps his private stash of coke. Wanna do a line?"

"Now you're talking directly to the hillbilly in me," I said.

She stood up and held out her hand for me to take. She led me around the couches and back down one of the hallways. We reached the end and she opened a door I'd previously thought was a closet.

Lilac swung it open, and I saw yet another set of stairs. These were actually so steep, they could almost pass for a ladder.

Lilac grinned at me seductively and said, "Ladies first." She started up the steps, and I was treated to a view of her bare ass for the second time that night.

At the top, she stopped to wiggle it for me a little, probably disappointed I had not yet made a mention of how nice it was. And it was rather nice.

"Oooh," I said.

"Oh, I like that sexy deep voice."

She reached a hand out and entered a code onto a keypad beside the door handle.

There was a beep and she opened the door. "Come on," she said.

I started up behind her, but when I reached the door, I pretended to trip. As I fell, I reached for the door handle and pulled it back shut.

"Whoops," I said. "May have had a little too much to drink."

I held the door handle tightly with both hands. She tried to turn it from the other side, but I was too strong.

"It's like it's jammed," she said through the door.

"Probably a glitch. Tell me the code and I'll bet it will open."

"I'm not supposed to—"

"Just tell me. You were going to let me in anyway."

"Yeah, I guess you're right." I felt her trying the handle again. "It really should open."

"It's just stuck. Probably a computer error. Everything will reset when I enter the code in again."

"Okay," she said. "The code is one-zero-zero-five."

"Got it." I entered the code, and waited until there was another beep and then opened the door.

We stood in a circular common space with three more doors. Beside each door was another keypad. Lilac led me to the middle door, and I watched as she entered the same code again.

She opened the door so I could go in first this time.

The room was larger than I expected. A huge window dominated one side of the space, the nearly full moon shining through the glass and creating natural light that revealed a semicircle of folding chairs around a large podium. I flipped on the lights, and my eyes were immediately drawn to the oversized framed photograph hanging on the wall just behind the podium.

The photo had been taken in a cornfield, almost certainly Lane Jefferson's. Twelve men stood in a semicircle, their faces somewhere between haughty and smug. I scanned them and wasn't surprised to see Taggart Monroe and Lane Jefferson. The two men who were talking about the hunt were there too, looking like the assholes they were.

I also recognized Frank Bentley's beady eyes starting back at me, and Jason, the kid that had been killed by Old Nathaniel just a few nights ago.

At the top of the photograph in big yellow letters it read, "The Agents of Change, 2015."

AOC mystery solved.

I looked again for any faces I might recognize. And there it was. Mayor Keith. Shit. If it wasn't the sheriff in this town, it was the damned mayor. Of course, I had to remind myself, it *was* actually both this time, though I didn't see Patterson in the photo. Then again, he wasn't even in town in 2015, which just meant he'd likely joined up later, after arriving.

The same was true for Jeb Walsh and Preston Argent, though I had no doubt those men were intimately involved.

These were the men behind the evil in Coulee County. Not only the snuff film, but also the ones who were making sure Jeb Walsh's book was taught at the local middle school, the same ones who made sure Jeb Walsh had access to the library and the town square whenever he needed it.

And I was pretty sure all of them stood to make money off Taggart's latest snuff flick.

"I always thought that photo was creepy," Lilac said. "Who stands like that? None of them are even smiling."

"Yeah, do you know what it is? The Agents of Change?"

"Old farts club," she said. "Men that get off on power and cruelty." She shook her head, looking at them. "I've been with over half of those guys, and nearly all of them have erectile dysfunction problems." She gave me a meaningful glance. "You don't have anything like that do you?"

"Hell no."

"Good. The coke is in here."

I turned and saw her standing beside a little desk with a computer on it. There was a safe on the ground next to it, and she reached down to spin the dial.

"He thinks I don't know the combination, but I know more than I let on."

She knelt, as she worked the combination. She was turning the handle when the door outside buzzed again.

"Oh shit," Lilac said, "he's coming. You've got to hide."

"Where?" I said, looking around the room.

"Hell, somewhere. Do it quick or you'll end up in the next movie."

I scanned the room frantically. Just as I'd decided to charge the door, gun drawn, I saw it. On the far side of the room there was one of those old movie projectors sitting atop a table. A checkered tablecloth hung almost to the floor. I didn't waste any time getting under it.

The fit was tight, and I had to draw my knees up to my chest and hold them there with my arms. I feared my boots would still show at the bottom, in the space where the cloth didn't quite reach the hardwood. I heard Lilac typing on the computer.

The door beeped and swung open.

47

"What are you doing?" It didn't sound like Taggart, but I recognized the voice.

"I'm checking on something for Mr. Monroe," Lilac said.

"Well, get out."

"Okay," she said. "Just let me log back out."

"Forget that. I need the room."

"Sure. I apologize, I was just—"

"I like that dress."

"Thanks, Mr. Walsh."

"Call me Jeb."

"Thanks, Jeb."

"Are you the redhead Frank was telling me about, the one who wants to be in movies?"

"That's me."

"I heard you've got some demons in you, girl. The kind that need to be exorcized."

Lilac said nothing. I'd closed my eyes now and was literally praying she wouldn't give me away.

"Sometimes," she said.

"Next time you get you a demon up in you, let Taggart know. I'll let you come over to my place and we'll tie you down on the bed, see if we can work it out. You like being tied down?"

"Sometimes."

"I'll bet you do. God almighty, I'll bet you do."

There was a smack and the sound of the door closing. I was pretty sure he'd slapped her ass on the way out. Jesus, I wished so badly that I could crawl out from under the table to confront him.

But I couldn't. I'd never get out of this party alive if I did that. Hell, I might not get out of it alive anyway.

I listened as Walsh paced across the room, going back and forth. He mumbled to himself, the words unintelligible. Finally, I heard the chair by the computer groan as he sat down in it.

There was a knock on the door.

"Shit. He would get here as soon as I sit down," he muttered. The chair groaned again and Walsh walked over to open the door.

"Mayor."

"Jeb."

"Thanks for taking a minute to talk."

"Sure. What's up?"

"It's about tomorrow night."

"You should have plenty of police protection, Jeb. They'll be deputies on every street—"

"I ain't talking about that."

"Well, what are you . . . ? Oh. *That.*"

"Yeah, Taggart's getting a little out of control. We agreed he'd only film if there was no heat."

"Well, to be fair, Sheriff Patterson has directed all the deputies to stay away from the cornfield. He managed to get the Atlanta police to finally stop sniffing around when he showed them the skull. And there's going to be a counterprotest, just like we hoped, so the whole area will be free of disruptions."

"Who was responsible for killing Jason?"

"Jason?"

"The kid. The kid that got mauled outside of the abandoned house at the edge of the cornfield. The one Tag just had to have to film some kind of scene at."

"I don't know who killed Jason."

"I liked that kid. He had potential. If it was Jefferson . . . shit. He's gone too far. All of this Old Nathaniel stuff has gone too far."

"Well, I think Lane believes that something supernatural is at work."

Walsh laughed. "Supernatural? Goddamn, what kind of idiots am I working with? So you mean to tell me he thinks Old Nathaniel is real? I thought he *was* the one dressed up?"

"He was . . . once. Now, I think he's got somebody else. I don't know. But that's beside the point, isn't it?"

"What is the damn point, then?"

"Tag and Lane've got the niggers believing it. They're scared shitless. Not only that, people have been downloading the scenes they've already filmed like crazy. According to Tag, he's already sold over ten thousand downloads, and once he gets the finale done, that'll triple."

There was a pause, and I wondered if Walsh was trying to do the math.

"How much per download?"

"That's the thing. Because it's a cop, a black female cop who is also very attractive, he thinks he can charge ninety-nine dollars a download for the last part."

"People will pay that?"

"Absolutely. Think about it. How often do you get to see a real person hunted and killed? And not just any person either. This is an uppity mulatto bitch with a hell of a nice rack. And a cop. It's pure gold."

I was squeezing my knees to my chest so tightly I could barely breathe. In my entire life, I didn't think I'd ever been so angry and not been able to act. It was killing me.

I didn't know how much longer I could hold out. The only thing keeping me from coming out, 9mm blazing was that I'd never get out of the house alive afterward.

"That's almost three million dollars," Walsh said. "Shit."

"That's what we've been trying to tell you. And, Jefferson's sure that if the product's good—which it will be—we'll have a lot of repeat customers."

"I still say he should wait until things calm down. The longer she's missing, the less people will think she might still be alive. And that would give us time to take care of her boyfriend."

"Marcus."

"He's been poking around. Based on Frank Bentley's description, the man who attacked him the other night was probably Marcus."

"And Sheriff Patterson had a run-in with him today."

"He did? I ain't heard that one yet. Did he arrest him?"

"No."

"Why the hell not? I told him to arrest him the next chance he had."

The mayor was quiet.

"Answer me, damn it."

The mayor made a squeaking sound in the back of his throat, and I thought he was about to break down. "Lane wanted to try to film Old Nathaniel killing him."

"Jesus. Lane and Taggart are going to fucking blow this."

"They've got some kind of thing in their mind about needing one more murder to make the movie complete. It's like the full moon shit."

Walsh paced the room. I saw his polished shoes under the tablecloth, drawing closer. He stopped at the table and pivoted. "Tell your boy that if he does something stupid like that again, I'm shutting the whole thing down. I'll talk to Tag tonight."

"Got it."

"Anything else?" Walsh said.

"Well, Marcus is still out there somewhere. And his damned blind friend. Shit, he's leading the counterprotest."

"That's okay. The counterprotests are good. Makes it more important for the police to be there and ignore everything else." Walsh hesitated. "I don't like that blind bastard, though. After the rally, I'm going to get Press on him."

"Make it clean," Mayor Keith said. "Please."

"He'll just vanish," Walsh said. "The same way I'm going to make Marcus vanish. Hell, Press is supposed to be over at his place right now. I'll feel better about everything once we've snuffed out that jackass's candle."

"Me too." Mayor Keith hesitated. "Well, do I need to talk to Sheriff Patterson about anything?"

"Tell him I still don't understand why he let the Thrash kid go."

"He said it would increase the chances of Marcus breaking the law, which would mean he could arrest him."

"Damn it!" Walsh exploded. "That's the problem with all of you! You take the hard way every damned time. You want to arrest somebody, fucking arrest them."

"But the DA—"

"I don't give a fuck about the DA. I'll handle the DA. Just tell Patterson to go arrest him. Next time he sees him. Either shoot his ass or arrest it."

"Okay. It's going to work, Jeb. I'm telling you it will. And once it does, we'll have enough to fund your campaign for the House."

"It'll take more than three million."

"Your cut is only half of that."

Walsh laughed. "Well, that's negotiable. Now, get on out of here and tell that little faggot to wrap this party up. Everybody needs their sleep tonight. And, Mayor?"

"Yeah, Jeb?"

"Tell that little queer I'm going to borrow his secretary for the night. I don't think he'll miss her."

I waited until I heard both men exit the room before leaning forward and lifting the tablecloth enough to see. They were gone. I stood on shaky legs. My hip screamed with pain as I limped over to the computer chair and sat down, trying to get my breathing under control.

I felt a little dazed by everything I'd just heard. At the forefront of it all was the knowledge that Walsh wanted me dead, which meant going back downstairs was rife with danger. I looked at the window above the computer.

I reached around the monitor and raised the window. The cool October air came in, and I let it flow over me like a salve. I felt a little more relaxed, tasting the cool mountain air. Even Sommerville Chase hadn't been able to corrupt that.

I climbed on the desk and stuck my head out the window, craning my neck to see what was above me. The roof. I twisted around and tried to reach it. I was close enough. Just barely. When I was ready to go, I'd climb onto the roof. From there, surely I could find a safe way down.

Or I could jump and take my chances. Even that felt safe compared to heading back down the stairs. I was beginning to realize just how lucky I'd been that no one had recognized me earlier.

I slipped back into the room and slid off the desk. Sitting back in the chair, I wriggled the mouse until the monitor came to life.

A clean blue desktop with two file folders on it greeted me. One was labeled "Paperwork" and the other "Cuts." I looked around for a flash drive to save them on but didn't see anything. Suddenly, I remembered the safe.

I slid out of the chair and turned the handle. I felt a rush of relief when it opened. Lilac had managed to enter the entire combination. Inside the safe was a heavy, solid steel orb-like paperweight with Taggart's name engraved on the side, two metal boxes, and a small stack of one hundred dollar bills. I moved the paperweight and the cash aside, placing them on the floor next to the safe, and opened the smaller of the two boxes. There were two Ziploc bags filled with white powder. I moved them out of the way to make sure there was nothing else. Placing the bags back inside, I closed the box and reached for the next one, which was larger and blue. It was locked. I sat it on the computer table and looked at the combination lock. I tried one-zero-zero-five, and it opened.

Thank God, Taggart used the same damn combination for everything.

When I saw the contents, my breath caught in my throat. It was a stack of DVDs in clear slipcases. The one on the top had writing on the shiny surface.

It read "Master: Sept. 27, Scenes 1–5."

My hand shook as I removed the DVD from the slipcover and inserted it into the DVD drive of the computer. I waited as the disk spun loudly. I clicked "Play" when the icon appeared.

Two phrases flashed across the screen: *Old Nathaniel* followed by *Part I, a film by Taggart Monroe.*

Faint banjo music played in the darkness, and I couldn't help but wonder if it was a nod to *Deliverance*, but then the tempo of the music shifted dramatically, and electric guitars cut through the rhythm, two strands of screaming feedback. The black screen gave way to a campfire in the woods.

Several kids sat around the fire, drinking light beer and laughing. One of them had a joint. Another—a pretty girl in her late teens—was wrapped in a blanket. A bearded man sat in a lawn chair. He was a little older than the others, and he seemed to be the center of the camera's zooming attention.

He reached down and clicked off a tiny speaker. The music stopped. At least most of it did. What was left was the music of the woods. Frogs and crickets and night birds pulsed in rhythm to the ghost of the song. It was really well done and made me hate myself for appreciating the artistry of it.

"You know what we're near, don't you?" he said in a deep growl.

All of the kids were still. The girl with the blanket pulled it up to her neck, her eyes shining. The camera panned from the gleam in her eyes, up through the trees, and into the open sky, where it moved slowly toward the full moon.

"It's called Skull Keep. It's where Old Nathaniel buries his skulls. I saw it once, when I was hiking back here in my younger days. Never been able to find it since, but that's okay." The camera dropped back through the trees, a little too fast, shifting slightly on the way down as if jostled by the branches. It landed back on the older, bearded man. He tapped his head. "I got the memory of it. Those skulls . . ." He shook his head and closed his eyes, breathing the night air. The camera crept closer, and I realized then that Taggart Monroe was subtly making the camera a character, or at least the eyes of a character.

". . . Those skulls," the bearded man continued. "They were only half buried in the hillside. The tops were uncovered, and they glowed in the moonlight, like little lights."

"Yo," the kid smoking the joint said, totally interrupting the flow of the story and the film, and I saw right away one of the problems with Taggart's films: besides being racist filth, of course—was that the actors were low quality. Of course, acting wasn't really the point in movies like this anyway, I reminded myself.

"Where did all these skulls come from?" the kids said.

"Old Nathaniel. He lives in the farmhouse not too far from here. He's so good at killing, nobody messes with him. Even the sheriff has him on speed dial when he needs to get rid of a thug."

A beep sounded outside the room again. I nearly jumped out of the chair. I reached for the eject button on the disc drive, but in my haste, I pressed it once and then again, confusing the machine. It began to eject, but then stopped, pulling the disc back in.

Footsteps were coming toward the door. I pressed eject a third time, this time steadying my hand so that I only hit it once.

The drive whirled, as if trying to decide what to do.

On the other side of the door, the footsteps stopped, and I heard the soft beeps as whoever it was entered the code. One beep, two beeps, three . . .

The disk was still stuck.

Four beeps.

Come on!

But the drive only spun, not releasing the disc at all.

The door buzzed, and I grabbed my 9mm out of my waistband and turned to greet whoever it was.

The door swung open to reveal Jeb Walsh. Neither of us spoke for a long second. He looked utterly confused by my presence. I hadn't exactly been expecting him to return, either.

"How'd you get in here?" he said.

"Shut the door."

He looked from the gun in my hand to my face, trying to read me. In the bathroom at Jessamine's, he'd correctly determined that I wasn't going to shoot him, gloating afterward that I'd missed my one opportunity and that I'd never get another one.

Now, I saw he wasn't so sure.

Because neither was I.

The thing was, I'd just heard the truth from him. I knew the kind of man he was. Before, I'd strongly suspected. Now there could be no doubt.

"I don't know what you think you're doing," he said, "but I'm pretty sure you're making a mistake."

"No mistake," I said. "I was right under that table earlier. I heard the whole thing. Heard how you were going to 'snuff out my candle.'" I lifted the gun a little so that the muzzle was aimed directly at his forehead. "Seems like you had that wrong," I said.

He held out his hands. "This is a complicated thing you've stepped into. That particular conversation was more show than anything else. See, I'm trying to infiltrate this whole ring. It's what my next book—"

I laughed. "You're pathetic."

He winced. "Okay, okay. I won't insult your intelligence. You're a bright man. You know what you heard." He reached for his pocket. I jabbed the gun in his direction.

"Don't."

"I'm not armed," he said. "I'm going for my wallet."

"Leave it be."

"I can pay you. More than you can imagine."

"That's the thing about morally bankrupt people. They naturally assume everyone else is the same way."

He sighed. "What do you want then?"

"I want Mary. I want you to tell me where to find her."

"You think I know? I'm only overseeing this operation. Helping with manpower and some of the finances. I don't know where they're keeping her. That's Lane's department. And that little queer, Tag."

"You have their numbers, right?"

"Excuse me?"

"On your phone, goddamn it. You can call them can't you?"

He nodded.

"Call Taggart. Get his ass up here. I want him to tell me where she is."

"I'm going to reach for my phone now, okay?"

I nodded, watching his hand closely as he moved it toward his pocket. He was almost there when I heard something behind me, a clicking sound, followed by high buzz.

The sound was just enough to give him the opportunity he needed. My attention was pulled away for an instant, and by the time I realized it was the sound of the disc drive finally opening, it was too late. He fired the snubnose twice, and one slug grazed my right shoulder. I managed to get off one shot myself before the pain became too much and I dropped the gun.

Walsh laughed, a cruel, cackling sound, and stepped closer to me until he was standing directly over me, the snubnose aimed at my face.

"Two chances to shoot me, and you failed both times. I heard you were the kind of man who liked to make noise but didn't actually know how to get anything done." He leaned closer, so I could see his face, the leer that was plastered on it like a frozen hook. "Only thing I regret is that I didn't teach that black bitch some manners."

I kicked out at him, but he stepped away, still leering.

I moved my hand slowly by my side, patting the carpet for something that I might be able to use as a weapon. My fingers touched something cold and metallic. Smooth and round. Not my gun, but maybe just as good if I could get my hand around it and make the throw count.

I slid my body up just a little, so I could reach the object more easily.

"Would have felt good, but I'm a man who knows he can't have everything. I reckon I'll settle for watching her get her head chopped off by Old Nathaniel."

He stepped forward again, just as the door behind him beeped. Someone was entering the code. Shit, I had to do it now.

I got my hand on the metal orb and threw it as hard as I could at his head. He fired off another shot just as the ball hit him in the right eye, but the shot went wide. I struggled to my feet and grabbed the DVD from the disc tray. The door swung open. One of the angry young men from downstairs stood there, stunned. For a moment, we were both frozen. Then his eyes went to the floor. I followed them and saw my 9mm. I lunged for it, scooping it up just before he could.

I pointed it at him and inched back toward the computer. I climbed up on the computer table, and I leaned out and tossed the DVD and then the gun up onto the roof. Then I swiveled at the waist until I had a good grip on the gutter. I pulled myself up and out of the window, just as I heard the young man start to yell.

I lifted myself up, my feet now dangling in the air as the gutter groaned and bent. A hand reached out from the window and grabbed onto one of my boots. The gutter groaned again. I managed to get one elbow up on the roof and then another.

He still had my boot. I made my foot straight and the boot slipped off.

I got one leg up, then the other.

On the roof, I lay flat for a moment, catching my breath, waiting. Hoping the man would be foolish enough to follow me.

A second later, I saw that he was. Two hands gripped the gutter as he tried to pull himself up. I waited until he'd twisted around and swung his legs free from the inside of the window. Then kicked his knuckles as hard as I could with my one good boot.

Two kicks was all it took. He fell silently until he hit the ground. Then there was only a dull, barely audible thud.

Grabbing the DVD and my 9mm, I stood on the slanted roof and moved toward the peak, looking around for a nearby tree limb that would allow me access to the ground. There had to be some way down. I couldn't accept that I'd made it this far only to get stuck on top of Taggart Monroe's roof.

When I saw it, my stomach sank. The best branch was a good seven or eight feet from the side of the roof. I'd never reach it without a death-defying jump. At least it looked sturdy.

I decided not to overthink it. That would just cause me to chicken out *and* waste time. I holstered my gun and tried to slide the DVD into my pocket, but it wouldn't fit, so I stuck it in my mouth and bit down on it. Then I took off.

Making the leap was no problem. If anything, I jumped *too* far. Still, I was able to grab the thickest part of the branch and hang on. The rest of my body collided with the tree trunk, and I felt a hot pain in my knee.

I held on. The DVD was still in my mouth, and I sucked air in around it. From this branch, I made my way carefully to another and then another until I was only about ten feet from the ground. I looked around, realizing I'd have to jump because there were no more branches . . .

Ten feet feels like thirty when you're falling and fifty when you hit the bottom. I rolled with it, and ended up going down a steep hill. The last thing I remember seeing before hitting my head was the moon, spinning in and out of my view, and each time I saw it, I realized how close it was to being full and how little time I had to do anything to save Mary, or myself.

48

When I finally heard my phone, it was almost dead. I reached for it, my hands grabbing kudzu vines and leaves. By the time I got it out of my pocket, it had stopped ringing.

The call was from Rufus. I sat up, trying to piece together what had happened. Instantly, my head hurt, and I decided to lie back down. Somehow I'd become tangled up in a bunch of undergrowth, but for the moment, I was content to just stay where I was and think.

It was morning, and I was at the bottom of a hill. Memories of rolling down it the night before came back to me. I felt something wet below my hip. I reached down to touch it and winced at the pain. When I pulled my hand away, there was blood on my fingertips. The landing—or maybe the rolling—had reopened the cut on my hip, and it had bled quite a bit while I'd been asleep.

Reaching for my phone again, I felt my shoulder light up with pain. I'd been shot. Jesus, how could a person forget that? I touched my shoulder gently, cautiously, and realized that it had bene bleeding pretty steadily for a while too. Luckily, the bullet had only grazed the hard top of my shoulder, tearing the flesh away, leaving me in pain but not otherwise incapacitated.

After some effort, I managed to rip off one of my shirtsleeves and tie it around my shoulder tight enough to stem the blood flow.

I picked up my phone and saw it was eleven forty-two in the morning. I'd been out for a long time.

My mouth was dry and tasted like blood. I'd have to find some water and some food. A sudden fear gripped me. What if I couldn't move my legs?

I bent both of them at the knees and relaxed a little. I was fine. I'd taken a blow to the head, but I was awake now, thinking clearly. I just needed to get myself out of the kudzu and make my way back to Susan's car. Then I could go to her place and finish watching the DVD—

Shit, the DVD! I patted the ground all around me, looking for it, but it wasn't there. I pulled myself up, ignoring the aching feeling in my head and searing pain in my hip and stood on shaking legs. I winced as I looked around. Now, I could see that I hadn't just rolled down the hill. Somehow I'd gone over a wooden fence and *then* rolled down the hill. The fence was at least ten feet high, and it seemed to stretch on forever. I realized with dismay that it most likely encircled the entire neighborhood. When I'd let go of the branch, it had been dark, and I hadn't realized I was effectively locking myself out of the neighborhood and away from Susan's car.

I walked along the bottom of the hill for a bit, trying to see if there was a gate or a break in the fence, or even a tree that I could use to climb back over. Unfortunately, all the trees on this side had been cut back precisely to keep people like me from getting in.

Never mind, I decided. None of it mattered without the DVD anyway. I focused my attention on finding it. It took some doing, but I was eventually able to locate the place where I'd come over the fence and rolled down the hill. I walked back up the steep hill, my legs burning with the effort, retracing my path from the night before. It was only when my legs were exhausted from the hill and I decided to take a short rest, that I saw the DVD hanging from a tree limb like a Christmas ornament.

"You better be worth it," I said as I extracted the disc from the branch and started back down the hill.

* * *

I didn't realize what bad shape I was in until I tried to call Rufus back. My phone was dead. Why hadn't I called him back immediately?

Just minutes before it had a charge, but I'd waited. Now it was too late.

Just like that, I was on my own, in the woods, with two pretty major injuries. I believed I'd been lucky because of where Walsh had shot me. No vital organs involved, and from what I could tell, it was a pretty clean wound. I was thankful for every piece of good luck, no matter how small.

I studied the location of the sun, trying to estimate how long I had to make it to the cornfield. The good news was I knew if I kept walking away from the fence, I'd run into it eventually. The bad news was that eventually could be too far away.

The night before, I'd stood on the high ridge, looking off over this valley, and what I'd seen were miles and miles of forest before the cornfield. I would have to hurry, especially if I hoped to watch the DVD before sunset.

As I picked my way down another hill, careful of rocks and roots, holding onto tree limbs, I tried to formulate a plan. If I could make it to the trailer park before dark, I could try to find Deja. She'd let me in her trailer to finish watching the DVD. If there was anything on it that would help save Mary, I wanted—no *needed*—to watch it.

I could also use her phone and call for some backup. I wouldn't ask Susan. Hell, she couldn't come anyway without a car, but I'd ask Ronnie. Surely, he'd help. I hoped.

Until then, I was on my own.

I kept walking, as the ground sloped ever downward, and the morning turned to afternoon.

The day was the coolest we'd had since last spring, and I would have liked nothing more than to be sitting somewhere in the Fingers with Rufus and Mary, polishing off a bottle of Wild Turkey and talking about religion or philosophy, or even the true nature of evil. It was an interesting topic when viewed at a distance. Up close, it was much less fascinating and quite a bit more troubling.

I tried to keep moving in a straight line, but that was more difficult than I anticipated. As the woods grew more dense, I often had to go around certain areas that were impassable due to deadfall or a sudden ravine. Often enough I ran into great sections of vines and snarled undergrowth that had entangled trees and boulders, creating something like a spider's web of greenery that I didn't dare try to pass through. After each obstacle, I found myself trying to see through the canopy of brown, green, and yellow above me to locate the sun. It had been a clear day when I entered the woods, but now only glimpses of sunlight were available, and most of that was diffused through a thousand leaves of every color so that trying to find the source of the day's fading light was like trying to find the brightest bulb in a room filled with shaded lamps.

After a while, I began to move on instinct. My father—who besides being a preacher had also been an excellent hunter and woodsman—taught me the best thing to do when you got confused in the woods was to sit down and seek God's counsel. Like so much of his advice, there was wisdom in the part that hadn't been warped by piety and his need to dictate people's lives. What he'd been right about was the sitting-down part. The being still. The very worst thing you could do when you were getting lost was to keep moving. All that did was increase the chances you'd become completely lost instead of just a little bit.

But stopping was not a luxury I could afford. I was keenly aware of the time I'd wasted because of the fall from the tree. Moreover, I was getting a little pissed that I'd done all of that for a DVD I might not even be able to watch. I kept walking, moving deeper into the woods because I was afraid to do anything else, because stopping would be giving credence to the creeping sensation that failure was right around the corner, that I had no real shot of saving Mary much less discovering what was really going on in Jefferson's cornfield.

The part that piqued my anger and dismay the most was that I finally thought I had a grasp of what was happening, and now I was lost, wandering the woods, in no position to do anything about it.

Evil, it seemed, never stopped. It always came back. My father had been an evil, vile man whose sole purpose on this earth seemed to be making others hurt for not believing the same things he did. I finally overcame him, only for Jeb Walsh to show up, a man who seemed to be cut from the same cloth as my father, a ruthless fanatic whose rules applied to everyone except himself. Then there was Lane Jefferson—a seemingly normal man, who might or might not don a killer's suit when the sun went down, to perpetuate some racist myth from the distant past. And how could I forget Taggart Monroe? A man willing to break every taboo for money and even a small piece of cult success.

But how to stop them? That was the question that was driving me insane. It was a question that might or might not be answered on the DVD I'd finally managed to wedge into my pocket (after ripping the corner just a little). Because if I didn't have some kind of edge, I was doomed to fail inside that cornfield. I'd been inside it before, and it was the kind of place that warped reality and favored the mad.

But maybe I did have an advantage. The mirrors had shown me the spokes. And the spokes all led to the center. Surely it was something they wouldn't expect me to know. Would it be enough to outsmart them, to stop Old Nathanial and the film?

Part of me wondered if it would even matter because this whole thing had become bigger than the individual players. Stopping some fool wearing an Old Nathaniel mask or some other fool holding a camera wouldn't stop the evil, would it? No, maybe it would save Mary, but what about the rest of the people who would cross the paths of these vile men? Their violence was systemic, and I intuitively understood that it was also comprehensive. Exhaustive. And the weight of it was heavier than anything one man could ever hope to lift alone.

I knew this was right, yet I also knew that if you could stop the button man, you could stop the killing. That was all I had to cling to as I kept moving in what I hoped was the right direction.

The next time I looked at the sky, the light was fading, and an early moon had already made its appearance in the late afternoon sky.

It was pale and soft, and beautiful.

And completely full.

49

At some point, my brain shut down. I didn't think so much as hallucinate. My body continued to plunge forward, but my mind drifted away to parts unknown. I was in church again, seated beside Mama, while Daddy stomped and raved and reached for another serpent. I was with Lester, sitting by Ghost Creek, drinking shine we'd swiped from Herschel Knott. I was with Mary, the last time we'd hiked in the mountains together, a thunderstorm fast approaching, her hand, small and urgent, in mine. She'd whispered in my ear that we should find a place to ride it out, and her tongue had curled and her breath had heaved on the word *ride*, and damned if I didn't know exactly what she wanted. We found the cave, and we found a moment or two that would forever be a part of me, and I hoped a part of her.

These memories and a thousand more came and went like gnats, worrying me for a few moments before dying away only to be replaced by the next ones.

When I came to the train tracks, I stumbled across them and fell face down on the other side, skidding down the rocky embankment along the tracks. I wiped blood off my elbows and noted the rips in my pants before touching my pocket to make sure that the DVD was still there, intact, and then I rose and kept walking, a zombie whose brain had been reduced to a single goal.

Following the tracks across the river.

* * *

I reached the train trestle at dusk, when the river below me had turned to its blackest pitch. I saw the moon reflected in its glassy surface, and my body wavered as I approached the midpoint of the trestle. Lack of fluids had made me unsteady on my feet, and for a brief second I lost my footing and lurched out toward the side of the tracks just the way I'd dreamed. I saw the black water, rising, reaching out for me.

But I managed to regain my footing and step away from the edge, leaning my weight back, centering myself despite the shotgun blast of pain in my hip.

I'm halfway home, I thought. Even as I thought it, I realized it didn't really make much sense. Home was in the mountains. Home was with Mary. I was only going to watch a DVD.

I nearly fell again but managed to only drop to one knee. I pulled myself back up and stumbled forward. Somewhere in the distance, I heard a train coming. The trestle began to vibrate.

When I made it to the other side, I went to the first trailer I could find and pounded on the door. An old man answered and held out his hands to steady me. "Deja," I said.

* * *

"Mr. Earl," she said, "drink some water."

She was holding out a plastic cup, one of those extra-extra-large ones you can get at the gas station. She pressed it to my lips, and I drank in the cool liquid.

Nothing had ever tasted better.

A few sips later, I felt more like myself.

We were sitting in her trailer on the couch. Her mother stood in the doorway between the kitchen and the den, watching us.

"You were shot," she said.

"I'm sorry." For some reason that was the only thing I could think to say.

"I tried to call the sheriff, but apparently everything in Riley is shut down because of that idiot's rally."

I nodded. "Yeah, they planned it that way."

"Deja said you're looking for the woman who disappeared."

"Yes."

"That's all I need to hear. We want to help however we can. Is your wound okay?"

"I think so. Please tell me you have a DVD player."

"A what?" Deja said.

"God, you're kidding me. A DVD player. It plays a DVD."

She shook her head. "You mean one of those disc drive things?"

"We have one," Deja's mother said. "It's on my laptop. Hold on and I'll get it."

"Thank you." I turned to Deja. "Can I use your phone?"

She handed me her cell phone.

I thought for a moment, trying to decide who to call first. I started to dial 911 but stopped after pressing nine. What good would it do to alert Patterson, which would be exactly what the dispatch would do?

I deleted nine and started over, dialing Ronnie's number.

Please, please, please answer.

"Hello," Ronnie said. He didn't sound drunk or high, just ornery, like a man thankful for a phone call just because he'd been too long without somebody to argue with.

"It's Earl."

"Earl? Are you shitting me? You okay? I been trying to call you all day. I even walked over to see if the blind bastard had heard from you, and—"

"Shut up and listen."

"Okay."

"I need you to do something for me."

"Sure. Except . . ."

"Except what?"

"I'm in downtown Riley, and it's a mess here. I hope you don't need me to go nowhere."

"That's exactly what I need. Get in your truck and start driving toward the cornfield. Keep your phone on you. I'm going to call you again when I know more. If you get here and you haven't heard from me yet, just keep coming. Head straight for the middle of the cornfield, and don't stop no matter what. You got it?"

"What's going on, Earl? Are you all right?"

"Yeah," I said.

"I ain't heard from you and . . . I don't know. I thought you might be dead."

"No, I'm okay. Just remember what I said. All the way to the middle of the cornfield. Drive hard and fast, Ronnie."

I ended the call as Deja's mother handed me the laptop. It was powered on, and all I had to do was slip the disc in the drive located on the side. I waited as it loaded.

The DVD started at the beginning, so I clicked the slider at the bottom and moved it ahead about a third of the way.

There he was—Old Nathaniel, or someone dressed like him—parting the dense stalks with a knife. The camera zoomed in on the knife. The reflection of the full moon was imprinted on the flat side of the silver blade. The corn opened up.

"Mr. Earl?"

"Hold on."

"You need to eat something."

I turned away from the screen and saw that Deja was holding a plate of ham and eggs. "Mama just made it."

I nodded and took the plate, eating greedily as I watched Old Nathaniel weave through the cornstalks in a seemingly random pattern. When he exited the corn, he was in the trees. The camera followed him from behind. It was shaky, poorly executed, but there was a rawness about the moment, a tension that I couldn't deny.

That tension reached a boiling point when the camera left Old Nathaniel and zoomed ahead through the woods. There were two people walking down a trail. One of them held a gun. The other one—

The other one was Mary.

They stopped, and Johnny Waters turned around, looking directly at the camera, but the light went out on the camera almost instantly, and the screen went dark. I heard jostling and then a scream.

The scream came from Johnny.

"Who are you?" Mary said.

"You can call me Nate," a modulated voice said.

The camera came back on and the cameraman ran to catch up, pausing just long enough to run the camera over Johnny, lying near the stream.

Someone grunted, and the camera flew back up—too fast, for a second everything was blurry—but when it finally did come back into focus, it showed Mary punching Old Nathaniel in the stomach. He bent over, huffing with pain. She started to run, but the man holding the camera spoke.

"Stop," he said.

Mary turned and looked directly at the camera. I didn't believe I'd ever been more proud of an individual in my entire life. Her look was defiant and unafraid.

"You going to shoot me?" she said. "Go ahead." Then she turned and started to walk away. She didn't get far before Old Nathaniel grabbed her, lifted her up like she was a sack of groceries, and tossed her into the air. Mary—she couldn't have weighed more than a hundred and ten soaking wet—landed hard against a tree trunk. She slid to the ground and lay there for a moment. Old Nathaniel walked over and said something I couldn't hear, most likely because his mic had already come off in the earlier struggle. Then he kicked her.

He picked her up and slung her lifeless body over his shoulder.

I swallowed. She was still alive. She was just out, I told myself. She was tough. Tougher than anybody I'd ever known, thank God.

The camera followed them as Old Nathaniel carried her back toward the cornfield.

"Shit," Deja said. "Was that real?"

"I'm afraid it was."

"It's your girlfriend."

It wasn't a question, but I answered it anyway. "Yeah, Mary Hawkins."

"Where's he taking her?"

"That's what I'm hoping to find out."

We watched, barely breathing as he moved deeper and deeper into the high stalks. Soon, he was dwarfed by them, and they seemed like cornstalks from a dream, instead of reality. I wondered if some special effect had been added to make them taller.

He came to a wall so thick with stalks that there appeared to be no seam, no way through. It was a dead end. He laid Mary down and pulled out his knife. He inserted it into the wall, creating a seam, using his other hand to separate the stalks.

He pulled them apart as wide as he could and turned back to Mary, taking her arm and dragging her through. The stalks closed, leaving the cameraman on the other side.

There was a cut, then the film resumed in a clearing, high stalks all around, a circular wall. Mary lay on the ground and Old Nathaniel stood beside a small metal hatch in the ground. The camera moved slowly closer until it was positioned directly over the hatch. Someone had painted the same symbol here as the one on the stickers—two axe handles and a skull. Old Nathaniel opened the hatch, and it groaned loudly.

At first, it looked like something electric inside. Whatever it was seemed to glow like starlight. But as the camera sharpened its focus, I could see that the glow came from gleaming white skulls. At least a half dozen of them, maybe more.

At the lip of the opening, I could make out the top of a metal ladder. Old Nathaniel climbed down until he was standing at the bottom among the skulls. Then he reached back up and found Mary's arm. He dragged her headfirst into the hole.

When he emerged a few minutes later, he stood over the hole, looking down. The last shot before he closed the hatch was of Mary, lying among the skulls.

Then the scene went dark.

50

I was shaking when I handed Deja the laptop. She took it and said, "You shouldn't go."

But I was already standing up, heading toward the door. "I'll be fine. At least until the police come."

Deja's mother came back in. "Do you have a gun?'

"Yeah," I said.

"How about a flashlight?"

Shit. Was I really about to go out there without one? "No, and I'd be really thankful if you had one I could use."

"I'll go get it."

I looked at Deja. "I hate to ask, but can I borrow your phone?"

She handed it to me without a word, but I could tell there was something she wanted to say, but hadn't been able to think how to say it yet.

"You okay?" I asked her.

"Do you think," she started, and then faltered. "Do you think one of those skulls is my brother's?"

I hesitated. My first instinct was to tell her no, that her brother was surely safe somewhere now, but I remembered how badly I'd wanted to know what happened to Mary, how I wouldn't let myself stop until I'd found the truth, even if it was bad. "I think it's a strong possibility," I said.

She nodded, a tear streaming down her cheek, and I found myself suddenly wanting to take it back, to tell her I was wrong, but that would have only made it worse. Once again, I was reminded that sometimes there were no right answers, much less easy ones.

"I'm going to try to make sure the men behind it are held responsible."

"Okay," she said. "I hope you do."

Deja's mother returned with the flashlight. I thanked them both and then left the trailer, walking quickly toward the bridge. I'd only gone a few steps when I began to run, hip and shoulder be damned.

I didn't stop running until I was on the other side of the river, looking at what I hoped was the same wall of corn where Old Nathaniel had entered with Mary.

I stepped inside and the corn swallowed me up as it always did, and there was a part of me that felt as if the real evil resided inside these stalks, where the corn silk flew wild and the light of the moon glazed everything in a thick honey colored glow. How much blood had fertilized this field? I had counted at least a half dozen in the video, but who knew how wide that underground space was and how filled it might be with the remains of the dead?

It all felt like a dream, but I was determined to wake up, to wake Mary up and walk the hell out of this damned cornfield forever.

The full moon made the cornstalks stand out, each one a scarecrow, each one deadly. I tried to find something that looked familiar from the video or from my view from the mirrors, but the problem was that it *all* looked familiar. Each stalk looked like the last.

Holding the flashlight in one hand and my 9mm in the other, I made a complete turn, looking for anything that might guide me.

There was nothing. I was in one of the spaces between the spokes, where the corn seemed random and stifling and impossible. I needed to pick a direction and bull through until I found a clear path that would lead me to the circle in the middle.

I holstered my 9mm and slipped the flashlight in my pocket. Then, using both hands, I began to swim through the stalks, pushing them aside and moving forward in small increments. It was a painstaking process, not only for my hip and tired arms, but also for my psyche. With each passing moment, I was more aware that I might not get to the bunker in time.

Sure, there was a possibility I'd arrive and not find her, that there would be one more skull among the others, but I was increasingly more convinced that they were keeping her inside until tonight. Until they could film the hunt.

The third and final climax.

When I broke free, it felt like I had been reborn, like I'd been underwater for a long time, and I'd finally found the surface and air that I could breathe again. I'd found a spoke. The straight row went on for a long, long time in both directions. The only problem was that in my long struggle to get here, I'd lost all sense of direction and didn't know which direction would take me to the hub in the middle of the wheel.

I pulled out my flashlight and lifted the beam toward the sky, waving it around until I saw the reflection from the mirrors to my right. That meant I needed to go in the opposite direction to reach the middle.

I hoped.

Turning left, I began to jog again, and then, the pain in my hip manageable—at least for the time being—I broke into a sprint.

When I saw the dead end in front of me, I thought I'd missed it somehow. I backtracked, slowly, taking care to move the flashlight around so I wouldn't miss the hatch. But I soon realized the hatch wasn't there. I hadn't passed it.

I turned back toward the dead end. I'd have to break through the wall. Surely it wouldn't be as hard as the last one I'd fought through.

Then I remembered what I'd just seen on the video, Old Nathaniel parting the stalks like a curtain. He found the seam with his knife, and . . . I reached out with both hands, feeling around for a gap or space that was invisible. My hand found a break, and I parted the stalks with both hands. They bent away from each other, and I saw that there was a path leading through to the other side.

I stepped through, turning sideways to keep the sharp, dry husks from cutting me. Emerging on the other side, I saw that it was a perfect circle of corn, that the moonlight had illuminated everything in its thick and lazy shine. It would have been a fantasyland, straight out of a Disney princess movie if not for the hatch set into the bare ground exactly in the center of the clearing.

I swallowed and moved slowly toward it. All of my impatience had slipped away, replaced by a chilled panic, a looming dread about what I'd find when I opened that hatch.

Two more steps, and the symbol on the lid came clear. The axes that framed the skull seemed more ominous in the light of the moon. I knelt beside the hatch, my 9mm in one hand, the flashlight in the other. The handle was there. All I needed to do was turn it.

I put the flashlight down, aiming the light at the handle. I felt a surge of despair. I felt as if I was poised before a moment that could go either way. The evil might be inside or it might jump into me, or maybe there was no such thing as evil and grief was all there was in the world. Maybe it was the grief that set off the evil, or maybe it was the other way around.

The only thing I knew for sure was that I didn't want to open the door. After all the struggle I'd been through, I didn't want to open it. Perhaps it was the realization that my struggle, in the end, meant nothing. The seeds of evil and grief had been planted so long ago, and we spent our lives opening the ground, tending the soil, nursing them to full health.

This one could kill me. Not just physically. This one would kill anything resembling my soul, my interior life, my faith in this godforsaken world.

I might have stayed there longer, wasting time I didn't have, putting off the inevitable, had I not seen the light flashing faraway, at what I guessed was the outskirts of the cornfield. Time was short now. They were almost here.

The handle was cold in my hand. I turned it hard and lifted the hatch.

51

Moments of joy—true ones, anyway—are the rarest things. I'm not talking about happiness. I'm talking about joy, true joy, the kind that aches as much as it lifts. The kind that makes you decide life might be worth it after all, even despite all the bad shit.

Maybe those moments seem more intense when they follow moments of despair. Despair is what I felt when I shined the flashlight inside the bunker and saw nothing but skulls so bright they seemed to glow. I eased down the ladder, gripping the metal rungs tightly, the sweat under my palms making each one slick.

At the bottom, I looked for a bare place to step and finally kicked one of the skulls out of the way with a hollow rattle. Once on solid ground, I smelled something horrible, something more pungent than old bones, and I immediately thought the worst. It was coming from my left, and I shined the light toward it and found . . . nothing. Well, not quite *nothing*. A closer look revealed what appeared to be human waste near the far wall of the bunker. Somehow, that gave me hope.

I turned the other way and that was when I saw her.

She was asleep, in the far corner of the bunker, which was a great deal larger than I'd anticipated. She was alive. She was breathing. She'd been fed.

And just like that I felt the joy.

It lasted only briefly, but it hardly mattered. When you feel it, real joy, you only need a shot. Mary's eyes opened under the glare of the flashlight. For a moment, her expression was utter disbelief, and then she smiled. I went to her and kissed her, and only then did she seem to believe that I was real.

"Earl?"

"I'm here."

"It's not a dream."

She sat up and hugged me so hard my hip hurt. I didn't care. I hugged her back just as hard.

"They're going to film me," she said, and she was crying and hyperventilating all at once. I pushed her hair back, stroking her face.

"Take it easy," I said. "I know all about it. Which is why we need to go. Right now."

Mary nodded, and I helped her to her feet. I must have winced when I did because she leaned in and kissed my neck. "You're hurt."

"Got shot by Jeb Walsh and cut in the ass by Old Nathaniel."

"Good Lord."

"Yeah, it's been one of those weeks."

We moved to the ladder. I let her climb out first, and then I followed her.

"Where?" she said. She seemed to be in shock, still unsure if my visit was real or a dream.

I looked around, trying to get my bearings. The corn looked the same on all sides, and it wasn't until I looked up and saw the moon that I understood which direction was which. Now I just needed to decide.

The dream always ended in the same place, the train trestle. The pervading sense I got from the dream upon waking was that Mary survived. I didn't necessarily get the same sense about myself, but the goal was to save Mary. That had always been the goal.

"This way," I said, pointing in the direction that I believed would lead us out of the cornfield and to the tracks.

* * *

Once inside the dense stalks again, another world revealed itself. It was a world of immense depth and layers. Complications upon complications, no sense or meaning other than plunging forward, looking behind to make sure Mary was still close. She'd become another dark shape among a million dark shapes, and I felt afraid of losing her again.

I lost track of time as we moved through the cornfield, and soon even my ability to read space seemed to suffer. Was the stalk far away or right in front of my face? Sometimes I couldn't tell. And where was the straight spoke that we needed, the path that would take us out of here?

Mary grabbed my hand and pulled me close. I started to speak, but she put a hand to my mouth and nodded off to the right.

The stalks weren't as dense here. It felt almost like a clearing, but there were still enough of them around to make it difficult to tell what was what.

One stalk in particular seemed different. The others glowed with pale fire, but not the one directly on our right. It stood crookedly and did not move when the breeze drifted down from the night sky.

I was transfixed. Was it an illusion or was that something more than a stalk, something closer to a scarecrow or a man? Mary squeezed my hand so tightly it caused my shoulder to hurt again.

"Who's there?" I said.

The stalk or man or scarecrow still didn't move.

Behind us I heard something crack dryly. A cornhusk breaking or a stalk snapping in two.

But I couldn't take my eyes off the unmoving stalk, the way it stood so crooked, so defiant . . .

Mary screamed and jerked my shoulder so hard, the wound reopened. I spun around and saw him.

The Hide-Behind Man, Old Nathaniel. He was flying at us, and I had just enough time to remember the old adage about when you see him, it's too—

"Don't kill them," a voice said. "Not yet."

The Hide-Behind Man stopped short of Mary, falling away back into the stalks. I lost him again.

A light burned my face.

"Howdy, detective."

It was Lane Jefferson. A cameraman and lighting crew stood behind him. They parted to allow a small man holding a flashlight to step into the little clearing. Tag Monroe. A man stood beside him, holding a rifle.

Tag nodded at me. "This is going to make for some great scenes. I want to thank you. Truly, Mr. Marcus, I couldn't have written it better myself. I have to admit, you fooled me at my party last night. I wouldn't have thought you'd be so ballsy. But never mind. It's all worked out for the best. Now we can do a dual scene at the Keep. We'll make it a ritual sacrifice. My adoring racists will eat it up. Uppity negress gets her head cut off while her guilt-ridden white boyfriend watches."

"I like it," Lane said.

* * *

Once back at the "Keep," Old Nathaniel appeared again. He had a knife and watched Mary and me like a hangman watches his victims. Tag spent some time talking to Lane as they discussed where to put us and how to light the scene.

The whole time, a man I didn't recognize held us at gunpoint. I squeezed Mary's hand in a way I hoped would be reassuring. *There was still hope* was the sentiment I was trying to convey.

For Mary's part, she looked defiant. She amazed me with her lack of fear. She didn't shrink from any of the men. Not even Old Nathaniel when he came over and held the knife out for us to see. It was a long, curved weapon, spectacularly sharp, and it was clear it would cut through flesh with little effort.

"Okay," Tag said finally. "It's time." He positioned Mary a few feet away from me and had her kneel. She refused, and several men came over and tried to force her to her knees. I was on my way over to help her when I heard it.

The rumbling.

I felt it too. Like an earthquake on the other side of the cornfield, whose ripples could be felt on the air, the wind, on the cornstalks, it moved closer, tumbling toward us, deepening.

"What the fuck is that?" Tag said.

I met Mary's eyes as they widened with understanding.

When the big headlights, like predator's eyes peering through the highest stalks, appeared, someone screamed. A monster was coming, leveling corn, shaking the very earth, and scattering men like leaves ahead of autumn's first breath.

I grabbed Mary's arm and pulled her out toward the corn as the monster crashed toward the clearing, growling again, a deep, sonorous, glorious thing that shook the very ground and, somehow, the sky.

Stalks fell over as a rippling wave shuddered through the field. Just behind the wave were the eyes, and I saw now that there were six of them. Two were lower to the ground and the other four were high and moved like spotlights. Somebody whooped, pure joy filtered through a rebel yell. I heard Mary scream, and realized I'd stopped moving, that I'd somehow become frozen in the great beast's bright gaze. Mary pulled my arm, dragging me into the cover of the stalks.

Behind us the engine died. Men shouted. Shots were fired. Bullets pinged off the undercarriage of Ronnie's truck.

We'd only plunged a short way through the corn before I recognized the moment, the feeling. Even the pain in my side and hip seemed familiar. My heart beat a familiar tattoo against the world. I was here. I was here, it seemed to say, but there was something implicit in it too, something unstated, like an echo . . .

Like a dream.

We crashed through the corn together. My shoulder burned, my hip began to bleed again, and I felt like I was running on a prop that wasn't really connected to my body, and I couldn't make the prop move fast enough, and I couldn't make it stop hurting.

Time slowed down and sped up all at once. We were in the field forever, and then we were free of it, and I remembered turning around and seeing him behind us.

Him. How was it even possible?

What followed us now was a myth come to life, a nightmare realized.

We ran through the woods for a long time before I fell.

Mary came back for me.

"No," I said. "Keep going."

She ignored me and braced me on my injured side, easing the pressure on my leg as we moved. I looked behind us. Old Nathaniel was closer. The knife was a silver streak in his hand. He seemed in no hurry, as if he already knew how it would all play out.

"You came for me," she said, and kissed my neck. "And I won't ever leave you."

"Yeah, but if you don't let go, he's going to catch us both."

"It's a chance we'll have to take. He may have a knife, but there's two of us."

"I dreamed this," I said. "We have to keep heading toward the train." Even as I said it, I was aware of two implicit things in the dream, the two things that I'd always known: Mary lived. I died.

It might not be the only way to make sure she lived, but it was the only way I knew about, so that was what we'd do.

As if on cue, I heard the train whistle. We adjusted our route slightly, heading for the tracks.

Somewhere far behind us now, I heard police sirens. I wondered if somehow Ronnie had gotten through to 911 and somebody had roused a deputy or two from the rally.

"You all right?" I asked.

"Fine. Got all the energy in the world," she said between deep gasps. "How about you?"

"Fine. Just need to keep moving," I lied.

"We're going to make it," she said, and I believed she meant it. "What happens at the train tracks?"

"We turn left and head for the train trestle."

"What about the train?"

"We'll have to outrun it." I didn't want to tell her about jumping.

"You can't outrun it."

"You can."

"I'm not leaving you. Remind me again why we need to go out on the bridge."

"It's the only way. It gives us an advantage." I knew even as I said them that my words lacked logic.

"It's not to our advantage to be foolish," she said.

But she kept going anyway.

Mary was holding me up now because my right leg was essentially useless.

The river came into view. I looked over my shoulder. Old Nathaniel was maybe twenty yards behind us and gaining fast.

Up ahead, the train whistle blared again, and I could see the bright headlight bearing down on us.

"We can't make it," Mary said.

"You can. If you let go of me, you can make it easy. Leave me on the tracks to deal with him."

"For the last time—I'm *not* leaving you."

"You *have* to," I hissed at her. "The dream—"

"I don't give a flying fuck about the dream."

She grabbed my hand and started across the trestle. She seemed determined to pull me across if she had to, but we were still going too slow. By the time we reached the middle of the trestle, two things were clear: Neither of us was going to make it to the other side before the train reached us and Nathaniel was going to catch us both before then anyway.

We stopped, and Mary turned to face Nathaniel.

"What are you doing?" I asked.

"I'm going to fight."

"No," I said. "We jump."

Mary looked down at the black water and shook her head.

"It's too far."

"No," I said. "We'll make it."

It was a lie. I felt like *she'd* make it. But beyond that, I had no idea what to expect.

Old Nathaniel was a few yards away from us now. Him slowing down had given the train even more time to get closer to us. Mary looked at it and realized the inevitable. Even if she were able to fend off Old Nathaniel, she'd still have to jump or be crushed by the train.

"Come on," she said, and grabbed my hand. I struggled to my feet with her help. "We jump at the same time, okay?"

I nodded. She counted to three and jumped. I let go of her hand, seeing the surprise in her face just before I turned to face Old Nathaniel.

The moment stretched out, as all the big moments do, and I saw the moon on the flat side of the blade, heard someone call out from far away, felt a whoosh of wind and thought it was a mighty breeze blown up from the river, but quickly realized it wasn't a breeze at all, but instead the uprising of air as Mary fell.

I waited as long as I dared, the train bleating at my back, Old Nathaniel coming hard at me from the front.

When I stepped off, I was in the dream again. Reality ceased. I was falling through sleep, in perfect silence, or I was floating, hanging in the air, and the water was actually rising up to meet me, to welcome me.

I spun as I fell and saw him above me, a dark-winged scarecrow who had infiltrated my very dreams, the way evil always infiltrates each one of us, sooner or later.

And then the black water of the river swallowed us up and I sank to the bottom, but my eyes never found the full moon, high above the world, flooding this dark river with its crazed light.

A dark shape, falling, blotted out the moon. I was coming up, the water rushing into my nose and ears, and as the dark shape sank, we collided.

I closed my eyes—because the light was gone anyway—and felt the prick of the knife somewhere in my gut.

Turning and twisting, I broke free of his grip and willed myself to the surface, my body broken and useless, but my eyes and lungs burning for the night air.

I broke through in a coughing fit, and Mary's hands were around me. She dragged me toward the shore where I lay, gasping, trying to tell her he was in the river too, but no sounds could break the shuddering violence of the train assaulting the night as it rumbled past.

When I saw him rise from the river, still clutching the knife, I pointed.

Mary turned to face him and he charged her, splashing water ahead of him. She sidestepped at the last moment, but he stuck out an arm and clubbed her shoulder, slowing himself. He spun, raising the knife and bringing it down in a flash, but somehow she'd slithered away, dodging the cut.

I stood, feeling like a dead man who just hadn't breathed his last yet, and lumbered over to Old Nathaniel. Because it really was him, wasn't it? No one else could be so relentless, so determined. All the others had found evil along the way. And he *was* the thing they'd found.

I grabbed him by the shoulders and threw my weight into him. He stumbled and swatted at me with the knife, catching the flesh on my right arm. As much as it hurt, that cut may have saved my life, and Mary's.

The knife got stuck in what the doctors would later tell me was a knotted tendon. As I pulled my arm away and fell to the ground in pain, the knife came with me.

He fell on top of me as I gripped the handle and tried to pull it free. He did not speak.

His hands went to my throat and gripped it powerfully. I could feel myself dying, the world growing dark, the very life being squeezed out of me until all that was left was a tiny glimmer, just the spark of a thing. He bore down again, and then the glimmer went out too.

52

Later, I pieced it together in fragments, the way you do when you've been dead and the world with all its light you take for granted goes on without you.

The first fragment I remembered was Mary crying, her tears covering my face like rain. I tried to speak but couldn't. She told me to rest. I closed my eyes and rested.

Then I remembered being in an ambulance as paramedics discussed how long I'd been dead.

"Ten minutes, according to the woman."

"Ten minutes is impossible."

"So is losing this much blood and still being alive."

After that the memories grew increasingly more scattershot. Mary's face. Rufus's hand on my shoulder. A deputy—no, two deputies—at my bedside, nodding, talking to themselves or maybe a doctor, maybe someone else.

Me, waking up and asking a nurse if they'd caught Old Nathaniel.

"Who, dear?"

"Old Nathaniel?"

"I know they caught a lot of men. You and your girlfriend did a good thing."

"What about Jeb Walsh? Did they catch him?"

She shook her head and pointed to the television I'd previously been unaware of. It showed Walsh taking questions at a press conference somewhere. His right eye was dark and swollen from where the metal paperweight had hit him. "Can you turn it up?" I asked, but the nurse was gone, and I was too sleepy to listen anyway. Later, I'd hear a replay of the conference. He was calling me a hero and saying how the county needed to move beyond its violent history. And that was why when he was in the House, he'd work hard to clean up areas of corruption like this one.

Me waking up sometime later and thinking how I might be the only man in the world to be bitten by a venomous snake, struck by lightning, and killed at the hands of a mountain legend. And yet, I was still alive.

That had to mean something, right?

I wasn't sure.

I'd never been very sure of much.

Except that wasn't true, was it? I was sure that I loved Mary Hawkins. Which is why the worst thing I've ever experienced wasn't dying. It wasn't being bitten in the face by that cottonmouth or being struck by lightning on top of a windy mountain.

The worst thing that ever happened to me lasted for eight days, the time in which I had to live without her.

* * *

While I was dead, Mary got the knife out of my arm and plunged it into Old Nathaniel's back.

That's what I was told anyway. It's easy enough to imagine. Mary's damned tough, tougher than me, and I don't say that lightly.

She watched him stagger back toward the river and then steady himself before stumbling into the swift water. She said the blood from his wound flowed out in front of him as the current carried him away.

They still haven't found him. Which—I won't lie—gives me pause. I still think about the strawberry-shaped tattoo on his neck. Every time I see a person I don't know these days, my eyes involuntarily go to their neck, just to see.

When he was gone, Mary gave me mouth-to-mouth. She pounded on my chest and did a lot of screaming. When the paramedics arrived, they said she was still screaming at me, and she didn't even realize I'd started breathing again.

People always ask me what I remember from those ten minutes. It would be nice to tell them I remember all the clichés, a long dark tunnel with a bright light at the end, that I saw my own body as I rose into heaven, or that my life even flashed before my eyes. The truth is, I don't remember any of that.

The only glimmer I have of my time on the "other side" was a feeling of being loved. That was it. I didn't have a body or a mind or anything except that feeling. It was a warm bath around me, and I think it sustained me. I think it proves all you really need to know about this world. Evil is planted and evil blooms and evil infects, but love transcends all of it. Even death.

* * *

The fallout was like nothing I'd ever seen. I thought taking my father's church down had been big. The Agents of Change had their fingers in nearly everything: local churches, banks, the sheriff's department, even the manager at the local coffee shop was arrested. But none of them had strawberry-shaped tattoos on their necks. I checked.

The worst part was who didn't go down.

Lane Jefferson was arrested and awaiting trial for participating in a criminal conspiracy, kidnapping, and attempted murder.

Taggart Monroe was in custody, awaiting trial for murder, criminal conspiracy, and attempted murder. The FBI, who were called as support, found his stash of snuff films and are actively trying to track down everyone else who was involved. The early estimate is that he was responsible for no less than eight deaths.

Sheriff Patterson was also in lockup, awaiting trial for so many charges I couldn't keep track of them all.

Frank Bentley, Jeb Walsh, Mayor Keith, and Preston Argent were still free men, and the scary part was they'd inserted themselves into the scandal as heroes, and most of the public seemed to be buying it.

Walsh was gearing up for his run for the House of Representatives, and Bentley and Keith were big supporters. Argent—I still couldn't believe this—was going to run for sheriff. And from the looks of things, he was going to run unopposed.

Then there was Ronnie. I might have suffered the most bodily harm during the whole ordeal, but Ronnie's suffering was the cruelest and the most unfair. Despite what he did to save Mary and me—not to mention ultimately expose the snuff film ring—he was arrested for manslaughter. When he'd come flying through the cornfield in that monster truck, he'd killed a man, and though both Mary and I pleaded his case, the FBI agents who ran the investigation took an immediate dislike to Ronnie's attitude and smart mouth. On top of that, the district attorney and Ronnie had a past. They'd had run-ins, and he didn't get the same leniency, the same benefit of the doubt that Mary and I did. His trial was still forthcoming, but they'd stacked the charges against him, and it didn't look good: breaking and entering, resisting arrest, manslaughter, some more drug charges for what they'd found in his truck.

He was being held in the county jail until his trial or until he made bail, which was set at twenty-five thousand, well beyond what Rufus, Mary, and I could scrape together.

I didn't even get a chance to explain about being in the hospital before he lit into me. I promised him I'd plead his case to the DA. And I did, but they didn't listen. Everyone there told me the same thing: Ronnie Thrash has had this coming for a long time.

I told them they were wrong, but it was like talking to a wall. One that didn't have any seams or a way through it.

Each subsequent visit with Ronnie was worse. He ranted and raved, accusing me of abandoning him. Telling me he'd always known I was using him. I promised him this wasn't the case, but I couldn't help feeling guilty anyway. I'd managed to get off free because the DA called my actions "necessary and even heroic." I'd called him repeatedly to tell him that I couldn't have done any of it without Ronnie, but he wouldn't listen.

"You're wrong to feel guilty for that little shit," he said. "He would turn on you the first chance he gets."

I might have believed that once, but not anymore. Ronnie was angry. He had a right to be. But when push came to shove, I actually wanted him in my corner. As crazy as he was, I'd take him in a heartbeat over most men.

Despite it all, I don't regret my friendship with Ronnie, only that it got so fucked by circumstances beyond my control. He's a little like me and maybe a little like Rufus. We were all shuffled out into the world hopeful and filled with light but found the rest of the world was crooked and there were dark corners in every part of it. We stumbled along, stretching that innate goodness out until we ran low and felt anger at the world and the way our parents had set it up. We lashed out and rebelled, but even in that there was a pureness, a grace. But somewhere along the way, we ran into dead ends, those empty places in the crooked darkness that didn't make sense, places we could not navigate.

Which is all to say, I get why Ronnie was angry. I get why he was hurt. I never did reciprocate the loyalty he offered me, and it took me far too long to trust him.

* * *

I was in the valley of the devil for eight days, but the repercussions lasted a long time afterward. Rehab took energy I didn't know I possessed. I wanted to quit so many times, and still do, even though winter is over and the spring is almost here. I'll be fifty-two next month, and a few people have told me it's time to make a change.

Mary was the first. We'd gone out together on a warm March day, me testing my hip and shoulder and how my side would hold it all together as we walked our old path in the mountains, leading toward the cave where we'd found the first skull, where I'd met Patterson for the first time, when she took my hand and squeezed.

"The special election takes place in June," she said.

"Yep. We need to get the word out for James Briggs."

"Yeah, except . . . well, when you were in the hospital, Rufus and me and Susan had a chance to meet Briggs. He's a great guy. He'd do wonders for this county."

"Hell," I said. "I'd elect Goose sheriff before I voted for that Argent crook."

"I know. But a lot of people don't know what you and I know, and if we try to get the word out, they'll just say its sour grapes and mudslinging."

I shrugged and tried to disguise a wince as my arm flashed with pain. "I don't know. I think he's going to lose. A lot of people are suspicious of Argent because he's an outsider. Briggs isn't."

"True," Mary said. "If I had to lay odds, I think in a fair election Briggs has a good shot. But my concern is what happens after he wins."

"What do you mean?"

"He's going to have to stand up to Walsh and Keith. I'm not sure he's cut out for that."

I sighed. "Not many are, unfortunately."

We walked a little farther until the cave at the top of the rise came into view.

"You're right," she said. "Not many are. But then, there are some who seem born to stand up to those who would abuse their power."

I knew what she was hinting at, but I didn't let on. The very idea was so foreign to me, so *inconceivable*. Sheriffs were men like Hank Shaw or Doug Patterson. Not men like me. I worked outside of the law and begged forgiveness later.

Mary let it go. But Rufus didn't.

* * *

We went to visit Virginia and Briscoe at their new foster home a week later. Susan came with us, along with a bag full of books she'd purchased after I told her about Virginia's love of reading. Mary had to work, so it was just the three of us. Rufus had been on me a lot to run for sheriff, but he'd yet to wear me down. It was a job for someone else, I kept telling him. Not me.

I had a good argument too: "We'll be fine no matter what happens. Hell, we survived the last one and his buddy's snuff films."

That had made Rufus go silent, but it was one of those silences that spoke louder than words. It was a waiting kind of silence, as if the right moment to reply hadn't turned up yet.

He found it when I sat down with Briscoe in my lap. The boy giggled at me and tugged on my beard.

Rufus sat on the couch beside me. The foster parents seemed like good people. Their house was nice, and they hadn't ruled out adopting both kids. I was rooting for that.

"Some weren't as lucky as us," he said.

"Huh?" I said. "What are talking about?"

"I'm talking about these kids and that brother of the girl in the trailer park. I'm talking about those other skulls."

"Rufus, this isn't the time . . ."

"The hell it ain't. This is the very best time. While you got that boy in your arms and that girl is here. That's why you have to run. Me and you and Mary will be all right. Even if Argent gets the job. But not them. Those kids need every chance we can give them."

It was my turn to be silent. I wanted to ignore his words. I wanted to sigh and tell him he wasn't in control of my life. But I was too busy looking at Briscoe's big brown eyes. I realized I wasn't really in control of my own life either. Sometimes you didn't have a choice. Sometimes, the choice came down to doing whatever it took to look at yourself in the mirror and sleep at night.

It was like the thing with Ronnie. He did what he had to do. There wasn't any reward except doing it. All things being equal, I think he would have done it again. And look what it got him.

Goddamn world.

There should be a better way. One where we don't have to fight so hard for a way to get along, to make sense, to find a damned place where we didn't have to worry about the undertow of evil that seemed so pervasive among us all.

I didn't want to run for sheriff. But I figured it wouldn't kill me, and there were a lot of things out there that would. I'd learned that much for sure.

Acknowledgments

Writing this novel was unlike writing any novel I've ever attempted. The threat of a looming deadline made this novel uniquely challenging. There were many times I felt as if this book was doomed and would never be satisfactorily finished. And perhaps it wouldn't have been without a few key people who all contributed to getting me to the finish line.

First up is Faith Black Ross who remains the consummate "writer's" editor because of her light, yet deft touch and a deep reservoir of patience, without which, she might have given up on me and this book. The first draft I turned into her was deeply flawed, but her calmness steadied me and her grace allowed me the time and space to make it right.

Jenny Chen may be the most efficient and competent person I've worked with in publishing. She is a marvel of goodwill, enthusiasm, and support. I can't imagine making it through this book without her.

Sarah Poppe is a fine publicist, always willing to go the extra mile to promote my books, and I shudder to think where either Earl Marcus book would be without her.

My agent, Alec Shane, is the very best agent I could have hoped for when I found myself looking way back in 2013. He's measured and smart, and works his ass off for me and my books. He's also teaching me patience (whether he knows it or not!), and that's a lesson I sorely need. I can't say enough how great it feels to be in the hands of an agent I trust.

I can't imagine writing anything without the advice, counsel, and critiques of my friend Kurt Dinan. Kurt is a young adult author who is the rarest kind of writer I know: insanely gifted in both writing *and* editing. He's probably helped me more than anyone else to become a better storyteller, and most of it boils down to one admonition I hear over and over again when he reads my work: "I need something to happen soon." I think of his words whenever I am writing, and I always try to write stories where he can't possibly use that critique (he still does, of course).

Last, I want to acknowledge my wife, Becky. I dedicated the first Earl Marcus novel to my daughter and this one to my son, but in a way all of my books could rightly be dedicated to Becky. Her faith in me as a person and a writer has sustained me when I would have otherwise given up. This book is as much hers as it is mine.